NATIONWIDE EXCITEMENT
for
LAWRENCE SANDERS'
BLOCKBUSTER NEW NOVEL
OF BLOODY AFRICA

THE TANGENT OBJECTIVE

PETER: A man with an explosive secret, willing to commit any sin to achieve his dream of power.

ANOKYE: The "Black Napoleon" who sacrificed everything for his violent destiny.

YVONNE: *The Frenchwoman seeking salvation in a doomed love.*

SAM: The Jewish mercenary whose one skill was murder, and one hope forgetfulness.

And the others—spies, whores, soldiers, princes—fighting for their lives in a whirlpool of oil, blood, sex, and politics . . . "WONDERFUL READING."
—*The Milwaukee Journal*

"CLASSIC INTRIGUE COMBINES WITH ACTION AD-VENTURE FOR EFFORTLESS AND IMAGINATIVE READING."
—*The Chicago Tribune Book World*

"PLENTY OF ACTION."
—*The San Francisco Chronicle*

The Tangent Objective

Lawrence Sanders

BERKLEY BOOKS, NEW YORK

This Berkley book contains the complete
text of the original hardcover edition.
It has been completely reset in a type face
designed for easy reading, and was printed
from new film.

THE TANGENT OBJECTIVE

A Berkley Book / published by arrangement with
G. P. Putnam's Sons

PRINTING HISTORY
G. P. Putnam's edition published 1976
Berkley Medallion edition / July 1977
Seventh printing / April 1982

ISBN: 0-425-05830-1

A BERKLEY BOOK ® TM 757,375
Berkley Books are published by Berkley Publishing Corporation,
200 Madison Avenue, New York, New York 10016.
The name "BERKLEY" and the stylized "B" with design
are trademarks belonging to Berkley Publishing Corporation.
PRINTED IN THE UNITED STATES OF AMERICA

Author's Note

The names of existing nations, organizations, and institutions have been used, but this is a novel, and individuals and events described are fictitious. Where actual official titles are used, no reference is implied to persons presently holding those positions, nor should such reference be inferred. Names and characters are wholly imaginary.

1

BRINDLEYS WAS A private club. Small enough so that one knew everyone. Large enough so that one didn't have to speak to them. So when Tangent saw Julien Ricard at the crowded bar, he found a place down at the other end and kept his eyes lowered.

It didn't work. He felt a heavy hand on his shoulder and looked up.

"Hullo, Ricard," he said, shrugging off the hand. "What're you up to?"

"This and that," the Frenchman said. He was a tall man. Not as tall as Tangent, but tall enough. On the right side of his face was a purple birthmark shaped like the boot of Italy. And there, on his neck, Sicily.

"How about a chop?" he asked. His voice was querulous, almost whining. He had the reputation of being a mean drunk.

"Can't," Tangent said shortly. "I'm waiting for Tony Malcolm."

Ricard didn't expect to be asked to join, and wasn't.

"Thick as thieves you two," he said nastily.

"Aren't we," Tangent said equably. "Here he is now. Tony! Over here . . ."

"Hullo, Peter. Ricard. I called for the corner table."

"Good. Let's grab it."

They walked away from the Frenchman. He looked after them, glowering.

"Bad-tempered scut," Tangent said.

1

"Isn't he," Malcolm agreed. "So you're off to visit your Zulus again? Good evening, Harold."

"Good evening, gentlemen," the old waiter said, pulling back their chairs. "The usual?"

"The usual," Tangent said. "And a rare steak for me. It'll be a while before I see a piece of beef I can trust."

They had a leisurely dinner. The dining room was crowded; there were others within hearing. So they traded small talk: the most recent London bombing, a movie star's suicide, the famine in Bangladesh. By the time they were on cheese and port, the room had emptied out; the tables next to theirs were vacant.

"Peter, you sounded excited," Malcolm said.

"Was," Tangent said. "Am. Tony, I need something."

"Ah?"

"You mentioned once you had a broker you used to buy stock on the New York exchange."

"That's right. On Lombard Street. Old, established firm."

"Can he cover for me? Buy in another name or something? Hide it somehow?"

"He does for me. No problems so far, knock on wood. Why? Onto something good?"

"Good? You wouldn't believe. Starrett Petroleum. I saw our top secret report on the Asante exploration today. We'll have oil coming out our ears. As an insider, I'll get my ass in a sling if I wheel and deal. Can your man get me five thousand shares and keep it under the table?"

"I don't see why not. Should I get in?"

"I'd advise it, Tony. One problem: our exploration lease expires in two months. That's why I'm going down there tomorrow, to renegotiate."

"Trouble?" Malcolm asked.

"In Africa? *Always* trouble. But I think I can swing it."

"They know about the oil?"

Tangent looked about casually. "No," he said. "We scammed their report. You won't have to tell Virginia about *that*, will you?"

"Not at the moment," Malcolm said.

"You bastard!" Tangent laughed. "Well, take care of my five thousand shares, will you?"

"Of course. Tomorrow. Now you do something for me."

"What?"

"Stop by and see my man in Mokodi. Bob Curtin."

"Dear old Bob," Tangent said. "Anything wrong? He been acting up?"

"That's just it," Malcolm said. "He hasn't been acting at all. He files once a week with Virginia. I get a copy, and believe me, Peter, it's nothing. His reports read like travel brochures. I can't believe Asante is that quiet."

"Believe me, Tony, it isn't."

"Maybe the sun's got to him."

"It wouldn't be the first time. But after that little deal he pulled in Germany, I'd have thought he'd be anxious to please."

"That's what I thought. Now I think maybe he left his nerve in that Berlin alley. Take a look at him for me, will you, Peter? I'd like to get your take."

"Sure. Want me to send a bullet?"

"No, no. When you return will be soon enough. No crisis. Curtin will probably ask you when I'm going to pull him out. Tell him he better change his luck."

Tangent laughed, and they debated awhile, lazy and uncaring, then decided on a cognac. The old waiters moved about slowly, setting up for the after-theater crowd. Brindleys allowed ladies in the dining room, but not in the bar or grill. And not, of course, in the small sleeping suites upstairs. Although there were stories . . .

"Tell me about Asante," Malcolm said.

"What do you want to know?"

"Everything. Well . . . about ten minutes of everything."

"Third-smallest country in Africa in land area," Tangent recited. "A population of about eight hundred thousand, although they've never taken a census. It's a thin, wedge-shaped sliver of land between Ghana and Togo. Runs north-south. About thirty miles wide on the coast. On the west is Lake Volta. On the east is the Mono River. South is the Atlantic Ocean. At the northern tip, Asante, Ghana, Togo, and Upper Volta all come together at a map position called Four Points. It's near the village of Dapango. But no one's ever surveyed or marked the national boundaries, so there's a lot of smuggling back and forth. The local politicos scream about it, but don't do much to stop it. Actually, it benefits everyone."

"My God, Peter, you're a walking atlas."

"Tony, it's my *business*. Let's see . . . Asante is now a monarchy. Used to be a French colony. Got its independence in fifty-eight. It's at a break in the West African rain forest. Like Togo and Dahomey. The savannas come down to the sea. There's a hilly area in the north with fine hardwoods, but generally Asante is agricultural. Cotton, wheat, coffee, yams, corn, citrus fruits, barley, cassava—stuff like that. They've got a brewery, two textile mills, a factory that makes African 'art' for export. It's all junk; you know that. There's also an asphalt plant."

"Minerals?"

"Phosphates, iron ore, one active gold mine. Every once in a while someone picks up a diamond."

4

"What about Mokodi?"

"Capital and largest city. It's on the coast, with a good harbor and port facilities. Offshore is the island of Zabar. It's connected with Mokodi by an old ferry that runs three times a day. We found the oil southwest of Zabar. It'll drive Shell over the edge. They spent millions off the Dahomey coast and have zilch to show for it."

"Mokodi endurable?"

"Very much so. Clean. Wide, tree-lined boulevards. The French know how to plan a city. Lots of public gardens and parks. The electric power works. The water's good. There's a serviceable telephone system."

"Radio or television?"

"One radio station. No television. One daily newspaper."

Tony Malcolm looked about benignly, a cherub in houndstooth. An unknowing member of Brindleys had once said of him: "There's less there than meets the eye." Those in the know who heard the comment had smiled secretly and kept their mouths shut.

"What's Asante's bottom line?" Malcolm asked.

"Need you ask? Hairy at the heels. Know any African country that isn't? Except possibly Nigeria and Zaire. France holds Asante's bonds and notes. Most of their funds come from tourism. The highest building is the Mokodi Hilton, on the beach west of the port area. That's where our offices are. Air-conditioned, thank God. Tony, it's not a *bad* country. The crime rate is very low. Get convicted of murder, and you get your head chopped off. Crooks work out their time in the phosphate mines. Owned by the King's brother-in-law. Naturally. The streets of Mokodi are swept every morning and hosed down every afternoon. There are nightclubs, theaters, restaurants, sidewalk cafés."

5

"Sounds like a tropical paradise," Malcolm said.

"That's Mokodi," Tangent said. "The only part of Asante that most tourists see. But in the small villages of the uplands and grasslands, kids paw through dungheaps looking for undigested nuts."

"Oh-ho," Malcolm said. "Like that, is it?"

"Like that," Tangent nodded. "King Prempeh the Fourth—calls himself the Avenging Leopard of Bosumtwi, for no apparent reason—is bleeding the country white, you should excuse the expression. Him and his relatives. They own everything."

"On the take?"

"Of course."

"Secret police?"

"What did you expect? Nasty thugs. The chief is called the 'Nutcracker.' Because when he—"

"Please." Malcolm held up a hand. "I can guess."

"The joke down there, when you hear of his latest depravity, is to say, 'That's what makes the Nutcracker sweet'."

"Very funny," Malcolm said. "Ha ha."

"Well, that's Asante. As African countries go, it's not as good as the best, not as bad as the worst. I like it."

"Oh? Why?"

"You'll have to go down there and see. It gets to you, Tony. Sooner or later."

"Well, it seems to have gotten to my man Curtin sooner. I've learned more about Asante from you in the last ten minutes than I have from Curtin in the last six months. You'll check him out, Peter?"

"Sure. And you'll take care of the stock buy?"

"A pleasure. When's your flight?"

"Noon."

2

THEY WERE IN position before dawn. Their attack was from the east, so the rebels would be blinded by the rising sun. Captain Obiri Anokye commanded the frontal assault by a platoon of joyous Ewe-speaking troopers armed with MAS 49 rifles and glaives, short machete-swords issued to every Asanti soldier. Their orders were to shout, scream, fire blindly, and charge bravely.

The rebels would then abandon their encampment and stampede down the path to the shore of Lake Volta. There, along the trail and on the beach, Sgt. Sene Yeboa and his men would be waiting for them with automatic weapons.

It had all been worked out on maps and sketches with the aid of the beautifully crafted lead soldiers belonging to Alistair Greeley, chief teller of the Asante National Bank. Captain Anoyke and Greeley had spent an evening bending eagerly over rough maps, moving the little soldiers about, soldiers in the brilliant dress uniforms of British dragoons and French cuirassiers. Sgt. Yeboa had been present and had looked on, bored. War was not his business. Battle was.

It was Captain Anokye who had suggested coming in from the east, with the new sun at the back of the attacking platoon.

"Very good, Captain," Greeley had nodded. "Very good indeed."

So it was. The Little Captain waited patiently until fire rose out of the earth. Then he led his men in a wild charge, shouting, screaming, plucking triggers. Rebels came popping from their lean-tos, squinted into the glare, then turned to flee down the trail to the lake. Only one unarmed rebel stood to face the attacking force. He folded his arms and regarded the onrushing soldiers with grave sadness. Captain Anokye shot him dead.

In a few moments they heard the chatter of automatic fire from the direction of the trail and lake beach. Captain Anokye ignored it; he knew Sgt. Yeboa's worth. He led his men in a quick search of the rebels' shelters. They found four women, three infants, a naked boy of nine, perhaps, or ten. Like the man who had been killed, the boy stood erect, folded his arms, regarded the soldiers gravely.

"You are a full man," the Captain assured him, in French. Then: "Do you speak Akan?" he asked, in that language.

The boy was silent, but his eyes flickered.

"Go alive," the Captain said, in Akan. "Tell your leader, tell the Nyam, that I am Captain Obiri Anokye, and I would speak with him. I will meet him at such a place as he wishes. I will come alone, with no soldiers, no weapons. If he wishes to kill me, he may kill me. But first, I would speak with the Nyam. Tell him that."

Then Captain Anokye went down to the shore of Lake Volta. The only rebel still alive was Okomfo, the traitor who had informed, telling of the location of the encampment, the number of people, the weapons. He was grinning.

"Was it not as I spoke?" he asked, in Hausa.

"It was as you spoke," Captain Anokye agreed.

"I will be rewarded?" Okomfo asked.

"Surely," the Little Captain said.

8

Lt. Solomon was put in command, with orders to bury the dead rebels, then march the soldiers back to the Mokodi barracks. Captain Anokye returned to his Land Rover. He sat in the back, alongside the traitor Okomfo. Sgt. Yeboa drove, his favorite Uzi submachine gun on the floor at his feet. The two soldiers put on large, aviator-type sunglasses. The sky was flaming. There were no signs of rain. Of anything.

They bounced through grassland to Asante's single paved highway. Then Sgt. Yeboa turned north. It took a moment before Okomfo realized what was happening.

"We are not journeying to Mokodi?" he asked.

"No," Captain Anokye said. He drew his Walther P38 from a hip holster and gently placed the muzzle behind Okomfo's left ear. "We are not journeying to Mokodi. We are journeying to Shabala."

Okomfo groaned softly. "I have a good wife and two small ones," he said. "They shall live?"

"They shall live," the Captain promised. And Okomfo was comforted.

Shabala was not even a village. It was a crosstrail accumulation of flattened gasoline tin huts, several of them broken, leaning crazily. The rebels had raided this place a month ago. They had killed most of the men. They had taken what food there was: wheat, barley, okra, a few pumpkins, shea nut butter, some yams. And they had driven off three cows and two goats. Okomfo had been one of the raiders.

Captain Anokye delivered the traitor to the survivors of the Shabala massacre. He and Sgt. Yeboa, sunglassed, sat silently in the Land Rover and watched as the rebel was lifted off the ground and his hands and feet nailed to a billboard that advertised, in French, "Coca-Cola: The

9

Pause That Refreshes.'' The men finished their job of crucifixion and stepped back. The women moved in. No one spoke.

Okomfo's singlet and trousers were cut away from him. He was wearing soiled underpants. These too were cut away. A hempen cord was knotted about his penis and testicles. At the end of the cord, between his spreadeagled legs, was attached a small reed basket. A stone was placed in the basket. Another would be added each day. Okomfo would be given water. Enough to keep him alive as his genitals stretched and stretched and stretched until the weight of the added stone burst penis and scrotum. Then the man might die.

"A good lesson for all traitors," Sgt. Yeboa said virtuously.

"Yes," Captain Anokye agreed. "Their traitors, our traitors. But there is another reason. The Nyam will hear of this death and understand. I, Captain Anokye, have given him Okomfo. Perhaps, in return, the Nyam will give something to me."

"Yes *sah*!" Sgt. Yeboa said, and both men smiled.

3

THE RULER OF Asante, King Prempeh IV, lived in a palace that had originally been the quarters of the French governor. It was a handsome, flat-roofted, four-storied building of imported stone. It was air-conditioned, but King Prempeh, in one of his extravagances, had decreed that the old, four-bladed electric fans, suspended from the ceilings, be retained and kept operative. They sent currents of chilled air drifting through the palace rooms. The effect was not uncavelike.

On the morning that Captain Obiri Anokye was defeating the rebels at Lake Volta and witnessing the crucifixion of the traitor Okomfo, King Prempeh IV was in his audience chamber on the ground floor of the royal palace. The King was seated at the head of a five-meter-long conference table, crafted of a single slab of pinkish mahogany. Prempeh sat in a throne-like armchair, the largest chair in the room, reinforced with iron braces to support his enormous bulk.

The current jape making the rounds of Mokodi's outdoor cafés, discotheques, and waterfront bars was that the personal tailor of King Prempeh IV was a direct lineal descendant of Omar the Tent-Maker. It was true the King's court uniform would have provided enough white silk for the saparas of two ordinary men. Sagging the expanse of white across the King's bosom was a dazzling array of medals and orders, many from other African

11

rulers, but most self-awarded.

At the moment, the King, who was fond of stroking his medals, was more fascinated by the gold Patek Philippe watch that encircled his right wrist. It was a gift brought from Geneva by Peter Tangent, who had had the foresight to order the watch attached to an expandable band twice the circumference of an ordinary band. It gripped the King's plump wrist comfortably, and he had been kind enough to accept it.

Two hours previously, there had been others present. Along one side of the table, on the King's right, in precisely spaced chairs, were seated the Crown's closest advisers: Prime Minister Osei Ware; Commander of the Armed Forces General Opoku Tutu; Minister of Finance Willi Abraham; and the King's personal secretary Anatole Garde, a Frenchman.

Opposing them across the gleaming table were four executives of the Starrett Petroleum Corp., headquartered in Tulsa, Okla., and New York, N.Y. The oilmen were led by Peter A. Tangent, Chief of African Operations, who worked out of Starrett's London office. The others were J. Tom Petty, General Manager of Starrett's Asante explorations; his legal counsel, Mai Fante, an Asanti; and Dr. Hans Apter, a German petroleum geologist employed by Starrett under contract. Apter had been brought along to provide whatever technical information might be required regarding Starrett's explorations off the southwest coast of the Asante island of Zabar.

Since the King was a Muslim, as were his advisers (except Garde, a Christian), no alcoholic drinks were served. But there was a thermos of chilled orange juice before each man, a plastic cup, and a small bowl of salted groundnuts. No one drank or nibbled until the King drank or nibbled. Since he did not, they did not.

The discussion was conducted in French, with Mai Fante whispering a running translation into the ear of monolingual J. Tom Petty. The leadoff speaker, at the King's command, was Minister of Finance Willi Abraham. He was a small, fine-boned, gray-haired man wearing a dark business suit of European cut. He was a graduate of the Wharton School of Finance. His personality profile in Peter Tangent's private file included:

"Phenomenal memory . . . soft-spoken but hard bargainer . . . does what he can to counter King's profligacies . . . refused two bribe offers . . . will accept contributions to Asante's schools . . . oldest son killed in war for independence . . . likes fine bindings . . . chess . . . HWC." This last was Tangent's shorthand for Handle With Care.

Speaking slowly in a clear, dry voice, without notes, Abraham reviewed the history of the Asante-Starrett relationship. A lease for preliminary oil exploration, including underwater explosions, had been granted for a period of three years, at a fixed annual fee. That three-year period would expire in two months. At that time, Starrett had the option to withdraw completely from Asante waters or, if they desired to continue operations, to negotiate terms of a new lease.

On the basis of the most recent report submitted by Starrett, the Minister said, tapping a heavy binder of documents on the table before him, it appeared there definitely was oil beneath the sea off the southwest coast of the island of Zabar. What did Starrett now propose?

"With all due respect, Minister," Peter Tangent replied, "I submit your use of the word 'definitely' is not justified by our findings. In fact, it is a word rarely used in petroleum exploration anywhere, at any time. Our indus-

13

try is, as you know, beset by thousands of unknowns and imponderables.''

"On page eighty-two," Abraham said, "under the heading 'Summary,' it is stated that there is a good possibility of a large field, somewhat oval in shape, that might prove to be recoverable by conventional offshore drilling techniques.''

"A 'possibility,' yes," Tangent said. "And 'might prove to be recoverable,' yes. But we are a long way, many, many months, from actually proving the oil is there. And we are years away from determining if it is recoverable in sufficient volume to justify the enormous outlay my people must make for development.''

"What do you want, Tangent?" Prime Minister Osei Ware asked bluntly.

"We respectfully suggest, Prime Minister, that the original lease be extended for an additional two years at the same annual fee. It will give my people the opportunity—''

A short bark of laughter came from King Prempeh IV, and Tangent ceased speaking.

"Impossible," the King rumbled. "I am sure you are aware, my dear Peter, that you are not the only people interested in profiting from Asante's oil.''

"Your Majesty," Tangent said, "with all due respect, it has not yet been proved beyond a reasonable doubt that oil actually exists beneath Asante waters. I would like, with Your Majesty's permission, to ask Dr. Hans Apter, our famous geologist, of world-wide renown, to describe exactly what we have and have not found.''

"It's all in the report, isn't it?" General Tutu asked impatiently.

"It is, General," Tangent acknowledged. "But perhaps Dr. Apter could expand a bit and convey to you

14

gentlemen the tentative nature of our findings. Your Majesty?''

''Oh, very well,'' the King said grumpily. ''Keep it short. This isn't my only meeting this morning, you know.''

Tangent nodded at Dr. Apter. Speaking a heavily accented French, the German scientist described the process of determining if fields of oil lay beneath the sea bottom. After five minutes of an extremely technical lecture that had General Opoku Tutu nodding sleepily in his chair, Peter Tangent interrupted . . .

''Yes, yes, Dr. Apter,'' he said. ''Very interesting, and we all appreciate the information. But what these gentlemen wish to know, I'm sure, is whether an oil field exists in the Zabarian exploration area.''

''I cannot say for a certainty,'' Dr. Apter said promptly. ''No one can. Perhaps yes, perhaps no.''

''So you can see,'' Tangent said earnestly, speaking to all the Asantis, ''an extended period of exploration is certainly justified under the terms of the original lease.''

''If you haven't definitely located oil in almost three years,'' Willi Abraham said, ''why do you feel more time will enable you to make that determination?''

''What we propose,'' Tangent said, ''is to bring over two offshore drilling rigs from the U.S.—at great expense to my people, of course—for drilling delineation wells. They should give us an answer to the question of whether there is or there is not petroleum in sufficient recoverable volume beneath your seas to justify further development.''

''You want to start drilling?'' the King said. ''Under terms of the original lease? What kind of fools do you take us for?''

''No, no, Your Majesty,'' Tangent said hastily. ''Not

commercial drilling. Not at all. Test wells, that's all. Merely a logical extension of our exploration to date.''

"Peter, Peter," the King said reprovingly. He waved a fat forefinger at Tangent. "The colonial days are over."

"I am well aware of that, Your Majesty. But what we propose is, I think a far cry—"

"You have told us what you propose," King Prempeh said. "Now I shall tell you what I propose. Willi?"

Peter Tangent attended to the Asante proposition without change of expression. But as he listened to Mai Fante's translation, J. Tom Petty's beef-and-bourbon complexion deepened; the big man rolled almost frantically in his chair. Tangent looked at him sternly. Petty gradually calmed under Fante's whispered entreaties.

What the Minister of Finance proposed was a two-year lease giving Asante seventy-five percent of all future profits derived from the sale of Zabarian oil. These terms would be subject to renegotiation at the end of the two-year period.

Tangent showed nothing of what he felt.

"I shall, of course, relay Your Majesty's suggestions to my people," he started.

"Not suggestions," Prempeh said. "Terms."

"Very well, Your Majesty. Terms. In all honesty, I must tell you they will find them unacceptable. Surely Your Majesty is aware that in many oil-producing nations of Africa and the Middle East, the customary division of profits is approximately fifty-fifty and, in several cases, sixty percent or more to the corporation or consortium providing the funds for exploration, drilling, the construction of pipelines, and so forth."

"And I am sure *you* are aware, Mr. Tangent," Willi Abraham said, "that in several oil-producing nations of Africa and the Middle East, *all* oil-production has been

16

nationalized completely, and the sovereign state is the sole owner of resources beneath its territory and the only party to profit therefrom.''

"True, Minister," Tangent acknowledged. "But those conditions only came about after many years of heavy investment by the oil companies and the development of productive and profitable wells over known oil reserves. Asante has yet to produce a single barrel of oil."

"And you think we won't?" the King demanded.

"I didn't say that, Your Majesty."

"Tell your people there are others who are interested, if they are not. Others from the East. Need I say more? You have heard our terms. Give us your answer as soon as possible. This audience is at an end. Peter, stay a moment. I wish to thank you personally for your gift."

The chamber emptied slowly, the others bowing themselves out backwards. Then the door closed. Prempeh motioned Tangent closer. The American moved around to take the chair on the King's right. He watched Asante's monarch hold his thick wrist aloft and turn his new watch this way and that, admiring the flashes of reflected light.

"Very handsome, Peter."

"Thank you, Your Majesty. May it bring a lifetime of health and happiness."

"Fourteen karat, I suppose," the King said casually.

"Twenty-four, Your Majesty," Tangent lied.

"Oh?" the King said. "Excellent. Peter, about this oil lease . . ."

"Yes, Your Majesty?"

"Your nation is so wealthy, and mine so poor."

"True, Your Majesty. But, of course, Starrett Petroleum is a very, very small part of the United States. I am sure Your Majesty has seen our most recent annual report. After-tax profits have declined alarmingly."

"Still . . . I have so many responsibilities, Peter. So many demands on my time and energies. And on my personal funds."

"I am sure you do, Your Majesty."

"You wouldn't believe how much I contribute to private charities. These are things never made public. I am not a man to boast. But I assure you the drain is enormous."

"I am certain it is. Is there any way my people may be of service to Your Majesty in this regard?"

"Peter, you know there is no disagreement between us. This matter can be settled between men of good faith."

"Of course, Your Majesty."

"Suppose, Peter, after a period of hard bargaining, I reduced my terms to fifty-five percent. For my Treasury. After expenses of production, distribution, and marketing have been deducted, of course. Do you think that would be evidence of my good faith?"

"It would, indeed, Your Majesty. But after such a noble concession, I would think it only proper for my people to make a concession on their part. Perhaps some means of assisting Your Majesty with the drain on his private funds."

"Oh? The idea hadn't occurred to me, Peter."

"I am certain it hadn't, Your Majesty. May I suggest to my people a fifty-five-percent share of all profits to the Asante Treasury, and an additional one percent to Your Majesty personally to insure continued support of those private charities Your Majesty mentioned?"

"Mmm . . . I think perhaps ten percent would enable me to do more for the poor of Asante."

"*Ten* percent, Your Majesty?"

"That is still only sixty-five, Peter. Ten less than my original terms."

"Quite so, Your Majesty. Of course. And the mechanics of delivering our aid to the private charities?"

"Oh, that can be worked out," the King said casually. He flapped one stuffed, beringed hand. "Surely you have business in Zurich?"

"Surely, Your Majesty."

"Well then . . ."

"I shall certainly present Your Majesty's generous offer to my people. I shall relay their answer before the expiration of the current lease. I hope a mutually beneficial arrangement can be quickly negotiated."

"Excellent, excellent," the King beamed. "I wish you success in all your endeavors. Will you be in Asante long?"

"Only another day or two, Your Majesty. Regrettably."

"It has been a pleasure to meet again with you," the King said. Then he switched to Akan. "Go in good health, and return in good health."

Tangent replied in the same language:

"May health, love, and wealth be yours; and time to enjoy them."

The King's secretary, Anatole Garde, was waiting outside the door to the audience chamber.

"All finished?" he asked.

"Completely," Tangent said.

Garde glanced about the corridor. Two members of the palace guard stood at parade rest at both sides of the chamber doorway. The guardsmen wore white spatter-dashes and carried Colt .45 automatic pistols in white leather holsters suspended from pipe clayed belts.

"You might stop by Minister Abraham's office," Garde murmured. "He wanted to speak with you."

"About what—do you know?"

"Not really. He said there was someone he wanted you to meet."

Tangent nodded, walked down the chilly hallway to the Finance Minister's suite. The receptionist was a young, perky Asanti woman, hair braided and corn-rowed, wearing a smart vermilion Apollo that came to her knees.

"Peter Tangent," he said. "The Minister—"

"Oh yes, Mr. Tangent," she said. Brilliant smile. She had spoken to him in English. But when she whispered softly into her intercom, it was in a language he did not understand. He thought it might be Twi.

"The Minister will be with you in a moment, sir," she smiled. "Would you care to sit down?"

"I'll stand, thank you," he said. "I've been sitting all morning. I need a stretch."

"Sir, you have a lot to stretch," she giggled.

He laughed, and nodded.

"Sir, I have been studying feet and inches in my English class," she said. "May I say that you are six feet tall and six inches tall?"

"*Very* good," he said admiringly. "Actually six-five."

"Is that tall for Americans, sir?"

"Yes. Quite tall."

"I want so much to visit America," she said. "I wish to visit Bahstan."

"Boston," he said.

"Are you certain, sir?" she said doubtfully. "My brother is studying to be a doctor there, and when he was back last year, he called it Bahstan."

He was saved from an explanation of American accents by the sudden entrance, from an inner office, of the Minister of Finance.

20

"Escort you to your car, Mr. Tangent?" he said, speaking French.

"An honor, sir."

"About that oil report . . ." the Minister said aloud. Then, as they came out into the corridor and he closed the door behind him, he said nothing more.

They exited the palace and walked slowly across the broad plaza that led to the Boulevard Voltaire.

"How much did he want?" Willi Abraham asked.

"Minister, I don't know what you're talking about."

"I'd guess ten percent," the Finance Minister said. "There's a man named Anokye."

"Who?" Tangent said. Bewildered. "What?"

"Obiri Anokye. He's an army captain. Look him up. You may be interested."

"Why should I be interested in an army captain, Minister?"

"A pleasure meeting you again, Mr. Tangent," Abraham smiled. "Captain Obiri Anokye."

He turned away and almost trotted back to the palace. Tangent watched him go, then began levering himself, joint by joint, into the Volkswagen he had rented. The other Starrett employees had arrived in the company's chauffeured white Mercedes-Benz limousine. J. Tom Petty had offered it to Tangent for his exclusive use during his stay, but Tangent thought it too conspicuous. Now he wondered if it was any more conspicuous than a red Volkswagen with the driver's head protruding through the opened sunroof.

4

"THAT NIGGER SONOFABITCH!" Petty said furiously.

"Watch your language," Tangent said sharply. "You keep talking like that and Starrett will be out of Asante completely, and you'll be peddling enchiladas in El Paso. Is that what you want?"

"But seventy-five percent? Jesus H. Christ!"

"It's not your problem," Tangent said coldly.

Starrett Petroleum Corp. had leased the entire penthouse floor of the Mokodi Hilton and, at great expense, had converted it into offices, a conference room, a "hospitality suite," living quarters for J. Tom Petty and his assistants, and bedrooms and baths for transient VIPs. There was an added advantage: On the hotel roof, up an outside iron staircase, was a helipad. It could accommodate the Sikorsky S-62 that made frequent flights to the *Starrett Explorer*, the ship engaged in searching for oil off the coast of Zabar. The *Explorer* had a helipad on her afterdeck.

Tangent and Petty were seated in the manager's office, an attractive room decorated with African art. Not the dross sold to tourists or exported by the shipload, but good pieces—ancient and modern—of wood, bronze, fabric, fur, shell, copper. None of it could be taken from the country without a special export license, difficult to obtain. But there were other ways . . .

"Well, what are you going to do about it?" Petty demanded. "Seventy-five percent? They sure got civilized fast!"

22

Tangent was silent.

"And look at this piece of shit," Petty went on, lifting and letting fall on his desk a copy of the exploration report submitted to the Asantis. "It cost Tulsa a mint. I knew it wouldn't work. That field proves out bigger every day. There's an ocean of oil out there!"

Tangent glanced about the office.

"I hope you're clean," he said.

"What?" Petty said. "Oh . . . sure. The whole floor is checked twice a week. No bugs."

"Don't count on it," Tangent said. "And don't go running off at the mouth about an 'ocean of oil.' I've got a report to file. I'll need the code book."

Petty opened a small desk drawer safe, handed the little red book to Tangent.

"Pete, I'm going to grab a drink and a chicken sandwich. You hungry?"

"Not right now."

"Christ, no wonder you're so skinny. Need me for anything this afternoon? I want to go out to the ship."

"No, you go ahead. I have enough to keep me busy."

He waited until Petty departed, then took the manager's swivel chair behind the desk. In spite of the air-conditioning, the leather seat cushion was uncomfortably warm. From Petty's heavy buttocks. With a twist of distaste, Tangent rose immediately, lighted a Players, and strolled about the office. Giving the cushion a chance to cool.

He liked this room. He had selected many of the works of art himself. There was one small bronze statue Tangent particularly fancied. Dogon workmanship, he thought. A squatting male figure with enlarged erect penis. The statuette had a dark green patina, but the extended penis was bright. Every visitor stroked it, laughing. The work-

23

manship had that sure, airy, amusing appeal that Tony Malcolm admired in African art. Tangent took the statue from its little teak base and slipped it into a manila envelope. Then he sat down on the cooled cushion to compose his report to the Tulsa office, with copies to London and New York.

He wrote it out in longhand (typewriter ribbons could be deciphered), keeping it as brief as possible. He detailed King Prempeh's final offer. He recommended that no decision be made at that time since almost two months remained of the initial lease period. He hinted that other options might be open to Starrett Petroleum, that he was exploring them and would report if they proved viable.

He then transposed his message into company code. He tore up and burned his original draft in the heavy marble ashtray on Petty's desk. He returned the code book to the desk safe and spun the dial. He rang for a secretary, an Asanti, and asked her to cable it immediately. Then he took the Dogon statuette in the manila envelope and headed for the elevators. He stopped suddenly, returned to the office area, knocked on Mai Fante's door and entered.

The Asanti attorney looked up from his littered desk, smiled, motioned to an armchair. Tangent slumped, hooking one knee over a chair arm. Fante sat back in his swivel chair, swinging gently back and forth.

"Quite a session, wasn't it?" he said. He spoke English.

"Beautiful," Tangent said. "Mai, I want to thank you for keeping Petty under control. The man is an animal. Out on the ship, an animal is exactly what we need. But not in a palace."

"My sentiments exactly," Fante laughed. "But . . ." He shrugged in the traditional Asanti gesture: shoulders heaved, hands raised with palms up, eyes rolled to the

24

heavens. Almost Italianate. "What can you do?" it said. Or, "It is the will of the gods." Or, "The entire world is mad, and every wise man knows it."

"Obiri Anokye," Tangent said. "An army captain. Do you know him?"

"The Little Captain?" Mai Fante said, grinning. "Everyone in Asante knows of Captain Anokye."

"I don't," Tangent said. "Tell me about him."

"A small man," Fante said. "But with a large pride. He leads his men personally, always. In every action he is out in front. That is rare for an Asanti officer."

"For *any* officer," Tangent smiled. "Is he to be trusted?"

"I believe so, yes. His men love him. They will follow him anywhere. He has become a legend, almost. There is a song about him, sung in our cabarets."

"Oh? Do you know it?"

"Difficult to translate in rhyme. Something like this: 'When the bullets begin to fly/Who is sure to be passing by? The Little Captain. When the action is at the front/Who is first to bear the brunt? The Little Captain.' Then the chorus goes: 'Bibi, Bibi, the big Little Captain who is first in the people's hearts.' Something like that. I told you, it is difficult to translate."

"It's interesting," Tangent said. "What is his background?"

"Born in Zabar," Fante said. "A large family. He had to end his schooling to help out. So he joined the army as a private. But he has continued to study on his own. He speaks French, of course, and English very well. Some German and Italian. Several African languages. He likes history, biography, political science. He is what you would call a quick study."

"Oh?" Tangent said. "How do you know all this?"

25

A mask came down over Mai Fante's face. Tangent had seen it many times before: The African asked a question he does not wish to answer and yet does not wish to appear rude by not replying.

"I have loaned him several books," Mai Fante said finally. "On occasion."

Tangent switched away from Fante's personal relationship with Captain Obiri Anokye:

"Is the Little Captain a friend of Anatole Garde?" he asked.

"The King's secretary?" Fante said. Astonished. "Friends? Not to my knowledge."

"Any connection?"

"Nooo . . . Unless, of course, it might be the Golden Calf." Fante giggled to indicate what he was about to say was a joke, of no significance. "Garde is a regular customer, and it is said that Captain Anokye is fond of Yvonne Mayer, who manages the Golden Calf." The attorney added quickly, "But all that is just street gossip."

"And Minister of Finance Willi Abraham? Any friendship or connection with Captain Anokye?"

Again the mask descended.

"Not to my knowledge, Mr. Tangent."

"Thank you," the American said, rising. "You have been most helpful, and I appreciate it."

"Please forgive my poor service," the attorney said, in Akan.

Tangent replied in the same language: "The wise man is never too old to learn and is thankful."

He could not endure the thought of folding himself once again into that rented Volkswagen. So he took the first taxi in line outside the Mokodi Hilton. To his pleased surprise, it was a 1968 Chrysler, spacious, spotless inside and out.

26

But around the passengers' compartment was displayed a selection of men's and women's leather sandals, tied to the upholstery, with pricetags giving the cost in West African francs, the CFA.

Since the cab was not equipped with a meter, Tangent thought it best to arrange terms before starting.

"The American Embassy, please," he said. "It is on the Boulevard Voltaire, one square north of the palace."

The driver turned to look at him. A face of a thousand wrinkles.

"But of course," the old man said. "I know it well. A splendid place. But a far journey."

"Surely not so far," Tangent protested.

"Far enough," the driver said. "But I shall drive you comfortably and in complete safety. What do you have— Dollars? Pounds? Francs? CFAs? Cigarettes?"

"I would prefer to pay in American dollars."

"A pleasure. A journey of such length will require ten American dollars. The dash is extra, of course."

"Surely the journey is not of such great length. It seems to me a payment of five dollars, including dash, would be generous."

"Oh, sir! Surely you make a joke? Five dollars including dash? Surely a joke! What would I tell my woman and little ones? So hungry!"

They warmed to their task. Other passengers entered cabs behind them, but no horns were honked. The game was going on everywhere.

"The smallest child needs medicine," the driver said. "A terrible pain. Here." He thumped his chest.

"I am not a wealthy man," Tangent whined. "I have arrived penniless in your beautiful country to seek my fortune."

They finally agreed on $6.50 for the fare, with the dash

27

extra, to be determined by the comfort, convenience, and speed of the trip. They started out in high good spirits—and with a sudden jerk that almost snapped Tangent's neck.

"Such a beautiful day, one is thankful to be alive," the driver said happily.

"One is indeed," Tangent murmured, as they barely avoided a collision with a slow-moving bus crammed with Asantis, and more clinging to the running boards. At the United States Embassy, Tangent climbed out trembling. He was still carrying the manila envelope with the Dogon statuette. He paid the driver the $6.50 and added a dollar dash.

"May you be blessed," the driver said.

"And you," Tangent said. "For driving me with such bravery."

"A trifle," the driver said modestly. "Sandals?"

"Not today, thank you."

"My wife's cousin makes them," the driver said sorrowfully. "The workmanship is not exceptional."

The Marine guard at the Embassy gate was chatting up a bird and paid no attention as Tangent walked across the tiled courtyard and pushed open the massive bronze door. The receptionist, reading an overseas edition of *Time* at her desk, looked up as he entered.

"Back again, Mr. Tangent?"

"Back again," he said cheerfully.

"The Ambassador's not here, you know. He's up in Monrovia for some kind of conference."

"I know," Tangent said. "It's Bob Curtin I'd like to see—your cultured Cultural Attaché. Is he in?"

"Let me find out . . ."

She picked up her white phone, dialed a three-digit number, spoke softly.

"He's in," she told Tangent. "Go on up."

"Second door on the left?" he said.

"Right," she said.

"Second door on the right?" he asked.

"No, on the—" Then she realized he was teasing her. "Oh, *you*," she said.

"Give my best to Selma, Alabama," he smiled.

"How I wish I could," she said. "I tell you I can't *wait*."

Bob Curtin was standing outside his door. He looked thinner, drawn, and the hand he proffered was soft and without strength.

"Peter," he said. "Good to see you."

"Bob," Tangent said. "You're looking well."

"And you're a liar," Curtin said. He laughed suddenly, a harsh bark.

They sat at opposite ends of a leather couch. Tangent handed over the manila envelope.

"Can you get this in the pouch, for Tony Malcolm?"

"Sure. What is it?"

"Take a look."

Curtin withdrew the Dogon statuette.

"Nice," he said. "Tony will flip. When you get back, ask him when the hell he's going to get me out of here."

"He told me you'd ask that. He said to tell you maybe you better change your luck."

"Don't think I haven't tried," Curtin said bitterly. "What's Tony been up to?"

"This and that."

"Are they still talking about me?"

"No one's talking about you, Bob. It's all past history."

"Not for me it isn't. I'm still stuck down here. Peter, it could have happened to anyone."

"Of course."

"I didn't panic, I swear I didn't. I really thought he was going for his gun. You know me, Peter; you know I'm not a trigger-happy kid. I've been in the business a long time. But I had to protect myself. I'd do exactly the same thing if it happened today."

"It was just bad luck, Bob. Everyone knows that."

"If he had just said something before he reached for his ID. I honestly believed he was going for a shoulder holster. It was his own fault."

"Look, Bob, be reasonable. The West Germans were very sore, and they had every right to be. One of their best men. So Virginia took care of his family and tucked you out of sight for a while. Memories are short; you know that. You'll be back in London one of these days. You haven't been put out to pasture."

"And you're full of shit," Curtin said morosely. "If I had any guts I'd resign, but what the hell would I do— write a book about Virginia?"

"I wouldn't advise it."

"I don't know—everyone seems to be doing it these days. Peter, I honestly thought the guy was going for his gun. That alley was dark, and he had been—"

"Bob, for God's sake stop brooding about it. It happened, and it's over. Finished and done with."

"Not for me it isn't."

"Tell me what you know about Captain Obiri Anokye."

Curtin looked up suddenly and stopped biting nervously at the hard skin around his thumbnail.

"What do you want to know about him for?" he asked. "He's just another army captain, with more balls than most."

"Is that how you see him?"

"Sure. What else? Do you know something I don't know?"

"I never heard his name until today."

"Where did you hear it—at the palace? When you were getting that reaming on the oil lease?"

"Oh, you heard about that," Tangent said.

"Peter, this is Asante. *Everyone* heard about it. Who mentioned Anokye's name?"

"Willi Abraham."

"That's odd. I don't know of any connection between Abraham and the Little Captain."

"There is none—if you can believe my local attorney."

"But you don't?"

"I just don't know. Is this Anokye politically involved?"

"Not to my knowledge. All he's interested in is military stuff. He's a steady customer at USIA. The *New York Times* every day. And they got him a lot of U.S. Army and Marine Corps field manuals he requested. Nothing classified."

"What kind of manuals?"

"Tactics for small infantry units, ambushes, street fighting, house-to-house fighting—stuff like that."

"Bob, have you filed anything on Anokye with Virginia?"

"Of course not. Peter, he's just a lousy army captain. They'd think I was really around the bend."

Tangent said nothing. Curtin blinked rapidly several times, bit angrily at the skin of his thumbnail.

"You think I *should* file on him?" he asked.

"Wouldn't do any harm," Tangent said. "Cover yourself."

"I guess you're right," Curtin sighed. "Even if nothing comes of it. Shows I'm on the ball—right?"

"Right," Tangent nodded. "You ever meet this Anokye?"

"No, I never have. But I heard him speak at a rally of war veterans. A real rabble-rouser. He had them screaming and crying and jumping all over the place."

"Oh? What did he speak about?"

"The usual crap—Asante for the Asantis. The glorious future that lies ahead. With liberty and justice for all. But he made it sound fresh and new. They ate it up. I think if he had said, 'Let's take the palace,' they'd have been right behind him."

"Better put that in your report to Virginia."

"I will. I'll get it off tonight. I guess I should have done it before. This sun down here is scrambling my brains."

"And you'll get that dingus off to Tony Malcolm?"

"Sure. In tonight's pouch."

"Thanks, Bob."

Tangent rose to leave.

"Sam Leiberman still in the country?" he asked casually.

"As far as I know," Curtin said. "Where's he going to go? If he goes back to Kenya or the Congo, they'll cut his nuts off."

"Can he get into Togo?"

"I don't see why not. What's your interest in Leiberman?"

"I've got a delivery to make in Lomé."

"If it pays enough, Sam will make a delivery in Cairo. He lives over Les Trois Chats down in the dock area."

"Thanks again, Bob. I'll find him."

"Tell Tony I'm doing a helluva job down here."

"I'll tell him. See you around."

5

THE ASANTE Royal Air Force consisted of two old Broussards and a twin-engined Piper Aztec. The Royal Navy included four motor launches, mounting searchlights and machine guns, assigned to antismuggling operations, and a smart corvette, *La Liberté*. This craft was a gift from the French government when Asante achieved independence in 1958. It was reserved for the King's exclusive use—for holiday cruises along the coast, close to shore; for ceremonial receptions for foreign dignitaries; and, it was whispered, for certain dockside revelries when King Prempeh and his ministers tired of their wives and orange juice.

The Asante Royal Army was somewhat more impressive. It consisted of two infantry brigades, the 3rd and 4th, with several smaller shared support units of light artillery, tanks, engineers, etc. The two brigades alternated in their occupancy of the Mokodi barracks. While one was stationed in the capital, the other was in the field, on maneuvers, and manning garrisons in smaller Asante towns and villages.

All the armed forces were under the command of General Opoku Tutu. Third Brigade was commanded by Colonel Ramon de Blanca, a cousin of the King, and 4th Brigade was commanded by Colonel Onya Nketia, the King's youngest son. But Colonel Nketia, only 25, spent most of the year in France, allegedly improving his military expertise. Mostly on the Place Pigalle, if foreign tabloids (not allowed in Asante) were to be believed.

In his absence, 4th Brigade was commanded by Major Etienne Corbeil, an ancient leftover from the French administration. He had stayed on to help organize and train the new Asante army. Now, arthritic and somewhat senile, he rarely moved from headquarters and left the training and day-to-day administration of 4th Brigade to Captain Obiri Anokye.

Following the action at Lake Volta and the business at Shabala, Captain Anokye and Sgt. Yeboa returned to the Mokodi barracks. The day was spent supervising close-order drill, calisthenics, lecturing on small-unit tactics, inspections, weapons instruction, map reading, a film on personal hygiene and, at 1900 hours, a Brigade review and trooping of the colors. The Asante national flag was alternating vertical stripes of red, white, and blue, superimposed with a large green star that bore in its center a fulgent sun. Brigade and company flags were somewhat more subdued.

Following the evening review, one-third of 4th Brigade remained on duty while two-thirds were allowed liberty, as was the nightly custom. Since most of the soldiers lived in Mokodi, or had girlfriends there, they went to their homes for their evening meal, taking their rifles and glaives with them. This custom resulted in a great saving of rations. Also, it was felt, the presence of armed, uniformed men on the streets of Mokodi was a deterrent to crime and civil insurrection.

Captain Anokye presided over the officers' table in the general mess hall. Officers ate the same food as enlisted men. That night it was an excellent, highly flavored shrimp and chicken stew, with eggplant chunks and tomatoes included. Side dishes were rice and fufu—yam dumplings. Dessert was fresh pineapple.

As was his custom, the Little Captain read a book while

eating. It was propped up on a specially designed stand of twisted copper wire his father had made for him. Oblivious to the chatter and laughter of his lieutenants, Captain Anokye spooned in his stew and read with great interest of the exploits of General Thomas Jackson during the American Civil War. Jackson's deployment of small but highly mobile forces against a numerically superior enemy was impressive. He seemed to depend on speed, Anokye noted, and the ability to feint, turn, strike, withdraw, strike again miles away. The loyalty of his men made it all possible, of course. Not so much their loyalty to the Confederacy, but loyalty to Jackson himself. He didn't command; he led.

Anokye finished his meal before anyone else, snapped his book shut, motioned to his lieutenants to remain seated, and strode away. He was still wearing his dusty, sweat-streaked field uniform: tan, camouflaged denim dungarees, canvas gaiters, leather boots, web belt, holster and pistol. His limp-brimmed forage cap was tucked under his belt.

He went to his office and spent two hours catching up on paperwork: Brigade accounts, records of courts-martial, inventories of weapons and supplies, muster rolls, etc. He stacked all the completed documents in his Out basket, for delivery to Major Etienne Corbeil. It was doubtful if the old man had the ability or desire to read the reports before scrawling his spidery initials of approval.

Then Anokye wrote out a terse account of the morning's action: personnel involved, huts destroyed, rebels killed. He singled out Sgt. Yeboa for a sentence of praise, and noted that the reconditioned MAS 49s had performed well. But he reiterated his frequent suggestion that his men be equipped with a modern weapon, preferably an automatic carbine or assault rifle. He favored the Kalashnikov

AK-47, but did not mention it in his report lest it might be thought he had been bribed by the Russians.

Paperwork completed, he closed up shop, turned off the lights, and walked rapidly to the compound gate, returning the faced-palm salutes of passing soldiers. He could have taken his Land Rover, but he didn't intend to return until dawn, and didn't wish to park a Royal Army vehicle outside the Golden Calf.

He walked on the dirt sidewalk of the Boulevard Voltaire. Farther downtown, of course, sidewalks were paved. But here they were packed dirt. After a while he paused to unlace his boots and remove them along with his wool socks. He stuffed socks into boots, tied laces together, and hung the boots about his neck. He strode along in his bare feet, grinning with pleasure at the feel of the good Asante earth beneath his toes.

A glorious night. A sky that went on forever, a million stars, a quarter moon as sharp as a glaive. Anokye was not a religious man. Technically, he was a Christian; his family were members of the small Mokodi Baptist community. But on such a night it was natural for a man's spirits to quest. Perhaps the old beliefs were best: the Onyame (from whom the Nyam had taken his name), the okra, the sunsum, the ntoro. Many, many beliefs and many, many gods. This night had room for all of them: Africa's and those of every nation on earth. It was all one.

He walked steadily for almost an hour before turning off on the wandering street that led, eventually, to the home of Professor Jean-Louis Duclos. He paused in a shadowed place to pull on socks and lace up his boots. Jean would not object to bare feet, but his woman, an Asanti, Mboa, whom Jean-Louis called Maria, would be offended by a barefooted Asanti officer entering her home.

Duclos was a Martinicain. He had journeyed to Paris to

complete his education at the Sorbonne, hoping to become a professor of history and political science. But in Paris, Duclos had discovered he was a Negro—and what that meant in France, Europe, the world. Unwilling to return to Martinique, he had brought his university degree to Asante where he obtained employment as a teacher of history at the Mokodi lycée. It was not the life he had dreamed.

He was drinking raw Algerian wine when Captain Anokye arrived, and had the exaggeratedly slow, precise movements of a man who has drunk too much and thinks to conceal his condition from observers. He was a handsome man, a light fawn, with straight hair, blue eyes. His study was lined with books, old and new. Over the door lintel was an angry red blotch where a bottle of wine had been shattered.

His woman, Mboa, or Maria, was small, blue-black, quiet and dignified. Her hair was corn-rowed, and she wore an ankle-length lappa in a tie-dye design of light browns. She spoke a mellifluous Akan and was inquiring, politely, of Obiri's health, that of his parents, his family, etc., when Jean-Louis interrupted angrily.

"Speak French," he shouted, in that language. "French, French, *French*! I've told you a thousand times."

Maria glanced timidly at him, then looked away hurriedly. She moved with a sinuous grace, bringing Captain Anokye a clean glass, pouring wine from a carafe, adjusting pillows on the low couch, opening the shutters wider to let in the cool night air.

"For the love of God, stop fussing," Jean cried. "Haven't you anything better to do?"

Anokye, familiar with such scenes, made no comment and kept his features impassive. It was their hell.

Stupid nigger,'' Duclos muttered, after Maria had left the room. "She remembers nothing."

Anokye took a small sip of the warm wine. He would have preferred a beer, but if he asked for it, and Duclos had none, the Martinicain's pride would be wounded and he would scream at Maria for not keeping a "decent house." So the Little Captain sipped his warm wine and told Duclos of the morning's action.

Jean-Louis listened intently. He said nothing of the slain rebels. His interest was solely in the possibility of a meeting with the Nyam.

"Is it necessary?" he asked.

"I believe it would be wise," Anokye nodded. "He is not totally without teeth. His men follow him bravely. Why should I wish to kill Asantis, my brothers? We all desire a free Asante. I will speak to him of this."

"Tell him that Africa's war is not one of class," Duclos said excitedly, "but one of race. Tell him that colonialism is not dead, but still exists in the white bankers who own our bonds, the white publishers who tell us what we may read, the white merchants who own our stores, the white profiteers who sell us guns and cars and beer and shoddy cloth." Duclos' voice became louder; he rose and began to pace about the room. "Tell him that Marxism is an invention of the white devils, a European religion that has nothing to do with African wants and needs and beliefs. The Nyam must be made to understand that the struggle is against *white* exploitation. That our black rulers are running dogs of the white imperialists. Look at this nation! This poor, impoverished nation! The King amasses a fortune in white European banks while his sons and daughters and cousins buy their whiteness in France with Asante taxes. Tell the Nyam there can be no freedom for us, no liberty, no happiness, until all white power is destroyed in this country, and eventually in all of Africa,

38

cut out like a malignant cancer. Only then can we build a black Asante and a black Africa, true to our color, our history, our traditions, our gods. Will you tell the Nyam all this?"

"No," Captain Anokye said.

There was a brief moment of silence. The professor looked at him in astonishment.

"No?" he repeated. "But—but I thought you believed these things. As I do."

"What you believe and what I believe are not important at this time. Words are not important. Actions are. If I was to tell the Nyam he must totally reject his Marxist beliefs, then *he* would reject *me*. I must persuade him to be pragmatic. Let him continue to read his thick books of Marxist philosophy and his thin pamphlets of dialectic and revolutionary tactics. It is not important. What is important is that now, *today*, he and I must join forces to destroy the monarchy and save our people from starvation. When the King is gone, and the palace is ours, then we may debate the nature of Asante's future. But now, *today*, that is not our problem. Our problem is to seize power. As soon as possible. And it will come sooner if we join forces and plan together. If I was to speak to him as you propose, I would be as great an enemy in his eyes as the King. Jean, do you understand? We need help from whatever quarter we can get it."

"I see, I see!" Duclos said. Almost shouting. "Expediency. Yes! Very good! Then, when the palace is ours, we shall rid our society of the white leeches and create a truly black Asante. Very wise, Bibi; very wise indeed. May I tell the others of this strategy?"

"If you wish," Captain Anokye said gravely.

"I will compose a letter," Duclos said. Filled with enthusiasm. "A magnificent letter to all the others. Explaining exactly what you have told me. The time for

39

action has arrived! How does that sound? The time for action has arrived!''

The Little Captain nodded. Professor Duclos rushed to his desk, pulled paper and pen forward, began to write frantically. Anokye watched him a moment, then went quietly into the kitchen. Mboa was sitting on a reed stool, knees spread wide. She was peeling a small eggplant. He stood before her, and she looked up. Timorous smile.

''For stew?'' he asked, in Akan.

She nodded.

''Do you grind the seeds?'' he asked her.

''Of course,'' she said. Laughter in her voice. ''Always.''

He put a hand lightly on her bare shoulder. His hand was almost as black as her matte skin.

''You love him,'' he said. More statement than question.

She looked down at the work in her lap, but her hands were still.

''He loves you,'' he said in a low voice. ''But he cannot say it. To you or to himself. Does he beat you?''

''Sometimes,'' she said. ''But not hard. Do you speak the truth? Does he love me?''

''Would he beat you if he did not? He is beating himself, his love for you.''

''Yes,'' she said wonderingly. ''That is true. Obiri, will he marry me?''

''That I cannot say. Yes, if he is to survive. But I cannot say.''

He bent swiftly to put his cheek against hers. Then he departed.

6

PETER A. TANGENT had visited 39 of Africa's 61 nations and knew well the myth of "this divine little native restaurant where prices are so *cheap!*" Claptrap. The best food was in Africa's big cities, because the best produce was sold there, for higher prices, and the best African chefs emigrated there, for higher wages. The price of an excellent dinner in Casablanca, Abidjan, Cape Town or Kinshasa was comparable to what Tangent was accustomed to pay in New York, London, Paris, or Rome. There was one difference in Africa: The service was better. It was cheerful.

His favorite restaurant in Mokodi was the Zabarian, specializing in seafood. It was close to the waterfront, within walking distance of the Mokodi Hilton. It was a modest building of whitewashed stucco with a red-tiled roof. The main dining room was air-conditioned. It was said that Felah, the Asanti bartender, was capable of mixing any drink a customer might name. Tangent had tested his expertise on a Pink Lady and a Bees' Knees, and hadn't stumped him.

But that night, Tangent was content with a Beefeaters martini, up, served in a frosted glass with a tiny prawn immersed, instead of the conventional olive, lemon peel, or onion. The American didn't object to the taste, but thought the little shrimp looked exactly like a miniature fetus floating in amniotic fluid. Not an appetizing fantasy.

He had called for a reservation and asked to be seated outside, on the open terrace. From his table, he could see the flickering torches of fishing boats and, beyond, the dim lights of the island of Zabar. Asante was on approximately the same latitude as Venezuela, and at that time of year, on the coast, the temperature rarely went above 85°F during the day, falling to 75°F at night. The rainy season would bring mugginess, but now the air was warm, clear, scented. Tangent wore a lettuce-green voile shirt, Countess Mara tie in navy blue, a suit of raw, cream-colored silk. He was comfortable.

After two martinis, he dined on an appetizer of crayfish lumps in a hot sauce, a broiled local fish similar in flavor to Florida's pompano, and a mixture of tiny eggplant chunks fried with groundnuts. There was a flinty '69 Muscadet and, later, coffee laced with a local brandy that was chocolate-flavored. He had, Tangent acknowledged, come a long way from Crawfordsville, Indiana.

He signed the bill and left a generous dash, in CFAs, for the waiter. He knew that in Asante the dash was customarily given before the meal was served. It was not a custom Tangent approved of or followed. He slipped an additional American fiver to the maître d', then stopped at the bar for a final Remy Martin.

"Felah," he asked the bartender, "do you know of a place called Les Trois Chats?"

The black did an exaggerated burlesque, rolling his eyes skyward until only the whites showed.

"Oh, Mr. Tangent, sir, please don't ask me," he begged. "I would not want it on my soul that I had directed you *there!*"

"That good?" Tangent asked.

"That *bad!*" Felah said. "All kinds of nasty-nice things there. Ask for Sweetpea."

"No, no," Tangent said. "You've got me wrong. I'm going to meet a man."

"Of course you are, Mr. Tangent," Felah said solemnly. "You are surely going to Les Trois Chats to meet a man. To be sure, Mr. Tangent, sir."

They both laughed.

"I'll summon you a taxi," Felah said. "A driver you can trust."

"Your cousin?" Tangent asked.

"How did you know?" Felah said. All mock innocence. "Anyway, he'll get you home safe. What's left of you."

"Another problem," Tangent said. "I need a bottle. Say, Johnnie Walker Red. You think your cousin might be able to help me out?"

"That cousin of mine," Felah nodded, "he's *helpful.*"

"Tell me, Felah—is there anything in this world money can't buy?"

"There is indeed, Mr. Tangent," Felah said. "The love of a good woman. But don't tell Sweetpea *that!*"

Twenty minutes later Tangent was seated in the taxi of Felah's cousin, drawn up outside a dockside bar. There was a neon sign, almost completely dark, and on the clapboard wall an enormous primitive painting of three cats fighting. Get that to a Madison Avenue gallery, Tangent thought, and your fortune would be made.

"This is it?" he asked the driver.

"Kootchie-koo," the driver said.

Tangent gave him 50 French francs.

"Please wait for me," he said.

"Kootchie-koo," the driver said.

"I won't be long," Tangent said.

The driver was still grinning when Tangent pushed through the wooden doors. Half-doors really. Swinging

43

wooden shutters. The Last Chance Saloon. He entered into bedlam. Noise. Dust. Music. Laughter. Shouts. A fight. But there were fascinated tourists in conducted tours. It might all very well be a put-on. "Harry, I got to tell you I was in this fantastic place in Mokodi, and you wouldn't *believe* . . ." It was possible.

He gave the fat bartender an English pound. His wallet was a file drawer of currencies.

The bartender was white. If washed. His hand devoured the bill.

"Sweetpea is busy," he said. "Sit down, relax, take off your shoes. She'll be—"

"Sam Leiberman," Tangent said. "Where can I find Sam Leiberman?"

The bartender jerked a thumb. "Outside," he said. "Around in back. Flight of steps. Upstairs."

Tangent looked about. The melee had quieted. People were sitting and drinking. Just another bar, tavern, cabaret. A thin young man at an upright piano struck a chord. His eyelids were sequined. Conversation ceased.

"When they begin," the young man whispered, "the beguine . . ."

"Play it again, Sam," Tangent said.

"What?" the fat bartender asked.

Carrying the Johnnie Walker Red in a paper bag, Tangent trudged up the outside staircase and rapped at a frame door covered with cloth mosquito netting.

"Sweetpea is downstairs," a hoarse voice shouted.

"Sam?" Tangent shouted back. "Is that you? Sam Leiberman? It's Peter Tangent."

He heard sounds. A light flickered, went off, came on again. A gas lantern. The door opened.

A black girl, giggling, wearing a man's shirt that came almost to her knees.

"Good evening," he said, in Akan. "My name is Peter Tangent. I'd like—"

"Cut the crap and come on in," the harsh voice called. "She don't speak the language. You bring anything to drink?"

"Johnnie Walker," Tangent said, entering and peering about.

"Red or black?"

"Red."

"That's right," the voice said. Throaty laugh. "I saw your latest annual report. Profits are down."

Tangent stumbled into a smelly inner room, following the voice. Sam Leiberman was lying in a net-covered hammock.

"Give the hooch to the cunt," he said.

Tangent handed it over. Leiberman spoke to the girl in a language Tangent did not recognize.

"What's that?" he asked. "What are you speaking?"

"Boulé," Leiberman said. "She's from the Ivory Coast."

"Sam, how many languages do you speak?"

"Eighteen," Leiberman said. "But I dream in Yiddish. Throw the clothes off that chair."

Tangent removed the soiled shirts with his fingertips and sat down cautiously in a wicker armchair. He sat on the edge.

"Get your raw silk dirty?" Leiberman jeered. "You're something, you are. Little Lord Fauntleroy all grown up."

The girl came back with two small jelly jars. One for her, one for Tangent. Both filled with Scotch. The bottle went to Leiberman. A hairy, muscled arm came out from under the mosquito net. A strong hand grasped the neck of the bottle. It disappeared under the net. The girl curled onto the floor, alongside Leiberman's hammock.

45

"What's with the net?" Tangent asked.

"Habit," Leiberman said. "I can't afford Atabrine. Thanks for the booze. Looking at you."

There was a sound of a gross swallow, a deep belch.

"I can't even *see* you," Tangent said, trying to peer through the net.

"I'm here," Sam Leiberman said.

"Who is she?" Tangent asked.

"The cunt?" Leiberman said. "Don't worry; she doesn't coppish English. Would I call her a cunt if she could? Actually, she's a dear, sweet knish who has been a great comfort to me in my old age. King Lardass really broke it off in you at the palace this morning, didn't he?"

"My God," Tangent said, "does everyone in Asante know about that?"

"Not everyone," Leiberman said. "There are a few herders up in the hills who won't learn about it until tomorrow morning. Their goats will hear about it soon after. What do you want?"

"I wouldn't be here if I didn't know you can keep your mouth shut."

"Cut the shit," Leiberman said. "All right, you bought me a jug. What do you *want*?"

"Can you get papers for Togo?" Tangent asked.

"No," Leiberman said. "But I can get into Togo. No problem, if the price is right. What is it?"

"You'll have to go to Lomé. For a day or so."

"Okay. So now I'm in Lomé. Then what?"

"There's a reporter named St. Clair. René St. Clair. He works for the *Free Press*."

"St. Clair?" Leiberman said. "I know him. A crud."

"Right," Tangent said.

"Buy him for a bottle of Algerian red," Leiberman

said. "*Or* a carton of Luckies. *Or* a fat young boy with sphincter intact."

"That's the man."

"We all have our price," Leiberman said. "Mine is Johnnie Walker Red. When I was young, it was Johnnie Walker Black. But we all get old, Tangent. Did you know that?"

"The thought has crossed my mind on occasion. This is one of them. Now, listen carefully. I want—"

"Wait a minute."

The hairy arm came out of the mosquito net again. The meaty hand slid into the girl's shirt, clamped on her bony shoulder, dragged her up and under the net. She rolled into the hammock. Giggling.

"I'm listening, Tangent," Leiberman said.

Tangent had stock options with Starrett Petroleum Corp., an excellent pension plan, an annual bonus, and a salary of 65,000 American dollars. Sometimes he wondered if it was enough.

"St. Clair writes a column for the *Free Press*," he said. "Political gossip."

"Blackmail," Leiberman growled.

"Sure," Tangent agreed. "But it's popular. Widely read, all over West Africa. I've used it before."

"So?"

"Back in nineteen sixty-one, there was a big flap between Asante and Togo. Over who owned the island of Zabar. It almost came to war."

"War?" Leiberman scoffed. "In nineteen sixty-one they were still shooting arrows."

"Anyway, it went to UN arbitration. Asante got Zabar, and Togo got control of navigation on the Mono River. Follow?"

"Way ahead of you. You want me to get into Togo, go

47

to Lomé, look up this crud St. Clair, and pay him enough to plant an item in his column saying there's been talk in high circles of the Togo government about reopening the whole Zabar question, and claiming rights to the island, adjacent territorial waters, and the oil underneath. You Jewish, Tangent?''

''No, I'm a goy.''

''You dress British and think Yiddish. It might work. Worth a try.''

''I just want an option, to give Starrett a chance to delay our answer. You sure she doesn't speak English?''

''I'm sure. She speaks mostly cock. You want to manufacture a flap.''

''Right. A minor flap.''

''Okay. How much?''

''A thousand francs. French. That's total. To you. For your expenses and the baksheesh to St. Clair. The lower you keep his dash, the more for you. But you've got to keep Starrett out of it. No connection.''

''How about fifteen hundred?''

''No way. Well . . . maybe. For a little additional poop.''

''Oh, you sly goyishe devil,'' Leiberman said. ''You *will* work your evil way with me. What more do you want?''

''Captain Obiri Anokye,'' Tangent said. ''Do you know him?''

''Sure.''

''You've actually met him?''

''Sure. He looked me up. I had heard of him before that, of course.''

''Why did he look you up?''

''Some of his men are equipped with reconditioned Garands. Okay, but old. He had read somewhere that during World War Two, the last *fun* war, some hotrods had modified the Garand to take a twenty-round magazine.''

''Is that true?''

''Sure, it's true. Gun nuts will do *anything*. The twenty-round magazines worked fine—for maybe two fast firings. Then the barrel burned out or the bolt jammed or something. I liked him. A nice young wog. Small. They call him the Little Captain. Eager to learn. Strictly no-crap.''

''What does he want?''

''Want? How the hell do I know what he wants? Just to be a good soldier boy, I guess.''

''Is he into anything political?''

''Anokye? Not to my knowledge. Nothing I've heard about. He just does his job of work.''

''The extra five hundred francs is to ask around about him,'' Tangent said. ''His family, education, how much he spends, who he sleeps with, friends in high places . . . the whole shmear.''

''No problem,'' Leiberman said.

''I'll be back down here in a couple of weeks,'' Tangent said. ''By that time I'll expect you to have the St. Clair item in print or scheduled, and I'll want whatever you've dredged on Captain Obiri Anokye.''

''It shall be done, O Great White Father,'' Leiberman said. ''Now get lost. The bartender downstairs can put you next to Sweetpea.''

Tangent rose, laughing. ''That woman has the greatest advance billing since Jenny Lind.''

''Worth it,'' Leiberman said. Then he simpered from under the net: ''Oh, Peter . . .''

''Yes?''

''Leave the money on the mantel, dear boy.''

7

CAPTAIN ANOKYE walked slowly through the soft darkness. This section of Mokodi was illuminated; corner street lamps with round globes leaked dim orange light, surrounded by frantic moths. Mid-block stretches were dark, but Anokye knew families lolled on screened porches, lay in outside, netted hammocks, perched on reed stools, sipped cold Benin beer, and watched his progress in the darkness. They knew; the Little Captain was on his way to visit Miss Yvonne at the Golden Calf. He could hear the gentle murmurs.

Beyond the business district, away from downtown, the Boulevard Voltaire became Asante Royal Highway No. 1, the nation's paved road running north 474 kilometers to Four Points. Intersecting roads were laterite, crushed stone, packed earth, or rutted one-track cart lanes leading away into the grasslands.

Less than a kilometer after street illumination ended was the Golden Calf, set in a handsome expanse of tended lawn and groomed acacia. It had formerly been the home of a wealthy *colon*. Now it was Mokodi's, and Asante's, most renowned, and most expensive, house of pleasure.

Prostitution, in Asante, was not legal. But neither were prostitutes persecuted; they were simply ignored, providing tourists were not cheated, beaten, or robbed. All went smoothly. A uniformed member of Mokodi's gendarmerie was customarily stationed on the porch, near the front entrance of the Golden Calf. His presence lent a certain quiet dignity to the activities of the maison. It was understood that clients might misbehave only within the privacy of the individual chambers. Public impropriety was rare.

The Golden Calf was ostensibly owned and operated by Yvonne Mayer, daughter of a *colon* family from the Saar. Actually, as most Asantis knew, the Golden Calf was truly managed by Miss Yvonne, but she owned only a third. The remaining two-thirds were owned by the widow of the King's older brother. This lady lived most of the year in St. Tropez and visited Asante as infrequently as possible.

It was a wraith of a white building, gently illuminated, floating in the darkness. All pillars and gingerbread trim. It seemed to soar. There were gables and minarets. And soft laughter.

Captain Obiri Anokye walked up the chalk driveway and around to the kitchen entrance. He entered without knocking and mounted the back staircase. None of the busy cooks and waiters appeared to notice him, but he knew his arrival would be signaled to Miss Yvonne. So it was; she awaited him outside the door to her private chambers on the third floor.

She was wearing a peach-colored peignoir. Her spatulate feet were bare. In her fingers, twirling, were her unusual spectacles, half-glasses actually, American, the type called Benjamin Franklin.

"Obiri! How nice!" She leaned forward for his cheek kiss.

As usual, they spoke French.

"Please forgive me," he said. "I smell like a goat. I have been in the field all day. May I shower?"

"Of course," she said.

She drew him inside her apartment, closed and locked the door.

51

"I heard about your adventure," she said.

"What?"

"This morning. At Lake Volta."

"Oh, yes. That."

"You killed them all?"

"All," he said. "Those were my orders." Then he saw something in her face. "Only the men," he said. "The women and children lived."

"Good," she said. "A beer? Benin or Heinekens? Now or later?"

"Later," he said. "When I am clean. I sent a message to the Nyam to meet with me. Wherever he chooses. I will go alone, without weapons."

"Was that wise?" she asked.

"Wise, not wise." He shrugged. "I am becoming impatient. I must move. We will speak of this later. Go on with your work. No, wait . . ."

He moved her to him. Kissed her closed eyes. His fingers pressed her thin back.

"Goat!" she said.

"I know," he laughed. "I am."

He showered slowly and carefully. He lathered his short, squat body thoroughly, paying particular attention to his armpits and groin. As usual, the size of his penis bemused him: so small in repose, large and ardent when excited. The American, Sam Leiberman, the mercenary, had told him an amusing story about a man with a short penis. The final line had been: "It ain't the size that counts, it's the ferocity." That was true. And not only in fucking.

"May I wear your kimono?" he called from the bathroom.

"Of course," she called back. "Do you have to ask?"

He padded from the bathroom, took the Japanese robe

from her closet. He left it unbelted. She was working at her desk, the funny glasses pushed down on her nose. He bent to rub his cheek against hers, to nibble her ear.

"Much better," she said approvingly, not looking up from her account book. "Now you smell clean and exciting."

"You are a blossom," he said, switching to Akan. "A white blossom blooming in the darkness, quivering to be plucked."

She spoke the language almost as well as he.

"Awaiting your fingers," she said. "To take me and press me in your heart."

He smiled, touched her lips. Then he went to the small office refrigerator. Benin was a light beer, tangy, Alsatian in flavor. He poured it slowly, admiring the froth. He brought the tall glass back to her desk. He sprawled in an armchair, the flowered kimono gaping open. He sipped, handed the glass to her. She took it absently, sipped, still peering at her ledger.

"A good month," she said. "Very good indeed."

"You work hard," he said. "You should own it all."

"Yes," she agreed. "But I cheat, you know."

"You'd be a fool not to."

"Still . . ." she said.

She took off the glasses, pushed the ledger away. She leaned forward to place her cupped palm lightly on his bared genitals.

"Love," she said.

They stared at each other. Nothing blocked them.

"What will you say to the Nyam?" she asked.

"At this time, I must tell every man what he wants to hear. I will tell him that I am his friend, that I desire what he desires—the end of the monarchy. Then I will tell him that he cannot succeed without me. That Okomfo was only

53

one of many traitors in his camp. That I am aware of every move he makes, before he makes it. That I have been ordered to kill him. That he and many good men will die if he continues to provoke the King. That my way is best. For everyone.''

"You think he will listen?''

"I believe so. He is not a fool. He will think to use me. Then, when I have helped him gain what he wishes—the liberation of Asante—he will kill me. That will be his thinking. What have you heard? Anything?''

"He met again with the man from Albania. Where are the arms? the Nyam wanted to know. Where are the weapons you promised? But the man from Albania was all soft apologies. Soon, he kept saying, soon . . .''

Captain Obiri Anokye laughed.

"They are having second thoughts," he said. "Perhaps they have invested in the wrong man. That is what they will think. Especially after what happened this morning at Lake Volta. The Nyam is a waste, they will think. The King's captain destroys him at his leisure. Why should we give such a victim valuable weapons? Another reason why the Nyam will speak with me.''

"I love you," she said.

"Yes," he said. "Anything else?''

"A man has been asking questions about you.''

"Oh? About me? Who?''

"A man named Peter Tangent. Do you know him?''

"I have never met him, but I know of him. The American from the oil company? Very tall, thin, elegant?''

"Yes. Too elegant.''

Anokye looked at her, then showed his white teeth. "Just because he has never visited your girls and dresses well . . .''

"Bibi, I *know*.''

"If you say so. What questions did he ask?"

"Who you are. Your family. What you want. Are you to be trusted. And so forth."

"Interesting. You believe Willi Abraham told him about me?"

"Yes. I think it may have something to do with the palace meeting this morning."

"About the oil lease."

"Yes. The King wanted seventy-five percent of future profits."

"But will settle for fifty-five with an additional ten to his Swiss account."

"That is what Willi guessed. Tangent wasn't happy."

"No, I do not believe he would be."

"He said he would have to talk to his people. Bibi, this American is very wise. He is in charge of all his company's African operations. But he never speaks of 'my company' or 'my corporation.' He always says 'My people.' That is smart in dealing with Africans. No, Bibi?"

"Yes," he agreed. "Very wise. You think this Tangent will come to me?"

"Yes," she said, "I think so. And I believe Willi thinks so. Tangent will come to you eventually. There is much money involved. The reports they showed the King are not true reports. There is oil there. Definitely. An ocean of oil."

He shook his head wonderingly. With great admiration.

"You know everything," he said.

"I listen," she said. "I listen and learn. My girls listen and tell me. Is anything a secret in Mokodi?"

"Not even in all Asante," he said. "The King sneezes in Mokodi, and in Four Points a border guard says, 'May your soul return'."

She laughed and leaned back in her swivel chair. She pulled her peignoir up to her waist and spread her legs. Her pubic hair was flaxen.

"My home awaits you," she said, speaking in Akan. "I bid you enter and find peace."

"I would share your home with great honor and pleasure," he replied. "Please forgive the poor gifts I bring."

"Your presence is gift enough," she said.

They never wearied of entwining the black and the white: arms, torsos, legs, all of them. To form sweated, abstract patterns. His dark loins locked in her pale prison.

"Do you believe in me?" he asked her.

"Can you doubt it?" she said. "But your ambitions are not important. They are, of course. But I would love you if you were a sweeper."

He started to say, "That is not the truth," but caught himself, and said nothing.

He watched her slow tongue. Her long, slow tongue. Fire rose in him. Just as the sun had bloomed from the savanna that morning.

Just before he entered into her, he said, "I shall conquer."

"Oh yes," she said. "My king! Hurt me!"

8

TWO DAYS LATER Peter Tangent was back in England. A company limousine met him at Heathrow, and he went directly to his suite at the Connaught. He had lived most of his adult life in hotels, and if he had ever felt the need to put down roots, he ascribed it to youthful romanticism. He might admire the personally decorated apartments of friends, their suburban villas, country cottages, beach houses perched on stilts. But there was much to be said for hotel living: its impersonality, instant service at the end of a phone, freedom from owning many *things*, or more likely being owned by them.

He showered quickly, changed clothes, took up two attaché cases and went back down again, to be driven to Starrett's London headquarters in an Edwardian town house in Mayfair.

"Good afternoon, Mr. Tangent," the uniformed commissionaire said, opening the limousine door. "Glad to have you back, sir."

"Glad to be back, John," Tangent said, and wondered if that was his first lie of the day. No, he had complimented a maid at the Connaught on her new hairdo. It had been dreadful. But that had been a white lie.

There it was again. White lie—small and innocent. Presumably a black lie would be large and evil. He had trained himself never to make such gaffes in his conversations with Africans. His thinking was something else again. That it was essentially racist he had no doubt. A product of his education, conditioning, growing up in Middle America. But at least he was aware of it. Which was more than you could say of J. Tom Petty and the warm-smiled, cold-eyed men from the Tulsa office.

There were no crises awaiting him. Most of Starrett's African fields had long since shaken down into routine operations. It was only when leases had to be negotiated, or when, following one of the frequent coups d'etat that racked African nations, the new rulers had to be placated and assured of Starrett's loyalty and support, that Tangent's personal intervention was required. In London oil circles, this latter process was sometimes casually referred to as "switching the dash."

"Where have you been, old boy?"

"South. Switching the dash."

"Ah."

On the afternoon of his return, Tangent found a confidential report awaiting him. It was his requested update on Asante's financial condition, prepared for him by the foreign section of Starrett's London bank. Tangent flipped through it quickly, automatically translating the cautious "bankese" and evaluating how it might affect Starrett's Asante investment.

The latest news was not encouraging. Asante's chronic balance of trade problem had worsened, exacerbated by the profligacies of King Prempeh IV and the ridiculous Asante tax structure which allowed the wealthy (mostly Prempeh's relatives) to escape income taxes almost completely if they established residence in a foreign land.

Most of Asante's bonds and short-term notes were held by French banks, investment funds, and institutions. The nation of Asante might have achieved political independence in 1958, but its economy did not. It was still heavily French-dominated. For instance, the Zabarian, Tangent's favorite restaurant, was French-owned. As were theaters, automobile agencies, insurance companies, the gold mine, office buildings, large cotton and corn plantations, the local Coca-Cola bottling plant, and many minor enterprises. The Asante National Bank—not the only Asante bank, but certainly the largest and most prestigious—was owned by a French-English-American banking consortium. The French had the largest share, by far.

So Tangent could understand why the French would be concerned by Asante's degenerating financial condition. He was certain that Anatole Garde, the King's personal secretary, was keeping the Quai d'Orsay informed as matters melted from bad to worse. Was it significant that Garde had directed him to Willi Abraham who had suggested the name of Captain Obiri Anokye? Did that mean France was giving tacit approval to the Little Captain? For what purpose?

Tangent put aside the financial report and flipped through phone messages that had accumulated during his absence. Most of the callers had left phone numbers, but not their names. Tangent recognized some of them, but not all. They would offer invitations to country weekends, request subscriptions to charities, announce gallery exhibitions. He tossed them all into his wastebasket. If they called again: "Sorry, my secretary must have slipped up; I didn't get your message." Then, standing at his desk, he dialed Tony Malcolm's private number on his outside line.

Malcolm's cover was unusual, a source of some amusement to members of Brindleys who knew the details.

In 1954, Virginia had invested in Schwarzkopf's Adventure Tours, a Liverpool-based travel agency, thinking to use it as a general cover for agents working Britain and Europe. The agency had been founded by Leon Schwarzkopf, an immigrant Pole, in 1950. His idea was to organize tours of European battlefields of World War II. He was certain British veterans would want to revisit places where they had fought, suffered, and watched friends perish. They didn't. At least, not in the 1950s. Schwarzkopf's was kept alive by infusions of Virginia funds. Its premises were gradually enlarged, offices were added, certain structural changes were made, and specialized equipment installed.

Leon Schwarzkopf died in 1959, officially of cirrhosis of the liver, although Tony Malcolm always claimed it was from an overdose of kielbasy. Virginia then hired Mrs. Agatha Forbes-Smythe, the widow of a British brigadier, as manager. To their astonishment, Schwarzkopf's Adventure Tours began to succeed, to prosper, to boom. Part of this was due to Mrs. Forbes-Smythe's managerial prowess and part to Leon Schwarzkopf's basic concept. He had been correct, but ahead of his time. In the 1960s and thenceforth, British veterans *did* want to revisit scenes of their World War II adventures, and profitable tours were arranged to the battlefields of France, Belgium, Italy, Germany, North Africa, Greece, and Crete. Schwarzkopf grew into a very successful chain of travel agencies. Virginia, now the sole owner, was delighted; there was talk of going public.

Tony Malcolm's title was "Director of Client Relations" in the London Branch. He had a private entrance, his own small suite of offices, and a permanent staff of nine. The Schwarzkopf schedule of tours provided an excellent cover for moving mules, couriers, spooks, and sleepers all over Europe and Africa. Which had been the original idea, of course.

Tangent got through to Malcolm with no delay.

"Tony? Tangent here."

60

"Peter! Welcome back. And thank you."

"Oh, you got it. Like it?"

"Delightful. I'm building up quite a collection. Thanks to you."

"Dinner tonight?"

"Fine. The club?"

"Sure. I'll see if I can get our corner table for nine. Meet you at the bar around eight?"

"You're on."

Brindleys was an infant compared to other exclusive private clubs in London. It had been organized after World War II and was housed in a relatively new (1925) town house on Park Lane that had suffered only minor bomb damage during the war. It had been completely repaired and renovated before Brindleys took possession.

Brindleys was mainly a dining and drinking club, although the two upper floors offered small sleeping suites for members who lived outside London, or for overseas guests. It was a wealthy club and an expensive club, a matter of little consequence to most of the members since their companies, multinational corporations, banks, and embassies picked up the tick. The chef had been lured away from a three-star restaurant in Lyons, and the serving staff were mostly ex-British army batmen who knew a good thing when they saw one. Brindleys had a fashionable dull gloss, quiet and gently gleaming. The atmosphere, Tony Malcolm said, was one of "blatant restraint."

What distinguished Brindleys from other London clubs was the youth of its membership and their occupations: corporation executives, diplomats, international publishers, United Nations representatives, trade officials, high military officers, and a hard-to-define group of multilingual commission brokers who seemed to have no home base but circulated confidently across borders, selling, buying, cajoling, persuading, as interested in Russian gold as they were in Greek tankers, Spanish real estate, South African diamonds, and stolen Etruscan art. The business of the world was discussed and sometimes concluded in the bar, dining room, library, and salons of Brindleys. The members, in their carelessly elegant suits of banker's gray, subdued stripes, and gentle plaids, spun easily in the interlocking orbits of government, diplomacy, banking, international finance, oil . . . and espionage.

Listening to the shoptalk at the bar, Tony Malcolm said, "This place is the Establishment's establishment."

"More like the world's most expensive men's room," Tangent said.

They exchanged only innocent gossip at the bar and, later, at their corner table. Talk of mutual acquaintances: who had been assigned where; who had succeeded and who had failed; marriages, divorces, and affairs; two unaccountable suicides, and one scarifying murder. They waited patiently, on their second brandy, until the surrounding tables were vacant before they got down to business.

"Did you see Bob Curtin?" Malcolm asked.

"Yes. For a short talk."

"What's your take?"

Tangent made a thumb-down gesture.

"Dump him, Tony," he advised. "He's lost his nerve. He'll fuck you up."

Malcolm sighed. "That's the word I get," he said. "Well . . . too bad. He was a good man."

"Good?"

"Good," Malcolm said, "not great. I'll get him on a stateside desk."

"An unimportant desk," Tangent said.

Malcolm looked at him, perplexed. He was a fleshy, pinkish man. He bounced rather than walked, and had the ebullient manner of a shoe salesman. He appeared to be a genial greeter and joiner, an intellectual lightweight, a grinning, slap-on-the-back chap, best company in the world. Believe all that, and you were doomed.

"Why so down on Curtin?" he asked.

"Something's going on there," Tangent said. "Curtin should be on top of it, and he's not."

He told Malcolm everything that had happened in Mokodi: the palace meeting, the mention of Captain Obiri Anokye, what he had been able to discover about the Little Captain. He told Malcolm he had hired Leiberman to dig further. He did not mention Leiberman's errand in Togo.

"Yes," Malcolm agreed, "something seems to be brewing. And Curtin should have been on to it. Peter, it'll take me a while to cancel him and break in a new bod. Will you keep me updated on what you get from Leiberman?"

"Of course. Can you get something for me from Virginia?"

"What is it?"

"What would their reaction be to destabilizing the Asante government?"

"All right," Malcolm said. "I should have word within a week."

"Think I should ask the French? I saw Ricard at the bar. I could go through him."

"Forget it," Malcolm said. "It'll take them a month of Sundays to come to any decision, and then your answer will be maybe yes, maybe no. If Garde sent you to see Abraham, then it stands to reason Paris won't object."

"Unless Abraham is playing his own game."

63

"Yes," Malcolm said, "there's that. Peter, you seem depressed."

"Oh . . . I don't know. Not so much depressed as subdued. A gray mood. One of those 'What does it all matter?' phases. You ever feel like that?"

"All the time," Malcolm said. "I know exactly what you need."

The two men stared at each other.

"You may be right," Tangent said.

"Let's go," Malcolm said.

Four days later, Tangent got a call at his Connaught suite.

"Peter? Tony Malcolm here."

"Yes, Tony."

"Feeling better?"

"Much."

"Good. That matter we discussed. The question you asked. At the club."

"I remember."

"I checked it out for you."

"And?"

"They couldn't care less."

9

ON THE FOLLOWING Saturday afternoon, Captain Obiri Anokye showered and dressed carefully at the Mokodi barracks. He donned his dress whites because he knew they would make his parents proud. Also, the whites would be easily identifiable later that night.

The dress uniform consisted of long trousers and a fitted tunic of white drill. A red ascot-type scarf was worn at the throat. A black, beaked officer's cap bore a brass Asante army insignia. Anokye wore two rows of ribbons and a gold aigulette signifying his staff status. The tunic's shoulder boards bore two small bars, captain's rank, and the trousers had an outside stripe of red. He was not armed.

Sgt. Yeboa waited in the Land Rover to drive him to the ferry slip.

"Yes *sah!*" the sergeant said, inspecting his captain. Both men laughed. It was their private joke.

They had been boyhood friends and had enlisted at the same time. In private, Sene Yeboa would never think of calling Anokye "sir." But they had seen many American films together, and the ones they liked best were war movies with Gary Cooper, David Niven, Douglas Fairbanks, Jr., Humphrey Bogart, etc. In these films, when the actors portrayed British officers in Africa and India, they gave commands, and their black soldiers, clad in khaki shorts and high stockings, stiffened to attention and snapped off a British salute, palm-faced, fingers together, the entire hand and upper arm quivering with tension. "Yes *sah!*" they always shouted. Anokye and Yeboa thought this hilarious. "Yes *sah!*" they kept shouting to each other as boys, and "Yes *sah!*" was still their private joke.

Yeboa was a thick man with the heavy neck and shoulder muscles of a born machine gunner. He lumbered, stooped, but his clumsiness was deceptive; he could move swiftly, lightly, silently, when needed. As the Little Captain knew. Yeboa had been "made in the bush," and was lighter in color than Anokye.

He drove slowly toward the port, hunched over the steering wheel. Anokye glanced at him, saw the puzzled frown, the furrowed brow.

"I must meet him alone, Sene," he said softly. "That was my word."

"I know. And without a weapon."

"Without a weapon," Anokye nodded.

"I could be there," Yeboa said. "In the shadows. They would not see me."

"Could you prevent my death?" the Little Captain asked. "Even if you were alongside me? They could use a long gun."

"Yes," Yeboa said miserably, "that is true. I fear for you, Bibi."

Captain Anokye touched the man's heavy shoulder.

"Do not fear, Sene," he said. "Auntie Tal cast the stones and saw a glorious future for me."

"Do you believe the stones of Auntie Tal?"

"No," the Little Captain said. "But still . . ."

At the ferry slip, Anokye got out, then leaned to speak through the open window.

"It will go well," he said to Yeboa. "Believe it."

"Will you then return to the barracks?"

66

"No. I have business elsewhere."

Yeboa nodded. "May the gods protect you," he said.

"And you," Anokye smiled. "My brother."

The trip to Zabar took almost half an hour, in a ferry that had once plied the waters of Chesapeake Bay. A refreshment stand that had formerly sold hot dogs, french fries, and Coca-Cola, now sold roasted yams, pepper chicken, and Coca-Cola. But there were few customers. Asantis had no money for ferryboat food.

At the slip in Zabar, Captain Anokye boarded a ramshackle bus to his village of Porto Chonin. He knew most of his fellow passengers, and there were warm greetings, embraces, jokes about his thinning hair, laughter. He took it as personal affection and was grateful; he knew their feelings toward the King, and he was the King's soldier.

At the village there were more friends to greet, a dozen invitations to decline regretfully. Little boys clustered about to stare wide-eyed at his splendid uniform. Old men and young pressed his clasped hands in theirs and muttered of prices, taxes, no work . . .

"Yes, yes," Anokye kept saying. "You speak the truth. I understand. These are evil times."

Finally he broke away, waving to all. He stopped at the butcher stand which offered a sad selection of three scrawny chickens, two miserably thin shoats, and a bony goat trembling as if with the ague. This butcher stand had once been the largest on Zabar. People came from other villages to buy its plump hens, cuts of bloody beef, and homemade pepper sausage greatly prized for stews. Now the poor stock, sagging tin roof, odor of spoiled meat gave evidence of its fate, of all Asante's fate.

Anokye picked out the largest of the chickens and watched while it was slaughtered, drained, gutted, plucked, wrapped in a week-old copy of the Mokodi *New Times*. He paid for it and started down toward the shore, holding the package away from him so it might not leak and stain his uniform.

"Uncle Bibi! Uncle Bibi!"

His older brother's children came running toward him, the four oldest racing like the wind, the baby stumbling after. They crowded around, hugging his legs, tugging at him, all speaking at once. He embraced them all, gave the oldest boy the chicken to carry, picked up the dusty toddler, and they all went down to their home, laughing and shouting.

First came the family. Then the sept, the tribe, the nation. But the family came first. The home was where a man was born and where he died. Between, if he was destined to journey to another place, he returned to the home and family to restore his strength and spirit. These were people *of* him. The same blood.

They were all there: grandmother, mother, father, older brother and his family, younger unmarried brother, younger unmarried sister. Also, uncles, aunts, cousins, some old, some young. A huge crowd it seemed, impossible to feed. But somehow it was done. Obiri's chicken was cut up swiftly and added to the enormous cast-iron pot simmering on an ancient wood-burning stove that bore a little brass plaque (kept carefully shined by his mother as a kind of juju). It read: "J.B. Freebly, Kalamazoo, Mich." Kalamazoo. What a wonderful word! "Kalamazoo!" the children called to each other. What did it mean? "Kalamazooooo!"

Captain Anokye gave up trying to keep his dress whites clean. Impossible, with dripping crayfish, a fish stew (and Obiri's chicken) with onions, beans, okra, fufu, rice, greens. Fresh oranges and pineapple. He knew what this homecoming feast must have cost them; they would all live on rice for a week to make up for it. But he could not mention their sacrifice; it would diminish their pride and their enjoyment.

After, leaving the women to clean up, the men strolled down to the shore, and Obiri passed around a package of Gauloises blue he had brought. They all lighted up and puffed importantly, coughing.

They inspected the Anokye fishing boat, pulled up onto the beach on rollers. Obiri admired the repainting of the small figurehead: an Ashanti chief in war regalia. Then the men sat on the sand and talked politics.

Obiri listened carefully, trying to judge their temper. Times were bad, they agreed, and getting worse. Food was increasingly scarce in Zabar and in Mokodi, but in upland villages, it was said, people were starving, and the old were wandering off so as not to be a burden to their families. How could such things be? Taxes were increased once, twice, three times a year. Now a tax on salt and matches? It was unheard of! Where did the tax money go? They turned to Obiri for an answer: Where did all the tax money go?

He could have told them, but did not. What could he say: The King is a thief? So he urged them to be patient. He said that certain men in high places were aware of what was happening and were determined to make things better. If they would be patient and endure for six months, things would change for the better. He was certain of that. His confidence comforted them. They would repeat his words to their friends. Soon all of Zabar would know what Captain Obiri Anokye had said. Perhaps it would help keep men with hungry children from doing something foolish.

There was a brief silence after Obiri had spoken. They

sat on the warm sands and gazed seaward. The night soothed them all. Far out they saw the lights of the *Starrett Explorer* rising and falling. The foreign ship searching for wealth beneath the sea. They dreamed of wells of francs, pounds, dollars—a constant flood of money pouring up from the center of the earth that would enrich them all.

Then it was time for Obiri to depart if he was to make the final ferry back to Mokodi. He embraced them all. There were tears, fond caresses. He finally tore himself away. His older brother, Zuni, accompanied him up the hill to the bus stop. They walked a few moments in silence. A half-moon paved the dirt path. Zuni was strong, slender with the sinewy muscles of a small-boat fisherman. He was darker than Obiri, burned black by the sun. He wore a small tuft of grayish beard. His forehead was already rippled with worry wrinkles; squint lines netted his eyes. An enormous blue marlin had left a pale scar along his right ribcage, from armpit to hip. Zuni had killed him. He rarely lost a big one.

"Our father grows old," Obiri said sadly.

"Yes," Zuni acknowledged, "but I cannot keep him from the boat. He demands to go. Every morning."

"I know," Obiri said. "Let him. What is he to do—sit and dream? You know he cannot do that."

"Nor can I," Zuni said. His voice was low. "When is it to be?"

"As I said, six months. Probably less."

"What may I do?"

"At this moment, do only what you have been doing. How many men can you count on?"

"Perhaps thirty men."

"Thirty *good* men?" Obiri asked.

"Yes. There are more, but some, I think, will not die."

"I understand."

70

"Weapons," Zuni said urgently. "We must have weapons."

"I know that, too. When the time comes, you shall have weapons. I promise you that."

"I believe you, Bibi. We all believe you."

"Kill me with your own hand if it is not so."

Zuni stopped, faced him on the dirt road, took him by the shoulders.

"Kill you?" he said. "You are my brother. How would I kill you?"

They embraced, and Captain Obiri Anokye left to return to Mokodi for his meeting with the Nyam.

During colonial times, the French had built a charming white boardwalk that ran along the shore from the foot of the Boulevard Voltaire to the site now occupied by the Mokodi Hilton. The boardwalk was wide, provided benches for the relaxation of sightseers, and afforded bathers access to the beach via several stairways decorated with ornate iron lighting fixtures.

Anokye's instructions, telephoned to him at his barracks office, had been precise: He was to be on the boardwalk, at the bench between the fourth and fifth lighted stairways, counting from the Boulevard Voltaire, at precisely 2400 hours.

He walked over from the ferry slip, sauntering slowly since he was early. It was a cleverly arranged rendezvous. Once on the boardwalk he would be in plain view of the Nyam's men on the beach or the landward dunes. If he was accompanied or followed, it would be noted. And the actual meeting of the two men at midnight would arouse no particular interest; a few bathers were still on the beach, a few tourists on the boardwalk and benches.

71

He paused to light a Gauloise before he crossed the wide Boulevard Voltaire. A movement to his left caught his eye. He turned slowly. Sgt. Sene Yeboa was standing in the shadows of the Asante National Bank building. Anokye looked at the night sky, strolled closer.

"Forgive me, Bibi," Yeboa whispered.

The Little Captain was silent.

"I can move *under* the boardwalk," Yeboa said eagerly. "On the sand. You know the hunter always looks ahead, behind, to right and left, but rarely up or down. They will not expect it."

Anokye did not speak.

"Do not feel anger toward me," Yeboa pleaded.

"I feel no anger," Anokye said. "Do what you must do. But do not interfere. Is that your word, Sene?"

"That is my word, Little Captain."

Anokye was quiet a moment.

"If I am killed," he said finally, "avenge me."

Yeboa nodded dumbly.

The Captain was moving past the second bench when two men rose and crowded him, one on either side. They were both wearing soiled tan raincoats and straw hats, the limp brims scraggly. They did not speak, but shouldered him roughly over to the seaside railing. Then, standing close to him, their bodies blocking him from the boardwalk, one held a knife point to the soft place beneath his chin while the other patted him down swiftly, expertly.

"I am without a weapon," Anokye said. "That was my word."

"Your word," the knifeman scoffed.

He was the taller and the angrier of the two. When the searcher reported Anokye was without weapons, the armed man pressed his point; Anokye felt it pierce his skin. Then the tall man removed his knife. Anokye

72

touched his throat, wiped away a few drops of blood, licked his fingers.

"You have cut me," he said tonelessly.

"It won't show on your pretty red scarf," the rebel said. He revealed broken, blackened teeth. "The Nyam is waiting. March, soldier boy."

Below, crouched in shadow, looking up through the slatted planks of the boardwalk, Sgt. Yeboa saw what had happened and heard most of what was said. When Captain Anokyè moved on along the boardwalk, Yeboa stayed motionless, watching the two rebel guards.

The Nyam was seated alone on the bench between the fourth and fifth lights. He was slumped far down, his legs thrust out before him. Like his men, he wore a soiled raincoat. A black beret was tilted rakishly over one ear.

Anokyé sat down next to him. The two men turned to look at each other.

The Nyam showed a hard, coffin face, a thick, black mustache, fervid eyes. He had not the gift of repose; the long body hidden under the raincoat was in constant movement, twisting, turning, straightening, slumping. His hands, too: clenching, unclenching, stretching wide, then fingers flicking off his thumbs, one fingertip after another: a compulsive tic.

"It is true," he said. "You are a *Little* Captain."

Anokyé said nothing.

"You wished to speak with me?" the Nyam said. "I am here. Speak."

"The killing must end," Anokyé said softly. "We are all Asantis, all brothers. We should not spill each other's blood."

"You are the King's soldier," the Nyam said. But he used the Akan word for "animal" or "creature."

"The King," Captain Anokyé said. "I cannot drink

water with such a man. You must know that I have spies within your camp. Okomfo was only one of many. You cannot succeed. Your weapons are few and poor. Your people are hungry.''

"So you say I should give my head to the King?"

"No," Anokye said. "I ask only that you end your foolish raids. They earn you nothing but the hatred of your victims. I want what you want—the end of the monarchy, the liberation of Asante. But your way is not the right way."

"We will fight on forever until the forces of democratic socialism defeat the imperialists and return the land to the popular will of the people," the Nyam recited.

"The words you speak are foreign words," Anokye said. "They are not the words of our people. But I did not come to debate political philosophy with you. I know your education and knowledge. You are wiser than I. I have no desire to change what you believe."

"Then?"

"I ask only for patience on your part, for an end to your raids and terrorism. When the time comes, you and I will join in creating a new Asante."

"And who will rule this new Asante?" the Nyam demanded.

"I am a soldier," the Little Captain said. "I told you, I have no experience in government. I know nothing of politics. My learning is not as deep as yours. But I can fight. That is all I propose, that we fight side by side to rid Asante of this evil that suffocates us all. Then, when the palace is ours, we may consider how best to rule our country so that the people do not starve and the rich do not steal our taxes for their personal gain."

There was silence then. The Nyam tilted back his head,

stared at the night sky, his eyes moving back and forth as if to read an answer in the stars.

"You counsel patience," he said. "How long?"

"Six months," Anokye said.

"Too long," the Nyam said promptly.

"You have been fighting almost five years," Anokye said gently. "Are you any closer now to a free Asante?"

"More people come over to us every day," the Nyam said angrily.

"That may be true," Anokye acknowledged. "But where are your weapons? The men I killed at Lake Volta were armed with spears and one Lee Enfield rifle without ammunition. Is this how you intend to storm the palace and liberate Asante, with spears and guns without bullets?"

"What can you offer?" the Nyam demanded.

"I command Fourth Brigade," Anokye said. "You know that to be true. The Fourth will follow wherever I lead."

"And the King's cousin commands the Third," the Nyam said. "You mean to lead your men against Third Brigade?"

"That will not be necessary," Anokye said. "Many officers and men of the Third feel as we do. They would not die for the King. I propose that liberation be planned for a time when my brigade is stationed in the Mokodi barracks, and the Third is in the field, scattered and divided. The Fourth will then take Mokodi and occupy the palace. Your forces, and men who feel as we do, will attack Third Brigade in the field to prevent a march to retake Mokodi."

"Weapons," the Nyam said. "Where are we to find the weapons for such attacks?"

The Little Captain reached slowly into the side pocket of his tunic and drew out a ring of keys. He selected two heavy iron keys and held them close to the Nyam's face.

"Keys to the arsenals," he whispered. "Master keys to the arsenals of Mokodi, Kumasi, Gonja, Kasai, to every arsenal in Asante. Even the armory of the guards in the palace. Pistols, rifles, ammunition, grenades, mortars, machine guns . . ."

The Nyam's eyes glistened. He stared at the glittering keys, hypnotized.

"It could be done?" he asked hoarsely.

"It could be done," Captain Anokye said definitely. "It shall be done. With you or without you. But sooner with you, and with less shedding of Asante blood."

Again there was silence. Anokye did not replace the keys in his pocket but let them remain in his open hand. The Nyam could not take his eyes from those keys.

"I know you love Asante as I do," the Little Captain said, his voice low and urgent. "Together, with those who will follow us, we will liberate our poor, suffering country and create a great new nation where children do not starve, and men and women may live in dignity and peace with the respect of their elected leaders."

The Nyam drew a deep breath.

"I will think on it," he said.

"You will give me your answer soon?" Captain Anokye asked.

"Yes," the Nyam said. His eyes turned to the sky again. "By the time of the full moon."

"A good omen," Anokye said. "May the gods protect you, brother."

He stood abruptly, turned, strode quickly away, not looking back. When he came to the bench where the two bodyguards were seated, he passed without glancing at them. He marched down the boardwalk, dress whites gleaming in the moonlight.

Beneath the boardwalk, Sgt. Yeboa watched his captain depart safely. Then he returned his attention to the two rebel guards. They waited until the Nyam came up to them. The three men spoke a moment in low voices. They walked slowly toward the Boulevard Voltaire. At the main stairway, they spoke again, and separated. The Nyam departed with one guard, the other, the thin, gangling man who had held a knife to the Little Captain's throat, watched them go, then shambled toward the dock area. Sgt. Yeboa moved after him, slipping through shadows on the other side of the street.

The rebel entered the first cabaret he came to, a crowded place with a noisy jukebox that could be heard from the sidewalk. Yeboa waited patiently outside, across the street, in a dark doorway. It was almost an hour before the rebel came out. His shambling walk had become almost a stagger. He reeled down the street, touching a wall occasionally to keep his balance. He went deeper into the dock area, a dark place of shuttered warehouses, pier sheds, loading platforms, immobilized forklifts and cranes. He lurched into another café, this one small, dim, with dirty windows and a torn canvas awning hanging almost to the pavement.

Sgt. Yeboa waited a few moments, then crossed the street and peered through the grime-streaked window. Bartender. Three men scattered singly along the bar. And the rebel seated by himself at a table. There was a glass of beer before him. His head was nodding.

Yeboa stepped through the swinging door. The bartender and the men at the bar looked up. He stared at them. They saw his field uniform: dungarees, boots, forage cap, web belt, holster, pistol, and they quickly looked away.

He went to the bar, asked for a Benin, and paid for it immediately, leaving the bartender a small dash. Then he took his bottle and glass over to the rebel's table, to the man who had dared hold a knife to Captain Anokye's throat.

"Good evening, brother," Sgt. Sene Yeboa said politely. "Have I your permission to join you?"

He spoke loudly enough so that he would be overheard by the other men in the smoky room. The rebel looked up. Not drunk, but dazed. He made a gesture. Yeboa dragged over another stool, sitting so his body was clear of the table. He poured a half a glass of beer, raised it to the rebel.

"To your continued good health, brother," Yeboa said loudly.

The man muttered something, raised his glass, took a deep swallow, thumped the glass down again. Yeboa leaned toward him, his voice now low, confidential.

"Is it true that you fuck your mother?" he asked pleasantly. "So I have heard. And the other women of your family as well? That is strange since it is known you open your ass to any white man who pays."

The rebel's head came up slowly, features twisted with shock and sudden sobriety. He did not believe.

"Oh yes," Yeboa nodded sadly. "It is said you fuck your mother. And it is also said you—"

The rebel gave a great roar of fury and anguish. Men at the bar whirled around. The rebel staggered to his feet. His stool went over with a crash. An open knife was in his fist. He fell toward Sgt. Yeboa.

The sergeant remained seated to take the charge. His right knee came up almost to his chest. He planted his boot in the rebel's midsection at the same time his quick hands went under the knife and gripped wrist and elbow. Then

Yeboa tipped back on his stool, using the attacker's momentum and weight, and cartwheeled him over his head onto an adjoining table, the straw hat flying. Wood splintered. The man was left stunned. Lying on his back in the wreckage. Eyes rolling dazedly.

Yeboa was on his feet then, standing over the fallen rebel. He brought one heavy boot high, slammed it down on the other's unprotected throat. Everyone in the room heard something break and crunch under Yeboa's grinding heel. The rebel's face empurpled. Blood welled from ears, eyes, nose, mouth. His chest made one rasping heave, caught, heaved again, stopped.

Sgt. Yeboa adjusted his forage cap, straightened web belt and holster, dusted camouflaged jacket and trousers. Then he looked at the frozen men at the bar.

"You all saw," he said coolly. "I spoke in friendship to this man. Yet he attacked a soldier of the King for no reason. Was he mad with drink? Who can say? But you all saw he drew his weapon and attacked me for no reason. Was that not how it happened?"

He looked slowly from man to man. Into their eyes. Each hastened to nod.

"It was so," one of them said. "I saw it. We all saw it. He attacked you for no reason."

They all agreed; it was so.

Captain Obiri Anokye was still charged when he arrived at the Golden Calf. He ran up the back staircase. Yvonne Mayer awaited him at the open doorway of her apartment.

"It went well?" she asked anxiously.

"I sold him his own tomatoes," Anokye said, paraphrasing an Akan proverb.

She laughed, drew him inside, closed and locked the door.

Within moments they were naked on her wide bed. His fears, tensions, turmoil, all were shoved within her. He thrust at life, hacking, splitting her wide with his fury. She wept with pleasure, urged him from crudity to cruelty, called him her "Little Captain," her "king," her "master." He continued to plunge, she to buck, until they were slippery with sweat and hot juices but could not stop their paroxysm until strength waned; they fell into a panting swoon, locked, insensate, teeth clamped to each other's fevered flesh.

Later, delirium faded, they showered, sat quietly a moment sharing a cold beer. Then they returned to the bed, which she spread with fresh sheets and pillowcases. He told her of his meeting with the Nyam.

"You have him in your basket," she said.

"I believe that is so," he laughed. "It was the keys that did it. He could not take his eyes from the keys. The keys to the arsenals. The keys to all his dreams."

"Could he steal the keys from you?" she asked.

"He could," Anokye said. "But to what purpose? The arsenals are empty."

"Empty?" she said. Astonished. "Bibi, all empty?"

"No weapons have been purchased for almost five years," he said. "And guns wear out, like shoes. Or are broken or lost. Ammunition is expended on the ranges, on maneuvers, in raids against the rebels. Money for new weapons goes instead to buy sports cars for the King's sons, diamonds for the King's wives and concubines, deposits to the King's account in Switzerland. The army's cupboard is bare."

"Then how will you get weapons?"

He quoted another Akan proverb: "Money is sharper than a sword."

"And where will you get the money?" she asked. "From Tangent, the oilman?"

"That is a possibility," he said. "Garde, at the palace, is another. There are others. Willi Abraham is a clever man. I do not despair. Do you?"

"Only when you are not with me."

She flung the covering sheet aside and began to lave him slowly with her tongue. He stared at the ceiling and listened to her tell what he might do to her.

10

PETER TANGENT FLEW from London to Paris, and thence to Togo via Air Afrique. At the Lomé airport, the Starrett copter was awaiting him, per cabled instructions from his London office. An hour later he was asleep in one of the VIP suites at the Mokodi Hilton.

His phone rang a few minutes after 0800 the following morning.

"Tangent," he said.

"Sam here," Leiberman's hoarse voice answered. "You awake?"

"I am now. How did you know I was in town?"

"I smelled your cologne," Leiberman said. "When do we meet?"

Tangent considered a moment, staring at the morning sunlight filtering through fishnet drapes at the picture windows. The risk of meeting Leiberman in public seemed minimal.

"All right," he said. "In an hour on the Mokodi Hilton terrace."

Tangent showered slowly, shaved carefully, donned a suit of white linen, yellow cotton shirt, black tie of silk rep. His benchmade shoes (size 13-AA) were black suede-and-white. His wristwatch was a complicated gold Omega chronometer, showing the time in Asante, London, New York, and Tulsa. Also, phases of the moon.

The Mokodi Hilton dining terrace was a broad sweep of Italian ceramic tile, facing the ocean, the world beyond. It was furnished with umbrella tables of wrought iron, chairs padded with cushions covered in African cloth. The waiters, some of them over 70, were friendly, energetic, understanding. Tangent ordered iced tomato juice, a carafe of black coffee, two croissants, a wedge of chilled Persian melon served with slices of lime. He was starting the melon when Sam Leiberman arrived. He took the chair across from Tangent, in the shade of the fringed umbrella.

The mercenary was wearing a short-sleeved safari suit of starched and pressed chino. A clean white cotton T-shirt was underneath. Sprouting above that was a mat of chest hair like steel wool. He wore light tan bush boots and carried a brown paper bag.

"You look prosperous," Tangent said.

"I am," Leiberman said. "I'm being kept by a rich goy."

"Breakfast?"

"Espresso and cognac."

"Cognac? It's only nine o'clock."

"So?" Leiberman said. "Somewhere in the world it's noon."

Tangent turned his head. Before he could signal, the waiter was at his elbow. The two men sat silently until the copper pot of coffee and balloon of brandy appeared. They stared, squint-eyed, at the glitter: gently rolling ocean, the smooth strand before the hotel, twinkling palm fronds. They listened to the soft laughter of tourists, digging into their chilled mangoes at surrounding tables.

Leiberman drained his small cognac and took a sip of coffee. Tangent summoned the waiter again.

"I think the bottle would be best," he said.

Leiberman fished into his paper bag, brought out a copy of the Togo *Free Press*. It had been folded open, and the item in René St. Clair's column marked with a red grease pencil. Tangent took his glasses from a leather holder clipped inside his jacket pocket and read swiftly.

"Very nice," he said. "Just what I wanted. Is this copy for me?"

"Sure. I even have two extras."

"Good. How much did you have to pay him?"

"I didn't pay him anything."

They were silent while a bottle of Courvoisier was placed before Leiberman, resting in a silver wine coaster. Leiberman took up the bottle and filled his glass.

"Nothing?" Tangent said. He finished his melon, dabbed his lips with the stiff, pink linen napkin. "How did you get him to run it?"

"You wouldn't believe me if I told you."

"Don't tell me," Tangent said hastily. "But can I still use him?"

"Anything you want," Leiberman said. "He'll do anything for me."

Tangent stared at him. The mercenary was a heavy, brooding man. Gray hair was brush-cut. Features were brutish: pig eyes, meaty nose, furrowed brow and cheeks. Wet, turned-out lips. Massive jaw. Creased, sun-bronzed neck. His bare arms were powerful, wrists particularly thick.

"You're not human," Peter Tangent said.

"Sure I am," Leiberman said. He took a swallow of his cognac. "That's my problem: I'm *too* human. You got what you wanted, didn't you?"

"Yes."

"Then cut the shit about what I am or am not. Or I might have to take you apart and see just how human *you* are. Would you enjoy that?"

"I doubt it," Tangent said.

"I do, too," Leiberman said.

They sipped their coffee. They looked out over the calm. Fishing boats, rented catamarans, girls in bikinis dashing along the beach. Not only the sights and sounds, but the scents of pleasure. Moneyed pleasure.

"How did you get on to him?" Leiberman asked.

"Who?"

"Anokye. Who tipped you off?"

"What the hell are you talking about?"

"Captain Obíri Anokye," Leiberman said. "Who told you what he's up to?"

"Will you start making sense?" Tangent said. "No one told me he's up to anything. That's what I hired you to find out."

"What made him worth five hundred francs to you?"

"Someone mentioned his name. Said I might be interested in him."

"Who mentioned his name?"

Tangent hesitated a moment.

"Willi Abraham," he said finally. "The Minister of Finance."

"Oh-ho," Leiberman said. "That makes the cheese more binding. Now I can put two and two together and come up with twenty-two. There's this organization called Asante Brothers of Independence. The ABI. They're all veterans of that shitty war against the French in fifty-eight. The Legion could have kicked their asses into Lake Volta, but Asante wasn't worth the trouble. Anyway, there's this Asante Brothers of Independence outfit. Branches in every town and village. Every once in a while they have a rally or a parade. But mostly they sit around their clubhouses and drink Benin and lie about the good old days. Like veterans everywhere."

"Weapons?"

"No, but they'd know how to use them if they got them. Guess who's the national leader."

"Captain Anokye?"

"Nah, he's too young. Willi Abraham."

Tangent signaled for another snifter and helped himself to brandy from Leiberman's bottle. The mercenary pulled his chair closer, put his elbows on the table.

"All right," he said. "Abraham has the ABI. A raggedy-assed bunch with no guns. But all the same, veterans and in every town. Anokye is CO of Fourth Brigade, a sharp outfit. His men love him. If he told them to cut off the King's balls, the fat bastard would be singing soprano before he knew what hit him. I went to see Anokye."

"You didn't!"

"Why not? Strictly a business proposition. I told him I know where I can get a thousand M3 burp guns, which I can, and asked him if the army and the palace might be interested. He said sure—which is a lot of shit. Asante hasn't got dime one for arms right now. But Anokye was interested in those guns—for himself."

"What does he want?"

"The Little Captain? He wants Asante. For starters."

"And then?"

"I'm not sure," Leiberman said. "The kid's got chutzpah. He's shacking up with Yvonne Mayer, who runs the fanciest cathouse in town. She wouldn't put out for a loser. Ever hear Anokye speak?"

"I've never met him," Tangent said. "Never even seen him."

"He'll mesmerize you. A great orator. Lots of drive, lots of power."

"Sam, he's just an army captain."

"And Hitler was just an army corporal. And Napoleon

86

started out playing with toy soldiers. That's another thing."

"You're going too fast for me. What's another thing?"

"The toy soldiers. The chief teller of the Asante National Bank is a gimp named Alistair Greeley. A Limey. Got a clubfoot. His wife's a monster. Real hatchet face. Last year Greeley's younger sister came down to live with them. A looker. There's been talk."

"Talk? About what?"

"Greeley's pretty sister and Greeley's ugly wife. It's interesting—but not important. What is important is that Greeley is a war nut. A military expert. It's his hobby. Studies tactics, diagrams battles. All that crap. And he owns a valuable collection of antique lead soldiers. Anokye goes over there all the time, and he and Greeley move the toy soldiers around on maps. Isn't that cute? That would have been a big help to me in the Congo. My ass! Anyway, Greeley is palsy-walsy with Anokye. That any use to you?"

"Yesss," Tangent said slowly. "Could be. Starrett keeps a nice balance at Asante National. I think I'll wander over and renew the acquaintance of Mr. Alistair Greeley. Perhaps he'll be kind enough to invite me to his home so I can meet the Little Captain."

"Can I come?" Leiberman asked.

"No," Tangent said. "What for?" he asked.

"I want to meet the sister and wife and see if it's true."

"See if what's true?"

"What they say."

Tangent looked at him, then closed his eyes slowly. After the damp chill of London, the strong, deep sun of Asante was a glory. He could feel it seep into his body, melt his bones. He opened his eyes to see a flight of gulls wheel and soar against the blue. It was all hot, live, vibran[t] with light. Tulsa, New York, London were cold, dead gray and gone.

"You're sore, aren't you?" Leiberman said.

"Sore?"

"About what I said. About taking you apart."

"Oh that," Tangent said. "Of course I'm not sore. If i[t] pleases you to flex your muscles, it doesn't disturb me."

"You could make one phone call and have me pu[t] down," Leiberman said.

"You know that, do you?"

"Sure," Leiberman said cheerfully.

"I think I better put you on the payroll," Tangent said.

"You're kidding?"

"Not the Starrett payroll, you idiot. My discretionary funds."

"I love it," Leiberman said. "How much?"

"Five hundred French francs a week."

"A thousand," Leiberman said.

"Seven-fifty."

"Done. Who gets the schlong?"

"Keep digging on Anokye and all his friends. And lin[e] up sources of weapons."

"Like what?"

"Small stuff. Infantry stuff. Pistols, rifles, machine guns, mortars, grenades, ammunition."

"How much of it?"

"Enough to take Asante," Tangent said dreamily.

"Oh-ho," Leiberman said.

"How will you get it in?" Tangent asked.

"No problem. Truck it over those open borders. Better yet, by lighter along the coast. Yes, that would be simpler. Money?"

"When needed. This is just exploratory. Make no commitments. Just make certain the stuff is available."

"Ah sahib, sahib, sahib," Leiberman sighed. "It is such a pleasure doing business with you, effendi."

"Go fuck yourself," Tangent said.

They finished the brandy. They watched two tall Swedish girls stride across the terrace, long blond hair whipping in the wind like flame. Out in the harbor were white yachts, brilliantly painted Asante fishing boats, the anchored *La Liberté*, showing a brave display of bright pennants. And above all, the endless Asante sky, the blazing Asante sun. Perfumed breeze: hot land, ripe land.

"It's not a *bad* country," Tangent said.

"Why don't you relax for once?" Leiberman said. "Why don't you admit it's a beautiful country?"

"I don't want to get involved," Tangent said.

They both laughed.

11

GONJA SAT ASTRIDE Asante Royal Highway No. 1, almost halfway between Mokodi and Four Points. It was Asante's second largest city, the army's midland base. Nearby were the phosphate mines. But Gonja was primarily a market center, gathering produce from surrounding farms, plantations, orchards, and shipping it by truck down to Mokodi for sale or export.

It was a flat, sunbaked, graceless town. Scrawny dogs prowled the streets. Wooden buildings peeled and warped. The one movie theater was shuttered. In the few restaurants and cabarets still open, idle waiters flicked flies from barren tables, looking for customers who never came. There was nothing in Gonja for tourists. In days of despair, there was little for Gonjans.

As recently as two years ago, the monthly meeting of the Gonjan chapter of the Asante Brothers of Independence would have been a riotous evening of good food, palm wine, laughter. There would have been a whole stuffed lamb, roasted over open coals, with kenkey, curried rice, beans, greens, eggplant, fufu, chicken, fish, crabs—as much as a man could eat. Later there would be speeches recalling the great victory over the French. Later still, some of the men, fired by food, wine, words, would leap to their feet and dance. Bare feet pounding on bare boards. To an intricate rhythm of clapped palms and a huffed chant.

But all that was two years gone. Now there was no feast, no wine, no dancing. Sullen, bewildered men hunched over plank tables and exchanged stories of hungry families, lost jobs, the cruelty of the King's tax collectors, who might seize a man's house—yes, even the clothes from his back and the food from his pot—if he could not deliver what the King commanded. Evil times. The veterans of Gonja agreed that Asante had fallen on evil times. Why had they fought and risked their lives? Had times been worse under French rule? No, they sadly concluded, times had been better.

Captain Obiri Anokye and Sgt. Sene Yeboa drove up from Mokodi in the Land Rover. The Little Captain was one of the scheduled speakers at the Gonjan ABI meeting. The other two were Professor Jean-Louis Duclos and Minister of Finance Willi Abraham. They had arrived earlier that afternoon in Abraham's limousine to consult with certain men.

The meeting was held in a deserted loading shed, the air thick with dust from bags of wheat, barley, rice. The hall was lighted by smoky kerosene lanterns. At one end, a platform of sorts had been constructed of planks set across small packing cases. Raw planks on trestles also served as tables and benches. There were not enough seats for all; many sat on the littered floor or hunkered on their hams, hugging their knees. Almost a hundred men waited patiently for spoken words that might lighten their misery.

The first speech, by Duclos, was a disaster. He spoke in French, in a fervent manner, with broad gestures. These men, most of whom were illiterate, had listened to griots from childhood. They respected the spoken word. It was sacred. It was their history, their meaning as a people.

But this downy black from across the seas could not move them. He spoke a lilting French they could scarcely

91

comprehend. Worse, he seemed to be saying that all their troubles were the fault of the white man. They looked at each other in puzzlement. Was the King not black? And his ministers, his soldiers, his policemen? All black. And had they not agreed that their lives had been better under the rule of the white French?

But the whites were *still* in command, Duclos argued angrily. From behind the scenes, they manipulated their puppets. In Paris, white bankers owned Asante bonds. In Asante itself, whites owned the plantations, the factories, the shops. Asante was still a colony. All patriots must work for the day when blacks would truly control their own destinies. In Asante, in Africa, throughout the world.

His speech, too long and too loud, was greeted with silence. Too polite to boo or hiss, the assembled veterans merely let him finish and step down. The tax collectors were black; that was all they knew or needed to know. This man spoke the truth as he saw it. But it was *his* truth, not theirs.

The second speaker, Willi Abraham, was more to their liking. He was of their age, of their blood. He had fought with them, and spoke a French they could understand. There was little fervor in what he said, but it all made sense to them.

He said that Asante was a very small nation; it could never hope to rival Russia or the U.S.A. Still, the land was fertile, rainfall was plentiful, the people were prudent and hardworking. With proper management, there was no reason why Asante should not prosper. There would be sufficient food for all, and enough for export. Tourism was increasing. With the revenues from the newly discovered oil field off the coast of Zabar, Asante could become a modest paradise, a showcase for all of Africa, a stable and flourishing nation where every man might work as hard as he wished at the trade he desired, and live with his family in peace, happiness, and dignity.

They liked that, and leaped to their feet, shaking fists at him in delight, stamping, slapping their own bare shoulders. Willi Abraham was one of them, a wise man, and he spoke their truth.

Then Captain Obiri Anokye strode onto the platform and they quieted, grinning to welcome him. He stood erect, proud, in his dress whites with decorations. He was youth and power. He was as they had been when they fought the French.

"Bibi, Bibi, Bibi!" they chanted. "Little Captain! Brother!"

He smiled down on them, and gradually they stilled to hear his words. He spoke to them in Akan.

"You are great men," he said, starting slowly, in almost a whisper, so they had to lean toward him to hear. "You are the sons of great men, great warriors, the Ashanti. Noble blood flows in your veins. Your ancestors held land that could not be crossed by a swift-flying bird in the time of a moon's turning. These grasslands, mountains, lakes and rivers, coasts and rain forests, were once all Ashanti land." He paused to stare at his audience, meeting their eyes. "And who knows?" he said. "They may be yours once again."

He was not a trained orator, but instinctively had sought and developed an individual style, at once impressive to his audience, comfortable to him. He stood with feet firmly planted, slightly spread, rooted. Usually he spoke with hands on hips, torso bent slightly backward. His barrel chest was inflated, chin elevated. He nodded frequently. His few gestures were short and explosive: the right palm brought down, edge foremost, in a sharp chop, or the left fist clenched and brandished. Gestures of an impassioned warrior.

"These are troubled times," he told them. "Believe me, brothers, I know what you suffer, and what your women and children suffer, and I grieve with you. I say that our salvation, and that of Asante, lies in our dedication to our history, to our blood. We must return to the spirit of the old ones, to their wisdom, and their sacrifice. I tell you now, you are not alone. You are not lonely men to worry and despair. You are a people. Draw your strength from your knowledge of what your people have done in the past and will do in the future."

He spoke for another twenty minutes, recounting their history, retelling the deeds of the Ashantis, describing the great cities they had created, the laws, the arts. What these men and women had done, he told them, they could do. They were, most of them, knowledgeable and wise in the breeding of cattle and horses and goats. Even chickens! Were men any less? Blood would tell; they knew that to be true. And in their veins they bore the blood of mighty warriors, wise law-givers, statesmen, philosophers, artists, and a people who had worked a mighty civilization out of raw wilderness.

"Do not despair," he finished. "I pledge to you my honor as a soldier and my life as a man that you shall enjoy better times. And sooner than you think! Even sooner if you remember, always, that you spring from the seed of men who were not afraid to follow their destinies. Tomorrow belongs to us!"

They surged forward then, to engulf him on the platform, weeping and crying out, stamping their bare feet, stretching to touch him, to touch the magic. Bibi. The Little Captain. He, too, was of their blood. He was a brother. They were all a family. He would give his life for them, and they for him.

Later, Anokye drove back to Mokodi in Willi Abraham's limousine, leaving Sgt. Yeboa to return the Land Rover to the barracks. The Little Captain sat in back, with Abraham. Jean-Louis Duclos, slumped and disconsolate, sat in front with the chauffeur.

"Were there secret police in the audience?" Anokye asked.

"Undoubtedly," Abraham said. "But nothing was spoken of a seditious nature."

"Alistair Greeley called me this afternoon. He invites me to join his family at his home tomorrow evening for drink and talk. And to meet Peter Tangent. Shall I go?"

Willi Abraham offered Anokye a packet of short, fat Dutch cigars. When the Little Captain shook his head, Abraham lighted one for himself, slowly.

"Yes," he said finally. "I think that would be wise. Yesterday morning Tangent met with Sam Leiberman on the terrace of the Mokodi Hilton. They had a long talk. Do you know what that was about?"

"No," Anokye said. "I told you Leiberman came to me offering to sell M3s. I gave him the impression I was interested. Perhaps they spoke of that."

"Perhaps," Abraham said. "Go to Greeley's home tomorrow night. Speak with Tangent. I believe he merely wishes to meet you personally, to see for himself what kind of man you are. It is amusing that you should meet him through Greeley. That will infuriate Garde."

"Will Tangent make an offer?"

"Tomorrow night? I doubt it. He does not yet know who you are, what you plan. Men like Tangent move prudently. He will seek to learn as much as he can, then report all he has learned to his home office. The offer must come from there, through Tangent.''

"Will he attempt to bribe me, Willi?''

"Perhaps. But in such a way that you could never say he had. Stop him. Immediately.''

"Of course.''

"Then he will be curious,'' Abraham laughed. "What kind of an African army officer is this who won't accept a bribe? It will intrigue him.''

"Intrigue?''

"Interest him. Perplex him. And so we will keep him off balance.''

They drove in silence then. Duclos was still slumped silently in the front seat next to the driver. Neither Anokye nor Abraham thought it wise to offer words of sympathy. They were approaching the outskirts of Mokodi before Willi Abraham spoke again.

"Bibi,'' he said. "I believe we will eventually receive an offer from Starrett, through Tangent, or from the French, through Garde. Or from both sources. When that time comes, it will be necessary to act. You agree?''

"Of course,'' Anokye said.

"You realize what it may mean to you and your family?''

"I realize. And you?''

"I realize. The Nyam desires the victory of the socialist proletariat. Duclos dreams of a racist war to remove every white from the sacred soil of Africa. I wish only a liberated Asante which I may help to become self-sufficient, prosperous, and reasonably happy. And you, Bibi? What do you want?''

"I want what you want,'' the Little Captain said.

"Do you?'' Willi Abraham said. "That speech of yours tonight . . . are you certain you don't yearn to withdraw

96

into the Africa of the past, an Africa that can never again exist?''

Captain Anokye turned to look at the Finance Minister.

''No, Willi,'' he said gently. ''I do not yearn for that. I told them what they wanted to hear.''

12

In Peter Tangent's private file in his London office, Prime Minister Osei Ware of Asante had been thumbnailed:

"Venal and shrewd . . . a Muslim who prefers Dom Perignon . . . scorn of Christians . . . a private jihad? . . . compliment on rose garden . . . story from T.M. re torture of French prisoners at Gonja . . . Islamic dress . . . do not use sex jokes . . . rumor of Jewish mistress in Beirut (circa a long time ago) . . . two fingers missing left hand . . . bad French, better English . . . hashish?"

"Prime Minister," Tangent said, "if you will allow me . . ."

He reached into a canvas carryall and withdrew a bulbous object wrapped in plastic. He placed it carefully on the Prime Minister's desk.

"A cutting of a new American rose," he said. "It's called 'Independence Day.' If you will accept it, I hope it may bloom in that famous garden of yours and give you pleasure every day of your life."

"A small gift for me," Osei Ware said. "How nice." He smiled coldly, took up the package, peered through the plastic wrapping. "You remembered my poor flowers. I shall graft it immediately."

They were speaking English, seated in the Prime Minister's private office in the palace at Mokodi. The room was scented by two large, artful arrangements of roses in

98

antique Asante jars. The ocher clay was decorated with black bands of stylized deer fleeing before spear-wielding hunters. As Tangent spoke, Prime Minister Osei Ware withdrew a pale yellow bloom from one of the vases and thrust his great hawk nose deep into the petals. He inhaled audibly, eyes lidding with pleasure.

"Prime Minister," Tangent said, "I have sought this audience because a matter of the gravest urgency has come to my attention, a matter I believe deserving of consideration at the highest levels of the Asante government."

He withdrew the copy of the Lomé *Free Press* from his carryall and placed it before the Prime Minister. He pointed at the item circled in red.

"Oh *that*," Ware said negligently. "A matter of little importance. It means nothing."

"With all due respect," Tangent said, "my people find it extremely upsetting. If that item accurately reflects the position of the Togo government, then our Zabarian investment is gravely threatened."

"The gossip of a journalist," Ware said. "It has no effect on our negotiations."

"But why should this man write such a story if there is no truth to it? What could his motive possibly be?"

"Who knows?" the Prime Minister shrugged. "Perhaps he is a writer of fiction. Perhaps he wishes to—what is the English expression—muddy the waters? And perhaps—" Here he raised his beak from the rose and looked directly at Tangent. Heavy lids; reptilian eyes. "—perhaps *you* persuaded him to write it."

"Excellency!" Tangent cried. Shocked. Horrified. "Do you know what you suggest? That I would deliberately endanger the friendly relations between two African nations for personal gain? Surely, Prime Minister, you know me better than that! My people, and I personally, desire nothing more than to develop a rich oil field in Zabarian waters, for the benefit of Asante—and for our benefit too, of course. But what are we to do now? If Togo brings this matter to the floor of the United Nations, the whole matter might be tied up in litigation for years. Dare we sign *any* lease agreement with Asante while this question remains unresolved? And I'm certain that other petroleum companies, *of whatever nation*, will feel the same. Quite frankly, Prime Minister, at this moment we don't know where we're at, or with whom we should deal.''

''Togo signed a treaty in nineteen sixty-one relinquishing all claims to Zabar and its territorial waters.''

''And the man who signed that treaty is now dead, as dead as the government he served. Why should the present rulers of Togo be fettered by the errors of the past? That, I fear, may be the way they feel. I know Your Excellency has had more than one experience with repudiated agreements. Governments change, and rulers, and circumstances. Perhaps rumors of a potentially profitable Zabarian oil field have reached Lomé, and that is the reason they talk of reopening the question of jurisdiction.''

''Get to the point. What do you want?''

''Would it be possible for your government, through its ambassador, to make discreet inquiries in Lomé? To determine if that published item is, as you feel, the concoction of a scandalmonger, or if there is any truth to it?''

The Prime Minister slowly lowered his nose back into the rose petals. When he spoke, his voice was muffled, hardly understandable.

''Our man in Lomé is not famous for his discretion,'' he said. No hint of irony in his tone. ''But perhaps you are right. Perhaps I should get to the bottom of this matter.''

''Excellent, Prime Minister,'' Tangent said enthusiastically. "I assure you it would help expedite a decision by my people on the King's lease terms."

"Ah yes," the Prime Minister said. "The King's lease terms. In that case, it may be best for me to handle this matter personally. I have been working very hard lately. A short vacation in Lomé—a beautiful city—combining pleasure and business—not an official visit—could do no harm."

"A wise decision, Prime Minister," Tangent said. "Go in good health, and return in good health."

Again the heavy lids rose, the eyes were revealed.

"And who knows?" Osei Ware said. "I may be able to discover how this item in this newspaper came to be published."

So Peter A. Tangent had to make another trip to the smelly premises above Les Trois Chats. Once again Sam Leiberman was in his hammock, hidden under a mosquito net. The girl from the Ivory Coast was curled on the floor, working a cat's cradle.

"I'm afraid our friend in Lomé may prove an embarrassment," Tangent said.

"All right," Leiberman said. "I'll take care of it. How much?"

"Keep it cheap," Tangent said.

"I had no choice, did I?" Alistair Greeley said. "What? What? After all, he is one of our biggest depositors. Or his company is. What was I to say: 'Sorry, Mr. Tangent, you can't come to my home to meet Captain Anokye'? What? What?"

He spoke in a whining, aggrieved tone, the "What? What?" calling upon God and the world to witness that he was a cripple, helpless before the cruelty of others, unable to defend himself because of a wretched accident of birth that had robbed him of strength and dignity.

"No, I suppose not," Anatole Garde said.

He took a sip of his Pernod and water and regarded his companion with some distaste. Greeley was bent, crabbed, with a gray skin that ten years of Asante sun had failed to brighten. Garde felt guilty about his own erect carriage, bloomy youth, vitality.

They were seated in the small outdoor café of the Restaurant Cleopatra, a reasonably priced establishment recommended in the guidebooks for its "amusing Egyptian decor" and the spécialité de la maison: broiled grouper with pepper sauce.

"Actually," Garde said, "Abraham would have brought them together one way or another. Perhaps this is best."

Greeley blinked uneasily.

"You think Tangent knows of my connection with you? What? What?"

"Calm," Garde said soothingly. "Calm. How would he know? But perhaps we should not meet again in public. I can come to your place occasionally, late at night. Better yet, we will transact our business on the phone."

"There won't be any—any danger, will there? What?"

"Danger?" Garde said, astonished. "How could there be any danger?"

"All this violence," Greeley said muzzily. "I don't like it."

"What violence?"

"You know—the niggers. Always cutting each other."

"Yes," Garde said. "Almost as bad as Paris and New York."

"Well, Maud doesn't like it either."

Garde stared at him a moment. The other wouldn't meet his eyes.

"Just how much have you told your wife?" Garde asked finally.

"Nothing. I swear, I've told her nothing."

"And your sister?"

"Jane knows nothing either. All they know is that Anokye visits occasionally, just as a guest. I take him into the study, and we talk about military things. The women aren't interested."

"Good," Garde said. "Keep it that way."

"They couldn't care less," Greeley said bitterly. "They've got each other."

Garde looked away in embarrassment from the other man's pain. He watched the sauntering pedestrians, a fascinating parade of gorgeous colors, fanciful hairdos, brilliant costumes. Smiles, laughter, a dozen musical languages.

"Charming," Garde murmured.

"What? What?" Greeley demanded. Then, when Garde didn't reply, the chief teller asked, "I will get the bonus, won't I?"

"You'll get it," Garde said. "It will come through the bank: a Christmas bonus."

"Then I'll send Jane home on the first flight out."

"Isn't Asante your home?" Garde asked.

Greeley didn't hear, or paid no attention. He looked down at his glass of Scotch and Perrier.

"It's been hell," he muttered. "Hell. A man can stand so much. What? What?"

Garde watched him lift his glass and drain it suddenly in two heavy gulps. His throat worked convulsively. A little dribble ran from the corner of his mouth. Greeley wiped it away with the back of his hand.

"Has Anokye said anything to you about his plans?" Garde asked. "Any talk of a possible coup?"

"No. Nothing yet."

"He will," Garde said. "The Little Captain respects your expertise. Keep me informed."

"Then what? What happens then?"

Garde finished his Pernod. He rose, left money and a dash, adjusted his white Panama.

"I have to go back to the palace," he said. "Don't talk too much tonight. Just listen. Then call and tell me how it went."

Greeley watched him stride away. Moving lightly, blithely, almost bouncing. The chief teller looked down at his own right foot, encased in a great, ugly, misshapen black boot. It wasn't fair.

Alistair Greeley's home was more hacienda than house. In colonial days it had been the main building of a large cacao plantation. As the city of Mokodi grew, the land was sold off to developers and builders. Only Greeley's home, centered in a hectare plot, remained of the original farm. He rented; building and land were owned by one of the King's cousins.

It was a low, sprawling clapboard structure embellished with a screened veranda, gingerbread trim, a precisely organized flower garden in the rear. An additional embellishment—of some embarrassment to the British ambassador to Asante—was a steel flagpole, planted in concrete in the front lawn, from which Greeley insisted on flying the Union Jack on such occasions as the Queen's birthday and the anniversary of Nelson't victory at the Nile.

Peter Tangent left his rented black Opel in the gravel driveway and stepped around the flagstoned walk to the screened porch. There was an orange light burning; he smelled citronella. He glimpsed dim figures seated on the veranda. The door was pushed open suddenly.

"Come in quickly," Greeley said. "Can't let the bugs in! What? What?"

Tangent was introduced to the two women, neither of whom rose to greet him or offered a hand. He joined them, folding himself cautiously into a fragile rattan chair. He was provided with a glass of desperately weak and tepid lemonade.

"Anokye called," Greeley said. "He'll be a bit late. But better late than never. What? What?"

The younger woman, the sister, Jane, began to ask about London. How was dear old England? Had he been to the theater ("thee-ate-er") recently? Anything new and good? What were women wearing these days? Was it true that two ministers were involved in another call girl scandal? Had he ever been to Brighton? Were prices as bad as everyone said? And when would the Prince marry?

The questions came rapidly, in a brittle, almost accusatory tone. Tangent answered as best he could, trying to draw Greeley and his wife into the conversation. But Jane Greeley dominated.

In the orange light her face appeared drawn, cavernous. The odd light empurpled her sulky lips and blackened her painted fingernails and toenails. She was wearing a tie-dyed pagne, a kind of sarong that showed a wedge of smooth, tanned thigh. A lush body whispered within that loose garment. Nipples showed through thin cloth.

In contrast, Mrs. Greeley was a sour Victorian matron, wearing a high-necked, ankle-length garden gown of white linen. All pleats and ruffles, threaded through with girlish ribbons. Sam Leiberman had been right; hers was a hatchet face. And a thin, sharp body hidden behind that curtain of white. Sudden, jerky movements. Grimaces rather than expressions. Unable, for more than a moment, to take her puzzled stare away from her husband's sister.

"Are you in Asante permanently, Miss Greeley?" Tangent asked.

"No," Greeley said sharply. "Just a visit. She'll be going home shortly."

The silence that followed that pronouncement was so taut that Tangent had to break it before they flew at each other's throats, biting.

"I understand you collect toy soldiers, Mr. Greeley," Tangent said.

"*Model* soldiers," Greeley said angrily.

"Show Mr. Tangent your collection, Alistair," Maud Greeley said. "I'm sure he'll be interested in what's keeping us poor."

It was the first time she had spoken. Her voice was unexpectedly young, lilting, with an Aberdeen burr.

Muttering something, the chief teller hauled himself up with the aid of the chair arms. Dragging his foot behind him, he led the way inside his home. Tangent followed and looked about. A museum reproduction of a shabby, genteel English flat, complete with photos of the Royal Family. Even the dusty, tea-scented, stale smell was *right*. They had reproduced Birmingham in Mokodi.

In the study, lined with books in glass-fronted shelves, the host displayed his treasures. They were a revelation: Greeley's dream.

Most of the model soldiers were single figures in *ronde bosse*. But there was one stalwart squad of Prussian grenadiers and an entire mounted troop of French hussars. There were musketeers and dragoons, fusiliers and cuirassiers, drummers and pipers, lancers, pioneers, guardsmen, carabiniers, and many others. They stood

106

frozen at parade rest, at attention, thrusting with pike or sword, rifle at shoulder, or charging at full gallop. Tangent had forgotten that men once dressed that brilliantly to die.

"Fascinating," he murmured. "Absolutely fascinating."

"What? What?"

Tangent donned his glasses and bent far over to inspect the models in bell jars and display cases. He clasped his hands firmly behind his back, the better to resist picking up one of the few bright figures standing uncovered in lonely splendor.

"Must have cost a mint," he said, not looking at Greeley.

"Oh yes," the chief teller said. He tried to laugh. "But when you're bitten, you're bitten. What? What?"

"Who is this chap?" Tangent asked, pointing. "With the curved plume."

"Bavarian cuirassier. About eighteen sixty-six."

"And this one, with the feathered hat?"

"Sardinian bersaglieri. About eighteen-sixty."

"Which are Captain Anokye's favorites?" Tangent asked casually.

"He seems most interested in the eighteen-sixty to eighteen-seventy period. About then."

"In Europe?"

"Yes. Now here are two you'll like. From your Civil War. Both are zouaves. The one on the right is Union, the Eleventh Indiana Volunteers. On the left is the Confederate, from the Louisiana Tigers."

Tangent sighed, straightened up, removed his glasses.

"I can see how a hobby like this could take over a man," he said. "So you'd spend every franc you've got on it."

"Can you?" Greeley said eagerly. "Can you see that? Maud can't. Most fascinating hobby on earth. When you read about the wars and battles, you can see history come alive. What? What? How they dressed, their weapons, their equipment."

"I should think—" Tangent began, but there was a knock on the door, and he stopped.

"Come in," Greeley called.

The door opened slowly. Captain Obiri Anokye, wearing his dress whites, carrying his cap under his arm, stepped into the room, smiling faintly.

Tangent saw a short man, surely not more than five-four, heavy through the chest and shoulders, with a hint of corpulence to come in a thick torso that swelled his tunic. He carried himself with an erect, head-up posture, leaning backward slightly, chest inflated, chin elevated. He moved lightly and gracefully on small feet. He avoided pomposity, but there was an almost magisterial quality in his slow gestures, his manner of turning his head rather than moving his eyes.

He was a very dark brown, not a blue-black, with a ruddy burnish on his mahogany skin. He was without mustache or beard, his hair a tight toque of closely cropped curls. No appearance of gray. His hands were small but broad, palms and fingers squarish. He wore a ring on the index finger of his left hand. It was hammered silver set with a loin stone.

Brow was high; eyes large, liquid, deepset; nose slightly hooked. The full somewhat protuberant lips were delicately sculpted. Jaw was rounded, heavy, with a sharply defined chin line. His face was unlined except, occasionally, when two small vertical wrinkles appeared above the bridge of his nose. Small ears were set flat to his skull. Neck was thick and muscular.

108

He had an imperiousness that belied his size. It was not arrogance so much as assurance: resolution and confidence. If he had doubts, he hid them well. But then he was too young to have been tried by failure.

They seated themselves at one end of a refectory table. Greeley served small glasses of an indifferent port.

"I've been admiring this—this marvelous army," Tangent said, waving his hand at the model soldiers. He spoke French.

"Please, Mr. Tangent," Captain Anokye said, in English. "Could we speak English? I desire very much to improve my efficiency in that language."

"Of course," Tangent said, in English. "You're doing very well. Much better than my Akan!"

"Oh? You speak Akan?"

"Badly. It is a very delicate, very poetic language."

"That is true," Anokye nodded. "After speaking Akan, English seems—hard."

"The language of action?" Tangent suggested.

Anokye considered a moment.

"Perhaps," he nodded. "Yes, I believe that to be true."

"I hate French!" Greeley burst out. "All those swallowed sounds. Can't get my tongue around them. What? What?"

"Captain, Greeley tells me the eighteen-sixty to eighteen-seventy period in Europe is your favorite."

"Oh? Well, I do admire the uniforms of that time. So much more colorful than our plain whites and khakis."

"That was the period of unification, wasn't it? In Germany and Italy?"

"Yes, Mr. Tangent, I believe it was."

"Bismarck and Garibaldi, if I remember my history."

"You remember it very well."

109

"Great men," Tangent persisted. "I've often wondered if great men make history or if history, the times and circumstances, produce great men. How do you feel about that, Captain?"

Anokye was silent a moment, his head turning slowly to Tangent.

"I do not believe it is either/or, Mr. Tangent," he said softly. "The man must be ready to meet the challenges of his day, if he is to achieve."

"The right man in the right place at the right time?"

"Precisely," Anokye said. He was not smiling. "Of course, much depends on what you would call luck or good fortune."

"But what the Asantis might call destiny or fate?"

Then Anokye laughed. "Oh, the Akan concept of destiny and fate is very complex, very involved. There is a destiny of the people, a destiny of the family, and of the individual. One is impelled by one's own fate, the requirements of ancestors, the demands of the tribe. I am not certain I completely comprehend it myself."

"But a faith that can be completely comprehended is not a faith at all, is it, Captain?"

Anokye was puzzled. The two little lines appeared between his brows. Then his face smoothed.

"Yes," he said. "You speak the truth. You are a wise man, Mr. Tangent."

"Thanks, but not really," Tangent laughed. "Just a good memory. I read it somewhere. Do you read a great deal, Captain?"

"As much as I can."

"Reading can be a wonderful escape."

"I do not read to escape."

It was not spoken as a rebuke, and Tangent didn't take it so. He turned the conversation to another topic, a coup d'etat that had recently occurred in Chad.

The president of that nation, Ngarta Tombalbaye, after 15 years of increasingly mercurial rule, had made a radio speech accusing the Chadian armed forces of being a corrupt "state within a state" that abused citizens and acted like "a conquering force, an army of occupation."

Ten days later soldiers stormed the presidential palace in Ndjamena, killed Ngarta Tombalbaye, and set up a military-dominated commission to run the government.

Tangent asked Captain Anokye if he believed the French assisted in the coup. Chad had originally been a French colony and retained strong economic, military, and cultural ties with France.

Anokye said he doubted if French soldiers stationed in Chad (ostensibly to protect the nation from Muslim rebels of the north) actually took part in the coup. But he had no doubt that the Chadian armed forces moved only with the acquiescence of the French, only after they had been assured French troops would not defend the government and palace of President Tombalbaye.

"Taking the palace and killing the president is one thing," Tangent said. "Ruling the nation wisely is something else again."

"That is true," the Little Captain acknowledged. "Any coup or revolt or revolution contains within itself the seeds of its own destruction if it is not broadly based, attuned to the needs of the people, and willing and able to meet those needs. Otherwise, Chad is merely exchanging one group of despots for another, military for civilian."

"You believe the military are ever capable of ruling wisely, of understanding and answering the needs of the people?"

Anokye's eyes widened.

"Why not?" he asked. "Are military leaders of the

higher ranks so different from high officials in government and business? Their training is quite similar."

"One big difference," Tangent said. "Officers are accustomed merely to giving commands and having their orders obeyed. Politics is another kettle of fish. In government, actions can only be taken and progress made by consensus. I'm speaking of governments other than dictatorships and absolute monarchies, of course. But in most governments, consultations, compromise, and agreement take the place of command."

"True," Anokye said. "But I see no vital discrepancy. History's great generals and admirals did not merely command, they led. Perhaps the processes of consultation, compromise, and agreement were not formalized, but they did exist. The military leaders realized, consciously or unconsciously, that their resolve was no stronger than the resolve of their men. Just as a ruler's resolve is no stronger than the resolve of the people he rules. Does what I speak make sense to you, Mr. Tangent?"

"A great deal. We call it feedback, a term used in computer technology. Now also used in sociology. If you will allow me, I would be happy to send you a book on the subject."

"I would like that very much, and I thank you."

After that, conversation became desultory. The port was finished, and since Greeley obviously had no intention of providing another bottle, of anything, and seemed uncomfortable in their presence, Captain Anokye and Peter Tangent rose almost simultaneously to thank their host and take their leave. Standing side by side, the two men made an odd picture. The slat-thin Tangent towered over the chunky Anokye. Neither man smiled at the disparity in their heights nor remarked on it. Tangent offered to drive the Little Captain back to the Mokodi barracks.

Anokye accepted the invitation gratefully. The Greeley women were nowhere to be seen when they departed.

As they headed back to the Boulevard Voltaire, Tangent said: "Captain, must you return to the barracks immediately?"

"No," Anokye said. "Officially, I am not on duty until tomorrow morning."

"It's a lovely night. I thought perhaps we might take a short drive. Perhaps north toward Gonja."

"I would enjoy that," Anokye said. "This car is very comfortable. After our military vehicles."

"To get back to the coup in Chad for a moment," Tangent said. "I'd like your advice. As you may know, I am in charge of African operations for Starrett Petroleum. We now have operating installations in eight African nations, with several others in the talking stages. One of our problems, a big problem, is the impermanence of African governments. The Chad coup is an example. Did you know it is the thirty-sixth coup d'etat in Africa since World War Two?"

"I was not aware of that, no. But it does not surprise me."

"Naturally, my people would prefer to deal with stable governments. I, personally, would like to be certain that the men I negotiate with today will still occupy their offices tomorrow. Tell me, Captain, why are African governments so volatile?"

"Volatile?"

"So explosive. Liable to change suddenly, usually by violent overthrow."

"Volatile. I must remember that word. Mr. Tangent, your nation recently celebrated its two-hundredth birthday. I know you are accustomed to think of Africa as a very ancient continent. But the new Africa is actually

113

quite young, no more than forty years old. We have, for the most part, thrown off the shackles of colonialism. Now you will find everything in Africa, from the most repressive dictatorship to a pure democracy. The revolts and coups are symptomatic of a people seeking, almost blindly, with few precedents to guide us, a form of government that is right for us, that uses what is best in Western Civilization but modified and reworked to fit our own unique traditions and culture and needs.''

"In other words, Africa is suffering from growing pains?"

"You might say that. Perhaps, at this point in our development, a military dictatorship—as much as you might dislike such a form of government—is what is needed to bring an African nation into the mainstream of the modern world. Or perhaps a democracy or a constitutional monarchy or a socialist state would serve better to develop resources, build homes, end famines, improve health, educate the people. No one really knows. So there is much fumbling about, much experimenting. That is the reason for the political instability you find in Africa.''

"But I gather you are confident of the future?"

"Oh yes, I am confident. We are young, and we are strong."

"And you shall overcome?"

"Yes," Anokye laughed. "We shall overcome."

They drove awhile in silence, passing the Mokodi barracks on Asante Royal Highway No. 1, and entering the unlighted stretch that led to Gonja.

"And Asante?" Tangent asked. "You have your problems here, too."

"Many problems," the Little Captain agreed. "Serious problems."

"But they will be solved?"

Anokye was quiet a moment, framing a careful answer.

"Our problems can be solved," he said finally. "I believe that. But perhaps, at the present time, we have not the resources to solve our problems by ourselves. It may be necessary to ask for outside assistance."

Now it was Tangent's turn to remain silent as he considered how far he might go.

"I presume," he said, "you mean such things as seeking financial assistance from other people?"

"Yes," Anokye said. "I believe that will prove necessary."

"I can understand why it might be," Tangent said cautiously. "But aren't you running a risk there? Surely no people would provide funds for Asante out of the goodness of their hearts. There would have to be a trade-off, a quid pro quo."

Anokye smiled. " 'Quid pro quo.' Strange, I looked in the dictionary for that phrase less than a week ago. A something for a something. Is that correct, Mr. Tangent?"

"Yes, that's correct."

"Of course there would be a quid pro quo," Anokye said. "It could be arranged. When two parties want the same thing for different reasons, they form a partnership, so to speak, and make an arrangement. Is that not so?"

"Usually. And usually the arrangement is formalized in a signed agreement. It prevents misunderstandings later."

"I see no reason why that could not be done," Anokye said. "For the greater good of Asante."

"Of course," Tangent said. "You are very perceptive, Captain, very understanding. Would you care for a cigarette?"

"Thank you, no."

"Do you mind if I smoke?"

115

"Not at all."

"Would you hold the wheel a moment, please, while I light up?"

Tangent took longer than necessary to take a packet of Players from his inside jacket pocket, pick one out, light it slowly. As his foot pressed harder on the accelerator. But Anokye's hand was steady on the wheel; the car didn't waver, although they were driving swiftly on the dark, deserted road, tree trunks flashing by on both sides.

"These problems of Asante . . ." Tangent said, taking back the wheel. "It seems to me—this is just the opinion of an observer—that they are increasing in severity and should be resolved as soon as possible."

"Yes," Anokye said gravely, "that is so."

"Within a month or two?"

The Little Captain nodded.

"Perhaps my people could be of assistance," Tangent said tentatively. "There is little of substance I can tell them at the moment, but I might make an initial presentation to see if the desire exists to come to your aid."

"Asante's aid."

"Of course. If they decide to provide assistance, I will need more details on the extent of the aid and how best it can be administered."

Anokye nodded. "The information will be made available," he said.

"It surprises me that Asante would not seek help from the French," Tangent said.

"Asante will thankfully accept aid from whatever source," Anokye said.

"And you believe there are others in Asante who feel as you do?" Tangent asked.

Captain Anokye turned his head slowly to stare at him.

"Many others," he said. "Many, many. Enough. I speak the truth, Mr. Tangent."

"I'm sure you do, Captain," Tangent said. "And you believe, with outside aid, that Asante's problems may be solved?"

"Not *all* its problems, naturally. But its most serious problems."

Tangent slowed, stopped, backed onto the verge, turned around and headed the car back to Mokodi.

"Assuming Asante's problems are solved," he said. "Not only its most serious problem, but other problems as well . . . Assuming Asante becomes a thriving, prosperous nation. Then what?"

"Why then we might become a showcase," Captain Obiri Anokye said dreamily. "A model for all of Africa. Who knows, our most important export might become our system of government with other African nations—the poor and the rich—seeking to follow in our path. Is that impossible?"

"No," Tangent said. "Not impossible. Captain Anokye, what you say impresses me."

"Does it?"

"I wonder how a man of your obvious talents and learning and vision could be content as an army captain."

"I am content."

"But surely your salary cannot be great."

"No, it is not great."

"And your family is large?"

"I am not married, but my family is large."

"Do you never think of seeking a position that might offer more rewards? Or an arrangement that might augment your income?"

"I am content," Anokye repeated, and Tangent let it go

at that, intrigued by this African army captain who would not accept a bribe.

Anokye asked Tangent to drop him a kilometer from the barracks gate. The American understood the Captain's motives and obediently pulled onto the shadowed verge and stopped. But the Little Captain made no immediate effort to get out of the car.

"Do you intend to stay in Asante long, Mr. Tangent?" he asked.

"This trip? Another day or two, at least."

Anokye sat in silence a few moments, considering.

"Mr. Tangent," he said finally, "there is an army general in Togo named Songo. Do you know him?"

"No. Never heard of him."

"A man of some influence in government. Very capable. His son, Jere Songo, was educated at St. Cyr. He has now returned to Togo and is a lieutenant in the Togolese army, assigned to his father's staff. He has been sent to Asante to observe our training techniques. A nice boy. He speaks French, Ewe, Twi, and Hausa. A little English. He is being escorted by Anatole Garde, the King's secretary. Tomorrow I will stage a military exercise for Lieutenant Songo. It is, I believe, the only one of its kind in the world. You may find it of interest. Would you care to join us as an observer? Lieutenant Songo will be present, of course, and Anatole Garde. It would be an honor to have you."

"Thank you," Tangent said. "You are very kind. I'd like to join you."

"I should warn you, you will have to cover a great distance on foot. Will that inconvenience you?"

This last was spoken politely, but the challenge was unmistakable.

"I think I can manage," Tangent said. "What shall I wear?"

118

"Dungarees, if you have them. Or old khakis. Certainly comfortable boots."

"I keep a change at the hotel," Tangent said. "Work clothes for my visits to the *Starrett Explorer*. They should do. A hat?"

"By all means. And sunglasses. I will provide a lunch. We start at exactly oh-eight-hundred."

"I'll be there."

"I will leave word with the gate guard at the Mokodi barracks to expect you. An escort will be provided to bring you to the staging area."

"I'm looking forward to it."

Captain Anokye got out of the car. He closed the door softly. He stood with hands on hips, torso bent slightly backward. His head was tilted up; he stared at the night sky a long moment. Then he leaned to speak through the open window.

"The moon is almost full," he said. "A good omen. A time to make important decisions. The sooner the better."

"I understand," Tangent said.

13

ON THE FOLLOWING morning, at 0745, Tangent drove his rented Opel up to the gate of the Mokodi barracks and stopped. A soldier immediately emerged from the guard hut and stalked toward him.

"How may I be of service, sir?" he called, in French.

"My name is Tangent. Captain Obiri Anokye said he'd leave word to expect me."

"Ah yes," the soldier grinned, not bothering to inspect the proffered passport. "Yes, yes. The Little Captain did say you are indeed to be admitted, Mr. Tangent, sir. You come to see the Hunt?"

"The Hunt?" Tangent asked. "Is that what it's called?"

"Ah yes!" the guard laughed. His mirth was so infectious that Tangent found himself smiling in return. "Much fun, the Hunt. Bim, bam, boom!"

His own words convulsed him, and Tangent had to wait until he calmed. Then he opened the gate and directed Tangent to the motor pool area where he would find parking space in the shade and where an escort would join him.

"Thank you very much," Tangent said.

"Bim, bam, boom!" the soldier repeated, and was still laughing as Tangent drove slowly inside the compound. He found the motor pool area, found a parking space in the shade of a large corrugated metal garage, and stepped out of the car, looking about curiously.

It was not his first visit to an African military installation. He was impressed with the neat cleanliness of this one: swept walks, trimmed foliage, no litter, garage windows washed. Good discipline and daily policing. There was a sign, in French, that read: "This is your home. Treat it so."

He was still looking about when an Asanti sergeant came around the corner of the garage, striding rapidly, right arm swinging, left arm crooked and holding a fly whisk clamped tightly between bicep and thick torso. He marched up to Tangent, froze to attention, saluted smartly.

"Mr. Peter Tangent, sir?"

"Yes, I'm Tangent."

"Sir, I am detailed as your escort for the day. My name is Sergeant First Class Sene Yeboa."

"Glad to meet you, Sergeant," Tangent said, proffering his hand—then, when Yeboa gripped it, trying not to sink to his knees in anguish.

"Is it all right to park here?" he asked, flexing his fingers behind his back.

"Perfectly A-OK," Yeboa grinned. "A guest of the Captain . . ." He left that sentence unfinished, then said, "A moment, sir." He looked into the rental car, reached through the opened window, removed the ignition key, and handed it to Tangent. "We would not like to leave temptation for a thoughtless child," he said, smiling. "This way, sir. I will take you first to the staging area. The other guests have already arrived."

The sergeant set a good pace, and Tangent lengthened his stride. They struck out across a wide parade ground, avoiding squads and platoons of soldiers going through close-order drill. They looked very professional to Tangent, and he told the sergeant so.

121

"They are indeed good soldiers, sir," Yeboa agreed. "But I would not care to tell them that."

Both men laughed.

"I understand this exercise is called the Hunt," Tangent said. "Is that correct?"

"Do you speak Ewe, sir?"

"No, I'm afraid not. Akan, and a little Kwa."

Yeboa immediately switched from French to Akan.

"In the Ewe language, the name for this exercise is a word that means hunt, search, or to fight on bravely—depending on how the word is used. We do indeed call it the Hunt, but it means other things as well."

The sergeant marched on steadily, slightly ahead and to the right of Tangent. They passed a row of wooden barracks where half-naked soldiers were washing clothes at iron troughs, airing bedding, playing with a couple of pye-dogs, reading the Asanti *New Times*, listening to a transistor radio, or just squatting on their hams in groups, gossiping and laughing.

"Free time for this company," Yeboa explained. "Soon they will be called to school."

"School? Weapons instruction?"

"Reading and writing," the sergeant said proudly. "Every Asanti soldier must know how to read and write."

"Oh?" Tangent said. "The whole army?"

"Oh no, sir," Yeboa said. "Only Fourth Brigade. It is Captain Anokye's order."

"Ah? Tell me, Sergeant, how do the enlisted men feel about Captain Anokye?"

Yeboa stopped suddenly and turned to stare at Tangent.

"We would die for him," he said, in such a tone that Tangent could not doubt it.

They passed through another guarded gate in the chain-link perimeter fence. Now they were in an area of scrub grass, dried gullies, rocky outcrops. Sgt. Yeboa proceeded rapidly along a barely defined path that led down into a ravine and up the other side. Tangent followed, thankful for broad-brimmed hat and sunglasses. He was beginning to feel the strength of the new sun.

They came up onto a large grassland plateau with wooded areas framing it on three sides, a horseshoe of trees with the open end on the dried riverbed they had just traversed. Almost precisely in the middle of this savanna, as if deliberately planted there, was a magnificent old iroko. In the shade of its thick trunk and branches, about 30 men stood or squatted or lay full-length on the ground. As Yeboa and Tangent came up to them, Captain Anokye walked forward smiling to shake Tangent's hand.

"Welcome," he said. "It promises to be a fair day."

"As always in Asante," Tangent replied.

He turned to greet Anatole Garde, and was then introduced to Lt. Jere Songo, the Togolese observer. Songo was a youth, open-faced, still flushing with pleasure at wearing a uniform and officer's bars, taking part in the world of men. He had a charming diffidence, a nervous laugh, an obvious anxiety not to behave badly.

The Captain glanced about, and without an order given, the lounging soldiers rose immediately to their feet, straightened, formed a loose circle around Anokye and his guests. The soldiers, Tangent noted, were not armed, but each carried a slung water bottle in a covering of woven straw and a stick about a meter in length, the thickness of a stick. Each stick was tied at one end with a bulbous wrapping of rags, tightly secured and dyed a bright red.

The Little Captain addressed his guests in French:

"The exercise you are about to witness is called the Hunt. I believe it is unique with us, although I have read of these coup sticks being used elsewhere in mock warfare.

123

By your Red Indians, as a matter of fact, Mr. Tangent. As you all know, Asante is a small nation, and I try to design the military training of Fourth Brigade to fit our special and particular needs. It would be useless, for instance, to train for amphibious landings. To what purpose? We do not possess the needed equipment, and have no desire for it. Neither are we capable of staging maneuvers of large military units, of coordinating tank and artillery attacks, of practicing airborne invasions.''

"What we are faced with in Asante is terrorism by Marxist guerrillas, the illegal traffic in smuggled goods and, of course, the basic need to protect our borders and national integrity from incursions and invasion.''

"Because of the geography of our country and the small size of our armed forces, it is necessary that every man in uniform be skilled in the very fundamental arts of individual survival, of tracking and avoiding pursuit, of knowing the land as he knows the palm of his hand, and being able to use the land to carry out his assigned duty.''

"So we have devised this exercise. A game of hide-and-seek. One soldier is assigned to act as the quarry. He is given a head start. His duty is to avoid capture. The remaining soldiers are the pursuers. Their duty is to track down and 'kill' the hunted man within eight hours. We do not kill the captured quarry, of course, since this is only practice. But the hunted man is considered 'killed' if one of his pursuers is able to get close enough to hit or touch him with a coup stick. That knob on the end of the stick has been dipped in a dye that will leave a mark, proving whether or not the hunted man has actually been tracked down and 'killed.'

"Before the Hunt begins, I shall point out the area in which the running man must stay. He can go anywhere in that area he wishes, hide wherever he likes—up a tree, in a cave, in a swamp. But he must remain free within that area for a period of eight hours. If he does remain undiscovered, he has won the Hunt and is rewarded with two days' extra liberty. If he is found and touched with a coup stick before the eight hours are up, he has lost—and must suffer the consequences."

The assembled soldiers burst out laughing, and several brandished their coup sticks, shaking them high in the air. Then the whole group clustered around a rough, hand-drawn map that Sgt. Yeboa spread on the ground. Captain Anokye pointed out the physical limits of the Hunt: the ravine behind them, Asante Royal Highway No. 1 to the west, a large wheat field on the north, a secondary dirt road to the east.

"Any questions?" Anokye asked.

There were none.

"Now it only remains to select the quarry," the Captain said. "Sergeant . . ."

Yeboa stepped forward and began to look slowly around the circle of grinning soldiers. It was obvious to Tangent that most of the men wished to be selected. They puffed their chests, pointed at themselves, even flexed their biceps, laughing. Finally Sgt. Yeboa pointed.

"Njonjo," he said. "You."

The chosen man gave a great roar of approval and leaped high into the air. He removed his boots and socks, handed his coup stick to a comrade, and immediately began a steady run toward the nearest shield of trees. Captain Anokye looked at his wristwatch.

"We allow the hunted man thirty minutes," he said.

The soldiers relaxed again, slumping onto the ground or squatting in groups. The Little Captain took Lt. Songo aside and spoke to him in a low voice. Tangent was left alone with Anatole Garde. The two men sat on the ground in the shade of the iroko, their backs against the massive trunk.

"Have you ever seen this before?" Tangent asked.

"No, never. I had heard of it, but I have never witnessed it."

"The Little Captain spoke of the consequences if the hunted man is found and touched with a coup stick before the eight hours are up. Then all of the soldiers laughed. What are the consequences—do you know?"

"Have no idea," Garde said. "Staying long?"

"This trip? No, not long. Another day or so."

"Any word from Tulsa?"

"Not yet. Is the King getting impatient?"

"What do you think?"

They were silent then. Tangent craned his head to look, but the quarry had disappeared into the forest.

"When do you think you'll hear?" Garde asked.

"This business in Togo . . ." Tangent said. He shook his head doubtfully. "It's fouled things up. It's made my people hesitant about making any deal."

"Nothing to it," Garde said "You can sign."

"Well . . ." Tangent said hesitantly. "The Prime Minister is going to Lomé to check it out. I think we better wait until he returns."

"Time is running out on the lease," Garde said.

"I know," Tangent said pleasantly. "It's a problem, isn't it? What do you hear from Paris?"

"Hear from Paris? What do you mean?"

"That's where your family lives, isn't it?"

"Oh. Yes, that's right. All's well, as far as I know. As usual, they complain about high prices."

"They should visit London."

"So I understand. I was hoping to get back for a week's vacation."

"Oh?" Tangent said.

"But I think now I'll stick around until this lease thing is settled. One way or another."

"Ah," Tangent said.

They watched Anokye and Songo stroll slowly up and down, conversing quietly. The Captain was shorter than Songo, but his arm was up and about the young lieutenant's shoulders.

"Nice boy," Tangent said. "Any problems?"

"No," Garde said. "He's anxious to please."

"I understand his father's a hotshot general."

"Who told you that?"

"I heard."

"Anokye," Garde said definitely. "Must have been. How did you happen to meet him?"

"Through Alistair Greeley at the bank. He invited me over for a drink, and the Little Captain showed up. Interesting man."

"Isn't he. Don't underestimate him."

"I don't."

"For instance, he's invited Songo for dinner tonight, with his family, at his home in Zabar."

"So?" Tangent said. "That's neighborly."

"I told you not to underrate him," Garde said. He laughed. "The Little Captain has a young unmarried sister. Name of Sara."

"Oh-ho," Tangent said. "Wheels within wheels."

"That's the Little Captain," Garde agreed. "Sometimes I think he's way ahead of us all."

Finally, the soldiers becoming restive, Captain Anokye looked at his watch, then nodded to Yeboa. The sergeant strode forward, and the men rose to their feet and clustered about him eagerly.

"Corporal Kibasu will be in command of the Hunt,"

the sergeant said. "You will follow his orders as if they came from the Captain himself."

The corporal, a short, pudgy soldier with a delicately trimmed mustache, puffed his chest and held up a hand from which three rings flashed.

"Pay heed to what I shall tell you," he said pompously. "First, we know that Njonjo is cursed with left-handedness." The assembled men groaned at this evidence of perversity. "Usually, a right-handed man, when faced with a fork in the path or choosing a way to escape, will move to the right, and a left-handed man will move to the left. Is that not so?"

The listening men, now serious, nodded their agreement, and one called out, "It is so."

"*But!*" Corporal Kibasu said triumphantly. "Second, we know that Njonjo is a sly, devious fellow. Recall what the Little Captain has told us of the need to understand the feelings and desires of the enemy, of trying always to crawl within his skin. Njonjo knows we are aware of his left-handedness. Therefore, he will deliberately turn *right* whenever possible to throw us off his track. Remember this. We will now divide into three squads. I take the center, Jomo the left, Malloun the right. Select the leader of your choice."

After a few minutes of confusion, of milling about, the soldiers divided into three approximately equal squads.

"Go!" Corporal Kibasu shouted, and the three teams began trotting toward the point where their quarry had disappeared into the trees, gradually diverging as they advanced. Captain Anokye followed at a steady walk, along with Garde and Lt. Songo. Tangent and Sgt. Yeboa brought up the rear.

"Do you think Njonjo will escape?" Tangent asked.

"No," Sgt. Yeboa said. "Jomo's team will 'kill' him."

"Is Jomo the very thin soldier without a water bottle?"

"That is the man. He is one of our best trackers. He is said to have Masai blood. I do not believe that to be true, but Jomo is very skilled. He has been the quarry three times and has never been caught."

"Is he better than you?" Tangent said. He meant it humorously, but the sergeant answered seriously.

"No," he said. "I am the best."

It was not a boast, Tangent realized. Yeboa merely spoke his truth.

"That business about being left-handed," Tangent said. "I know how Africans feel about the left hand, but is Njonjo clever enough to do as Corporal Kibasu said he would?"

Sgt. Yeboa laughed. "Oh, that fool Kibasu!" he said. "Njonjo is more clever than that. He will know how Kibasu thinks—that he will turn right to confuse the hunters. Therefore, Njonjo will turn to the left. He will be one step ahead of Kibasu in his thinking. But Jomo will pay no attention to left or right. Jomo will follow only the signs. He will reject the false signs and follow only the true ones. You will see."

Then they were into the trees, not a true rain forest but thick enough. Sgt. Yeboa led the way, bringing Tangent up behind Jomo's squad, who were moving slowly and carefully, peering left, right, up, down, forward, back. There was an exclamation from one, and almost immediately Jomo was at his side, examining a twig that hung broken to the left. Tangent watched, fascinated, as Jomo waved the other men away and dropped to his knees. He sniffed the ground slowly, exactly as a bloodhound might. Then he rose to his feet, motioned directly ahead. The men moved off silently.

129

"How did Jomo know it was a false lead?" he asked Yeboa.

"When a green twig is broken deliberately in that manner, the stem is slightly pinched on both sides of the break by the man's fingers. Jomo saw that, and smelled no scent of human passing to the left. Now we will stay back a little. It is important the pursuers make as little noise as possible."

"Sorry," Tangent apologized, having just snapped a dried branch under his foot. "I'm afraid I'm not doing Jomo much good."

"No, no, it's all right," Yeboa assured him. "Njonjo is far ahead at this moment. But when they close in, we must move slowly and carefully and silently. If you become thirsty, please tell me."

"Thank you," Tangent said. "But not yet."

After hearing the Hunt described by Captain Anokye, Tangent had thought he would be bored. He was not. As the initial quartering settled down, and the trackers began moving stealthily through the forest about him, he found himself caught up in the chase.

There was a low whistle off to the left, and Sgt. Yeboa led him toward it. They came to a broad-trunked plane tree where Jomo was pointing out the direction he wanted his men to take.

Jomo saw Yeboa and Tangent come up and gestured briefly at the tree before disappearing again. Yeboa moved close to inspect the tree trunk.

"What do you see?" he whispered.

"A tree trunk," Tangent whispered back.

"Feel it."

Obediently Tangent ran his fingertips down the smooth-barked surface.

"Dampish," he said.

"Now smell your fingers."

Tangent sniffed cautiously. "Sweat," he said. "Human sweat."

"Very good, sir," Yeboa chuckled. "We will make a tracker of you yet. Njonjo entered into the woods a distance and immediately set about laying false trails, doubling back to his starting place. He worked very hard, very fast. Now he is finished. He is sweating. He leans against this tree to catch his breath a moment, considering what his true path should be. This is his starting place, not where he entered the woods."

The morning went faster than Tangent could have believed. They moved slowly and deliberately, Yeboa following where Jomo's trackers led. After a while Tangent began to learn how to place his feet, how to avoid low-hanging limbs and refrain from scraping against rough surfaces. They waded quietly through several marshy areas, after Yeboa showed Tangent how to cinch his trouser cuffs inside his boot tops to keep leeches out.

The trail led generally northward, as far as Tangent could determine from infrequent glimpses of the sun overhead. Some of the wood was in dappled shadow; most was dimness with birdcalls, unexplained grunts, and occasionally the sudden crash of escaping animals.

"Warthogs?" Tangent asked. Somewhat nervously. "Deer, d'you suppose? Or what?"

Sgt. Yeboa didn't answer. He was too intent on following the path of the elusive Jomo, who was following the trail of the elusive Njonjo. Occasionally he pointed out the signs to Tangent: usually nothing more than a fallen leaf, or a forest orchid with one petal scraped loose and dangling. In one swampy area, apparently the hunted Njonjo had tripped over a submerged root and fallen. He had attempted to brush away the marks of his fall with a leafy

131

branch, but time was running out; the branch itself had been concealed but the pale scar where it had been stripped from a sapling had not been smeared with earth; it gleamed whitely in the forest gloom. And the swept area of silky mud was apparent even to Tangent's untrained eye.

After moving northward, almost to the wheat field boundary, Njonjo had left several clever false trails, then returned to his junction to begin a wide circle westward toward the paved highway. The pace of the chase increased.

Sgt. Yeboa knelt suddenly to place his fingertips in a small depression in the leaf-rank earth.

"A heelmark," he whispered to Tangent. "Fresh and deep. Njonjo is getting careless. Now I think Jomo is no more than ten minutes behind him."

"Njonjo knows this?"

"Oh yes, Mr. Tangent. He hears things, feels things. Perhaps the birds are still as he passes, then chatter angrily, then are still again. Perhaps Njonjo hears the crash of animals behind him as Jomo advances. The hunter is close behind, so Njonjo runs and becomes careless. I think you will have your lunch sooner than you expected, Mr. Tangent."

Tangent found himself trembling, and not from fatigue.

"I would like to be in on the 'kill,'" he whispered.

Sgt. Yeboa looked at him a moment, then showed his teeth.

"Jomo moves very quickly, very silently," he said, "but I will try to move up on him. Please follow me closely."

"Where are the others?" Tangent asked. "Captain Anokye, Garde, Lt. Songo?"

"Behind us," Yeboa laughed. "Following Corporal Kibasu, who moves like a sleepy water buffalo. This way now, with care."

Tangent's khakis were sweated through, somewhere along the way he had lost his sunglasses, his face had been rasped with vines, and his bare forearms and hands oozed blood from a dozen small cuts and insect bites. He didn't care. He wanted Njonjo "killed."

They made a wide circle, moving faster now as the trees thinned, and there were grassy glades where Tangent could see the sun. Looking up, to judge their direction, he stumbled into a shallow ravine, fell, slid, went rolling to the bottom. He lay a moment, fighting for breath.

Sgt. Yeboa was at his side, hauling him to his feet.

"Are you all right, Mr. Tangent, sir?" he asked anxiously. "Shall we go back?"

"No, no," Tangent said. "I'm all right. I want to go on. How close are we now?"

"Jomo is directly ahead, and no more than five minutes behind Njonjo. I think Njonjo is heading to the grassland where we started. He means to enter the ravine and run along that. He hopes to gain time that way. But Jomo runs faster; you will see. There is no reason for quiet now, Mr. Tangent. Now he cannot escape Jomo."

The pace increased. Tangent found himself running with an agonizing stitch in his side. But that eased, he caught his second wind, and went crashing after the speeding Yeboa, marveling how lightly and effortlessly the heavy man moved.

Within a few moments they were in sight of Jomo, loping steadily ahead, scarcely pausing to glance at signs of the hunted man's passing. Jomo's head was up, he seemed to be sniffing the air. He turned suddenly to the left and began to run faster. Now he carried his coup stick

133

shoulder-high, plunging back and forth like a barbed spear.

"He sees him," Yeboa shouted back over his shoulder. "He will 'kill' him before the ravine. Hurry, please, Mr. Tangent. Hurry! Hurry!"

Tangent dug in, disregarding the ache in his thighs, his straining lungs. Sweat stung his eyes, coursed in rivulets from scalp, neck, shoulders, back, groin. He smelled himself and didn't care. He ran dementedly. Everything was in the running.

Then they came bursting from the trees, out onto the wide savanna. Ahead was the iroko tree, shading three squatting soldiers who had brought bottles and boxes of drink and food for the Captain and his guests. They saw the running men, jerked to their feet, began to leap about excitedly and yell in a language Tangent could not understand.

Njonjo, the hunted, was in the lead. He saw he could not make the ravine and sprinted desperately across the grassed plateau, hoping to reach the forest on the other side. But Jomo, the pursuer, head still high, lengthened his stride; he seemed to be taking giant leaps, almost floating, both feet apparently off the ground. Now he carried his coup stick extended, the dyed knob forward. After him came Yeboa and Tangent, and then others burst from the forest behind them, calling and shouting, everyone running, screams rising in intensity, earth rumbling from the pounding feet, coup sticks brandished, torsos glistening with sweat, the hunted man frantically plunging, almost falling forward as the relentless Jomo gained on him, gained, gave a cry of triumph and made a final great lunge to slam the knob of his coup stick against Njonjo's back, the blow heavy enough to topple the fleeing man and send him somersaulting, rolling, twisting, until he came to rest on his back, spread-eagled, and then they were all on their backs, chests heaving, but yelling, screaming, cawing, barking, growling, Tangent as loud as the others.

Finally, slowly, they quieted, and men began to rinse their mouths with water, to pour water over their heads, to strip off sodden shirts and shorts, some to stand naked in socks and boots. Njonjo rose groggily to his feet, emptied a water bottle onto his upturned face. He clapped Jomo on the shoulder. The two men embraced, called each other "brother." Captain Anokye went to them and spoke quietly. Within a moment they were grinning, nodding, looking about proudly in hopes others had heard the Captain's praise. Tangent glanced at his watch. He was amazed to see it was 1500. The hunt had lasted almost six hours. He could hardly believe the time had run so swiftly.

Sgt. Yeboa stepped forward, gave a command in Ewe. The soldiers began to form two ranks, facing each other, a meter's space between. They reversed their coup sticks, gripping them with both hands just above the dyed knob. They held the staffs as men of other countries might hold bats or sledgehammers. The Little Captain came sauntering back to where Tangent, Lt. Songo, and Garde now stood in the shade of the iroko tree, nervously waiting.

"Running the gauntlet," Anokye said pleasantly, looking at Tangent. "An ancient custom, known in many lands. The price the loser must pay. He proves his manhood by how slowly he moves between the files. He may run swiftly or he may stroll. The choice is his to make."

Njonjo, head high, chose to stroll. The blows that fell upon his bare back were not light. They made a ripe, smacking sound, some of them powerful enough to knock him forward. But he never hurried his pace. Tangent saw that buttery black back suddenly riven with red. Then

135

flowing. By the time Njonjo emerged from the gauntlet, now moving shakily, he was wearing a crimson cape, blood dripping onto his legs, onto the thirsty African soil. But he had not cried out. After the last blow had landed, the punished man turned to his tormentors, tried a grin, raised a wavering fist above his head.

Then a great roar of approval went up, coup sticks were tossed high into the air, his comrades rushed forward to hug his bloody torso. A sling of crossed fists was fashioned, Njonjo was seated, and the soldiers departed with the "killed" man carried aloft in triumph.

Tangent turned to Anatole Garde.

"What do you think of that?" he asked, his voice high.

"Appalling," Garde said. "You?"

"Thrilling," Tangent said.

14

IN THE PAST year or so, a strange thing had been happening to Josiah Anokye, the 82-year-old father of the Little Captain. His three sons—the oldest Zuni, Obiri, and the youngest Adebayo—had spoken of it amongst themselves. Their first thought was that their father, because of his age, was going soft in the head.

He would say odd, unexpected things that had nothing to do with what was being spoken at the moment. For instance, he might—very intent—suddenly say, "When the wind is from the west, as it is today, and it is difficult to breathe, and the clouds move fast and high, then pull the boat far up on the beach." Zuni, who captained the Anokye fishing boat, already knew this.

Or Josiah might say, "When a man you scarcely know becomes suddenly friendly and claps you on the shoulder, he plans mischief toward you." Or, "When gutting a fish, always move the blade away from you."

Or he might repeat ancient Akan proverbs: "Poverty has no friends," or, "When a rich man gets drunk, he is indisposed." (This latter very similar to the English-language saying: "The poor man is crazy; the rich man is eccentric.")

So his sons thought that Josiah, reciting these things at odd times, might be getting soft in the head. But then they realized it was not that. The old man sensed the onset of death, and since he had no wealth to leave to his sons, he was determined to leave them the accumulated experience and wisdom of his 82 years. He just wanted to help them; he was not soft in the head.

That night, for instance, the three sons and their father sat on the sandy beach of Zabar and watched as sister Sara and Lt. Jere Songo waded in the warm water up to their knees, laughing, chattering, whispering.

"He is a fine boy," Zuni said. "But shy."

"Yes," the Little Captain smiled. "But not with Sara."

"What do you know of his family?" Josiah asked.

"In his country," Obiri said, "his father is a man of importance, a general in the army and with power in the government."

"What would he pay for Sara?" the old man asked.

His face was a walnut, his head almost completely bald, covered always with a watch cap of blue knitted wool topped with a pompon that had once been red. The old man's body was all rope and twine, muscles and veins distinct through thin, wrinkled skin. He had once killed a shark with a knife, in the water with the big fish. That was the truth; men who had witnessed the fight still spoke of it with awe.

"Pay for Sara?" Obiri said. "It is too early to speak of such things."

"Not too early," Adebayo said in a low voice, hesitant to state his opinion in the presence of his elders. "See how he touches her hand? And she is drawn to him."

"How can you say?"

"She comes alive in his presence." Then, when they laughed, the young man said indignantly, "Well, is it not so? You see. She has a love for him."

"When I was their age," Josiah said, "we bought our wives. As I did your mother. That was the mark of a man's love: what he would pay for a woman. Now, today, this is

138

said to be old-fashioned and bad. Now they must love each other, and that is enough. But I do not see that marriage is better for it. Love goes, but an investment lasts. A man who gives part of his wealth for his wife does not wish to be thought a fool for making a bad bargain. When he has given nothing of value for her, or she has brought no dowry, why should they remain together if their love goes? An investment insures the marriage will last until they are grown together, two edges of the same knife. Bibi, will you marry soon?''

''Yes, Father,'' Obiri said. ''Soon. But I have work to do first.''

''It goes well?'' Zuni asked quietly.

''Yes.''

''And the Nyam?''

''When a man wishes to take a wife,'' the old man intoned, ''it is best to deal with an uncle, not the father. It may be necessary to say the woman desired is without beauty, she has a squint in one eye, she is a bad cook, and so forth. A father might respond to these things with anger. But an uncle, being once removed, will understand they are but bargaining, and he will praise the woman, pointing out her strength, her soft voice, how she always grinds the eggplant seeds.''

''The Nyam sent word,'' Obiri said to Zuni. ''He will end his terrorism, and will join us if we move within a period of one month.''

''And if we do not act within a month?'' Zuni asked.

''An uncle,'' Josiah nodded. ''An older brother of the woman's father is best, since he has lived longer and has more experience. A gift is brought to him to prove good faith. He will then provide food and drink, a good meal to show the wealth of his family. Then the talk may begin. The man who wishes to marry should not speak for himself, but should be represented by his father, an older married brother, or by an uncle.''

"Then the Nyam will resume his raids," Obiri said.

"You agreed to this, Bibi?" Adebayo asked hesitantly.

"Yes," the Little Captain nodded. "Since I had no choice. Also, things now move swiftly. I have been approached by a man named Tangent who represents the oil company. The money for the weapons may come from him. Or from the French, who are not happy with the reign of King Prempeh."

"The talk may take days, weeks, even months," Josiah said, remembering. "Your mother's sister, your Aunt Jemin, was not purchased until talk had continued for almost a year. It is not a matter to be taken lightly. But if the man and woman come from good families, an agreement may be reached that benefits both. Do not speak loudly or shake your fist or stamp the ground. Speak softly, gravely, and with respect. The other family will think more of you for this. Act with dignity. It is a matter of importance."

Zuni considered a moment, then addressed Obiri:

"You mean to play the oil company against the French?"

"Not I. But I believe that to be Abraham's plan. He has so acted that both Tangent and Anatole Garde, the King's secretary who represents the French, know of each other's interest. It is, I think, a good plan. Abraham is a wise man and knows more of these things than I do."

"You trust him?" Zuni asked.

"If the man truly wishes the woman, and cannot live his life without her, and would give all his wealth for her," Josiah went on steadily, "the man who speaks for him should not mention this. That is why it is best the man does not speak for himself. The man who speaks for him—the

140

father, older brother, uncle—says only that man who wishes to marry is not certain in his own mind, that he wants only a woman to make his home, that he thinks frequently of other women. And so forth. The passion must be concealed. Or the price goes up.''

''Abraham?'' Obiri said. ''Yes, I trust him. I must trust others; I cannot do it all myself. Abraham says he acts from his love of Asante, and I believe him. But he is not a simple man. He delights in riddles and puzzles. He plays chess very well. He wishes to solve problems. He finds pleasure in that.''

''And he believes he can solve Asante's problems?''

''He believes so,'' the Little Captain nodded. ''And I believe he can. Most of Asante's problems are money problems, and Abraham is skilled in moving money about. Like chess pieces.''

''In the end,'' the father said, ''it usually happens that the man gives more than he first intended. The time spent in talk has made him impatient. He wishes to make his home. The woman begins to seem more valuable to him as the bargaining continues. So, finally, defeated by desire, he offers more than he knows is wise, and his offer is accepted. Then he may become sorry, and wonder if he has acted the fool. But the agreement has been made, and he cannot withdraw. Usually it turns out well.''

The four Anokye men were silent then, watching Sara and Lt. Jere Songo frolicking in the surf, splashing each other, laughing. Occasionally touching.

''You will marry soon, Bibi?'' Josiah asked again.

''Soon, Father.''

''Good,'' the old man said. ''If not, who will make your fufu?''

15

STARRETT PETROLEUM, INC., leased a small suite at the Savoy for the convenience of transient VIPs. It was there the Man from Tulsa and the Man from New York stayed during their short visit to London. Tangent considered holding the conference dinner there or at a private dining room in Brindleys. But because of security problems, he finally decided to have them over to his Connaught suite. His premises were "swept" electronically twice a week. He was, he admitted to himself, paranoiac in his fear of shared secrets.

He had gone to a great deal of trouble and expense in planning the menu and selecting the wines.

"You're bribing us, Pete," the Man from Tulsa said, helping himself to more of the smoked salmon flown down from the north of Scotland.

"If I'm going to be bribed," the Man from New York said, holding his white beaujolais to the light, "this is the way to do it, Peter."

They were dressed like twins. Artfully tailored suits of some dark, sheeny material, pale blue shirts, silver satin ties. And tasseled black patent moccasins to prove their swinging informality. Their fingernail polish was colorless, but it was fingernail polish. They smiled frequently. Up to their eyes. They were not quite twins; one wore a toupee. But which, Tangent never could decide.

He had planned his presentation carefully. He waited until coffee and cognac had been brought, Cuban cigars offered, the door softly closed behind the departing serving staff. Then he listed their options.

"First," he said, "we can give Prempeh exactly what he wants—fifty-five to Asante and ten to him."

"Sheeyut," the Man from Tulsa said.

"On a two-year lease?" the Man from New York said. "And no guarantee that he won't raise the ante next time, or kick our ass out? No way."

"Second," Tangent said, "we can knock Prempeh. It could be bought. But to what purposes? He has five sons, a dozen bastards, countless brothers, uncles, cousins. Get rid of him, and we'd have another one just like him to deal with."

"Sheeyut," the Man from Tulsa said.

"Third," Tangent said, "withdraw from Asante completely."

They both stared at him, and he added hastily, "All right, all right, I just wanted to explore all our options, no matter how ridiculous."

The Man from New York ran a vividly red tongue around the rim of his brandy snifter.

"Peter," he said gently, "we know you didn't bring us three thousand miles to tell us to pick up our chips and go home. What are you finagling?"

"Spell it out, son," the Man from Tulsa said.

Tangent talked steadily for almost 20 minutes, telling them about Captain Obiri Anokye. He told them about the Little Captain's reputation in his own country, the loyalty he inspired, the bodies he owned. He spoke of the dreadful conditions in Asante, the poverty and starvation outside of Mokodi. He told them of the French investment, the role of Garde. He mentioned—casually, briefly—what he had already done to locate sources of weapons. He suggested Starrett finance a coup d'etat.

143

They were interested. The questions began.

"Did you check this out with State?"

"No. State is cold on Africa. No interest. I checked it out with Virginia. They couldn't care less."

"The French?"

"A problem. They hold the bonds. And they're jealous of their hegemony in Africa."

"Hegemony?" the Man from Tulsa asked.

"Power. I don't know how they'll jump."

"What guarantee would we have?"

"The very minimum would be a signed statement from Anokye before we started. X percentage for Y years. On paper and on tape. We get it first, or no guns. If he shits us, we release it to the world press. It would kill him in Asante."

"This Abraham—what's his gimmick?"

Tangent took a chance. "He wears dark suits, like yours. Blue shirts and silver ties, like yours. Tasseled patent moccasins, like yours. You can talk to him."

Both men laughed.

"Pete, you really are a red-ass," the Man from Tulsa said. "You know that?"

"All right," the Man from New York said. "Now let's get down to the nitty-gritty. How much?"

"Maybe a mil," Tangent said. "Maybe half a mil. Within those limits. I can't tell you exactly until I get a report from Leiberman. But in situations like this, I'd rather go for more than less. If we skimp, we're dead."

"Who gets the dineros?" the Man from Tulsa asked.

"Ah," Tangent said. "Good point. No one does. We buy the weapons and deliver to Anokye. That's my plan. I'll have to go through Leiberman, a thief. But his kickbacks will be mild compared to what we could lose delivering cash to a bunch of hungry niggers."

His language was brutal and deliberate. He knew his audience. But he had the uneasy feeling he might be trying slang in a foreign language. They'd know.

But— "Makes sense to me," the Man from Tulsa said.

"I'll buy that," the Man from New York said. "What about time?"

"Immediately," Tangent said. "I've stalled as long as I can with the Togo ploy. It's all smoke, but it served to scare off the competition. Now we've got to move. I don't want the French getting in before us."

The two men stared at each other a long time.

"Want me to leave the room?" Tangent asked.

"Don't be anal," the Man from New York said. "We're trying the permutations and combinations."

"There's a pisspot full of oil out there," the Man from Tulsa said. "You know that, don't you, Pete?"

"Sure."

There was silence again while Tangent poured a little more brandy into their balloons.

"How much can you get from Anokye?" the Man from New York finally asked.

"Forty-nine percent tops," Tangent said. "No one can get more. I'll stake my life on it. I'll ask for sixty, of course. And a twenty-year lease."

"And his lagniappe?" the Man from Tulsa asked.

Tangent stared at him, amazed that such a man should know such a word. Even if he pronounced it "lanny-yappy."

"Not a cent," he said. "I swear to that."

"Seems to me you're swearing to a lot tonight, Peter," the Man from New York said. Eyes cold. "And 'staking your life' on a lot. I'm just repeating what you've said."

"That's right," Tangent agreed. "I'm going all the way on this. My cock."

145

Again they were silent, but moving about, tasting cold coffee, warm brandy, crossing and recrossing their legs. Tangent said nothing.

"Your bottom line looks real good to us," the Man from Tulsa said finally.

"Glad to hear it," Tangent said.

Then the two men looked at each other. If a signal passed, Tangent didn't see it.

"Sheeyut," the Man from Tulsa said. "We got no choice, do we?"

"Keep the cost down," the Man from New York said. "We'll go a mil, but we'll scream. Over, and you're out. Half a mil will make us real happy."

"Got it," Tangent said, rising. "And now, gentlemen, I've lined up some entertainment for this evening that I don't think will disappoint you."

"Lead me to it," the Man from Tulsa said.

"I'll just call the ladies and see if they're ready," Tangent said. "Sorry I can't join you, but I want to get moving on this Asante thing. Cables, and so forth."

They didn't seen disappointed at his inability to spend the evening with them. Relieved, rather. Tangent felt it and turned back to address the Man from Tulsa.

"By the way," he said, "the lady you'll meet tonight really is a Lady."

"What?"

"She's a Lady. Peerage. Lady Sybil."

"Wow," the Man from Tulsa said.

"Six months ago she had a dose of the clap," Tangent said cruelly. "But I think she's okay now."

Two hours later Tangent was seated at a small banquette, with Tony Malcolm, in the grill at Brindleys. It was a Saturday night; the bar was crowded. The decibel

146

count was satisfactorily high. They could lean toward each other and talk briskly.

"You're taking an awful risk, Peter," Malcolm said. "I mean *you*, personally."

"I know," Tangent agreed. "They as much as told me. If it goes sour, I'm out."

"Nice boys." Malcolm said.

"They do their job. I don't like them any more than they like me. But who says you have to like the people you work with?"

"Not me," Tony Malcolm said.

"They're such cold cruds," Tangent said, looking down at his glass, using the wet bottom to make interlocking circles on the wooden tabletop. "They make it all seem tawdry."

"What you're doing in Asante?"

"Yes," Tangent said. "No," Tangent said. "I'm not making much sense, am I?"

"No, you're not."

"How's this: When I'm in London, especially when I'm here at Brindleys, trading grins with all these slick movers and shakers, what I'm doing in Asante seems tawdry. Cut-and-dried. Cheap. But when I'm in Asante, I come alive. It's exciting, and worth the candle. It moves me."

"Moves you?" Malcolm said. "Oh boy."

"Yes, moves me," Tangent insisted. "You haven't met Captain Obiri Anokye."

"He moves you?"

"Yes, goddammit, he does. He believes in himself. Utterly. Do you or I? He's a complete man: No doubts. No doubts at all. Oh hell, I suppose that occasionally at three in the morning he wonders. But the impression he gives is of absolute purpose. That he can't miss."

"Can't miss what?"

"Taking Asante. And then on. And on. And on."

"Like what?"

"All of Africa."

"Peter, you're joking?"

"I swear I'm not. This is my take on the man. He sweats power. Tony, you know I'm very perceptive about people, and I tell you Anokye wants all of Africa, and if anyone can do it, he can. He's got balls. Did you get rid of Bob Curtin?"

"Goes home on Monday."

"Good. Replace him yet?"

"No."

"Don't until all this is over. Or Virginia will get blamed for it."

"We'll get blamed anyway," Malcolm said mournfully. "We always do."

"That's true," Tangent laughed. "Ready for another?"

When Malcolm nodded, Tangent looked around to signal the waiter. He pointed toward their empty glasses. A man at the bar caught his eye, smirked, winked lewdly.

"Julien Ricard's at the bar," Tangent said. "Drunk as a skunk."

"Oh?" Malcolm said. "This Little Captain of yours—how old is he?"

"Twenty-six."

"Twenty-six!"

"So?" Tangent said. "Napoleon was a general at twenty-four. Michelangelo finished the *David* at twenty-nine. Mozart—"

"All right, Peter, all *right*. You've made your point."

"And Keats—"

"Gotcha!" Malcolm said. He burst out laughing

"Keats was fucking *dead* at twenty-six."

"Well, you know what I mean," Tangent said. "Anokye is alive and well and ambitious at twenty-six."

"A young Alexander," Malcolm murmured, and they were silent while their new drinks were served.

"How's he going to do it?" Malcolm asked.

"Anokye and Africa? I haven't the slightest at this stage. I doubt if he knows. But it's on his mind; I know it is. Tony, it makes sense. The whole continent is balkanized. Every time you pick up the *Times*, there's a new nation. And most of them smaller and poorer than Jersey City. They've got no political or economic clout. But the potential! Oil. Minerals. And a consumer market that hasn't even been tapped. Don't think the French don't know it. They want—"

"And speaking of the French," Malcolm said, rising. "Hello, Julien. Join us?"

"Thank-oo, no," Ricard said. "Siddown, siddown. Dropped by to see what mischief you two were plotting."

He stood before them, swaying slightly, his features trying for a sardonic smile. He settled for a vacuous grin.

"No mischief," Tangent said. "Just exchanging dirty jokes."

"I know a dirty joke," Ricard said, trying to drain a few drops from an empty glass.

"Tell us," Malcolm said.

"There's this Frenchman and this American and this Jew," Ricard mumbled.

"I like it already," Tangent said.

"How does it end?" Malcolm said.

Ricard stared at them. Slowly his face congealed into a scowl.

"Smartass," he said. "Isn't that what you'd say, Tangent?"

"No," Tangent said. "I really don't believe I'd say that."

"How does it end?" Ricard muttered. "You'll find out. And soon."

He turned abruptly, walked stiffly back to the bar, banged his glass down, shouted something. Men turned slowly to look at him with distaste.

"Nasty bastard when he's drunk," Tangent said.

"Isn't he?" Tony Malcolm said. "The French should stick to wine. By the way, Peter, there's another Frenchman I wanted to speak to you about. A man named St. Clair. In Togo. Do you know him?"

"St. Clair? René St. Clair? A newspaperman in Lomé? Writes a political column?"

"That's the man."

"Sure. I know him."

"He's dead. Died a few days ago."

"I'm sorry to hear that," Tangent said. "He did some favors for me. Years ago. Was it in the London papers?"

"Of course not. Our resident in Lomé sent me a bullet. St. Clair is supposed to have died in a car accident, but our resident doesn't think it was kosher."

"That's odd," Tangent said.

"Isn't it? St. Clair did some favors for us, too. I'm understandably concerned."

"Of course."

"Peter," Tony Malcolm said, "you *are* telling me everything you're doing down there, aren't you?"

"Tony, have I ever held out on you?"

"Not tonight—I hope."

16

SAM LEIBERMAN, CLEAN, sober, well-dressed, rented a Datsun in Mokodi and, with his Ivory Coast girl giggling beside him—her lap filled with presents for her relatives—drove at a sedate speed along the coastal road to Accra. At the border, he offered their passports, properly validated, each containing within its pages a "sincere dash," not too large, not too small. They were waved through with grave courtesy.

They spent the night at Sekondi-Takoradi, drank two bottles of Spanish white, ate four crayfish swimming in a sauce of cream, paprika, tiny shrimp, and little chunks of hot pork sausage. Then they made love on the floor of their hotel room. The Ivory Coast girl sat astride Sam Leiberman, squeezed his balls, and he had never been happier.

They were on the road again early the next morning (another bottle of chilled Spanish white on the seat between them), and were into Abidjan by 1400. Leiberman turned north and delivered his girl to her squealing family at Sikensi. Gifts were bestowed, the Spanish wine was finished along with a bottle of Algerian red, and by 1700 Leiberman, alone now, was eating a peppery fish stew at a hotel restaurant in Ndouci. He washed it down with two jugs of millet beer and couldn't stop belching.

He drove west from there, toward Agboville, and turned off the improved road onto a one-lane earth track. It led back into the rain forest and ended at wrought-iron gates suspended from two painted concrete pillars. One bore a brass plaque: "R. Firenza. Antiquities." Leiberman nudged the unlocked gate with the Datsun's front bumper, and the wings swung wide. He drove slowly onto a graveled driveway before a pillared mansion that resembled an antebellum Mississippi plantation home. Complete with verdant lawn and mossed trees.

"Frankly, my dear," Leiberman quoted aloud, "I don't give a damn."

He pulled the brass plunger, and the small black who answered the door let him in without question. Leiberman followed the ancient houseman into the shaded entrance hall, then moved closer and goosed him. The old man leaped, turned, grinned.

"Oh *you*!" he said in English.

"Me again," Leiberman said. "Stay loose, Saki."

Doctor Ramon Firenza was, as usual, in his paneled study, behind his splendid old American rolltop desk which had, somehow, found its way to this corner of Africa. And, as usual, the Doctor was examining a scarab with the aid of an enormous magnifying glass with a carved ivory handle.

"Ah," the Doctor said, looking up but not rising. "Peck's Bad Boy."

"Pecker's bad boy," Leiberman said. "Ask me to sit down and offer me a drink."

"Won't you sit down?" Firenza said. "And would you care for a glass of champagne?"

"Yes and yes," Leiberman said.

He flopped into a leather club chair and said nothing until the houseman brought a bottle of chilled Piper, two glasses, and served. Leiberman took a deep swallow, smacked his lips noisily, wiped his mouth on the back of his meaty hand, looked around at the museum. All small antiquities, displayed and mounted with loving care. Bone fragments, ivory chips, stone carvings, incised jewels, hammered gold, jade pendants, religious relics, raw diamonds.

"Worth a king's ransom," Leiberman said. "Except kings aren't worth much these days."

"True," Firenza chuckled. "They are not. And how may I serve you? Cleopatra's personal dildo? A shinbone from St. Peter? A Cro-Magnon horse? Perhaps Napoleon's penis, removed after his death on St. Helena. The provenance is impeccable. It's mummified now, of course."

"I've got one in the same condition," Leiberman said. "Actually, I'm looking for something a little more modern. How are you fixed for AR-15s? Or Kalashnikovs? Or Uzis?"

Doctor Firenza sighed. He was a tiny man, squirming in a shiny black alpaca suit. Leiberman didn't know what he was—Spanish, Portuguese, Berber, Egyptian, Lebanese; it was impossible to tell. He spoke dozens of languages, all with the accent of another. Once, as a joke, Leiberman had memorized a few phrases in Choctaw and tried them on the Doctor. He was answered immediately in that language, although later Firenza confessed he spoke Choctaw with a Cherokee accent.

"What is it, exactly, you desire?" he asked. Speaking French now, in a light, frilly voice.

Leiberman pulled his shirt from the front of his pants, unzipped a money belt, took out a folded square of onionskin paper. He smoothed it out before he tossed it onto Firenza's desktop.

"My shopping list," the mercenary said.

The Doctor used his magnifying glass to read the numbers and types of weapons.

"You intend to invade Egypt?" he asked finally.

"Something like that," Leiberman said. "Well?"

"Most of it, but not all of it," Firenza said. "Where I cannot provide, suitable substitutions can be made."

"Let me be the judge of that," Leiberman said. "What about the mortars?"

"Most difficult."

"I didn't ask that. Can you get them?"

"I'll need time."

"How much time?"

"Three months."

"Forget. Give me my list. I'll try Darami."

"How soon then?"

"A month."

"Oi vay," Doctor Ramon Firenza said. "A month? Well, of course, on special orders, the price goes up. Naturally."

"Naturally," Leiberman said. "I need an estimate to take to my people. How much? In American dollars?"

"In the neighborhood of a million," Firenza said.

"That's a rich neighborhood for a poor nebbish like me," Leiberman said. "Try again. Try a neighborhood of half a mil America. A real ghetto."

"Absurd," Firenza said. "But surely we can work something out. We each give a little, we each take a little. It's the story of civilization. Whatever we agree upon, I would prefer Swiss francs."

"It can be arranged," Leiberman said. "Delivery?"

"Oh no," Firenza said. "No no no. FOB Sassandra is the best I can do. After that, it's your problem."

"Keep the list," Leiberman said. "If it's go, I'll send a signal. See how I trust you, Doctor?"

Firenza spread his hands wide. He leaned toward Leiberman, sincere.

"Why should we not trust each other?" he asked.

154

Earnestness in his voice. "Have we not worked together pleasantly and profitably in the past? Your five percent, of course. I accept that. I welcome it. You labor hard, you risk your life, you are entitled. But trust between us is everything. If we have no trust, then what have we? We deliver our lives to each other. Because we have faith in each other's integrity."

"You're fucking-ay right," Sam Leiberman said.

He drained his champagne and was about to rise when a French door leading to a patio opened suddenly. A youth stood posed. Soft, slender, tawny, wearing a tiny bright pink bikini brief.

"My ward," Doctor Ramon Firenza said hastily.

"Another one?" Leiberman said. "What a kind, generous man you are."

"Am I interrupting, Uncle?" the youth caroled. In Boulé.

"Not at all, Michael," Firenza said. "Come in, come in. Our business is concluded. This gentleman was just leaving."

The long-haired youth entered, came close to Firenza's side, pressed his nylon-sheathed load against the doctor's arm, slid a squid hand across the doctor's shoulder, caressed his neck.

Firenza blinked at Leiberman.

"It is not the fact that he is a boy," he said, in French. "It is the youth."

"I understand," Leiberman said gravely.

He drove away from the shaded mansion, down the dirt track, then stopped the Datsun about 100 meters before it joined the improved road. He got out of the car, raised the hood. Then he took three signet rings from the canvas musette bag on the rear seat. He put the rings on the index, middle, and third fingers of his right hand. One of the

155

rings was steel, the other two a cheap pot metal. They were all heavy studs.

He waited patiently, sure, leaning against the warm front fender. It was almost 20 minutes before the trim Fiat sportscar came tearing down the earth track from the home of Doctor Ramon Firenza. Michael, the ward, was driving. He was wearing a yellow short-sleeved sports shirt with a little alligator embroidered on the breast, and white linen slacks. He slowed to a halt behind the parked Datsun. Leiberman walked toward him slowly, smiling.

"Something is not working," he said, bending at the window at the driver's side. "I have stalled and cannot get started. Do you know machinery?"

"No, I do not," Michael said crossly. "I must get on. I will push you off the road. Then I will send you a mechanic from Ndouci."

"Perhaps if you took a look. . . ?"

"I tell you I know nothing of machinery."

Leiberman sighed, jerked open the Fiat's door suddenly, grabbed a handful of the long hair, and dragged the shocked youth out onto the road. He spun him around, set him up, and crashed his armored fist twice, rapidly, into the boy's face. The nose broke on the first blow; blood sprayed. The second smash splintered the front teeth. The slender youth fell curling into the dust.

He wasn't carrying it, but Leiberman found it in the glove compartment of the Fiat: a sealed envelope addressed to M. Anatole Garde, Royal Palace, Mokodi, Asante. It was marked "Personal." Leiberman didn't even bother opening it; just tore it into small bits and tucked the pieces of paper into Michael's hip pocket.

Then he pulled the boy to his feet, propped him against the side of the car, slapped his face lightly. Michael didn't come around. Leiberman left him propped there, got a

156

water bottle from his Datsun, poured some on the youth's head, some onto his face, some into his mouth. The blood thinned, running down the yellow sports shirt, the white linen slacks.

"Better?" Leiberman asked solicitously.

Michael nodded groggily.

"I think you better go back to Doctor Firenza," Leiberman said. "I think you better tell him what happened. Tell him his letter is in your hip pocket. Got that?"

The youth looked at him dazedly.

"Understand what I just said?" Leiberman asked.

Michael blinked his eyes.

"Good. Tell the Doctor I'll be in touch, and that trust between us is everything." Leiberman paused to inspect the boy's shattered face. "Mike," he said, "your career as a ward is ended. Sorry about that."

17

IN FRANCE, IN PARIS, on the Avenue Montaigne, stands a restaurant that has had, during its distinguished history, one name, L'escargot d'Or, and a dozen façades—all of which have carefully preserved the scars of three musket balls fired into the original plaster during the French Revolution.

The two-star restaurant serves the public only on the ground floor. But there is a secluded dining room on the second floor available for private parties, conferences, discreet meetings of industrialists, labor leaders, church dignitaries, bankers, diplomats, etc. It is said that this dining room was once connected, via a secret sliding panel, to a bedchamber. But there is no evidence of that today.

On the third Wednesday of each month, the second floor of L'escargot d'Or was reserved for a banquet of Le Club des Gourmets. This prestigious association of food and wine fanciers never numbered more than 24. New members were elected only upon the death (frequent) or resignation (rare) of an existing member. Dues were nominal, but each member, in turn, was required to plan and pay for the monthly banquet at L'escargot d'Or for the entire Club.

A member's reputation as a gourmet depended upon the creativity of the dinner he provided, in consultation with the restaurant's master chef and executive staff. It was said that, on occasion, Club members had gone into debt to finance a memorable banquet. But it was also known that certain members had greatly advanced their careers by the originality and daring of the feasts they had furnished. Members of Le Club des Gourmets came mostly from the Bourse, Quai d'Orsay, Elysée Palace, and from multinational corporations and international cartels. There were also a few Parisian merchants, of newspaper publishing, auto making, asparagus canning.

The dining chamber itself was long and narrow, barely wide enough to accommodate table and chairs, and to allow room for serving. It was mostly dark mahogany and stained glass, both patinaed with the cigar smoke of generations. There were four rather scruffy chamois and mountain-goat heads mounted on the walls, and a series of faded chromolithographs showing the Eiffel Tower under construction. Otherwise, decoration was minimal. The business was eating.

On this particular Wednesday evening, the menu was the responsibility of Julien Ricard. It included pheasant pâté en croute, ris de veau à la financière en vol-au-vent, langoustes à la Parisienne, and riz à l'impératrice. But the only unusual dish was the soupe aux truffes Elysée. The original recipe was the creation of master chef Paul Bocuse for a luncheon at the Elysée Palace during which he was awarded the Legion of Honor by the President of France. The soup, baked with a pastry topping, had been craftily selected by Julien Ricard in homage to the Man from the Palace, one of Monsieur le President's closest advisers, and himself President of Le Club des Gourmets. Wines served included a '47 Château Margaux, Pouilly Fuissé, Krug '28. Coffee, Kirsch, Grand Marnier, and Remy Martin were offered from a sideboard after the cheese and sauterne. Cigars were available.

Members congratulated Ricard on his dinner, to his

face. But amongst themselves, during private after-dinner conversations, most agreed that except for that truffle soup, it had been a pedestrian affair. Palatable, but undistinguished.

Unfortunately, Julien Ricard worked out of the same Quai d'Orsay office that employed Anatole Garde, in Asante. And the upper floor of L'escargot d'Or had been completely and cleverly equipped with listening devices and recording apparatus. So that on the following day, Ricard was able to hear tapes of the private comments of his fellow Club members. He was not amused.

The room had emptied out by midnight. The table had been cleared, lights dimmed. Julien Ricard remained. And two other men. Both were portly, wearing heavy, dark suits with high vests draped with golden chains. One, the Man from the Bourse, wore the ribbon of the Legion of Honor in his lapel. The other, the Man from the Palace, the President of the Club, had been a hero of the Resistance and bore the scars: a black patch over one eye, a steel hook for a hand. Thin white hair did not conceal a small metal plate set into his skull.

They dawdled over a final cognac while Ricard filled them in on what was happening in Asante. He spoke rapidly, vehemently, with the truculence they expected. He told them it was evident, from Garde's reports and other intelligence, that Asante was on the verge of a coup d'etat.

Ricard was a Cassius, dark, saturnine, with the body of a fencer. Nose and chin were long, skin olive, lips pale and compressed. No one doubted his intelligence or his patriotism; it was his judgment that was questioned in some quarters. He made his anti-Americanism superfluously evident, and it was known that on his frequent trips to England, he gambled heavily at a private London club.

160

He seemed to win more often than he lost. But still
. . . was it wise for a man in his position?

Ricard could not sit still, but paced about the darkened
dining room, touching his birthmark as he related the most
recent developments in Asante. The other two men, hands
and steel claw folded comfortably over their bellies, listened in silence. They followed him with their eyes as he
stalked about.

"As I see it," he said, "we have three alternatives.
One: We can instruct Garde to do everything in his power
to smash this coup and provide him the means for doing it.
Two: We can take certain steps to remove Captain Anokye
from the scene. It would be arranged. Three: We can offer
assistance to this Anokye. In effect, take over the coup
ourselves. Well?"

"Or four," the Man from Bourse rumbled, "we can do
absolutely nothing."

"Nothing?" Ricard said angrily. "And let the Americans take over Asante?"

"Julien, Julien," the Man from the Palace said mildly.
"You must not let your dislike of the Americans affect
your good sense. Surely things are not as bad as you
suggest. We agreed to let Starrett Petroleum develop
Asante's oil resources. We had Prempeh's assurance they
would eventually be expropriated. Let the Americans
spend their dollars."

"And what if this Little Captain takes over with the aid
of the Americans?" Ricard asked. "What guarantee do
we have that he will honor Prempeh's assurance?"

"There is that, of course," the Man from the Bourse
said. "Have representations been made to this man, this
Anokye?"

"Nothing definite."

"Why not?"

161

"Because at this point we have no definite proof of his intentions. We have a hook into him: the chief teller of the bank, a man Anokye consults on military matters. So far, according to Garde, no mention has been made of a coup being planned. Still, the evidence is overwhelming: the economic condition of Asante, the starvation and unrest in outlying districts, the terrorism of Marxist guerrillas, Anokye's personal popularity, Abraham's leadership of the veterans' organization, Anokye's sudden friendship with Peter Tangent, who is Starrett's man in Asante. It all adds up to a military coup. We ignore all these danger signals at our peril."

"I think you exaggerate," the Man from the Bourse said. "As far as I can see, nothing has yet occurred to justify alarm."

"Still . . ." the Man from the Palace said.

"Prempeh is a dolt, a pig, a thief," the Man from the Bourse said.

"Agreed," the Man from the Palace said. "But rather the devil you know . . ."

"The loss might be considerable," the Man from the Bourse said. "But I have no wish to create a dangerous precedent. I need hardly tell you we have other interests in Africa, of more importance."

"And of more value," the Man from the Palace said.

"Gentlemen," Ricard said, the birthmark livid, "if your purpose is to confuse me, you are succeeding admirably."

Both men stared at him, without mirth.

"In situations like this," the Man from the Bourse said slowly, "my instinct is to preserve the status quo."

"I think I agree," the Man from the Palace said slowly.

"Therefore?" Ricard asked impatiently. "Shall we remove Anokye?"

"Oh, I wouldn't do that," the Man from the Bourse said. "Until it becomes absolutely necessary."

"Your first alternative," the Man from the Palace said. "Instruct Garde to do everything in his power to smash this coup. He's a clever chap; he'll know what to do. My wife's cousin, you know."

"I hadn't known that," the Man from the Bourse said. But he had. "I concur with your decision."

"Thank you, gentlemen," Ricard said gratefully. "Shall we finish the bottle?"

They begged off, and all departed and went their separate ways. Ricard drove first to his office at the Quai and dictated a long letter of instruction to Anatole Garde that would be included in the morning pouch. Then he nodded to his night staff and drove home alone to his apartment in the 16th Arrondissement, arriving at approximately 0200.

His Vietnamese wife roused sleepily.

"Julien?" she mumbled. "Is that you?"

"No," he said. "It is Mickey Mouse."

"That's nice," she giggled. "Come to bed, Mickey."

"Soon," he said. "In a moment, dear."

He waited for her soft snore before he went into his study and turned on the light. He composed a short, terse message revealing the decision regarding Asante that had been reached that evening in the private dining room of L'escargot d'Or. Then he transposed the message into code.

He used a book code, based on the number of page, paragraph, and word of a certain edition of "The Collected Works of Edgar Allan Poe." Ricard was charmed

163

to find that he could select most of the words he required from "The Purloined Letter." He then tore up his original draft and flushed it down the toilet. The coded message he handled carefully, by the edges. He folded it, slid it into a plain white envelope, sealed it, stamped the envelope, addressed it to a box number in Liverpool, England.

Tony Malcolm should have it in a few days. He also admired Poe.

18

Minister of Finance Willi Abraham was not present at the palace conference. Tangent thought this curious, possibly significant. During a brief pause in King Prempeh's denunciation of Starrett's unwillingness to reach a decision, Tangent said:

"Your Majesty, with all due respect, my people are not unwilling to come to a decision, they are unable to. I am sure that if Finance Minister Willi Abraham was present, he would say—"

"I am not interested in anything Willi Abraham might say about this matter," Prempeh shouted. "You understand that? Do you?"

"Completely, Your Majesty," Tangent said humbly.

The others at the table—Prime Minister Osei Ware, General Opoku Tutu, Anatole Garde—all looked at Tangent coldly, trying to conceal the glee they felt at his humiliation. Their obvious enmity confirmed what Tony Malcolm had told him before he left London: Garde had been ordered to forestall the coup.

"Surely, Your Majesty," Tangent said, "under the circumstances, an extension of the current lease for three months would cause no hardship or loss of revenue to the Asante treasury."

"Not three months' extension," the Prime Minister thundered. "Not one month, not one week, not one day! Not even one hour's extension. The lease expires when our signed agreement says it expires."

"You take us for fools?" General Tutu screamed. "Poor little ignorant black boys? Your pickaninnies who know no better?"

"General, I assure you—"

"You assure me of nothing!" Here Tutu slammed a meaty hand down on the mahogany table. "I do not like you, Tangent. I hope I make that obvious. More important, I do not trust you."

"We don't need you," the Prime Minister continued the assault. "We do not need Starrett Petroleum, Incorporated. We have other friends, many friends. As wealthy as you."

"Wealthier," King Prempeh IV murmured. He was fondling his medals again. The gold Patek Philippe watch, Tangent's gift, was not on his wrist.

"But we are gentlemen," Osei Ware said. "We will observe every last detail of our signed agreement. No one will be able to say we are uncultured. But as for an extension—no, no, and no! If we have received no word from you by the expiration date, we will consider the lease null and void."

"And should that happen," King Prempeh said ominously, "should that happen, I suggest you make preparations to leave Asante within twenty-four hours. You personally, your staff, your ship, your helicopter, your equipment—everything. If you have no interest in Asante's welfare, then I have no interest in yours. If you remain on our soil more than twenty-four hours after the lease has expired, I cannot be responsible for your personal safety."

"Your Majesty! I wish—"

"No more. This audience is at an end."

Tangent was pleased to find he was not trembling. And during the taxi ride back to the Mokodi Hilton, he was able to chat quite casually with the driver about the mealy taste of frozen shrimp and the difficulty of finding properly ripened mangoes. Still, it was not easy to forget the hooded stare of Prime Minister Osei Ware, the lupine grin of General Opoku Tutu, the pity of triumph in the blue eyes of Anatole Garde.

Worst of all was the King's delight in his exhibit of naked power. Beheading was the punishment of those Asantis convicted of capital crimes. Tangent could imagine the vengeance Prempeh wreaked upon his political enemies. It would not be as quick as decapitation.

He went at once to the office of Mai Fante, the Asanti legal counsel of Starrett Petroleum. Fante was on the phone, and waved Tangent to a deskside chair. It was obvious, from Fante's conversation, what the matter concerned. An Asanti fisherman claimed his boat had been scraped by the *Starrett Explorer* while it was changing position. His attorney had called Mai Fante, announcing that if damages of thirty-four dollars and fifty-two cents were not paid immediately, legal action would, of necessity, be initiated in Asante courts.

Mai Fante, urbane, confident, soft-spoken, replied by suggesting a personal meeting between himself and his caller to arrive at an equitable solution of this "tragic problem." It was not so much what the lawyer said that bemused Tangent as the language. Speaking Akan, Fante inquired after his caller's health and that of his family. Did he find the weather uncomfortably warm? And how was he enduring the grievous demands of the legal profession? Yes, surely, it was a difficult and yet a rewarding career. Justice was a fine ideal to which a man might devote a satisfactory life. The truth was worth fighting for, and who could deny that the law demanded much but offered more.

It went on and on, and Tangent listened with fascination as the Akan poetry spread its magic. It was truly a language designed for speaking: mellifluous, lilting, with delicate shades of meaning and emphasis indicated by change of voice pitch rather than breath force. The conversation ended by Mai Fante inviting the plaintiff's attorney to have lunch with him at the Zabarian.

"Beautiful," Tangent breathed, after Fante had hung up. "Do you know the man?"

"Never met him in my life," the lawyer grinned. "But before you came in, we discovered that his oldest uncle's cousin is married to my mother's aunt's youngest child. So you see, we are related! I think we shall come to a satisfactory agreement."

"Is everyone in Asante related to everyone else?" Tangent asked.

"Everyone in Africa," Fante said soberly.

He was a handsome, smooth-faced man, with features that seemed experienced in smiling. It was difficult to judge his age; he moved youthfully, step and gestures were full of bounce. But hair was gray, eyes old. He dressed with restraint, but the elegance was in the man himself, casual and sure.

"How may I be of service, Mr. Tangent?" he asked, in French.

"I wish to ask a favor of you," Tangent said, speaking Akan. "This is a personal matter and does not concern Starrett. If you cannot grant my request, I will understand completely, and it will in no way affect your employment or our friendship."

"Ah," Mai Fante said.

"I wish to meet with Captain Obiri Anokye," Tangent went on. "At a place and time of his choosing. As I say, this has nothing to do with Starrett. But for reasons I

168

believe sufficient, I do not think it would be wise for me to call Captain Anokye at the Mokodi barracks.''

''No,'' Fante said immediately. ''That would not be wise.''

He began to swing back and forth in his swivel chair, looking at the ceiling. Tangent waited patiently. Africa had a rhythm of its own. It was not Europe's rhythm, and even less America's. That did not make it better or worse; it was simply different.

''Yes,'' Mai Fante said suddenly. ''I shall arrange it and let you know the details as soon as I learn them.''

''My gratitude is poor reward,'' Tangent said.

''The pleasure is in serving,'' Fante replied gravely.

Tangent rose to go.

''Mai,'' he said, ''you're due for two weeks' vacation, are you not?'' Now he spoke French.

''Yes,'' Fante nodded. ''Beginning next month.''

''Why don't you take four weeks?'' Tangent said. ''Take a nice, long trip. Perhaps to London. We can devise some reason for it. The company will pay. Take your wife and children. Get out of the country for a while. Give you a whole new perspective on things.''

The two men stared at each other. Then Mai Fante resumed his gentle swinging back and forth in his swivel chair. But his eyes never left Tangent's.

''I thank you for your kind and generous offer, Mr. Tangent,'' he said. ''You are a true friend.''

Tangent made a gesture.

''But I believe I will remain in Asante,'' Fante said. ''It is my home.''

Tangent spent the next day drawing up a contingency plan, in case rapid evacuation of Starrett personnel became necessary. They would be flown by the Sikorsky copter to the *Starrett Explorer*, which would then haul ass for international waters. In case of attempted interception by Asante gunboats—well, that particular crisis would have to be handled when and if it arose. Tangent knew the *Explorer* carried only a small arsenal of handguns, rifles, and shotguns. But in its holds was an enormous store of dynamite, gelignite, nitroglycerine, and other explosives. In his imagination, Tangent saw the Starrett copter taking off from the ship's helipad to drop a huge bundle of short-fused explosives on an attacking launch crewed by Prempeh, Ware, Tutu, and Anatole Garde. It was a succulent fantasy.

Late in the afternoon he received his precise instructions, relayed through Mai Fante. He was to drive a dark-colored rental car to the Golden Calf, attempting to arrive at precisely midnight. Once inside, he would be accosted by a small black girl wearing a scarlet evening gown. Her name was Sbeth. Tangent was to accompany her upstairs, playing the part of a client. She would conduct him to a meeting with the Little Captain.

It went smoothly and without incident. Tangent entered the Golden Calf, barely had time to look about curiously, to note the surprisingly attractive interior, become conscious of the decorous, almost sedate atmosphere, when a small black girl wearing a scarlet evening gown was at his elbow. She smiled up at him, murmuring a crazy stream of copybook English as though she had memorized the phrases but had no idea of their meaning: "Hello, sir. How are you, sir? My name is Sbeth. I am well, thank you. Is it not a delightful evening? Shall we go upstairs, sir? Drink and food are also available at popular prices. Please to follow me, sir."

Tangent followed her up the wide, gracefully curved

170

staircase. The second floor was active—clients arriving and departing, maids scurrying about with towels, waitresses hustling loaded trays—but Tangent's guide continued up to the third floor, and brought him to a closed door.

He offered her a dash, but she shook her head, smiled, slipped away.

The woman who answered his knock was pale-haired, pale-skinned. A curious face of cameo features with a tough, distrustful cast. Strong hands and long, bare feet. The body appeared slender, the naked arms were sinuous. She wore a bottlegreen cheongsam. The blond hair was plaited into two thick braids, small gold rings in her pierced ears. Tangent guessed her age at 32-35, in that range.

"Come in, Mr. Tangent," she said, not smiling. Her voice was unexpectedly resonant, deep. "I am Yvonne Mayer."

He stepped inside and while she closed and locked the door behind him, he looked about slowly. He knew who she was, and guessed this to be her personal apartment. He was about to compliment her on the comfortable charm of her sitting room when three men entered from an inner chamber. Captain Obiri Anokye led the file, followed by Willi Abraham, and a man introduced as Professor Jean-Louis Duclos.

The four men drew up chairs about a small, round ormolu table. Yvonne Mayer sat at a desk, slightly withdrawn.

"Mr. Tangent," Captain Anokye said. "I have taken the liberty of asking these friends to be present during our discussion. They share my plans and my hopes. I vouch for all of them, completely."

171

Tangent nodded. He turned first to Willi Abraham. His challenge was almost brutal.

"Minister," he demanded, "are you in disfavor at the palace?"

"Yes," Abraham said promptly. "And I am fortunate it is no worse than 'disfavor.' I am protected by my association with the Asante Brothers of Independence; the King doesn't wish to antagonize the veterans. That is Anatole Garde's advice. Also, I am allowed to continue my work, to occupy my office. There are many things about the finances of Asante that only I know."

Then Tangent turned to Anokye.

"Captain, may I speak to you openly and honestly?"

"That is always best in the affairs of men," Anokye said.

Tangent looked at him sharply. Was the Little Captain putting him on? Anokye's expression seemed grave and intent. As did that of the others in the room.

"Are you planning a coup against the present regime in Asante?"

"I am."

"Do you intend to take over the government yourself?"

"I do. With the aid of those you see here, and others."

"What support do you have?"

"Fourth Brigade, without question. Certain officers and units of the Third. Amongst auxiliary companies—artillery, tanks, supply, and so forth—the most I can count on is neutrality, until they see how things are going. The same is true of naval and air personnel. But they are not numerous enough to be important. I also have the Asante Brothers of Independence. Trained men, but unarmed."

"What about the Marxist guerrillas?" Tangent asked.

"They will join us," Anokye said. "I have the Nyam's word. If we move within a month."

172

Tangent opened his mouth to speak, then closed it suddenly.

"Would you care for a glass of water?" Willi Abraham asked unexpectedly.

"Yes, thank you," Tangent said gratefully.

"Perhaps a glass of cold white wine?" Yvonne Mayer said, rising.

"Please don't go to any trouble."

"No trouble. I have it here."

She brought deep glasses and poured wine around to all. They lifted glasses in an unspoken toast, sipped, sipped again.

"You have a plan?" Tangent asked. "A military plan? Tactics, and so forth?"

"Only the basics," Anokye said. "That it must take place while the Fourth is in Mokodi, and the Third is in the field."

"You feel Mokodi is the key to Asante?" Tangent asked.

"Of course," Anokye said. "And the palace is the key to Mokodi."

"Difficult," Willi Abraham said.

"Why is that?"

"The palace guard," Abraham said. "A company of men, heavily armed. About two hundred, I think. Bibi?"

"Less than that," Anokye said. "Perhaps a hundred and fifty at full strength. But they are—as you would say, Mr. Tangent—very tough babies."

"I wouldn't say it," Tangent said, "but I know what you mean. Can they be bribed?"

"No," Anokye said. "They are all Muslims and will die happily for their faith. Particularly if they die while killing infidels. Then they will achieve paradise. Others in the army may be bribed, but not the palace guard."

"Then how do you intend to take the palace?" Tangent asked.

"I don't know," Anokye said frankly. "It would be foolish to plan until I know what weapons are available."

"Surely you could destroy the palace with mortars," Tangent suggested.

"Would you like your White House destroyed?" Professor Duclos said angrily.

"What Jean-Louis means," Willi Abraham said smoothly, "is that the palace is a symbol. The seat of government. Of law and authority. The heart of Asante. We would not care to see it reduced to a heap of rubble."

Tangent was silent, clinking his wineglass gently against his teeth. Finally he sighed, drew a deep breath.

"Let me tell you what my people want," he said. "Then you tell me what you want. Perhaps we can find a middle ground satisfactory to us both."

"No voice in our government," the Martinicain professor said determinedly. His fawny skin was flushed.

Anokye turned his head slowly. His gaze seemed to concentrate. Duclos lowered his head.

"We will listen to Mr. Tangent," the Little Captain said, mildly enough. "Then, as he has suggested, we will state our desires."

"We'll advance half a million American dollars," Tangent said, "for the purchase of arms, the exact number and types of weapons to be determined in consultation between Captain Anokye and our representative. The actual purchase will be done directly by us; no sums will be released to you. The weapons will be delivered where and when you want them. In return, my people want a twenty-year lease of the Zabarian oil fields with forty percent of the profits to Asante, and sixty percent to us. The moneys

174

we advance to accomplish the coup will be subtracted from our first year's payment. And for Professor Duclos' benefit, we have absolutely no desire to interfere in any way in the government or interior affairs of the new Asante. All we want is oil. That does it, I think.''

"Willi," Captain Anokye said.

"Let us take it point by point," the Minister of Finance said. "I see no objection in funds for the weapons being paid directly by your people. But we will require an additional two hundred thousand American dollars for other purposes. For propaganda, for instance; for bribery of staff members of the Asante *New Times* and the radio station. And gifts to certain army officers in return for either their loyalty or their neutrality. But most important, to provide food, medicine, and the basic necessities of life for our supporters in cities, towns, and outlying villages, to prove to them that we have the resources to answer their needs. When you are starving, Mr. Tangent, a tough chicken and an unripened melon mean more than all the political promises in the world. As for the Zabarian oil fields, we propose a five-year lease, with sixty percent of the profits to Asante, forty to you. I have finished.''

"Now," Captain Anokye said, smiling faintly, "shall we get started?''

The bargaining continued for almost an hour. Voices rose gradually in volume, fists were clenched and brandished, palms were smacked together, feet were stamped, men rose and stalked about the room angrily. Yvonne Mayer quietly brought more cold wine and kept the glasses filled. The disputants drank thirstily, but were hardly aware of her presence.

Finally, they had narrowed the area of disagreement. Starrett was to purchase the weapons and provide a slush fund in cash, not to exceed one hundred thousand American dollars. The oil lease would run for twelve years. It was on the division of the profits that there was no meeting of minds. Abraham was willing to accept a minimum of 55 percent for Asante. Tangent was willing to accept the same minimum for Starrett. Neither would budge, and all were reduced to a morose silence, slumped in their chairs, staring moodily at nothing.

Finally, the Little Captain spoke:

"Mr. Tangent, to you this is a business proposition, and you seek the most favorable terms. As you said, all you want is oil. I do not condemn you for that. Indeed, you are to be congratulated; you have argued most persuasively. But you must understand that to us it is more than a business proposition. We are talking about the future of Asante, the future of our people. And we are talking about our own lives, which all of us are willing to sacrifice to make our dream of a new Asante come true. We have won many Asantis to our cause. We have done this by convincing them they are being robbed and cheated by rulers who care only for their personal wealth, who steal Asante taxes to fatten their Swiss bank accounts. Now, assuming the coup succeeds, and we become rulers of Asante, and we then announce that we have given more than half of the profits of Asante's oil to a foreign company—what would be the result of that? Would not the people feel that once again they have been robbed and cheated, that they have merely exchanged one gang of thieves for another? And would you blame them for feeling that way?"

There was silence again. Tangent sat hunched over, hands clasped between spread knees, head bowed. Finally he straightened up.

"All right," he said. "Fifty-one to Asante, forty-nine to us."

"Done," Willi Abraham said.

176

A sigh of relief ran around the room. The Asantis stretched wearily.

"Now," Tangent said, "I have another condition."

Duclos leaped angrily to his feet.

"We have come to an agreement," he shouted. "I, personally, feel we have given too much. But I will go along with the others. But no more conditions, no more demands! You take us for fools? Do you think we are poor little ignorant black boys?"

"Exactly what General Tutu screamed in the palace yesterday," Tangent said coldly. "I have not accused you of racism, Professor. Please have the courtesy not to accuse me."

"What is your new demand?" Willi Abraham asked.

"It is not *my* demand," Tangent said. "I have complete faith in what you have promised. But I am an employee—a servant, if you will—of a large, faceless corporation located thousands of miles away. I am empowered to make this agreement, yes, if I can provide proof that you—who are strangers to them—will honor this agreement if the coup is successful."

"*When* the coup is successful," Yvonne Mayer said, and they all looked at her in surprise, realizing it was the first time she had contributed to the discussion.

"What kind of proof?" Willi Abraham asked.

"A signed statement from Captain Anokye that he agrees to those terms affecting the oil lease. The twelve-year period. The fifty-one/forty-nine split. That he will honor those terms when he becomes ruler of Asante. Also, this statement must be repeated, in his voice, on tape."

The Little Captain burst out laughing. "Oh, Mr. Tangent," he said, "what kind of proof is this your people demand? What if I do not become ruler of Asante? What if the coup succeeds and Abraham becomes ruler? Or Duclos? Or any other man? Where is your proof then?''

Tangent stared at him. Gradually Anokye's mirth faded, the two small vertical wrinkles appeared above the bridge of his nose. His features took on that somber, magisterial quality Tangent remembered from their first meeting. Anokye may admire Garibaldi, the American reflected, but he resembles Mussolini.

''I'll take that gamble,'' Tangent said. ''Will you sign and dictate such a statement?''

''I will,'' the Little Captain said.

The remainder of the meeting was spent in discussing ways and means. Willi Abraham named Mai Fante as the man he wanted to act as go-between, to deliver the Starrett slush fund and to obtain Captain Anokye's signed and recorded statements. Tangent named Sam Leiberman the man who would consult with Captain Anokye on the numbers and types of weapons available, and make arrangements for delivery.

All agreed on the necessity of secrecy and the need for fast action. The expiration date of Starrett's present lease was less than a month away.

''As is the Nyam's pledge,'' Captain Anokye remarked.

They were all, suddenly, sobered and shaken by the magnitude of the events they had set in motion. They could hardly meet each other's eyes as they shook hands and departed, one by one, at five-minute intervals. Duclos first, slipping down the back stairs. Then Tangent, stalking steadily down the main staircase, ignoring the music and dancing now going on in the main floor parlor. Then Abraham, out the front door, pausing on the porch to light a stubby Dutch cigar and gossip about the price of tobacco with the Mokodi gendarme on duty. Abraham gave him a cigar before he left, and the man never saw him.

Upstairs, Captain Obiri Anokye, his tunic unbuttoned, sat sprawled in the upholstered chair at the desk. Yvonne Mayer moved quietly about the room, straightening up, emptying ashtrays, collecting glasses, bottles, corks. She opened the windows wider. A vagrant breeze came in to dissolve the smoke, freshen the room with cool night air.

"More wine, Bibi?" she asked.

"Thank you, no. I am grateful for what you have done."

"I did nothing."

"Come here."

Obediently, she came over to him, sat on the floor at his feet. She grasped one calf, put her head against his knee. He stroked her smooth hair absently, then curled his fingers about one of her plaits, caressing it gently.

"What do you think of him?" he asked.

"Tangent? A very capable man. I would like to have him working for me. Think of what he has done for his people tonight. A twelve-year lease. Forty-nine percent of Asante's oil. And all moneys advanced to be repaid by Asante."

"Oh yes," Anokye agreed. "A hard bargain. But did we have a choice? We know from Garde's actions that we can expect no help from the French. They will continue to back Prempeh. Starrett was our only chance."

"Tangent knew this, of course."

"Of course. Yvonne, when you climb a steep ladder, it is foolish to take more than one step at a time. This agreement with Starrett is my first step. Tangent represents money and power. I need money and power if I am to succeed."

"You trust Tangent?" she asked.

179

"Why not? It is in his interest, the interest of his people, to see Prempeh overthrown."

"And after, when you become ruler of Asante? You mean to honor this agreement?"

"To the letter. There are other matters in which Tangent and his people may be of help. I must establish a relationship of trust with them. They must learn the kind of man I am."

"Why should they want to help you further?"

"If it is in their interest, if they can see profit or potential profit, they will help me. That is the nature of things." He was silent a moment, stroking her hair slowly. "This Tangent puzzles me. He said it was merely a business proposition, that he was interested only in the oil. But I have a feeling there is something else."

She rose to her knees, bowed her pliant back, rested her forearms on his thighs, looked up into his face.

"You saw that, did you, Bibi? I did too. He is excited by your plans."

"By the idea of a coup? Of overturning a government by force?"

"Nooo," she said thoughtfully. "Not entirely. I know men. Why should I not? Haven't I had enough experience? Yes, Tangent is excited by the violence of the coup. But he is also excited by you, Bibi. *You* excite him."

"I? Why should I excite him?"

"The same thing that excites me. Your sureness, your resolve, your ambition, your singlemindedness, your power. He senses all this, and he responds to it. It excites him because he knows he lacks it."

"I think you exaggerate."

"I did not. Bibi, would Tangent die for Starrett Petroleum, Incorporated?"

"Of course not."

"Because it is merely a job of work to him, nothing more. If not Starrett, then some other company or corporation. But you would die for Asante. He knows it. Since he cannot feel that, he wants to share the feeling of one who can and does. It makes him important. It is significant. There has been nothing of significance in his life until this."

He looked at her with wonder.

"You believe this to be true, Yvonne?"

"I do. I think you are right, that Starrett will continue to support you if they can see a profit in it. But Tangent's motive is more complex than that. You *must* succeed, and he will do everything in his power to help you. For if you are crushed, he is crushed. He loves you, Bibi. That is *his* profit."

"Now you speak nonsense," he murmured.

"No." She shook her head. "I speak the truth. I recognize it because that is the way I feel."

"Shall we go to bed now?" he asked.

"Of course."

"Let me shower first. Go to bed and wait for me."

"Don't be long. Please."

She lay naked in bed, staring at the ceiling, awaiting her lover. It was as she had said of Tangent; there had been nothing of significance in her life until Anokye. The pain she had known, the humiliation, fear, the dread—all had been endured. Repetition reduced them to a dull ache. But hope never died. Never. Not even in the starving or the condemned. The dying await the miracle. This man was hers.

He arranged her on hands and knees, her head down upon the pillow. He kneeled behind her, between her spread legs so that he might admire the sweet flare from narrow waist to smooth hips. He held her two braids as a rider might hold the reins of an eager, blooded horse.

When he entered into her, she cried out once and lurched back against him. He pulled on the plaits, and her head came up as though she held a bit. They rode with grunts and gasps, became sweated, their flesh raw and tumescent. They stopped a few moments and began again. They stopped a few moments and began again. They stopped a few moments and began again.

When, finally, they could pause no more, both victims of their lust, she called him, as she always did, her "master," her "king," her "ruler." He did not speak, but with intent ferocity rent the pale heart and continued to plunge even after she collapsed prone and boneless, a continent conquered by his hard blows.

19

THE DAY'S CATCH had been a good one—bluefish, bass, cod, a small tuna—and the Anokye family had a fine peppery stew from the best of the lot. The remainder were sold to a merchant in Porto Chonin. He would select the best of his purchase for his own table, and take the remainder across to Mokodi in his boat, for sale to hotels and restaurants. It was quite possible that Tangent, dining that night at the Zabarian, would eat a bass that had threshed futilely in the Anokye nets.

After the evening meal, Josiah, Zuni, and Adebayo went down to the beach to mend nets stretched over drying racks. Obiri stayed in the kitchen, listening to the talk of his sister Sara and their mother, who had been given the name Judith when her family converted to Christianity.

Sara was trying very hard to keep her conversation ladylike and dignified. But her youth defeated her. She was constantly breaking into an impish giggle, covering her blushing face with both hands, or betraying her delight with a smile of such radiance that it lighted the room. Judith and Obiri watched her and listened to her with loving indulgence; she was the youngest of the Anokye children, the beautiful "baby," and she could do no wrong.

The matter under discussion was this:

Lt. Jere Songo had returned to Lomé, to resume his duties with the Togolese army, on his father's staff. He had written a short letter to Josiah Anokye, as was proper, thanking him for the hospitality that had been shown him. The lieutenant had also written a personal letter to Sara. It was couched in most respectful terms. It mentioned his pleasure in meeting her and her family, and it concluded with an invitation to Sara to come to Lomé, to stay at his home and meet his family.

Sara, who had never been out of Asante, wanted very much to go. Her mother said it was completely, utterly, irrevocably out of the question; young girls did not travel alone to meet young men in another country, men they had met but once. Judith conceded that the lieutenant had made a good impression. He was open, cheerful, polite. Shy, too, of course. But that was to his credit; he did not push himself forward. Still . . .

It was more discussion than argument. There was never any possibility of Sara disobeying her mother's edict. But she wished to state her side, and in the process create a fantasy of the delightful new experiences that awaited her. Also, she was old enough to travel by herself. Also, how could she be expected to behave properly in the world outside Asante if she was not allowed to learn? And so forth . . .

She was sixteen, a tall, willowy girl-woman, tremulous with dreams but saved from sappiness by a ready sense of humor and a recognition of life's absurdities. She attended the lycée in Mokodi, and planned to become a teacher, nurse, secretary, airline stewardess, actress, fabric designer, or artist. All subject to change without notice. She was lively, the best swimmer of the Anokye children, and kept a picture of Alain Delon on the wall above her bed.

Then, the kitchen shining, pots and utensils set out for the morning meal, the two women sat down at the table and looked to Obiri expectantly, awaiting his judgment on the proper response to Lt. Songo's invitation. As usual he considered gravely and made no attempt to treat the matter lightly.

"Sara," he said finally, "join your father and brothers for a few minutes."

"I don't see why I—" she began indignantly, but the Little Captain rose and touched her twigged hair fondly.

"Please, Sara," he said. "We understand how you feel. Perhaps something can be worked out."

Satisfied with this vague promise, she flashed them both a bright grin and ran lightly from the room. They watched her go, smiling. It was impossible to resist her fresh charm.

Obiri sat down across the table from his mother. They stared at each other. She seemed suddenly smaller to him. Not older, but shrunken, the skin tighter on a body as corded as her husband's. She continued to work as hard as ever, her mind alert, but the rhythm of her life was slowing, slowing. Sometimes, late in the evening, she would sit silently, mending untouched in her lap, and stare about her home as if seeing it for the first time. Or the last.

"Sara cannot go to Togo," she told Obiri. He knew that tone well: the final judgment.

"Not alone," he agreed. "It would not be proper. But if you accompanied her . . ."

"I? No, I am too old."

"Nonsense. You would enjoy the trip. I would make all the arrangements."

For an instant her eyes brightened as she thought of the adventure. But her good sense conquered.

"No," she repeated. "I cannot leave Father. And now I am sometimes weary. Is it so important that Sara visit this boy?"

"And his family," Obiri said. "Yes, it is important. For her and me. For all of us. I would like you and Sara to be in Togo in about three weeks' time."

She knew his plans, of course; it was impossible to conceal anything from her, and he valued her counsel. Now she looked at him in much the same way Mai Fante had looked at Tangent when he suggested a vacation in London.

"So soon?" Judith breathed.

"Yes. I will feel better if you and Sara are not here." The old woman thought a long moment.

"Sara may go," she said finally. "Zuni's wife will go with her. I will remain here."

"As you wish," Obiri said. "Also—"

He stopped speaking. But she knew his thoughts, as she always did.

"Also," she said, "it will be good for Sara to marry this boy. Then, if you succeed, you will have important relatives in Togo."

"Yes," he said, "that is my thinking."

"And Adebayo?" she asked ironically. "What do you plan for him?"

"Nothing, Mother," he said, smiling. "Not yet."

She shook her head, recognizing that this son had grown beyond her. He was engaged in enterprises, dangerous enterprises, foreign to her. She could not see the limits of his ambition, and what drove him she did not know. She knew only that he was her strongest, loneliest, and most loving child, and for that she could cherish him.

"Live a long life," she told him. "Be happy and do good in the sight of God."

He lifted her feather hand from the tabletop and kissed her worn fingers.

20

"MUST YOU SIT around like that?" Alistair Greeley said. "What? What? You're half naked!"

"Oh, much more than that," Jane Greeley said languidly, and Maud laughed.

The chief teller glared at the two women, furious, feeling he should tell them a thing or two, but not knowing what—or how.

They sat on the hot, shadowed veranda; a pitcher of warm lemonade between them. Lately they had taken to spiking the insipid drink with sloe gin, ignoring Greeley's anguished reminders of what the gin cost. He dragged his clumsy boot up and down the porch, rehearsing in his mind all the clever, cutting things he might say.

"Oh, do sit down," his wife said. "You're making me nervous. You act like a Piccadilly tart waiting for her soldier boy."

This time his sister laughed. They were always laughing at him, one or the other or both. To his face or behind his back. He knew, he knew. They thought him a weak cripple, half a man. But they'd see, they'd see. When he got the bonus from Garde, they'd come sucking around, and then it would be his turn. What? What?

He waited impatiently for Captain Anokye, pacing, dragging his boot back and forth, pleased that he was annoying his wife. He avoided looking at his sister. She sat slumped far down in the cushioned wicker chair, her long bare legs thrust out. And spread! Between brief white shorts and a flowered scarf tied about her heavy breasts, a gap of soft, rippled flesh was insolently displayed. The whore! His own sister—a whore!

And his stick of a wife taking it all in with covetous eyes, leaning forward to murmur, touching the bare shoulder, playing up to the younger woman like a—like a— Greeley didn't know what. But it was poisonous to see. And even when he didn't look at them, even when he was away, at work in the bank, he knew they were together, alone in the big house, slopping down their gin and—and God knows what. Sickening!

"He's here," Greeley said loudly, watching Anokye's Land Rover pull into the driveway. "Jane, will you please straighten up and try to act like a lady for a change."

He thought she said, "Go flog yourself," but he wasn't sure, and didn't want to cause a scene with the Little Captain already mounting the steps.

"Good evening, Captain," he called out cheerily, flinging open the door. "Right on time. The only time you'll be late is for your own funeral. Then you'll be the late Captain Anokye. What? What?"

"That is true," the Little Captain smiled. "Good evening, ladies."

They nodded, and Greeley hustled his guest into the house.

"Strutting little peacock," Maud said.

"Oh, I don't know," Jane said lazily. "Some of those little men surprise you. Or maybe it just looks bigger because they're so small."

"Jane, I wish you wouldn't talk like that."

"Do you? I thought you liked pig-talk. Get me some more ice, there's a sweet."

Maud took longer than usual to return with a shallow bowl of stunted ice cubes.

"The fridge is acting up again," she reported. "I waited to hear if it clicked on, but it didn't. Do you suppose it's stopped completely?"

"Who cares?" Jane said. "Home, sweet home. Have another peg, sweetie. Good for what ails you."

"It makes me all perspiry," Maud said. "I'm all wet."

"The gin's not what makes you wet," Jane said. "I know what makes you wet."

"Oh *you*!" Maud said. "I could hear them plain as anything in the study. Always talking their wars and battles and soldiers. Like two little boys."

"Has the gimp said anything more to you about sending me back?"

"Not a word. But I know he's up to something. He gets that smirky look."

"Christ, I couldn't stand England again," Jane said. "Not after this sun. I'd like to spend the rest of my life in the sun. Lying naked in the sun. And you could keep me all oiled. Would you like that?"

"Oh yes," Maud whispered. "I would, I would."

Jane laughed throatily. "Not much chance of it if he sends me back," she said.

"He won't," Maud Greeley said fiercely. "I won't let him."

"I have a problem I hope you can help me with, Mr. Greeley," Captain Anokye was saying.

"Of course, of course. Anything at all."

"Next month—say the first two weeks in August—I'd like to plan a brigade-strength tactical exercise, something designed to test the initiative of my junior officers and noncoms. Of course, being stationed in Mokodi, the area in which we can operate is necessarily limited. No farther

189

north than Gonja, certainly. Any suggestions, sir?"

"Mmm, let me think," Greeley said. "I gather you're ruling out the reenactment of a set battle. What? What?"

"Oh yes, sir. It would have to be a situation in which small units—squad- and platoon-strength—would operate more or less independently, with only the most basic orders—assignment of objectives and time allowed."

"Tank and artillery units available?"

"No, sir. This will be mainly or wholly an infantry maneuver. You know approximately the number and type of vehicles assigned to Fourth Brigade."

"Yes, yes," Greeley nodded. He stumped about the study, turning his face away from the Little Captain. He was on fire, almost convinced Anokye was leading up to the planning of a coup, the action Anatole Garde had been waiting.

"Perhaps an invasion?" Greeley suggested. "An amphibious invasion with landings at the harbor?"

"No, I don't think so," Anokye said. "The area of hostilities would be too limited, and merchants would be certain to complain if we tied up traffic on the waterfront."

"True," Greeley said. "I hadn't thought of that. Ah, Captain, I have it! An insurrection! An attempted coup d'etat by the Nyam's rebels or any other bunch of crackpots. How does that strike you? What? What?"

"Yesss," Anokye said slowly. "That might do. We'll plan an imaginary coup, plant 'enemy' forces in certain key positions, and then see how effectively Fourth Brigade roots them out. Yes, Mr. Greeley, I think that will serve excellently. It can be staged in the area south of Gonja, and will necessitate several small units operating independently without specific tactical instructions."

"Good, good, good," Greeley chortled, rubbing his

hands together. "Now let's get out the map and start planning how such a coup might take place. That's the first step. What? What?"

"Yes, Mr. Greeley," Captain Obiri Anokye said. "That's the first step."

After Captain Anokye departed, Alister Greeley announced he was going directly to bed. After all, he said, he needed his sleep if he was to get to work the next morning and earn enough money to keep them swilling sloe gin. He waited for their rejoinder. When there was none, he slammed angrily back into the house, leaving them sitting together on the dark veranda.

They assumed he had gone up to his bedroom, so when Maud Greeley went into the kitchen to scrape more ice fragments from the stubborn refrigerator, she was surprised to hear her husband's voice coming from the study. She pressed her ear against the wall.

"—doubt about it," Alistair Greeley was saying. "Certainly I'm sure, Mr. Garde. He's pretending it will be a military exercise, a maneuver. What's that? Next month. First two weeks in August, he said. Well, we'll plan the coup as if it was actually taking place. The soldiers playing the 'enemy' will take over the key positions selected. Then Anokye will designate teams to retake the positions. But I'm sure he's not interested in that. All he wants is my ideas on the coup itself—what positions to seize, vital crossroads, the timing, and so forth. Well, of course, it's all a game. Maneuvers are supposed to be a game. What? What? It's all play-acting. Practice for the real thing. But in this case, it *is* the real thing, what? Of course, Mr. Garde. Yes, sir. No, just preliminary work tonight, deciding exactly how we will approach

191

the problems of planning. Next time he will bring me the numbers of troops and units involved in staging the coup, and the numbers assigned to the counter-coup operation. Yes, Mr. Garde. Of course. I'll report every meeting. Yes, sir. Thank you, sir."

Maud Greeley heard him hang up the phone. She went swiftly back to the porch.

"Ice?" Jane asked.

"Sorry, no more," Maud said. She stood directly behind the other woman, looking down at the naked shoulders. Gleaming. She stood there quite a long time while her sister-in-law finished her warm drink. Then Jane rose, yawned, stretched her full body like a satisfied cat. She looked curiously at the still silent Maud.

"Penny for your thoughts," she said.

"Oh, they're worth more than that," Maud Greeley said. "Much more."

21

IT BEGAN RAINING that night. It began suddenly; one moment the sky was clear, the next it was clotted, and rain fell straight down, not driven by gusty winds but simply dropping steadily, heavily, at the same rate for hour after hour. It might, Asantis knew, continue for a day, three days, a week, two weeks. But few complained. The rivers would gush full, trees would flower, the baked earth would bloom verdant overnight.

Tangent spent the afternoon in the office of J. Tom Petty at the Mokodi Hilton. He lounged on the leather couch, idly scanning the pages of the Asante *New Times*. Perhaps he was imagining it, but it seemed to him the tenor of local news articles had already changed perceptibly. The slush fund had been delivered only two days previously, yet there were such items as: "The Minister of Agriculture denies that near-starvation conditions exist in the northern provinces," and, "Authorities state supplies of beef, pork, veal, goat and chicken will be drastically reduced in the coming months due to a serious shortage of feed." Etc., etc. The items were cautiously worded to reflect the official position, but even mention of such matters was significant. Heretofore, the *New Times* had been a palace house organ.

Pleased with this early evidence of media manipulation, Tangent tossed the paper aside and turned to look out the window.

"It's never going to stop," J. Tom Petty said grumpily.

"It's going to keep raining forever, and the whole god-damned country will float away."

The big man was in his shirtsleeves, seated in his swivel chair, hunched over the desk. He was smoking a fat cigar as he struggled with cost estimates and payrolls.

"The dry season starts in August," Tangent remarked.

"Bullshit," Petty said. "This place ain't got a dry season. Unless you call a week a season."

His phone rang, and he jerked it angrily off the hook.

"Yeah?" he said. "Yeah, he's here. Who? Okay. I'll tell him. Hold it a minute." He covered the transmitter with his palm. "Peter, you got a visitor. A lady. Says her name is Mrs. Greeley. Want to see her?"

Tangent unfolded slowly from the couch, straightened, tugged his jacket smooth.

"Why don't you run down to the bar and have a couple of slow ones, Tom?" he suggested. "Help you forget the paperwork and the rain."

"Best idea I've heard all day," Petty said. "Maybe there's some of that Swedish gash hanging around. Send the lady in?"

Tangent nodded, and Petty spoke over the phone. He grabbed his jacket and headed for the door. He was no sooner gone than an Asanti secretary ushered in Mrs. Greeley. She stood a moment, looking about in awe at the big, richly furnished room. She was wearing a clear plastic raincoat, a plastic hood. She carried a man's black umbrella.

Tangent came forward smiling.

"So nice to see you again, Mrs. Greeley," he said.

"What an unusual room," she said. "I've never seen anything like it."

"Marvelous view," Tangent said. "Except on days like this."

194

He took her wet hood, raincoat, umbrella, and hung them away. Then he conducted her on a short tour of the office, telling her something of the artwork displayed, pointing out rugs, drapes, and curtains of African fabrics and design.

She was wearing one of her calf-length Victorian gowns, white again, with the usual pleats and ruffles. She was, he decided, the kind of woman who didn't remove her undergarments until she had donned her nightdress. At the moment, she was visibly nervous, twisting her gold wedding band or reaching up to poke tendrils of hair into her spinsterish hairdo.

She did not seem the type of woman who would welcome informality. So rather than seat her on the couch, he drew up a club chair to the desk while he took Petty's swivel chair. Then he leaned forward, clasped his hands on the tabletop, smiled pleasantly.

"And how is your husband?" he asked. "And your sister-in-law?"

"All right," she said vaguely. "They're all right."

Then she was silent, looking down at her bony hands, twisting that ring again. Tangent stared at her, perplexed.

"Mrs. Greeley," he said, "how may I—"

She looked up suddenly.

"You're a good friend of Captain Anokye, aren't you?" she demanded.

Tangent leaned back slowly. He stopped smiling.

"I'd hardly call us good friends," he said. "I know him, certainly. I met him for the first time at your home."

"Well, I have some information that could be worth a lot of money to Captain Anokye," she said. Almost definately. He noted that she was blushing; deep pink blotches mottled face and neck.

"Oh?" Tangent said. "But why come to me? Why not go directly to Captain Anokye?"

She looked at him in astonishment.

"But he's a darky," she said.

"Ah, yes. I see."

"Besides," she said, "he's in the army. Men in the army don't have any money. Everyone knows that."

Tangent knew at least three millionaire colonels and one private first class worth a great deal more, but didn't feel the moment right to mention it.

"Do I understand you correctly, Mrs. Greeley?" he said gently. "You have some information you believe would be of value to Captain Anokye. You want to sell this information. But you don't wish to contact the Captain directly, and since you believe he could not afford to pay in any event, you have come to me, thinking I would pay you. Is that right?"

"Yes. That's right."

"Why on earth should I pay you for information about Captain Anokye?"

She became confused.

"I—I—I thought you were good friends. You left together. That night at our place. This is important information. I know it is. I need the money. I *need* it. I—"

Suddenly, to his discomfort, she began weeping. She bowed her head so he couldn't see the tears. But he heard her snuffling. She pulled a small square of white from her knitted handbag, held it to her face. She wasn't weeping because she needed the money desperately, he decided. It was the shame.

He waited patiently until she calmed. Finally she raised her head, lifted her chin, looked at him directly.

"I'm sorry," she said.

It was the wrong moment to offer sympathy. He looked at her sternly.

"I *may* be able to help you," he told her. "Right now, I don't know how, but perhaps it can be done. What is this information you have?"

"I get paid first," she said firmly.

"Oh no, Mrs. Greeley. No no no. That's not the way it's done. Why should Captain Anokye or I or anyone else buy a pig in a poke? What if, for instance, I pay you what you ask, and your information turns out to be worthless? I'd look a proper fool then, wouldn't I?"

"It's not worthless!" she cried. "I swear it's not."

"That's for the buyer to decide," he said grimly. "Either you reveal what you're selling, or I'm afraid this meeting must end."

"But that means I have to trust you!"

"Exactly," he nodded. "If you wish to profit from what you have, you must first reveal it. To me or someone else. Would you buy a home, a car, a dress, even a mango sight unseen?"

She was silent again, and he gave her all the time she wanted. He did not think her a stupid woman, but a troubled one. Under severe stress. Racked. He could guess her problem, but it was no concern of his. Everyone had problems. It was the name of the game.

"All right," she said finally. "Here it is: Captain Anokye came to our house last night. He went into the study with my husband. Then, later, he left. Mr. Greeley said he was going to bed, but he didn't. I went into the kitchen, and I heard him. He was in the study, talking on the telephone."

Then she recounted Greeley's conversation. To Tangent, it sounded like she was repeating it word for word, and he never doubted that such a conversation had taken

197

place. He listened closely, his face expressionless. When she had finished, she looked at him expectantly. He leaned back in the swivel chair, arm outstretched, fingers toying with a steel letter opener. He sighed.

"Frankly, Mrs. Greeley," he said, "I fail to see why that conversation would be of value to Captain Anokye. I know it is certainly worth nothing to me. As far as I can tell, your husband was merely calling a Mr. Garde to tell of a military maneuver that is being planned. Nothing secret about that. Maneuvers are frequently held in the open, on public property, in the city or countryside, where anyone can witness them."

"But they talked about a coup!" she said desperately.

"I didn't get that impression at all," he said coldly. "It sounded to me, if you have repeated the conversation precisely, that the coup they discussed was merely to be—what was it your husband said?—'play-acting,' just an excuse for military practice. They do it all the time. Armies, I mean. They practice invading and repelling invasions, they run through old battles and devise new ones. Hardly valuable information."

She collapsed, defeated.

"However," he said, "I could be wrong, although I doubt it. Suppose we do this, Mrs. Greeley: Suppose I take your information to Captain Anokye. Perhaps his reaction will be different from mine, and he will be willing to pay you for your interest. How much were you thinking of asking?"

"Five thousand pounds," she said dully.

"Mmm," he said. "Quite a sum. Well . . . do you want me to try Captain Anokye?"

"Might as well," she said.

"All right. Suppose you call me at this number tomorrow afternoon. Here, I'll jot it down for you. Call about noon. I'll make it a point to be here, and I'll try to have some word for you."

"Thank you," she said, in a voice so low he could hardly hear. "You've been very kind."

"Not at all, not at all," he protested. "It's a pleasure to be of help."

He walked her to the elevator, talking enthusiastically of her husband's collection of model soldiers. When the doors closed her away, he hurried to the office of Mai Fante and burst in without knocking.

"Mai, I've got to see the man," he said. "The sooner the better."

"Tonight?"

"Has to be."

"I'll set it up," Fante said, "and get back to you. Trouble?"

"You might say that," Tangent said.

"That's the name of the game," Mai Fante said, and Tangent winced.

He drove slowly, hunched over the wheel, peering through the smear of the windshield wipers. Occasionally he reached to palm moisture from inside the glass. It didn't help much; it was almost midnight on Asante Royal Highway No. 1, on the unlighted stretch from Shabala north to Gonja. Tangent strained his eyes for the dirt track he had been instructed to seek. When he found it, it looked like a quagmire, and he feared bogging down if he made the turn. So he pulled onto the slightly raised shoulder of the road, keeping the left wheels on the paved highway.

He switched off the lights, kept the motor idling, opened the windows slightly to let in the cool, damp air, but not the rain. Then he waited . . .

Mai Fante had said "about midnight," but it was more than twenty minutes past the hour when he saw blurred headlights coming from the direction of Gonja. Gradually he made out the distinctive silhouette of a Land Rover, and when it was close, it slowed, crossed the road, and pulled up in front of him, bumper to bumper. Through the two windshields he could see a hand beckoning him. He dashed out into the rain, climbed hurriedly into the rear of the Land Rover, stretched his long legs sideways. Sgt. Sene Yeboa was driving. Captain Anokye sat beside him. The sergeant switched off motor and lights, and then they were all disembodied voices. It bothered Tangent that he could not see expressions, reactions, gestures.

Tangent was prepared to waste no time on preliminaries, to plunge right in. But the Little Captain inquired politely after his health, asked if the weather was inconveniencing him, assured him the rain was needed and welcome, and mentioned that he had had two satisfactory meetings with Sam Leiberman and they had reached an agreement on the numbers and types of weapons required. Tangent forced himself to reply in kind. Only after all courtesies had been exchanged did he begin to relate what had happened that afternoon. He did not question the presence of Sgt. Yeboa. If Anokye had brought him along to such a meeting, Tangent could speak freely.

The two soldiers listened to Tangent's rapid French without interrupting, though when Garde's name was mentioned, Tangent was conscious of Yeboa stirring restlessly in the driver's seat. When he had concluded, they all sat in silence at least a minute before Captain Anokye sighed.

"I have acted foolishly," he said.

"Not foolishly," Tangent said. "Carelessly, perhaps."

"I thank you for your kindness," Anokye said. "Greeley is a difficult man to like. Very difficult. But he is educated in military history and has an excellent tactical sense, though of course he has never seen active service. He has been of help to me several times in the past. I thought he enjoyed it—an opportunity to put his learning to the test. He never mentioned politics. I believed him to be nonpolitical."

"I think he probably is," Tangent said. "I don't think he is betraying you for ideological reasons."

"What then?"

"Money. I should have suspected him before this. The French control the Asante National Bank. Anatole Garde represents French interests in Asante. How better monitor your activities than through Greeley? I suppose he would do it for a promised promotion or raise in pay or something like that."

"For money," the Little Captain repeated in a low voice. "He did it for money."

"It's hardly catastrophic, Captain. There are several solutions."

"At the moment," Anokye said, "the only solution I desire is to eliminate Greeley."

"Yes *sah*!" Sgt. Yeboa said softly.

"But that is my blood talking," Anokye went on. "It would not be wise."

"No, it would not," Tangent agreed. "No matter how cleverly done. Garde would be suspicious, and angry. Can't you merely stop visiting Greeley? Give him some excuse—military secrecy, press of business, whatever. Simply end all personal contact with him. I'll tell Mrs. Greeley her information was of no value to you, and there's an end to it."

Again there was silence. Windows and curtains were

closed; the interior of the car became oppressively hot. Tangent pulled his tie loose, opened his collar, struggled out of his jacket. And waited . . .

"May I light a cigarette?" he asked finally.

"Of course," the Little Captain said. "Strike your match near the floor, please, in your cupped hands. Probably an unnecessary precaution, but still . . ."

"You, Captain?"

"Thank you, no."

"Sergeant?"

"Thank you, sir."

Tangent bent far over, struck the match in cupped hands near the floor, lighted his Players. Then he handed a single cigarette to the sergeant and held the burning end of his own steady so Yeboa could light up. Now there was a slight illumination in the car. When Yeboa took a deep drag, Tangent could see his heavy, sensual features. Captain Anokye remained in shadow.

"My personal situation is delicate, Mr. Tangent," the Little Captain said slowly. "I have tried to move carefully, obey all orders, to make no speeches that could be considered seditious. But I am certain the secret police are aware of my association with Yvonne Mayer, with Minister Abraham and Professor Duclos. They cannot be unaware of the personal loyalty of my troops and my popularity with the Asante Brothers of Independence. I do not mean to boast; I merely state facts. We now know, from Garde's recent actions, that they fear an attempted coup. If I break off all contact with Greeley, the palace may feel their best course of action would be to arrest me. Or assassinate me."

A low growl came from Sgt. Yeboa.

"Yes," Tangent said. "I can see that. If they feel you are under adequate surveillance, that Greeley is reporting on your plans, they'll probably allow you to remain at liberty. For the time being, at least."

"Another factor also," Captain Anokye said, almost dreamily. "By maintaining my contact with Greeley, I will be able to pass along false information to Garde. On the plans for the coup, the numbers involved, the tactics to be employed, and most important, the timing."

Tangent smiled in the darkness.

"Congratulations, Captain," he said. "You have converted a difficulty into an opportunity."

"The mark of a professional soldier," Captain Anokye said. Then he added dryly, "Or so Alistair Greeley has told me."

22

THEY WERE IN Abidjan, Ivory Coast, and their destination was on the road to Grand-Lahou, near the mouth of the Bandama River. Leiberman had described it to Tangent as a cluster of ramshackle safari cottages around a main restaurant-bar building.

"It was built for tourists," he explained, "but now it's a pirates' den. Every smuggler and nogoodnik along the coast drops by. We'll find our man there."

Leiberman had wanted to take a boat from the foot of the bridge in Treichville and make a lazy trip down the lagoon. Tangent had vetoed the plan as too time-consuming, and insisted on renting a Simca at the Hôtel Ivoire.

"You're running too close as it is," he told Leiberman.

"Deliberately," the mercenary said. "We're dealing with gonifs. The less time you give a gonif between making the deal and the delivery, the less time you give him to start brooding on how underpaid he is. Then you get the shaft."

"When are you scheduling the first delivery?"

"I told you—next Tuesday night."

"Did you coordinate that with Anokye?"

Leiberman was driving, and took his eyes off the road long enough to look sideways at Tangent.

" 'Coordinate,' " he repeated. "You guys kill me. I said we'd deliver at midnight on Tuesday, and Anokye said okay. If that's coordinating, then I coordinated."

"Where's the first drop?"

"Off Zabar. His brother is taking delivery. Just small arms and grenades."

"What do you think of him now?"

"The Little Captain? A pisscutter. He'll go far, if he stays alive."

"What do you mean by that?" Tangent asked.

"I've seen guys like him before. They think the bullet hasn't been made with their name on it. They die with the most surprised look on their face. But the kid's got moxie, I'll give him that. I think he'll do all right."

"Your job is officially over after the last delivery is made," Tangent said. "But I'd feel better if you stay around until this thing comes off. I'll keep you on salary."

"Why not?" Leiberman said. "In for a penny, in for a fart. I want thirty percent combat pay plus a paid-up life insurance policy."

"All right," Tangent agreed. "I'll arrange it. Stick close to the Little Captain. We've got a lot riding on him."

"My cock, for starters," Leiberman said.

They drove in silence awhile, watching the north side of the road for a sign Leiberman said would indicate five kilometers to the Hôtel d'Azur.

"You know who puzzles me in this whole business?" he asked Tangent.

"Who?"

"You. I know you been involved in things like this before, but since when did you ever go along to make a deal? You leave that to expendables like me. Are you coming along on the delivery?"

"I think I may."

"What are you trying to prove?"

"I'm not trying to prove anything."

"Ho ho ho," Leiberman said. "And I suppose you'll

205

be there in your raw silk suit and Countess Mara tie when the balloon goes up?''

"Yes," Tangent said determinedly. "I'll be there."

"What's the matter," Leiberman said, "backgammon lost its thrill? Listen, you're nuts, you know that? What can you do, except get in the way? Or get your ass shot off. Have you ever fired a gun?"

"Certainly I've fired a gun. I happen to be a rather good shot."

"With what?"

"A twenty-gauge Franchi over-and-under."

"Beautiful," Leiberman said. "I can tell you're a real killer."

They pulled into the small asphalt parking area. Leiberman rolled up the windows tightly and locked the doors.

"Take off your rings, sit on your wallet, and don't drink anything that doesn't come in sealed bottles," he advised Tangent. "And if you've got gold fillings, keep your teeth clenched. Let me do the talking."

Smells hit them first: human sweat of a dozen nationalities, frying oil, stale beer, spilled wine, spices, incense, pomade, hashish, and antique urine. Then the noise: shouted conversation, roared laughter, screamed delight, bellowed curses, a scratchy jukebox playing "The Last Time I Saw Paris," in English, competing with two live musicians, mandolin and drums, wailing an African lament, in Boulé. Then the sights: men and women, black, brown, tan, yellow, white, pink, wearing a thrift shop's inventory of costumes, mostly bright colors, jeweled with glass, hung with brass, flashing, twinkling, bare feet, naked torsos and bulging breasts, a zoo of ruffians and their women, a few dancing, kissing, rubbing, groping.

"It's the bishop's summer day-camp," Leiberman said. "Over here; we'll share."

They sat down in two empty chairs at a table for four. One of their partners was a tall, incredibly skinny black man wearing a red bandanna knotted about his head and a gold loop through the lobe of his left ear. The other man, wearing a seaman's cap, had his head down on his folded arms and was sleeping.

The black glanced up as they pulled out their chairs.

"Sam," he said.

"Yakubu," Leiberman said. "How they hanging?"

"Down," the black man said. "Who's your friend?"

"This is Pete," Leiberman said. "Pete, meet Yakubu, the best pimp in Abidjan."

"The best but not the richest," the black man said. "Buy me a beer?"

"Sure. How about your friend here?" he motioned toward the man flopped on the table, snoring gently.

"No friend of mine," Yakubu said. "He's out. I think someone rolled him."

"Oh? You checked, did you? Hey, waiter! Three Heinekens, the colder the better." He looked slowly around the crowded room. "Shagari been in?"

"He's here," Yakubu said. "Probably out in the kitchen trying to bang the cook."

"How's he doing these days?"

The black shrugged. "Eating thistles, I hear. You got something for him?"

"Could be."

"Need a hand?"

"Could be. What happened to your women?"

"They keep falling in love," Yakubu said. "Then they start giving it away. No business sense."

"Things are tough all over," Leiberman sympathized.

The beers were slammed down. Bottles, no glasses. Tangent paid.

"Take your beer and go find Shagari for me, will you?" Leiberman said to Yakubu. "And hang around; there may be something for you."

The black nodded, picked up his beer, slouched away.

"You know everyone here?" Tangent asked.

"Not everyone. Most of the bad boys."

"Is Shagari one of the bad boys?"

"Not so bad. Stupid, mostly. And a drunk. But his cousin is a fisherman, and he owns a trawler."

"How many men will you need?"

"Shagari and his cousin. Yakubu. And you and me. That should take care of it. They'll do the work; we'll ride shotgun."

"You don't anticipate any trouble, do you?"

"Always," Leiberman said. "I always anticipate trouble. Hello, Shagari, pull up a chair."

"You sonnenbitch Leiberman!" the man shouted. "You no good Jew bastard!"

"Not so loud," Leiberman said. "I'm trying to pass. Meet my friend, Pete."

"You sonnenbitch Pete!" the man shouted. He insisted on crushing their hands between his two filthy paws. Then he signaled wildly for the waiter, almost falling off his chair.

"You're in great shape," Leiberman said. "Too bad. I was going to offer you a job of work, but you couldn't navigate your way through a Tunnel of Love."

"You show me money, see how goddamned fast I sober up," Shagari said. "How's Dele?"

"Okay," Leiberman said. "She's out at your place. Dele's my girl," he explained to Tangent. "She's his daughter. He sold her to me."

"You beat her?" Shagari demanded.

"Only on national holidays," Leiberman said.

"Got more daughters," Shagari grinned at Tangent. "You want one?"

"Thank you, no."

"Sing, dance, cook, plenty push. Cheap."

Tangent shook his head, and Shagari shrugged. He was a short, dirty, walnut-colored man, wearing a sailor's blue dungarees and a soiled white singlet. He was barefoot, unshaven, gap-toothed, with dripping nose, rheumy eyes, ears stuffed with thick clumps of black hair. He smelled rankly of fish. Dead fish. Long-dead fish. Tangent had a sudden vision of the Man from Tulsa and the Man from New York stalking in unexpectedly and witnessing how Tangent was spending Starrett's money. He felt sick.

"Your cousin still got that trawler?" Leiberman asked.

"Sure."

"How's fishing?"

"Lousy."

"Maybe these waters are fished out," Leiberman said. "Maybe you can make more money off Asante or Togo, around there."

True to his word, Shagari seemed to sober up instantaneously.

"What you got?" he asked in a hoarse whisper.

"Cargo."

"What cargo?"

"Farm implements."

"Where from?"

"Sassandra. Your cousin still got that electric winch aboard?"

"Sure."

"Good. These implements are heavy."

"What about crew?" Shagari asked.

"You, your cousin, Pete here, me, and Yakubu."

"Yakubu? Why him?"

"Because he's fast and don't give a damn."

"One trip?"

"One for starters. Maybe more if the price is right."

"When we go?"

"Figure on being off Lomé at midnight next Tuesday. Better give it two days. So we load next Sunday. You can make it in two days, can't you?"

"If weather holds."

"It'll hold," Leiberman assured him. "I slipped God a dash. For you, a thousand francs, French."

Suddenly Shagari was drunk again.

"Joke!" he shouted. "You make funny joke!" He pounded Leiberman on the back. "Plenty funny, Sam! Good laugh!"

They settled for 1,500 French francs, and Leiberman agreed to pay for fuel, food, and wine for the trip.

Later, Tangent said, "I hope it's a seaworthy boat."

"The *Queen Mary*," Leiberman assured him. "And you remember what a great swimmer *she* was."

They drank more beer, had some lunch, then rented one of the safari bungalows. They took a nap, fully clothed, on straw ticks covered with coarse unbleached muslin sheets. Leiberman got a man to come in and spray sheets, ticks, and cots before he'd let Tangent take off his shoes.

"Can't send you back to London with crabs," he said cheerfully. "Give West Africa a bad name."

It was darkling when they awoke. They splashed water on their faces from a stained enamel basin, dried on a flour sack, combed their hair in a mirror tacked to the wall. It could be tacked because it was a disk of polished tin, looking like one end of a No. 10 can. Tangent told himself he was enjoying all this.

210

They went back into the restaurant-bar-tavern-cabaret. It was smellier, louder, dirtier, more crowded. Leiberman grabbed a table when two black men got up to dance together. When they came back, the mercenary told them to get lost.

"I cut you," one of them said menacingly. In English.

"Sure you will," Leiberman said.

"I slice you up."

"Of course," Leiberman said.

"I take you for a ride," the other one said.

"Naturally," Leiberman said.

"I rub you out."

Then they were all laughing, the blacks so hard they could hardly stand up. Tangent bought them drinks, thimbles of Pernod, and they went off, giggling and happy.

"Nice girls," Leiberman said. "Hold the fort, Pete. I'm going to explore the kitchen and see what I can promote. I'll send a bottle of wine from the bar. If I can find something that won't burn with a wick."

They had a meal of broiled chicken, one lobster they shared, yams, rice, fresh greens, cold papayas. Everything tasted good. The Algerian wine was harsh but palatable. Leiberman got some ice chips to put in their glasses, and that helped.

They were just finishing when Shágari returned, Dele trailing behind him. She was carrying a knotted scarf holding her personal belongings, ready for the trip back to Mokodi. She squealed with pleasure, jumped onto Leiberman, clamped her arms about his neck, kissed him frantically.

"Here, here," Leiberman said. "This ain't Paris, you know."

More chairs were pulled up. More food and wine were ordered. Friends and acquaintances of Leiberman came

211

crowding around. The mandolin and drums struck up a mournful tune, and between swallows of chicken and rice, Dele sang the words for them, in Boulé, in a sad, sweet voice.

"It's about this woman who's going to marry a rich farmer," Leiberman translated for Tangent. "It's really his younger brother she loves, but her intended owns four pigs, three goats, and two cows. So she marries him. But his barn catches fire, and he and his pigs and his goats and his cows become overdone bacon. So she goes back to the younger brother and says it was him she loved all along, and he tells her to fuck off. It's a very romantic song."

"You're kidding me," Tangent said.

"I swear I'm not. It's called 'Four Pigs, Three Goats, Two Cows.' Right now, it's number one on the Hit Parade in Abidjan. Want a woman?"

"Not at the moment, thanks."

"Didn't think you would," Leiberman said.

"What the hell's that supposed to mean?" Tangent demanded.

"Jesus Christ, don't be so goddamned touchy," Leiberman said. "Just that you look happy enough with your wine. My God, you're hostile."

"Sorry," Tangent said, and tried to grin.

They drank more. Tangent started out matching Leiberman glass for glass, and then decided that was a mistake, he better slow down. But it was too late; he was seeing everything through a pleasant haze of rosy smoke that swirled, billowed, bloomed.

"The cottage is second down on the right when you need it," Leiberman said.

"I know where the cottage is," Tangent said, speaking slowly and precisely.

"Sure you do," the mercenary said. "One more bottle

212

and you won't be able to find your ass with a boxing glove."

People came and went. Once Tangent danced with Dele. He was so tall and she was so tiny that he tired of bending over her. So he picked her up and carried her gravely about the dance floor. People cheered and sent more drinks to their table. Only now it was three tables, pushed together, a great noisy banquet of sweating men and women, falling all over each other.

Tangent, beginning to slump, felt caution leak away. He was a long way from Brindleys, a long way, and he was delighted he could still feel joy. Fun. That's what had been lacking in his life.

"Fun!" he yelled at Sam Leiberman.

"You're fucking-ay right," Leiberman said, kissing Dele, who was sitting on his lap. "Who's your girlfriend?"

"Who?" Tangent said, confused.

"Next to you," Leiberman said, motioning.

Tangent turned slowly. A white woman was sitting close to him, rubbing the cloth of his jacket sleeve between her fingers.

"Nice material," she said, her voice low and husky. "You in the business?" She spoke English.

"No," Tangent said. "I sell farm implements."

"That's good, too," she said. "How's business?"

"Fine," he said. "You in business?"

"Yes," she said.

"What do you sell?"

"I sell me," she said, not smiling.

"Oh," Tangent said. "Well, how's business?"

"Comme ci, comme ca," she said, flipping her hand. "Right now I'm having a seasonal slump, but it'll pick up in the fall."

"I hope you're watching your cash flow," he said, but it didn't faze her a bit.

"I'll get by," she said, "until the tourists return in the fall."

"Like the swallows to Capistrano?" he giggled.

"Exactly like the swallows," she nodded gravely.

He focused his eyes, with a conscious effort, and looked at her more closely. A fleshy woman, about 40, thickly made up. Black, oily hair. A shiny black dress cut low enough to reveal massive breasts pushed together. Sweat was trickling down her throat and chest, disappearing into the tight cleavage. Her body was heavy, but it did have shape. She stared at him with dark eyes.

"I know what you need," she said.

"What?"

She leaned forward and whispered in his ear. He listened intently. She pulled away and looked at him questioningly. He considered it carefully. It might be amusing. And pleasurable. As long as he didn't have to touch her. She might be diseased.

23

PROFESSOR JEAN-LOUIS DUCLOS had been asked by Captain Obiri Anokye to submit ideas for the restructuring of the Asante government after the coup had destroyed the Prempeh monarchy. Duclos approached the task with none of the trepidation he had brought to all the other important challenges and decisions he had faced in his disappointing career. He had confidence in his own intelligence, ability, talent. But at the same time, a worm gnawed. The world's rejection of his merit mocked his self-assurance.

He ascribed this scurvy treatment to his color; it was that simple. Because of his skin pigmentation—only one of thousands of inherited physical and mental characteristics, and a minor one at that—he had been denied the prizes that should rightfully have been his. It was difficult not to despair—to hate!—when he saw white men of lesser quality reap money, honors, esteem, as if such rewards were their inalienable right.

But recognizing the accident of birth that seemingly doomed him was one thing; ignoring it or rebelling against it was quite another. Until he met Captain Obiri Anokye. Then hope flared that he might help change the unjust order of things. Blacks had once been great rulers, great leaders in Africa. As the Little Captain had said at Gonja (why couldn't *he* have spoken those inspiring words?), blacks had created African civilizations that had lasted for millennia and produced a culture equal to any that history recorded.

And now Captain Anokye had asked him to design the political foundation of a new nation that might one day produce a new civilization, a black civilization that would answer the needs of Africans and provide a vehicle by which Africa would become equal or superior to the other great world powers of the 20th century. Professor Jean-Louis Duclos opened a blank notebook, filled his fountain pen, and—a stack of reference books on the floor beside him, a bottle of wine on his desk—set to work with passion and delight.

Each day, because of his poverty, he was forced to teach summer classes at the lycée and to tutor the doltish sons of government officials. But even as he discharged these mechanical tasks, his brain was working feverishly, and he rushed home each evening to his growing pile of notebooks, fervid with new ideas, bold ideas. Never had he felt so creative, so masterful. A new world began to take form beneath his speeding pen, and the gnawing of self-doubt was vanquished.

During this period, he had little time for Mboa. He gulped down the food she put before him, answered her questions in monosyllables, discouraged her attempts at conversation, fled to his study as quickly as he could to refine and make elegant the political paradise he was designing.

There was one interruption when Captain Anokye summoned him to that meeting with the oilman, Tangent. Professor Duclos had done what he could to prevent a complete capitulation to the white interlopers, but all those military and financial details really did not concern him. He saw himself as a political scientist, and if *his* efforts did not succeed, the labyrinthine plans, hopes, and ambitions of the others would come to dust.

A second interruption in his vital work came that week

in an engraved invitation (all the teachers of the lycée got one) to attend a reception at the palace given by King Prempeh IV to honor the new President of Dahomey. Such an invitation, of course, was tantamount to a command; there was no question but that he would attend. It infuriated him; an evening lost from his work.

Captain Anokye, who had also received an invitation (all officers of the armed forces had), promised to call for Professor Duclos in his Land Rover. All that remained was to dress as formally as his limited wardrobe allowed.

''Maria!'' he wailed. ''My white shirt! I can't find my white shirt. The one with the stiff collar.''

Obediently, Mboa took the white shirt, wrapped in tissue paper, from the bottom dresser drawer. She also found his cuff links and black silk hose, polished his black shoes with a scrap of cloth and palm oil, whisked his shoulders, adjusted his maroon bow tie, and stepped back to admire him, smiling, her head cocked to one side.

''You are beautiful, Jean,'' she said softly.

''Handsome,'' he said. ''Men are handsome, women are beautiful.''

''To me, you are beautiful.''

He inspected himself in the dresser mirror, squaring his shoulders. She came up close behind him, put her arms about him. He saw her face, over his shoulder, in the mirror. As always, her coal-blackness came as an unpleasant shock. Such a contrast to his tawniness. He was no darker than a suntanned white. A woman in Paris had told him that. In bed. Once.

''I wish I was going to the palace with you,'' she said sadly.

''Don't be silly,'' he said. ''The invitation came to me, personally. It said nothing of bringing a guest.''

"If we were married, it would be for both of us. Wouldn't it, Jean?"

"I suppose so. If we were married. Don't wait up for me; I may be late."

"I'll wait up. I want to hear all about it. I wish I was going. I could, if we were married."

He made a sound of impatience, broke the clutch of her arms, stepped away from her. He smoothed his jacket where her tight embrace had wrinkled it. He went to the front window to peer out, hoping Anokye would come soon.

"What are you going to do tonight?" he asked, his back still turned to her.

She didn't answer, and he turned to look at her. She was still standing in front of the mirror where he had left her. She was weeping, arms down at her sides, looking at her tearful image in the glass.

"Now what, for God's sake?" he shouted angrily.

"Nothing, Jean, nothing. I am sorry I am crying."

"What are you crying about?"

"Nothing. It is nothing."

He stared at her in baffled fury. She was wearing a sun-yellow lappa that made her skin even blacker. Her hair was still corn-rowed, a fashion he found detestable. "Jungle style," he called it. There was no denying the dignity in her slim body, but her features had a Negroid cast: wide-spread nose, protruding lips. Put bones through her ears, he thought, and brass rings about her neck, and she might paint her breasts and dance naked under the moon. He shook his head at the insanity of this vision, and without being aware of it, ran a finger down his own straight, patrician nose and lightly touched his delicate lips.

Then, thankfully, there was a short horn beep from outside.

"The Captain," he said loudly. "I'm on my way."

"Jean," she called, but he didn't turn back.

During the short ride to the palace in the Land Rover, chauffeured by Sgt. Sene Yeboa, Professor Jean-Louis Duclos lectured to Captain Anokye:

"History teaches us that most governments fail and fall because of inability or unwillingness to respond to the needs of the people. Governments—even new governments—by their very nature tend to become conservative, bureaucratized, slaves of the status quo. Political arteries harden. Government officials resist change, since change may threaten their power. Instead of serving the people, the government becomes a self-serving entity, its own continued existence its most important responsibility.

"What I have designed for the new Asante is not unusual in its organization, with one vital exception. Basically, Asante will be a republic, government by an elected chief executive, a unicameral legislature, and an independent judiciary. Universal suffrage, but with a literacy test for voters."

"Excellent," Captain Anokye said.

"The unique feature of my plan is this—and I have given it many hours of careful thought—the constitution submitted to the citizens for ratification would mandate change. For an initial period of, say, five years, the chief executive would have extraordinary powers. To overrule decisions of the judiciary, for instance. To veto laws passed by the legislature. The purpose of this is to provide a transitional period, from absolute monarchy to parliamentary democracy, to acquaint Asantis with participant government, to improve education in order to bring greater numbers into the electorate. During such a period of growth and confusion, a strong chief executive with almost unlimited powers would be a necessity.

"At the end of the initial five-year period, the chief executive's power would be greatly reduced. The powers of the legislature—representatives of the people—and the powers of an independent judiciary would be increased. The chief executive's veto could be overridden by a two-thirds vote of the legislature, for instance, and he could overrule decisions only of the courts of appeal and the highest court. During this middle period, greater freedom would be granted to the communications media and to opposition political parties.

"During the third five-year period and thereafter, the people would be granted unlimited freedom, of speech, worship, the press, political dissent, and so forth. The judiciary would be absolutely independent of the chief executive, and the legislature could override his veto by a simple majority.

"By this schedule, I hope to mandate change as the law of the land. I feel this design will not only be sensitive to the needs and desires of an increasingly sophisticated electorate, but it will reduce social unrest to a minimum. Why plan a revolt or revolution when the constitution clearly states the democratic goals you seek will become law within a few years?"

"Interesting," Captain Anokye said. "And I presume this constitution, after it has been ratified, could be amended, altered, or even totally rescinded?"

"Of course," Duclos said. "By plebiscite."

"Good," the Little Captain said. "That is what I wanted to hear."

The palace gleamed whitely in the glare of floodlights. Fountains splashed. From the flat roof hung garlands of flowers and huge national flags of Asante and Dahomey.

220

Across the plaza, up to the palace door, a double file of guards stood at parade rest in their uniforms of black trousers with white spatterdashes, red tunics, white kaffiyehs bound with agals of goat's hair. All were armed with MAT 49 submachine guns and Colt .45 automatics suspended from white leather holsters.

"Handsome turnout," Anokye said, returning the salute of the lieutenant in command.

"Thank you, sir," the guards officer said languidly, turning away, not at all interested in the opinion of a mere infantry captain.

A sergeant major at the door took their invitations, checked their names off on a master list, and motioned them to the grand ballroom on the ground floor. More prestigious guests were directed up the graceful mahogany stairway to the second-floor landing where King Prempeh IV, the new President of Dahomey, and high-ranking officials of both nations formed a reception line.

"Was Willi Abraham invited?" Duclos whispered to Anokye.

"Oh yes. They were being most correct. He is probably upstairs."

The ballroom blazed with the light of three magnificent crystal chandeliers, inherited from the former governor. French doors to the terrace had been thrown wide, but the room was uncomfortably hot, crowded with at least two hundred perspiring guests. Palace servants circulated with trays of nonalcoholic drinks in paper cups, and a buffet offered sliced meats, side dishes, fresh fruits, and petit fours which, it was said, had been flown in from Paris that morning. A small military band, stationed on a platform at one end of the long room, played a medley of popular airs, one of which was, unaccountably, "Deep in the Heart of Texas."

221

The guests were predominantly male and predominantly black. There was an eye-blinking variety of costumes and uniforms, from embroidered girikes to European-style dinner jackets. The military attaché of the British Embassy wore trews and a white mess jacket, and a Yoruba chief wore a splendid cloak of fine furs and seemed the coolest man in the stifling room.

The few women present displayed as much variety in their dress and hairdos. Curiously, most of the whites wore African fashions, and most of the black women wore Western-style evening gowns and tailored suits. Near the bandstand, a few couples danced sedately, but most of the guests merely stood or circulated slowly. Conversations were muted; even laughter was quiet.

Anokye and Professor Duclos were separated in the crush. The Captain moved casually about the room, nodding to acquaintances, stopping to exchange a few words with fellow officers. He was inspecting the platters of sliced meats on the buffet when he felt a light touch on his arm. He turned to face a white man clad in a dark suit of tropical worsted. The man had obviously suffered a bad sunburn; his entire face seemed to be scaling, and the shoulders of his jacket were covered with a thick scurf.

"Captain Obiri Anokye?"

"Yes."

The man held out a peeling hand.

"Jonathan Wilson. Cultural Attaché at the American Embassy." He spoke a lame French.

They shook hands.

"Too much Asante sun?" Anokye smiled.

"Like an idiot," Wilson nodded. "In bed three days. Didn't realize how close to equator we are. Stupid."

He seemed a pleasant enough young man, only a few inches taller than Anokye, but of a slender build, with narrow shoulders and a flat stomach.

"What happened to Curtin?" Anokye asked.

"Transferred," Wilson said. "Step outside a minute? Get a breath of air?"

The Little Captain nodded and followed Wilson through the crowd, out the French doors onto the tiled terrace. There were fewer people there; they were able to find a relatively secluded place at the balustrade, overlooking a beautifully groomed formal garden dominated by a fine beobab tree in full bloom.

"Tangent not invited," Wilson said. He was not facing Anokye, but spoke softly, his lips barely moving.

"No," Anokye said, "I did not think he would be."

"Asked me to look you up."

"Oh?"

"Said you might be interested."

"In what?"

"Know the French intervention force?"

"I have heard of it, yes. A division stationed near Toulouse?"

"Right. Just moved a regiment to Senegal. Paratroops."

There was a pause.

"I see," Anokye said slowly. "Thank you, Mr. Wilson."

"Pleased to meet you, Captain." Wilson waved, moving away. "Hope we meet again."

The Little Captain sauntered around the terrace. He looked up, but the floodlights obscured the stars. He followed the terrace to the rear of the palace and thence to the other side. There were few people there, some sitting in the shadows on iron settees. A servant came by with a tray, and Anokye took a paper cup of orange juice. It was warm.

He began to retrace his steps. In the rear of the palace, standing at the parapet, a young woman, short, rather plump, turned to face him. It would have been uncultured to ignore her.

"Good evening," he said.

"Good evening—" she said. She glanced at his shoulder insignia. "—captain. Is your drink as warm as mine?"

"Warmer." He smiled. "My name is Captain Obiri Anokye, Headquarters Staff, Fourth Asante Brigade."

"Happy to meet you, Captain," she said, holding out her hand. "I am Beatrice da Silva. From Dahomey."

"Da Silva?" he said. "Portuguese?"

"Yes," she laughed. "My family were Brazilians. Freed slaves."

"You were coming back when most of the others were going?"

She laughed again. "Just so," she said.

Her ring finger was bare.

"And your father?" he asked. "In the army?"

"No," she said. "Government. He's the new Premier."

"Ah," Anokye said, startled for a moment. "Then I presume he is upstairs with the President?"

"I suppose so. I was too, but it got so boring I came down."

"I fear it is not too exciting down here either. I have never been to Dahomey. Tell me about it."

"I don't know as much as I should. I've been away at school in France for the past ten years."

"And you are now home on vacation?"

"No, for good. I've graduated."

"Congratulations!"

"Thank you," she giggled. "There were times I didn't

224

think I'd make it. Anyway, Mommy died last year, and Daddy needs a kind of hostess now, so I came back to stay."

"You miss France?"

"Of course, but I'll get over it. Dahomey is my home, and Daddy really needs me; he's so busy. We do a lot of entertaining. I like that."

They began to stroll slowly back to the ballroom.

"Brothers or sisters?" Anokye asked.

He learned a great deal about her, listening intently to everything she told him. Her ancestors originally came from Abomey, were sold to Portuguese slavers in Porto-Novo, and ended up in Brazil. In 1864 her great-grandparents were part of the exodus of liberated slaves returning to West Africa from South America. They were all called "Brazilians," and applied their new talents, skills, sophistication, and ambition to developing an elite managerial class that won wealth and privilege during the time Dahomey was under French control. After independence was granted, in 1960, the "Brazilians" continued to dominate, in government, business, education, and the arts.

She had two sisters and a brother, all younger than she. Her family was Catholic. Her father was very intelligent and worked very hard. She loved West African food, especially pepper chicken. French food was too bland. She liked to swim in the sea, but the undertow along the Dahomeyan coast could be treacherous. Green was her favorite color. She owned a bicycle. If he must know, she was eighteen and resigned to being an old maid. She had several male "friends," but wasn't serious about any. Had the Captain ever eaten crocodile meat?

All this came pouring from her in an open, ingenuous flow. As she chattered, he listened and, when they came to

225

the lighted doorway to the ballroom, inspected her more closely.

She was almost as dark as he, but there was a rosy undertint to her skin while his had the deep glow of burnished cordovan. She *was* plump, but well-formed; she carried herself with a jaunty youthfulness. The short, beaded evening dress she wore (green, of course!) showed good legs; slender ankles, muscled calves.

Like his sister Sara's, her hair was twigged, braided into short plaits, a dozen at least, tied with small green ribbons. He thought perhaps she was wearing rouge, but no lipstick. Little jade chips hung from pierced ears on tiny golden chains. Her perfume was fruity and sweet.

Open brow. A smooth face, untouched by worry. Or even, he thought, reflection. Laughing mouth. A warm, bubbling, confiding manner. She touched his arm frequently. She was disappointed when he confessed he could not dance, and said, "I must teach you." Young. In years and in spirit.

They spent almost an hour together, a pleasant hour. He spoke little, but her conversation never flagged. He was amused by her often shrewd observations about passing guests:

"Look at that man over there by the buffet. First decent meal he's had in weeks. See how he chomps! There—that lieutenant! Is he holding his breath? No, he's wearing a corset! I swear it! See that woman? It's a wig; I can tell. And not even hair! Some kind of synthetic. Or perhaps wood shavings!"

A Dahomeyan major, wearing staff aiguilettes, came up discreetly, bowed slightly, and informed Miss da Silva her father wished her to rejoin him.

"Bye!" she said to Captain Anokye, gripping his arm.

"Thanks for putting up with my nonsense. Will I see you again?"

"I hope so," he said.

She looked into his eyes, suddenly serious.

"Try," she said.

In a few minutes, there was silence from the military band, then a fanfare that seemed never to end. But it did, and at its conclusion, the closed doors to the entrance hall were thrown open, the band played the Asante national anthem, and King Prempeh IV waddled in, escorting the President of Dahomey. Following came dignitaries of both countries, generals and ministers, ambassadors and colonels, diplomats and majors. All ranked with stiff regard for precedence.

Captain Anokye, on tiptoe, trying to see over the crowd, caught a glimpse of Beatrice da Silva, walking solemnly beside a tall, distinguished man with gray hair and a silvered beard. She kept her eyes straight ahead, but seemed to be biting her lower lip. The Little Captain could guess how close she was to hilarity.

Then the speeches began. King Prempeh conferred upon his dearest friend, the President of Dahomey, the Asante Order of the Triumphant Lion with Laurel Crown. The President conferred upon King Prempeh a newly created Medal of Extreme Valor with Golden Cluster. They embraced. Applause was enthusiastic. Chairs magically appeared. The rulers and a few of their top ministers and aides sat down. Others in the ballroom pressed back to the walls to clear a space on the parquet floor.

Into this area came bounding members of the Asante Royal Dance Company, a troupe supported by the state, that had appeared to great critical acclaim in Moscow, Paris, London, New York, Tokyo, and many other cities. They presented an abbreviated version of their most famous dances: Harvest Celebration, Welcome Home to the Warriors, Full Moon, Young Love, To the Sea God, and River Magic. Accompaniment was provided by a band of flautists and drummers who played everything from tiny bongos to great hollowed logs. The audience responded to the ancient rhythms, clapping their hands, swaying, stamping their feet lightly, chanting softly.

When the entertainment ended, King Prempeh and his honored guests returned to the second floor where, it was said, a lavish state banquet for fifty was being served. The uninvited on the lower level began to straggle toward the exits. Captain Anokye looked about for Professor Duclos and finally found him, pacing impatiently outside the main doorway.

"What a waste of time," Duclos said angrily "Ridiculous! Can you take me home?"

"Of course. Sene is waiting. This way."

Once again they passed between that double file of armed palace guardsmen. Captain Anokye looked at the Muslims closely and was impressed. Big men, with a professional air about them. Many mustached, with short tufts of beard. Hard eyes. He knew they would not die easily.

On the return trip the Little Captain said to Duclos "Tell me more about the duties of the chief executive under this proposed constitution of yours. For instance would he be commander of the armed forces?"

"Of course he would," the Professor said enthusiasti cally. "Commander-in-chief actually, ruling through minister of defense."

"Could he conclude treaties with other nations on hi own authority?"

"During the first five-year period, yes. During th

second period and thereafter, he would require the consent of the legislature."

"Could he declare war?"

"The same conditions as pertain to treaties," Duclos said. "During the first period, the chief executive would be empowered to declare war on his own authority. After five years, he would require the consent of the legislature. An added factor: After ten years, the nation could not go to war without the approval of the electorate. A simple majority would suffice."

"But such things take time. What would the chief executive do in case of invasion or obvious threat of attack—wait for a vote?"

"Not at all. The chief executive would be empowered to use the full strength of the armed forces in time of invasion or national emergency without consulting the legislature or the electorate."

"I am glad to hear it," Captain Anokye said. No irony in his tone. "How many years does the chief executive serve?"

"Five," Duclos said. "He cannot serve two consecutive terms. But he may serve five years, remain out of office for five, then run again for another term. The same holds true for legislators. This is just another factor to insure change and growth, to make certain the government is constantly served by an infusion of new blood, fresh ideas, bold approaches to problems."

"You have thought of everything," the Little Captain said admiringly. "I presume the chief executive is served by a cabinet of ministers?"

"Naturally," Professor Duclos said. "During the first five-year period, the chief executive may appoint whom he pleases. During the second period, his choices must be confirmed by the legislature. During the third period, cabinet positions become elective posts. Everything has been designed to make the new Asante government a living, growing organism.''

"You have all this written down?'' Anokye asked.

"Yes. Roughly. In notebooks. I am almost finished. Then I will organize the material formally, type it up, and submit it for comment.''

"I would not care to have it fall into the King's hands,'' Anokye said. "Guard it well.''

"With my life!'' Professor Jean-Louis Duclos said fervently.

As they turned into the road leading to Duclos' home, Sgt. Yeboa leaned forward suddenly, staring through the windshield.

"Captain,'' he said warningly.

Anokye and Duclos craned to look. At least twenty people milled about in the packed-earth yard in front of Duclos' house.

"What is it?'' the Professor said. "What are they doing? What's happening?''

The crowd saw the Land Rover pull up, rushed to peer through the windows. When they saw Professor Duclos, a loud wail went up, and all began to jabber at once. Captain Anokye climbed from the car, faced the frenetic throng. All the men were speaking loudly at once, all the women were weeping, some rocking back and forth, aprons thrown over their heads in grief. The Captain held up a commanding hand.

"Silence!'' he thundered. When they had quieted, he pointed at one man. "You, speak. Say what happened.''

With frequent interruptions, the story came out. About an hour previously, neighbors had been startled and frightened to hear a loud scream from the Duclos home

They had rushed to investigate and had found Mboa lying on the floor of the kitchen. Her slashed wrists were spouting blood. A fish-scaling knife lay nearby.

While some tried to tie rope and twine tightly about her arms, others had run to the corner fruit and vegetable market, which had the only telephone on the street. They had broken the locked door and had entered to call the gendarmerie.

"Nothing was stolen at the market," the speaker assured Captain Anokye.

A red squad car had soon arrived—"A matter of minutes, sir"—and the gendarmes had taken Mboa to the Mokodi Royal Hospital. Neighbors had called just a few minutes ago, and had been told that while she was still alive, her condition was critical and blood donors were needed. Immediately, several had set off to give blood for Mboa, but since they were walking, and the Hospital was at least two miles away, who knew if they would arrive on time?

As Jean-Louis Duclos listened to this report, his features grew ashen, and he slumped back against the car. Sgt. Yeboa moved to support him. Anokye went into the Duclos home. Stepping over a frighteningly large pool of blood on the kitchen floor, he took a bottle of wine from the cupboard, went back outside, and made Duclos take several small swallows. Then the Professor pushed the bottle away, put his hands to his face, began moaning.

"Sergeant," Anokye said, "take him to the Hospital. Stay with him as long as necessary. Then return to the barracks."

Yeboa assisted Duclos into the front seat of the Land Rover. The Professor seemed in shock.

"I love you, Maria," he kept repeating.

Anokye turned to the neighbors.

"You have done well," he told them. "I am proud of you."

They looked down, shuffled their feet, smiled shyly.

"Mboa is a fine girl," one of the women called loudly and the others nodded.

"Always ready to help," another said.

"Yes," the Little Captain said. "Now please, return to your homes and pray for her recovery."

They dispersed slowly. He stood there until the street was empty, then went back into Duclos' home. He found the notebooks in full view on the desk in the study. He had to go back into that dreadful kitchen—flies and roaches already feasting on the spilled blood—to locate Mboa's string shopping bag. He put all the notebooks inside, then added several pages of rough notes and scribbled references. He turned off the lights and, carrying the bag started walking to the Golden Calf.

He walked slowly; there was much to consider. And he knew, because of the many visitors in the city for the King's reception, Yvonne and her girls would be busy.

There were clouds moving slowly across the moon. The air smelled damply of rain. It intensified all the odors of Asante: the spicy aromas of cooking, perfume of sweet flowers, tangy scent of resinous wood, and beneath all, like a deep diapason, the stirring smell of the land itself, rich and fecund. It seemed to him a land that had lain fallow long enough and was now bursting to be sown.

As usual, he entered the Golden Calf through the kitchen. He went directly to Yvonne Mayer's apartment. She was not there, but the door was unlocked and he entered. He took off tunic, shoes, and socks, and sat down heavily at her desk. She came flying in breathlessly a few moments later, informed of his arrival. She kissed his cheek, told him the house was crowded, with clients waiting in

232

the downstairs parlor, and that she must oversee everything for at least another hour or two.

"Of course," he said. "I understand."

"You promise to wait, Bibi?"

"I promise. Perhaps I shall take a short nap. Before you go back, would you put these notebooks in your safe? Duclos' work on the new government."

She locked them away in a heavy safe built into the wall behind a curtain. Then she kissed him again and was gone.

He locked the door behind her, went to her liquor cabinet and poured himself a small glass of Italian brandy. Then he undressed and, taking the brandy with him, went into the bathroom for a tepid shower. After he dried, he put on Yvonne's kimono, sat down again at her desk, and phoned the Mokodi Royal Hospital. He identified himself and was told that Mboa Aikpe—it was the first time he had heard her surname—was slightly improved, and the prognosis was now guardedly optimistic. Satisfied, he took a deep swallow of brandy. Then he sat stolidly, chin on chest, staring at the complex design of the Chinese rug.

He was still sitting thus, planning, rejecting, accepting, when Yvonne returned almost two hours later. Her face was slack with fatigue. She took the brandy glass from his hand, drained it, shuddered slightly, then smiled wanly.

"I feel tied in knots," she said. "I must have a hot bath. Come in and talk to me."

In the bathroom, he sat on the closed toilet seat and watched her loll in the sudsy water, steam rising. Her eyes closed in bliss. The oiled and scented water slicked her white arms and breasts. Beneath the glimmering surface, pale torso and legs wavered and moved feebly, like a limpid underwater plant bobbing on currents.

He made her laugh with her description of the reception, how the King had made his waddling entrance after a long fanfare of trumpets, how he had received a medal for "extreme valor" from a man he had met that day for the first time and to whom he referred as his "dearest friend."

He told her of what happened later, how they had returned to Duclos' home to discover what Mboa had done, or attempted to do. Yvonne's face showed shock, horror, pity. Her eyes brimmed with tears, but she wiped them away. She was encouraged by the report Anokye had received from the Hospital and vowed to visit Mboa the very next day.

Later, clad in nightgown and peignoir, she sat at the table with the Little Captain and shared a platter of "small things" she had sent up from the kitchen: radishes, cucumbers, pickled melon balls, squares of cold yam, goat cheese, chunks of smoked beef tongue. They cleaned it all up and traded belches. Then sat back, both quiescent, eyes lidded with weariness.

"What happened to Mboa," Anokye said, "is the result of Duclos not speaking what he felt. When he feared she might die, then he knew his love for her and would have spoken of it. But it was almost too late."

"You believe they will marry, Bibi?"

"If she lives, yes, I think so."

"It is a lesson to him," she said, almost angrily.

"A lesson for me, also," he said, looking at her. "I must tell you how I feel toward you."

Her eyes widened in alarm.

"You're leaving me?" she said. "You've come tonight to say goodbye?"

He smiled at her.

"No, Yvonne, not to say good-bye. But you must know I cannot marry you. If the coup succeeds or fails, no difference; we cannot marry."

"Oh *that*," she said, relieved. "I knew that from the

start. I never expected it, never let myself think of it. I am content the way things are, Bibi. I want nothing more from you than what I already have.''

''I speak to you this way because I love you,'' he said. ''I do not believe it is your kind of love, but it is mine. I love you, my family, Sene Yeboa, Willi Abraham, Professor Duclos. Even Peter Tangent. Yes, I love you all.''

''Surely you love me in a different way than you love the others?'' she protested.

''No, Yvonne,'' he said gently. ''I love you all for the faith you have in me.''

''And in bed?'' she asked. ''Does that not count?''

''Surely, it counts,'' he said. ''It is a great happiness for me, but it is not why I love you. Yvonne, I speak so truthfully because of what happened to Duclos tonight. Also, I know your intelligence, your knowledge of people and why they act as they do. I have told you more of my plans and hopes than I have told anyone else. Because I value your counsel and your friendship. You know this?''

''Yes.''

''I want to continue that friendship. But I must tell you this: tonight at the reception I met a woman I wish to marry.''

She stared at him, puzzled.

''You met her tonight? For the first time?''

''Yes. I do not know if she wishes to marry me, or will wish to if I am able to see her again. Or even if her father will allow her to marry me.''

''Who is her father?''

''He is the new Premier of Dahomey.''

''Ah!''

''Yes. At this time, there is no question of love between this woman and myself. I spoke to her for only an hour. But I feel she is interested in me. It would be an advantageous match. If I can convince her. And her father.''

"If you wish to, you will," she said. "And me? If you marry?"

"I would want things to continue as they have been," he said. "That is my wish. But the decision is yours to make. That is why I tell you this now."

"But *could* we continue?" she asked. "It would be difficult."

"Difficult, yes," he agreed. "But I believe it could be done. If you desire it."

She tried to laugh.

"I knew you could not marry me and I was content," she said. "But now I am not so content, sharing you with another woman."

"I would not change to you."

"I know that, Bibi, but still . . ."

"I said it was your decision. If you wish not to see me again, I will accept that. It will sadden me, but I will understand."

"I don't know," she said. She rose, began to pace about the room. "I don't know what to do, what to say."

"It is not necessary to decide now, at this moment," he said. "Consider it for a time. I may never marry this woman."

"But if not her, then someone else?"

"Yes," he said, "that is true. Eventually. If not her, then someone else."

"Is she beautiful?"

"No, not as you. She is short, heavy, young."

"Oh!" she said bitterly. "Young!"

"It means nothing to me," he said. "You know that."

"But her father means something?"

"Yes. Will you consider it, Yvonne?"

"I suppose so."

"Do you wish me to leave now?"

"Yes. No. Yes. I don't know what I want. *Tell* me, Bibi!"

In bed, he lay beside her, a few inches away, their naked bodies not touching. But he stroked her with his strong fingers until her rigidity melted, the knot within her loosened, limbs relaxed, flesh became warm and yielding.

"I don't care," she said. "Don't care. I can't give you up. *Can't!* Please, Bibi, never go away from me. Swear it."

"I swear it."

She dug a hand, an arm, beneath him and pulled, tugged, until he rolled over on top of her. She spread her thighs wide, bent her knees, linked her ankles behind his back. She gripped his hair fiercely, pulled his face close to hers.

"If you desert me," she whispered, "if you deny what you have sworn to me, then I will do what Mboa did tonight. But I shall succeed. And after I am dead, I will come back and put a curse on you. All you have worked for and dreamed will come to nothing. You will fail. If you desert me."

He shivered and pressed closer.

"Do you believe what I have said?" she demanded.

"I believe."

Then she was all molten heat, seeking his brutality, clutching him and moaning and calling him "lord," and "King," and "master."

24

"NO, NO, MR. GREELEY," Captain Anokye said. "I don't think that would work at all."

"What? What?" the chief teller barked. Indignant.

They were standing at Greeley's study table, looking down at a map of Asante. Perched on the city of Mokodi, covering the suburbs and port area, was a French chasseur-à-cheval, a trooper of the 19th Century Imperial Guard. His little carbine and sword were finely detailed.

"In planning this military maneuver," Anokye patiently explained, "I have tried to put myself into the mind of a rebel leader planning a coup d'etat. I assume his resources are limited, perhaps no more than a few hundred trained and armed followers. Even granting the citizens were sympathetic to his cause, how could he hope to take Mokodi?"

"Strike for the jugular!" cried Alistair Greeley.

"No, sir," the Little Captain disagreed. "Not armed only with rifles and sidearms. Not when taking Mokodi means taking the palace. That would mean attacking the guard—superbly trained, well equipped, almost fanatical professionals. The rebellion would bleed to death on the plaza before they could get close enough to toss a single grenade through a palace window."

"Then what do you suggest? What? What?"

"Here," Anokye said. He lifted the model soldier gently and set it down so that it covered a circle marking the city of Gonja.

238

Greeley looked up in puzzlement. "Why there?"

"Gonja is almost in the exact center of Asante. It dominates the north-south Royal Highway. It is the hub of all these secondary roads—here, here, and here. Hardly a kilo of food reaches Mokodi that hasn't first passed through Gonja. In addition, the pipeline bringing fresh water from the north runs alongside the highway. The main pumping station is here, a few kilometers south of the city. If you control Gonja, you control the capital's food and water."

"Starve 'em out?" Greeley asked.

"Exactly. But there are other factors just as important. The Gonja armory is the largest in the country outside of the Mokodi barracks. If the rebels took Gonja, they'd have an excellent source of weapons and ammunition to supply their own needs and to arm their supporters. The Gonja garrison, including the arsenal, is lightly manned and guarded. A determined insurgent cadre could capture it easily. Then, with a greater force adequately armed, it could move down the highway to lay siege to Mokodi."

"Softening it up by cutting off the food supply and water?"

"Precisely. Under the circumstances, I think the public would force the capitulation of the government to the rebels' demands. The palace would be surrendered without a shot being fired."

"That is how you intend to do it?" Greeley asked. His eyes were wise.

"That is how I believe it *could* be done," Captain Anokey corrected him. "Do you agree with me, sir?"

"Absolutely!" Greeley cried. "Very ingenious, Captain. My congratulations."

"Your teaching," the Little Captain smiled. "You have repeated many times that 'War is geography.' "

"But what about Kumasi and Kasai?"

"Of minor importance. Once Gonja is taken, those towns would simply wither, to surrender after the capital falls. Besides, they are outside the physical area in which I will conduct this exercise."

"But you feel the rebels' main thrust would be at Gonja?"

"Correct," Captain Anokye nodded gravely. "The city itself, the garrison and arsenal, and the pumping station. This is the problem I mean to assign my junior officers the morning of the maneuver."

"And when will that be?" Greeley asked.

Captain Anokye, studying the map intently, looked up.

"Pardon me, sir? I didn't hear."

"When do you plan this maneuver to take place?"

"I've scheduled it for the twelfth of August. To start in the morning."

"The sooner the better," Greeley said excitedly. "What? What?"

"True, Mr. Greeley," Anokye said. "The sooner the better."

The agreement between Anokye and the Nyam specified that each could be accompanied by a single aide. The meeting was to be held in the back room of a waterfront bar. It happened to be the place where Sene Yeboa had stomped to death the rebel who had threatened the Little Captain. But the sergeant said nothing of this as he and Anokye drove directly to the rendezvous from the home of Alistair Greeley. The Captain and Yeboa wore civilian clothes. Both were armed. They parked several blocks away, locked the Land Rover, walked through the darkened streets to the bar.

240

The Nyam and his aide had already arrived, wearing soiled raincoats and black berets. They sat at one table in the empty, dimly lighted room. Anokye and the sergeant sat at a table facing them, about two meters away. No greetings were exchanged; no drinks were offered or ordered.

"The weapons?" the Nyam asked at once. "Where are the weapons?"

As before, he could not sit quietly, but thrust his feet out, drew them back, changed his position, straightening, slumping. His fingertips flicked off his thumbs constantly in a tic he could not control. But his burning eyes never left Anokye's face.

"You will receive them within a week," the Little Captain said. "A hundred Russian assault rifles with sufficient ammunition."

"Kalashnikovs?" the Nyam asked.

"Yes. Will you require instruction on their use?"

The Nyam's aide laughed suddenly, a brief, harsh sound in the shadowed room.

"No," the Nyam said. He showed large, yellowed teeth beneath the thick black mustache. "We know how to use them. What else?"

"That is all."

"All? No machine guns? No mortars?"

"Machine guns are primarily defensive weapons," Captain Anokye said. "You will have no need for them. The few mortars we have will not be available to you. But you will be able to obtain others?"

"Oh? And how may I do that?"

"By attacking and capturing the garrison and armory at Gonja. Whatever weapons you liberate are yours."

The Nyam straightened, leaned forward eagerly.

"And vehicles?"

"Vehicles also. Food. Equipment. Whatever the garrison contains."

"How many men are stationed there?"

"Sergeant?" Anokye said, turning his head slightly.

"Not more than fifty, sir," Yeboa said. "Probably less."

The Nyam, in turn, glanced at his aide. The rebel nodded briefly.

"A surprise assault," Anokye said. "You should have no problems. Discipline is lax in Third Brigade. There is one guard at the gate. No perimeter defense. The morning meal is at oh six hundred. I suggest you attack then."

"And where will you be?"

"In Mokodi."

"Ah? Taking the palace? Installing yourself as president—or king?"

"No, I will not be doing that," Anokye said sternly. "My men will be taking over the Mokodi barracks, neutralizing the navy and air force, the tank, engineer, and supply units, seizing the power station, newspaper and cable offices, and establishing control of all roads leading into the city. The assault on the palace will not commence until you and your men arrive from Gonja, after you have captured the garrison."

The Nyam stared at him a moment, his heavy lids drooping.

"You give your word on this?" he demanded.

"It is not a question of giving my word," Anokye said. "I will not have sufficient men to do everything that must be done and assault the palace by myself. I will need your help, and I will wait for it. I suggest that as soon as the Gonja garrison is taken, you bring your men to Mokodi as quickly as possible. In captured military vehicles or in commandeered civilian trucks and cars."

The Nyam thought awhile. Perhaps he had a mental image of a glorious armed convoy speeding south to Mokodi. Himself standing erect in the leading jeep, an automatic rifle cradled in his arms. Flags and pennants snapping. Citizens along the way cheering and throwing flowers . . .

Anokye and Yeboa waited patiently, expressionless.

"How do you intend to assault the palace?" the Nyam asked finally, and they knew they had won.

"With the mortars we have," Anokye said. "And those you bring."

"Good," the Nyam said, eyes glistening. "We will bury the running dogs of the colonial imperialists in a fitting tomb, the ruins of their own palace."

"Yes," the Little Captain said tonelessly. "Be prepared to move any day after the first of August. I will give you twenty-four hours' notice. Is that sufficient?"

"Yes, enough," the Nyam said. "Where will we receive the weapons?"

"Can you receive them on the coast? Or shall we truck them inland?"

Again the Nyam looked to his aide. The rebel bent forward, put his lips close to the Nyam's ear. The two men whispered a moment.

"The coast," the Nyam said finally. "We will make our own arrangements."

"As you wish. I will inform you when and where they will arrive. Is there anything else?"

"Yes," the Nyam said. "The King must die. Or he will remain a constant threat to the new Asante."

Captain Anokye shrugged. "What will be, will be. The battle itself will dictate who lives and who dies."

"Do you intend to take prisoners?" the Nyam demanded.

243

"The men of Third Brigade, yes. They are loyal Asantis, but badly led. I believe many will surrender and come to our side. The palace guard will not surrender. It will be necessary to kill them."

"Good," the Nyam said. "We will meet again before the attack?"

"Once again. To decide on timing, passwords, and so forth. Is there some way your people can be identified? By clothing or insignia? So my men will not fire upon them?"

The Nyam pondered a moment. The aide leaned forward again to whisper in his ear.

"Yes, good," the Nyam said. "Katsuva suggests a piece of red cloth tied around the right arm."

"Excellent," Anokye said. "I will have my people informed that those wearing red armbands are to be treated as brothers."

"Have you thought more on the organization of the new government?" the Nyam asked.

"No," the Little Captain said. "As I told you, I am a soldier, not a politico. I leave the formation of a new government to you. I would like to be commander of the armed forces."

"Of course," the Nyam said.

The Captain and Sgt. Yeboa departed first. The Nyam and his aide watched them go. They waited in silence a few moments. Katsuva went to the curtained doorway and peeked out, making certain the soldiers had departed. Then he came back to the Nyam.

"You trust him?" he asked.

"So far and no farther," the Nyam said, grinning. "We will capture the Gonja garrison, then go to Mokodi to assist in the destruction of the palace." He paused to stare at his aide. "As he said, the battle will dictate who lives and who dies. Can you take care of it?"

Katsuva nodded. "He will die a hero's death," he said. "All Asante will grieve."

"Mrs. Greeley!" Peter A. Tangent caroled. "What a pleasant surprise!"

As planned, they had met "accidentally" on the sidewalk near the Restaurant Cleopatra. It was their third meeting. At the second, they had agreed upon a final price of three thousand British pounds. Mrs. Greeley received half of this as a down payment. She was to receive an additional 500 each time she reported to Tangent on her husband's telephoned conversations with Anatole Garde, until the final payment had been made.

"In the event the number of your reports of the telephone calls exceeds the agreed-upon total payment of three thousand pounds," Tangent had explained precisely, "payment for the said additional reports will be made at a rate of fifty pounds per report. Is that satisfactory?"

"What?" Mrs. Greeley had said.

It was not that Tangent expected her betrayal of her husband to be of any further value. They already knew what they needed to know. It was just that he wanted to foreclose the possibility of her hawking her wares elsewhere. Like informing Anatole Garde of what she had told Tangent. He wanted her secure. Money would do it.

Now, chatting loudly for the benefit of any observer/listener, he steered her into the dim, cool interior of the Cleopatra. At that hour, the place was almost empty, as he knew it would be. They sat at a far corner table, and Tangent handed over his folded copy of the Asante *New Times*. Within its folds nestled her payment of 500 pounds. Without peeking, she put the paper into her tapestry knitting bag. When the waiter came up, she ordered a sloe gin fizz. Tangent had a vodka gimlet.

After the drinks had been served, he said, "Well?"

Like a schoolgirl reciting a memorized theme, she rattled off what her husband had said to Anatole Garde on the phone the previous evening. Tangent listened closely, not interrupting. When she had finished, they both took sips of their drinks. Then he leaned forward over the table. She leaned forward. Their heads almost touched.

"Two points," he said in a low voice. "You're certain he told Garde that the main attack would be at Gonja?"

"Absolutely."

"And he told him the maneuver would start on the morning of August twelfth?"

"Absolutely."

"Thank you." Tangent said back, smiling. "And how is your lovely sister-in-law?" he inquired.

"Very well, thank you," Maud Greeley said primly. She could not meet his eyes.

"A small problem, Mrs. Greeley," he said. "I'll be away for two or three days. So don't panic if you can't contact me. I expect to return by Wednesday morning. If you have anything to report, just save it till then."

"Taking a little vacation?" she said archly.

"Something like that," he said.

25

AFTER THAT WALPURGISNACHT at the Hôtel d'Azur, Peter Tangent was nagged by the fear that he had hired a bunch of drunken clowns. But when he boarded the trawler late that Sunday night at the Sassandra wharf, he was gratified to find an unexpectedly sober and professional crew of mercenaries.

They went about the task of loading with the ease of long experience. The boom swung in and out like a metronome, the electric winch whined efficiently, the wooden crates set down into the midships hold with a solid thump. The men rarely spoke. When they did, it was mostly in obscenities directed toward inanimate objects:

To a crate of rifles: "Get up there, you motherfucker."

To a coil of rope: "Get out of my way, you shit-brained cock sucker."

To a case of grenades that came apart: "I'll get you for that, you cunt-lapping whoreson."

And so forth . . .

Sam Leiberman was directing the loading with gestures and grunts. Yakubu, tall, skinny, still wearing his red bandanna and the gold ring in his left ear, manhandled the crates into the cargo net on the dock. Shagari, as dirty as before, a villain, unloaded the cargo net below. The winch was operated by Shagari's cousin, who seemed to be known to the others simply as "Cousin." He was short, fat, wearing a dark green undershirt bulged by almost feminine breasts. He chomped a cold, wet cigar.

The whole operation seemed to be taking place with little effort at secrecy or concealment. Leiberman had assured Tangent that the dock watchman, the Ivory Coast gendarmes, and the harbor master had all been adequately dashed. But it still seemed incredible to Tangent that they were loading, quite openly, a shipment of arms to be used in overthrowing a legitimate African government. He felt, somehow, there should be bull's-eye lanterns, muttered passwords, armed lookouts.

When he mentioned this, the mercenary looked at him in astonishment.

"Guns go out of here every day in the week," he said. "For God's sake, it's *business*."

But Tangent's most serious doubts were reserved for the trawler itself. It was called *La Belle Dame*, and after one look, Tangent thought the *Sans Merci* could well be added.

It was certainly the strangest boat he had ever seen. He was ready for an old boat, even an ancient boat. And he guessed it would be filthy, cluttered, smelly, and uncomfortable. But he was not prepared for that design, if design it was and not just a crazy, haphazard joining of disparate sections.

A lofty pilothouse (with small cabin and engine room below) was shoved far aft. The foredeck, which appeared to be planked with sections of used crates still showing the original stenciling, extended only three meters back from the clumsy prow. Between this flimsy deck and the aft pilothouse was, almost literally, nothing. Only a large open hold from which a leaning mast and cargo boom protruded. On both sides of this enormous black hole, narrow catwalks ran fore and aft.

What worried Tangent was the freeboard, the distance between the surface of the water and the low gunnel of that midships hold. As *La Belle Dame* was loaded, it sank farther and farther until it seemed to Tangent that a wavelet in a park lake might be sufficient to lap over and swamp them, let alone the open sea.

He mentioned this to Leiberman.

"Nah. I been out in this tub before. She'll do."

"What if we run into rough weather?"

"Then she won't do. You want off?"

"No," Tangent said. "I can swim."

"Bully for you," Leiberman said. "I can't. But I'm not worried because my heart is pure. That's the last load. Now we add the fish."

And so they did. Not even bothering to use a tarp over the crates of weapons, but shoveling fish on top and spreading them around to make a reasonably effective cover. Within moments it appeared the trawler's hold was filled with a fine catch.

"Never stand any kind of inspection," Leiberman said, "but nothing else would either."

Final preparation included loading demijohns of wine and water, bread, cooked meats, some cold fufu, baked yams, fresh fruit, tins of sardines, cans of orange juice, paper cups and plates, etc. Coffee. Two bottles of Scotch and one of brandy. And two large cardboard cartons containing Leiberman's personal gear: an M3, two Uzis, three fragmentation grenades, an old Springfield with telescopic sight, a Colt .45, a Smith & Wesson .38, a delicate .22 with pearl grips, an old Very pistol with two flares, ammunition, a flashlight, a mayonnaise jar filled with a plastic explosive, caps, fuse, wire, a metal tea box filled with black gunpowder, binoculars, and a small tin mezuzah.

"Nearer, my God, to Thee," Leiberman said cheerfully.

They got underway about 0230, running lights rigged, and Tangent took as a good omen the fact that the engine farted into life almost immediately, and settled down to a comfortable pant. They headed out of the harbor, Cousin at the wheel, and within minutes were chugging slowly eastward, close enough to the coast to mark the lights of Sassandra, Grand-Lahou, Dabou, and Port Bouet.

"Ah, this is the life," Leiberman sighed. He was sitting on the midships catwalk, his legs dangling down into the hold. "Give me a stout ship, a merry crew, and a fair wind. Then Ho! for the Indies. How about a wee bit of the old nasty before we turn in?"

Tangent joined him, bringing a bottle of Scotch and paper cups. They filled their cups, then passed the bottle up to Shagari and Cousin in the pilothouse. Yakubu had taken a demijohn of wine to the foredeck and was sprawled out on his back, staring at the night sky and crooning softly.

"What's he singing?" Tangent asked.

"Some bush thing," Leiberman said. "About a warrior who turned into a snake. I know a guy who took a cunt for a drive and turned into a motel. Here's looking at you."

They sat silently awhile, sipping their Scotch.

"Nice night," Tangent said, looking about.

Leiberman grunted, leaning back against the gunnel. He held his paper cup atop his thick belly.

The offshore breeze brought the sultry smell of the land, sweet and stirring. The wake gurgled pleasantly. Above, the stars whirled their shining courses.

"So many," Tangent murmured. "So close. So much brighter than at home."

"Home?" Leiberman said. "Where you from, Tangent? Ohio?"

"Indiana."

"No shit? I never would have guessed it. You know how I tell guys from Indiana? They never untie their ties when they get undressed at night. They slip the knot down on the short end and pull the tie off over their heads. After a while the tie gets worn, and the stuffing starts to come out. You see a guy with the stuffing coming out of his tie, and the odds are ten to one he's from Indiana. Bet you can't guess where I'm from."

"Burbank, California," Tangent said.

Leiberman turned to look at him.

"You sonofabitch," he said softly. "You got a file on me, haven't you?"

"That's right," Tangent said equably. "I like to know who I'm hiring."

"How did you get in the oil business?"

"The money's good," Tangent said. "How did you get in the war business?"

"The money's good," Leiberman said. "If you live to collect. No pension, but you don't have to kiss too many asses. You're a queer duck."

"Queer? How?"

"I told you. I can't figure your angle on this Asante thing."

"Strictly business."

"Bullshit. You act like it's some kind of personal crusade."

"That's ridiculous," Tangent said. "Oil is what it's all about."

"If you say so," Leiberman sighed. "Get that bottle back; I need a refill. And get me another paper cup; this one is beginning to leak."

Tangent obeyed, rising cautiously and stepping carefully along the catwalk to the pilothouse deck. Shagari was asleep, wedged into a corner, snoring heavily. Cousin was still at the wheel, his eyes half-closed. The wet cigar, unlighted, was clamped in his teeth, chewed down to a butt. Tangent took the opened Scotch bottle and paper cups back to Leiberman.

"Married, Tangent?"

"No."

"Ever been?"

"No. How about you?"

"You mean it's not in that file of yours?" Leiberman jeered. "Shit, I got wives and kids all over the place. Of course, most of them were bush marriages, performed by some joker wearing a coconut mask and a feathered jock-strap. But I guess they made as much sense as saying 'I do' in a Stateside church and having a handful of rice tossed in your kisser."

"What's going to happen when you get old?" Tangent asked softly.

"In my business, no one gets old. But *no* one."

"How old are you?"

"On the sunny side of forty-five."

"Which side is that?"

"The other side," Leiberman said. "The down side. But I can still outfight and outfuck you any day of the week and twice on Sundays."

"I believe it," Tangent said. "Ever been scared? Not when you're fucking, when you're fighting."

"Scared?" Leiberman said. "Goddamned right. All the time. That's the kick. Feeling it and putting it away from you. Ever been in a firefight, Tangent?"

"No, I never have."

"If you go along with the Little Captain when he makes his move, you'll be in a firefight."

"I know."

"You're liable to shit your pants."

"I suppose so," Tangent sighed. "I'm not very brave."

"Who the hell is?" Leiberman asked. "The last party I went to—this was in the Congo—this big stud came at me with a sticker about ten feet long. I was carrying a machine pistol, some piece of Polish junk. So this guy came at me with this sticker, and I pulled the trigger, and the gun fell apart. I mean the whole goddamned gun literally fell apart. Lousy Polish joke."

"What did you do?" Tangent asked breathlessly.

"I started reciting the kaddish."

"No, no kidding, what happened?"

"He tripped," Leiberman said. "Can you believe it? This jungle-trained paskudnyak tripped over a vine and went flying ass over teakettle."

"Did you kill him?"

"Kill him, shit," Leiberman said. "I ran like a goosed golem. That's what I'm trying to tell you. There are times to be brave and times not to be stupid. Enough of this philosophy; let's get some sleep."

They slept in the tiny, bare cabin, taking off their shoes but not undressing. Tangent was certain he would be long awake in those strange surroundings. But he fell asleep almost instantly. He awoke once, toward dawn, and opened his eyes to see Leiberman up, yawning, trying to work the stiffness out of his shoulders and knees.

"Taking the wheel for a while," the mercenary whispered. "Go on back to sleep. I'll wake you if we sink."

Tangent closed his eyes and drowsed. After a while he awoke, looked at his watch, saw it was almost 0900. He heard Leiberman's footsteps overhead. It had to be Leiberman; the other three were barefoot. Tangent rose cautiously; he could not stand upright in the cramped cabin. Leaning against a bulkhead, he pulled on his shoes,

253

then climbed the short ladder and stepped out onto the narrow deck that circled the pilothouse.

It was a blazing morning, hot and clear. To the westward, directly aft, the Atlantic Ocean stretched to a far horizon, heaving gently. Off the port beam was the green coast of Africa, a section of rain forest that came down almost to the sea. There were other boats in the area, small fishing craft, a rusty freighter directly ahead, and far out to starboard a white, rakeo-stack cruise ship. *La Belle Dame* chugged on, slowly and steadily. Tangent was pleased.

"Where are we?" he asked Yakubu.

"Off Ghana," the black said. "Past Cape Three Points. Coming up to Cape Coast."

"Right on the old kazoo," Sam Leiberman said. "We may have to kill some time before the meet. Have some breakfast."

Tangent had a can of warm orange juice, ate two slices of dry bread and a mango, drank three cups of black, chicory-laced coffee. Like the other men, he pissed over the side. There was a small head off the little cabin, the zinc toilet flushed by seawater, but the closet was so smelly that Sam Leiberman preferred to let down his pants and underdrawers and sit on the midships gunnel, his great white ass stuck out over the sea. Shagari şaid something to him in Boulé. Leiberman replied in kind, and the three blacks got hysterical.

"What was that about?" Tangent said.

"Shagari said a shark would come up out of the water and bite my ass off. I told him sharks won't eat kosher meat."

"Hilarious," Tangent said, and opted for self-imposed constipation before he would follow Leiberman's example or dare the stench of the below-decks head.

Cousin showed him the compass, pointed out the heading, and handed over the wheel without comment. He went below with Shagari. Yakubu went to his favorite spot on the foredeck. Leiberman began to disassemble and clean the tools of his trade on the pilothouse catwalk. Tangent was left alone, nervous at the wheel, making little adjustments to keep his course exact.

"Relax," Leiberman called from outside. "Take it easy. If you go off, you can always correct. We got plenty of bottom around here. You're not going to pile us up."

After that, it was fun. Standing erect at the wheel, feeling the throb of the engine through his soles. Most of the pilothouse windows were broken; a cool sea breeze came billowing through.

"Haul down your mains'l stays'l fores'l jib," Leiberman yelled. "Run out the port battery. You may fire when ready, Gridley."

Tangent grinned. He really did feel that way. He gripped the wheel firmly, surveyed the ocean grandly. In a few moments they ran into a brief rain squall, mild as mist. Then they were through, and he saw a rainbow. He didn't want to be anywhere else.

The day went pleasantly. By nightfall, they were coming up to Accra and nearing the coast of Asante. Cousin slowed the engine until they were barely making headway, sea mercifully calm, sky clear. Shagari put a line over the side and caught a nice bass which he gutted, skinned, and cut up. The three blacks and Leiberman ate it raw, but Tangent passed. He ate half a roast chicken, fufu, yams, and some canned fruit salad. He was ravenous.

At dusk, Leiberman took a loaded Uzi and extra magazines to the foredeck where he had a long, huddled conference with Yakubu. The weapon and ammunition were left there, concealed under a scrap of greasy canvas.

255

Leiberman came back to the pilothouse. He pulled the Colt .45 from his box of tricks and handed it to Tangent.

"Ever fire one of these?"

"No," Tangent said. "My God, it's heavy."

"This little gizmo here is the safety. Off. On. There's another safety in the grip, so you've got to grab it hard or it won't fire. This dingus releases the magazine. See—full clip. You jack one into the chamber. When you want to fire, grab the gun with your right hand. Support your right hand with your left. Tight! Hold the gun out in front of you, two-handed. Try it."

Tangent did.

"Bend your elbows a little. Bring it in closer. That's it. Okay, let's say the safety is off. You're gripping it hard with both hands. Then you point it at what you want to hit, close your eyes, and blast away. Keep pulling that trigger until the gun is empty. And hang on, or the whole damned thing will go flying away over your right shoulder."

"You must think I'm some kind of an idiot," Tangent said.

"Behind a desk you're a genius," Leiberman said. "Out here you're an idiot."

"Why should I close my eyes before I fire?"

"Because you'll be too spooked to aim. Because you'll close them anyway after the first shot. This thing makes a noise like a one-oh-five howitzer. Just spray bullets. You may hit something. All right, give it back. I'll keep it for now."

They were nearing Asante waters, and Leiberman started giving orders. For the rest of the trip he wanted one man awake at the wheel and one man awake on the foredeck, as lookout. On the first four-hour trick, Shagari took the wheel, and Tangent went forward. At first, he liked it up there; the trawler was heading into the wind, and he couldn't smell the strong odor of rotting fish coming from the hold.

Like most African nights, this one came suddenly. One minute the swollen red sun was bobbing on the western horizon, the next minute it was gone. Darkness moved in; Tangent shivered. There was a waist-high rail about the prow. He hung on to that and strained his eyes for lights, shapes, anything. He kept turning, as Leiberman had instructed, making a 360-degree inspection of the sea about them. There were a few lights, far off, but these soon faded. Then *La Belle Dame* seemed alone in a black world, puffing quietly eastward, kicking up sprinkles of phosphorescence at bow and stern.

Tangent kept glancing at the luminous dial of his wristwatch. He thought it had stopped, but it hadn't; time had. It was, he thought, the longest four hours of his life.

And the darkness was not only out there; it entered into him. Now he saw the Asante coup d'etat as an act of madness, doomed to failure. Captain Anokye was just another military opportunist. Sam Leiberman was an over-the-hill buffoon, not to be relied on. And Tangent himself was a foolish romantic, hoping to cure the sour desperation of his life with this wild fantasy, a comic opera of armed peasants coming down from the hills, singing; a gorgeously uniformed young officer flourishing a sword, singing; a fat bemedaled tyrant robbing Asante's treasury, singing. Sigmund Romberg could have plotted it. Or Victor Herbert. It lacked only a 40-piece orchestra and a blond heroine, singing, with Mary Pickford curls, six dirndl skirts, and a laced bodice.

Finally, the fantasia became so grotesque he began laughing, silently, and was still laughing when Yakubu relieved him, and he could go aft for a paper cup of whiskey and try to sleep.

There was a thick morning fog the next day, billowing right down to the surface. The sea moved oilily, not even a tiny whitecap to be seen. The fog burned off by noon, and they changed course to pass the island of Zabar to port. But they were close enough to see villages, fishing boats drawn up on the beach, donkey carts on the roads. Beyond, Mokodi was hidden in a shimmering haze, glowing. The Promised Land.

"We'll run down to Lomé to waste time," Leiberman decreed. "Turn around after sundown and run back. If anyone stops us before dark, we're on our way to Lagos."

"And if anyone stops us after dark?" Tangent asked.

Leiberman looked at him.

When they made their turn at dusk off Togo, Cousin took them farther out to sea so they might approach Zabar directly from the south, keeping the land mass of the island between them and Mokodi. Leiberman and Tangent went down into the stifling, fume-choked engine room. They smeared heavy black grease on their white faces, arms, backs of their hands. When they came back up on deck, Shagari was lowering the cargo boom to make it ready to swing over the port side. It would carry a green light, the signal for Zuni Anokye to bring out his fishing boats.

Leiberman handed the Colt .45 to Tangent. "Don't stick it in your belt," he advised. "You're liable to shoot your balls off. Stay inside the pilothouse. Sit on the deck. Make sure your head is below window level. Keep the gun close to you. Someplace where it won't slide around."

"Where will you be?"

"Don't worry about me. Just keep down out of sight. And stay there until I tell you otherwise."

Tangent obeyed, beginning to feel a tightness. Not fear, he told himself. It wasn't fear; it was just a tightness, a kind of tension.

"A tot of rum all around," Leiberman said, opening the second bottle of Scotch. "Cures the fantods and narrows the sphincter."

South of Zabar, out in the Gulf of Guinea, the sea was rougher. Waves began to lap over the midship gunnels, splashing down on the fish below. But then Cousin spun the wheel, changing course to head directly for Zabar. Then it was a following sea, and they shipped no more waves.

The engine was throttled down. Now it was almost purring. The trawler was barely moving.

Leiberman stood near Cousin in the pilothouse, staring directly ahead. He was holding a Uzi cradled in his arms. The S&W .38 was pushed halfway into his side pocket.

"Looking for three red lights," he explained to Tangent. "One on the beach, one farther inland, one on a hill. When we get them lined up, we're in position."

In a few moments, Cousin made a small sound and jerked his head to port. Leiberman went to a window.

"That's one all right," he said. "Bring her around a little, Cousin. There's another. Hold this course."

They finally found the third red light, almost hidden in the dim glow coming from a small village. Cousin worked the wheel carefully until they had the three red lights lined up. Then *La Belle Dame* retreated about two kilometers until the lights dimmed and could barely be seen. The engine was stopped, running lights extinguished. The boom was swung out over the port gunnel. At its end was fastened a battery-powered lantern showing a green light toward the shore of Zabar.

"Now we wait," Leiberman whispered. "Keep the

259

noise down. No smoking. Tangent, what time you got?"

"Twenty-three forty-three."

"I make it forty-five. Close enough. If anything is copesetic, they should be here in ten-fifteen minutes."

"Anchor?" Tangent whispered.

"Nah. Probably too deep for what this tub carries. Besides, we might want to haul ass in a hurry."

They waited in the darkness. Sitting on the deck of the pilothouse, Tangent could see nothing but a dim night-glow through the broken windows. The tightness was swelling in him. His bladder felt full, and he realized he was gulping rapid, shallow breaths. He forced himself to breathe deeply, slowly.

Cousin hissed something, in Boulé.

"What?" Leiberman said.

Cousin repeated, louder.

"Son of a bitch," Leiberman said. "He says he hears a boat engine. Off to starboard. Not our boys. They got nothing but sails."

In a moment they all heard it: a faint rumble, growing louder. Yakubu shifted position on the foredeck, squatting on his hams near the scrap of canvas covering the Uzi. Shagari moved to lean against the pilothouse door.

The sound grew louder—a throaty cough. Cousin said something.

"He can see running lights," Leiberman reported to Tangent. "A launch, he thinks."

The sound increased—a burbling roar. Suddenly a searchlight snapped on. A yellow beam began to sweep the sea. It moved toward them slowly.

" 'Mother of God,' " Leiberman quoted, " 'is this the end of Rico?' "

He kneeled near Tangent, peering over a window ledge.

But when the searchlight caught them, he ducked down, the Uzi held across his chest.

The light grew brighter, the engine louder, as the boat came up to them. Cousin muttered something.

"Asante navy," Leiberman whispered to Tangent. "One of their lousy motor launches. Looking for smugglers."

The launch came up on the starboard side. The engine diminished to a low growl. The searchlight probed back and forth slowly, finding Yakubu on the foredeck. Then it returned to glare on the pilothouse and remain there.

"Asante naval launch *Griselda*," someone shouted, in French. "Stop your engine."

"We are already stopped, excellency," Shagari yelled back. "We are not moving. Our engine has failed."

"Who are you?"

"Fishing trawler *La Bella Dame*, sir. Out of Accra."

"What are you doing in Asante waters?"

"We went to Lomé to sell our catch, excellency. But no one would buy. We were on our way back. But our engine died."

"Where are your lights?" the voice yelled.

"They went out when the engine failed, sir. All we have is that green battery lantern."

"Nice try but no cigar," Leiberman whispered to Tangent. "He'll know that's a lot of bullshit."

"How many men?" the voice called.

"Three, sir."

"Stand by. We are coming aboard."

"That does it," Leiberman muttered to Tangent. "Son of a *bitch!* Keep your head down."

The launch backed, then came forward slowly along the starboard rail. There were five men on deck. One sailor operated the searchlight; one stood behind a .30 caliber machine gun mounted on a swivel atop an eye-level pipe. A third was at the wheel in the open, lighted cockpit. An officer stood near him. The fifth sailor reached toward the trawler's gunnel with a boat hook.

"Whew! What a stink!" the officer yelled. "No wonder you could not sell your catch."

"We have been drifting out here all day in the hot sun, excellency."

"Why didn't you throw your fish overboard?"

"In Accra we can sell them for fertilizer," Shagari said. "Please not to come aboard, excellency. You will soil your uniforms."

For a moment, Leiberman thought it might work. But then the two boats crunched together.

"Go over and take a look," the officer commanded the sailor with the boat hook. "Make sure they have nothing but rotting fish."

Using his boat hook as a balancing pole, the sailor stepped up lightly onto the catwalk alongside the trawler's hold.

"Put the light down here," he called to the man on the launch.

The searchlight was lowered to illuminate the hold. The Asante sailor probed down with his boat hook, pushing it through the fish. Everyone heard the metal head strike the top of a crate.

"Lieutenant!" the sailor shouted excitedly. "Here is—"

Leiberman straightened suddenly.

"Yakubu!" he screamed.

He poked the muzzle of his Uzi through the pilothouse window and opened fire. Almost at the same instant Yakubu began firing from the foredeck. Tangent lurched to his feet, scrambled about wildly for the Colt.

Leiberman's first burst took out the man at the machine gun. Bullets stitched across his torso, slammed him backward, head thrown up, arms flying. Leiberman turned to the open cockpit, sweeping the muzzle back and forth. The helmsman's face and head exploded. His lifeless body fell forward over the wheel. The officer turned as if to dive overboard. Bullets ripped into his spine. His body arched, hands clawed around. He fell to his knees, crumpled forward.

Now Tangent was at the window next to Leiberman. He was vaguely conscious of Cousin and Shagari flat on the deck. He shoved the Colt .45 through the open window, held it in two hands, pointed it at the Asante motor launch, pulled the trigger again and again and again, not hearing his shots in the stuttering crack of Leiberman's machine pistol, next to his ear.

Yakubu's first burst killed the man at the searchlight. Now the light was swinging wildly, making swift patterns of light and dark across both boats. Yakubu's second target was the sailor who had come aboard with the boat hook. He was down, lying across the gunnel, legs over the side, his head, arms, shoulders dangling into the hold. The boats drifted slowly apart.

Suddenly, silence. Cousin and Shagari raised their heads cautiously. A final burst from Leiberman's gun shattered the searchlight. Then they were in darkness again, except for the green lantern at the end of the boom and the launch's running lights.

Tangent, numb, stood at the window. His arms and hands were outside, the automatic pistol still pointing at the launch. Leiberman put down his Uzi, pulled him gently back inside, helped him sit down on the deck. He tried to take the pistol from Tangent's grasp.

"Let go," he said.

"What?" Tangent said. "I can't hear you."

"Let go of the gun."

"I can't."

"Loosen your fingers."

"I just can't," Tangent said. "I can't move them. They're numb."

Leiberman worked the pistol back and forth, twisting. Finally it came free. Leiberman smelled the muzzle, then gave a hoarse bark.

"This little gizmo here," he said. "The safety. Off. On. Never mind. You tried. You did good."

He got his flashlight, switched it on. Cousin had tossed a small grappling hook onto the launch, caught its rail, pulled it close again. Leiberman jumped down onto the deck, his revolver held out in front of him. He inspected the two in the cockpit, then the sailors who had manned the machine gun and searchlight.

"Fini," he called back to the trawler. "Where's the other guy, the one with the boat hook?"

Yakubu, carrying his Uzi, began searching from the port catwalk. Leiberman looked down into the sea between the two boats.

"Where the hell is he?" he said angrily. "I don't like loose ends. Shagari, check the hold. Maybe he fell in on top of the fish."

Tangent had climbed shakily to his feet, stumbled out onto the pilothouse deck. Now he looked down, fighting sickness, and saw something in the water, something white.

"Here," he said weakly. But no one heard him. He tried again, louder: "Here he is. Back here."

Leiberman came running along the deck of the launch. Yakubu climbed the ladder to the pilothouse and stood

264

alongside Tangent, peering down. The others joined them.

A white-clad arm came out of the water. Fingers scrabbled at the trawler's hull. The face of the sailor bobbed up, mouth gaping for air, eyes showing white completely around the iris.

"Grease him, Yakubu," Leiberman ordered.

The black fired a long burst. The sea churned a red froth. Jumping and dancing.

"Enough," Leiberman yelled. "He's finished."

The water calmed. The body was gone. Bits of white and gray stuff floated, bobbled, drifted away.

Leiberman came back aboard and gave orders to Cousin and Shagari, in Boulé. They went below, came back with an ax and a long crowbar. They jumped down into the launch and began opening the hull, jabbing, chopping, thrusting, letting in the sea.

"Did you have to do that?" Tangent demanded of Leiberman. "That last wounded sailor—did you have to kill him?"

"No," Leiberman said, "we could have fished him out, patched him, and you could have put him up at the executive suite of the Mokodi Hilton. Have your brains turned to shit? Witnesses we don't need. Are you going to be sick?"

"I don't think so."

"If you are, puke over the side. This tub stinks enough as it is."

The launch was already settling, water in the cockpit knee-deep, when Cousin and Shagari scrambled back aboard the trawler. They all lined the rail and watched as the launch went deeper and deeper, the sea rushing into the torn hull. It settled slowly, slowly, going down evenly. In the weak glow of Leiberman's flashlight they saw it sink below the surface, hesitate a moment, then it was gone. A few plank scraps swirled to the surface. An empty thermos bottle bobbed. A life preserver drifted. A sodden copy of the Asante *New Times* . . .

"I could have used the grenades," Leiberman explained to Tangent, "but someone on Zabar or Mokodi might have heard or seen the explosions. This is as neat and clean as I could make it. The bodies may come up in a few days, but we'll be long gone by then."

Tangent said nothing.

Leiberman decided to remain where they were and wait.

They made a few efforts to destroy the evidence: tossed empty cartridge cases over the side, washed the sailor's blood from the starboard catwalk, chopped his boat hook into small pieces and flung them into the sea. Because the wood shaft had *Griselda* burned into it. Then they waited, Leiberman cleaning the Uzis and reloading. He made no effort to talk to Tangent.

They waited about an hour and were almost ready to give up when Cousin spotted a cluster of three white lights bobbing toward them slowly. Leiberman stood in the pilothouse, armed now with the M3. Yakubu returned to the foredeck with a cleaned and reloaded Uzi. Tangent held the Colt again, trying to remember—"Little gizmo. Off. On." Shagari and Cousin crouched on the pilothouse catwalk.

Cousin waited until the lights came close enough. Then he snapped on Leiberman's flashlight. Long enough to identify three brightly painted fishing boats. He turned off the light. The boats slipped up alongside, sails whispering down.

"Leiberman?" a voice called.

"My God," the mercenary said, "it's the man himself. Captain, is that you?" he called.

"Yes. We thought we heard firing. That is why we are late. Was it you? Trouble?"

"Nothing we couldn't handle. Can you come aboard? Need a ladder?"

"Thank you, we shall manage."

In a few moments, Obiri and Zuni Anokye were in the pilothouse, shaking hands with all, grinning.

"At the last minute, I decided to come along," the Little Captain said. "It was not that I felt Zuni could not do it"—here he put his hand on his brother's shoulder—"but it is the first delivery, and I wanted everything to go smoothly. Apparently it did not."

Leiberman shrugged. "Bad luck," he said. "The Asante navy picked this night to go cruising for smugglers."

"The navy?" Anokye said sharply. "Where are they now?"

"Sunk," Leiberman said. "No choice."

"Survivors?"

"No."

"Good. Any casualties here?"

"Only Tangent's pride."

The Little Captain turned. "How is that, Mr. Tangent?" he asked.

Tangent laughed shortly. "I forgot to take off the safety," he said. "I must have pulled the trigger a dozen times."

Anokye smiled. "I did exactly the same thing in my first action."

Tangent appreciated the lie.

"Next time you will remember," the Captain said.

267

"My God, what is that stink?"

The flashlight was turned down into the hold.

"The guns are underneath," Leiberman said.

"Please," Captain Anokye said, "next time use bags of rice."

At Zuni's command, men came swarming over from the fishing boats. With Cousin at the electric winch, crates and cases began to fly up from the hold, to be deposited on a fishing boat's deck. As soon as one boat was loaded to capacity, it moved sluggishly away, and another took its place. In less than two hours, the trawler's hold was emptied of arms. Zuni Anokye insisted his men help clean up. Buckets of rotting fish were hoisted out and dumped overboard. Within minutes scavenging fish were in the area, darting, gobbling the unexpected banquet.

More handshakes as arrangements were confirmed for the next delivery. The last fishing boat slipped away into the darkness, the Little Captain waving. The trawler's boom was swung inboard and lashed, running lights were rigged, the engine was started. *La Belle Dame*, dancing high out of the water, headed back for the Ivory Coast. Full cups of brandy were poured. Tangent took his forward, sat on the foredeck, his back against a rail stanchion. He listened to the hiss of the cutwater, thinking back on what had happened that night, wondering what it meant, wondering if it meant anything.

But he found it difficult to think, impossible to concentrate. All he could feel was an immense weariness, physical, mental, nervous. So he sipped his brandy, conscious of his breathing, conscious of his heart pump, knew he was alive. At that moment it seemed enough.

Sam Leiberman came rolling carelessly along the catwalk, bringing the half-empty brandy bottle and fresh paper cups. He flopped down next to Tangent, poured him a new drink.

268

"Well," he said, "you didn't shit your pants after all."

"You seem to be anally oriented," Tangent said.

"Not me," Leiberman said. "I'm prickally oriented."

"Well, no one was firing at *me*," Tangent muttered.

"True," Leiberman said. "Still, it was hairy, and you tried to help. You didn't have to. No one asked you."

"Didn't do much good."

"Don't pick at it," Leiberman advised.

Tangent didn't answer, and they sat in silence a long time, finishing the brandy.

"What's eating you?" Leiberman asked finally.

"Nothing's eating me. A little shell-shocked, that's all. I've never seen—never been through anything like that before."

"Shocked to see what your money buys?" Leiberman asked.

"Yes," Tangent said.

"It's only the beginning," Leiberman said.

26

SGT. SENE YEBOA was a great favorite with the Anokye family and relatives. Especially with the children, since he always brought gifts and delighted to teach them new games, new riddles, and such marvelous arts as building sand forts on the beach, making little boats from scraps of bark, and flying kites constructed of reeds and pages of old newspapers.

Since Yeboa had no family of his own, he had become an adopted son of the Anokyes and was encouraged to visit frequently. In return, he could not do enough for them. He insisted on helping all, even assisting Judith in the kitchen, cleaning fish, washing utensils, serving meals—women's work. The Anokye men were amused by this and called him "Auntie" Yeboa. But their jibes were without malice, and Sene took it all with elephantine good humor.

On Sunday morning, Sene Yeboa and the Anokyes walked to church, two kilometers west of Porto Chonin. Sara was missing since she was visiting Lt. Jere Songo in Togo, chaperoned by Zuni's wife.

The Baptists on Zabar had erected a one-room church, used as frequently for social gatherings as for religious services. It was a low, graceless structure, a weathered gray, but with adequate ventilation through wide doors at both ends and screened windows along both sides. A cloth-covered table on a low platform at one end served as a rude altar. The congregation sat on wooden benches. An ancient harmonium, foot-pumped, was placed at the right of the altar.

The usual Sunday service consisted of an opening hymn, a prayer, more hymns, the offertory, church announcements, and the award of colored picture cards to children who had distinguished themselves in Sunday School. Then it was the custom of this church to follow the minister's sermon with an address by a lay member.

It had been announced the previous week that Captain Obiri Anokye would speak on the following Sunday. As a result, by the time the Anokyes arrived the benches were almost full, with more people squeezing in every minute. When the wheezy organ sounded the chords of the first hymn, the church was jammed, all seats taken by children, women, and elders. Men stood at the back and along the walls. Many found no room inside, but clustered outside at the open windows and doors, waiting to hear the Little Captain speak.

He was introduced by the preacher with a quote from Isaiah: "A little one shall become a thousand, and a small one a strong nation." Captain Anokye's text came from Ecclesiastes: "Whatever thy hand findeth to do, do it with thy might."

He stood before them, wearing an undress uniform of khaki drill, an overseas cap tucked into his belt. His short-sleeved shirt was open at the throat. He assumed the familiar position: feet firmly planted, torso bent slightly backward, chest inflated, chin elevated. As he began speaking, in Akan, his hands rose to his hips and stayed there, except for the short, violent gestures he used to emphasize a point. He looked slowly about the church, locking eyes with his audience. They leaned forward eagerly, staring with fascination at those grave, magisterial features, impressed by his intensity.

"I am a soldier, as you know. Like soldiers everywhere, I am expected to do my duty, even though it might

271

be difficult, it might be painful, even though it might result in my own suffering, or my own death.

"To whom do I owe this duty as a soldier? I owe it to our King. Is this duty absolute and supreme? It would be easy to say Yes. It would simplify a soldier's life, since then it would only be necessary to obey the orders of a superior officer to be a good soldier.

"But I say that my duty as a soldier of the King is not absolute and is not supreme. I believe that I have a higher duty, as you do, and you, and you. This duty, the *highest* duty, is to God.

"Our duty to God, as we know from the Bible, is to walk in the paths of righteousness. That is no easy thing. But though we may fail occasionally—as fail we must since we are but human, with all the weaknesses of humans—that should not discourage us from seeking always to obey God's commandments and follow the teachings of Christ.

"Now I ask you this: What must a soldier do when the duty he owes his superior conflicts with the duty he owes to God? This is no simple matter to decide. For to disobey a superior officer, who speaks for the King, is a serious thing and, in some cases, may be punishable by death. And yet to disobey a commandment of God may condemn you to eternity in the fiery pit.

"When such a conflict arises, I say it is necessary for us all—soldiers and civilians alike—to listen to the voice of God and follow His orders. That is what I believe.

"How may one know what God commands? His order may not come from a voice from Heaven or a visitation of angels. But I believe each of us will feel it, will *know* it, in his soul. And since God is Our Father, that small whisper in our souls is His. There are so many of us and only one of Him, His voice and commands are divided amongst us all, and come to each of us only as a whisper. We deny God's whisper at great peril. He is telling us the way, and if we disregard His command, if we disobey, then we fail in our duty and will be punished for it.

"The time may come—sooner than you think—when it may be necessary for you to make this decision between duty to the King and duty to God. I urge you to listen to God's small whisper in your soul and then to think on how best you may obey His command. And whatsoever thy hand findeth to do, do it with thy might. To the greater glory of God."

With that he finished his address, and stepped down, taking his place along the wall with the other men. There was no applause. The congregation looked to each other in puzzlement, not certain what the Little Captain intended. In low voices they agreed it was an eloquent sermon, but he seemed to be hinting at more than he said. What did it all mean?

The Anokyes walked slowly home from church, the Little Captain alongside Sene Yeboa. Both had taken off boots and socks and luxuriated in the feel of the warm, powdery dirt beneath their bare toes.

"A good speech," Yeboa said.

"No, Sene, it was not," Captain Anokye said. "They did not understand. But the fault was mine. I could not make it clear to them. I am certain the secret police were there, listening. I went as far as I could. To say more would have endangered everything. But perhaps they will understand next week. Then they will remember what I said, and it will have meaning for them. Meanwhile, perhaps I have planted a seed."

"What seed is that?" Yeboa inquired innocently.

The Little Captain laughed. "That obedience to God's will sometimes demands disobedience to the King's. A revolutionary doctrine. I hope some day it does not return to haunt me. Now listen, Sene, here is what I want you to do . . .''

Briefly, concisely, he outlined Sgt. Yeboa's role in the coup d'etat. The big sergeant listened closely, interrupting frequently to ask questions, to make certain he understood precisely what would be expected of him.

"Bibi," he said finally, "Can't I be with you? In Mokodi?"

"You will be," Anokye patiently explained. "I will not start the assault until you and Leiberman join me. You have a very important part to play. You see that?"

"Yesss," Yeboa said. Dubiously.

"Another thing . . . If I am killed, or if I am wounded so badly that I cannot command—do not look at me so; such things may happen; you know that—the attack is to continue under the command of Willi Abraham. I expect you to give him the same loyalty you would give me. You agree? Sene? Well, do you?"

"I agree," Yeboa said in a low voice.

Anokye clapped him on the shoulder, the heavy, muscled machine gunner's shoulder. "But I do not intend to be killed or seriously wounded. That is *my* whisper from God. You and I shall live to enter the palace together."

"Yes *sah*!" Yeboa said, grinning.

The Sunday afternoon dinner was meager: a fish stew with mashed plantains. But the stew was mostly onions, tomatoes, beans, and okra. The fish scraps were just for seasoning; there was no meat on them.

After the pot had been scraped clean, Sene Yeboa passed around a packet of thin cigars he had brought as a treat. It would have been impolite to refuse, so even Judith lighted up one of the dark Spanish cigarillos.

The table was cleared, and Zuni spread a large, hand-drawn map of Zabar. It showed the island's roads, villages, and important installations, such as gendarme headquarters, ferry slip, a small army post, governor's office, etc. These had been marked with numerals indicating the order in which they would be captured by the Zabarian chapter of the Asante Brothers of Independence, commanded by Zuni Anokye.

Obiri and Sgt. Yeboa listened carefully as Zuni explained his plan of attack. He would first capture the telephone office to cut off all calls to the mainland. He would then take control of the ferry slip. From there, his men would move to gendarme headquarters, army post, and governor's office. They would move as rapidly as possible to surprise the King's forces on Zabar. Officers and officials would be jailed; soldiers and gendarmes would be given the option of joining the revolution or jail. Those offering resistance would be shot.

The Little Captain nodded agreement with this plan, knowing how easily Zuni's timetable could be bollixed by any number of things: an unexpected firefight, a truck that failed to start, excessive caution on the part of Zuni's men. He warned his brother of these things.

"You promised us weapons, and we received weapons," Zuni said. "I promise you Zabar."

Obiri reached up to touch his arm, smiling.

"I believe you, Zuni," he said, "and your plan is a good one. But do not be discouraged if things do not go as you have planned. You must be prepared to revise your tactics on the spot if circumstances dictate. You understand?"

"Of course."

"One final thing: If a ferry arrives while your attack is in progress, seize it and hold it here until you have taken control of Zabar. Then, if it is possible, send to me in Modoki as many armed men as you can spare. Not you.

275

You will be needed here. But if you can send men, I can use them in Mokodi.''

"I will go," Adebayo said excitedly. "I will lead the men to Mokodi.''

Judith Anokye stretched out a hand and seemed about to speak. Then her hand dropped, she said nothing.

Obiri looked at his younger brother.

"I can do it," Adebayo said defiantly. "I am not a boy. I have learned to shoot the rifle. I know how. I can help you in Mokodi.''

"Zuni will decide who goes and who stays," Obiri said sternly. "You will take your orders from Zuni. You understand that?''

"I understand," Adebayo muttered, lowering his eyes.

"Then there is nothing more to be discussed." The Little Captain rose, pushed back his chair. "Sene and I must return to the barracks. Zuni, you will receive twenty-four hours' notice of the time to begin. That will be sufficient?''

"Yes, enough.''

"Good. We shall not see you again before it starts. God bless you all and keep you well.''

Then all rose. The family embraced Obiri and Sene with kisses and pattings, murmurings and hugs. Josiah began weeping, tears running down the deep walnut ravines of his face. The Little Captain took him aside and spoke softly to him a few moments, and the old man calmed.

Then Captain Anokye and Sgt. Yeboa departed, walking up the hill to the village. They turned once to look back. Judith, Josiah, Zuni, and Adebayo were standing outside the Anokye home, looking at them. No one waved.

27

THE PASTRY CRUST of the Beef Wellington was soggy, but Peter Tangent was too excited to notice. Too excited, in fact, to do anything but stab at his dinner as he described the action off Zabar. Tony Malcolm listened, but didn't neglect his food. Finally, his dinner and Tangent's recital finished, he pointed at Tangent's plate and said, "Eat your food, Peter. If you insist on buckling swashes all over the place, you'll need your strength."

Then, when Tangent, blushing faintly, turned his attention to the rare beef, Malcolm said, "This Leiberman, he plays rough."

Tangent, talking around a mouthful, said, "That was my initial reaction. But then I started thinking about it. Tony, what else could he have done?"

"I suppose you're right," Malcolm murmured. "Still . . ."

"What amazed me," Tangent went on, chewing and still talking excitedly, "was how fast he reacted. Almost as if he had planned it."

"I imagine he had," Malcolm said. "Not consciously perhaps, but a man with his experience would have contingency plans. Do B in case of A. Do Y in case of X. So he was able to move almost instinctively."

The dining room at Brindleys was sparsely occupied; they were served at their favorite corner table with some degree of privacy. The other diners seemed as secretive as they; heads met over tables in whispered conversations.

"When is the coup scheduled?" Tony Malcolm asked.

"First week in August. I don't know the exact date. Garde has been told the twelfth. Have you heard anything more about what the French are up to?"

"They don't seem too concerned. Your Little Captain picked a good time. In August, everyone in Paris goes on vacation."

"The paratroops are still in Senegal?"

"As far as I know."

"Tony, I've got a wild idea I want to try on you. Would it be possible to put some of our ships in that area—just as a signal to the French?"

"No, it would not be possible."

"I'm not asking for the Sixth Fleet. I had in mind, say, a destroyer and a couple of escorts. Or perhaps a minelayer or two. Just showing the flag. A symbol of U.S. interest, that's all. It might make the French think twice before making a move."

Malcolm pondered a long moment, twirling the stem of his wineglass. For a plumpish man, he had unexpectedly long and elegant fingers.

"I could send a bullet to Virginia," he said finally. "But something like that would be bucked to State."

"Exactly," Tangent said eagerly, bending over the table. "And I could get Tulsa to have our man in D.C. lean on State. We've done them enough favors. My God, I'm not asking for the Marines—just a couple of small ships visiting, say, Accra, Lomé, or Lagos. Close enough to signal the French we have an interest in the Little Captain's coup and wouldn't take kindly to their dumping a regiment of paratroops on him."

Malcolm looked at him curiously.

"You're expanding this thing, Peter. It started out as just another army revolt in just another two-bit African country. Now you've got French troops on standby in Senegal, and you want some of our warships making an excursion into an area where the U.S. has no vested interest. Starrett Petroleum does, but not the U.S. Do you know what the hell you're doing?''

Tangent leaned back, took out his packet of Players, offered them to Malcolm. They both lighted up slowly, glancing about casually to see if anyone was interested in their conversation. No one was.

"I know exactly what I'm doing, Tony," Tangent said in a low voice. "Let me fill you in . . . There's a clique in the Secretariat for African Affairs in State that thinks the U.S. is missing the boat in Africa. Right now, most of the radicals are young and black and don't have much clout. They claim State and the White House are paying too much attention to West Europe, Russia, China, and the Middle East, and not enough attention to Africa. They argue it's an enormously rich continent, still largely uncommitted politically, and it's going to be a hell of a market in the future, besides being an incredible source of cereals, oil, minerals, and so forth. But all the White House does is give a free lunch to any African leader foolish enough to go to D.C. looking for help. Anyway, I happen to agree with the dissidents in African Affairs. I especially agree with their warning that we're letting African markets and raw materials go to France and Britain by default. I think Starrett's lobbyists in D.C. could work with this group and get State to okay a friendly cruise of a few piddling U.S. Navy ships off the Asante coast. If you could get Virginia's okay, it would be in the bag. It's not just Anokye's coup I'm interested in, Tony—although I admit it's important to me and important to Starrett. But it goes beyond Anokye. I want to see the U.S. make a dent in the French hegemony in Africa. If the Little Captain is

279

successful—and I think he will be—we'll have Asante in our hip pocket. And with his ambition and drive, who knows where it might lead? Will you try Virginia?''

Malcolm considered a moment, staring into Tangent's eyes without seeing him.

''All right,'' he said finally. ''I'll get off a request. No guarantee.''

''Good enough,'' Tangent said happily. ''And I'll get my people on it. I'll tell the Little Captain what we're attempting. Even if it doesn't come off, we'll make Brownie points for trying.''

They were silent while the table was cleared, and coffee and brandy were served. Years later they were both to remember that dinner. It marked a turning point, though neither was aware of it at the time.

''What about tonight, Peter?'' Malcolm asked lazily.

''Sorry, we'll have to let it go. I want to get a long cable off to Tulsa, and then I have to pack. I'm leaving for Asante again in the morning. Tell me, what does one wear to a coup d'etat?''

Malcolm shook his head. ''You're demented, you know that? This Little Captain has scrambled your brains.''

''Tony, if the coup comes off, I'd like you to come down to Asante.''

''What for?''

''To meet Anokye. I think you should.''

''Well . . . maybe. I'll have to get shots, won't I?''

''Shots? What for?''

''Tsetse flies. Rhinoceros bites. Things like that.''

''Don't be an ass. Besides, there are no shots for what you're going to catch.''

''And what's that?''

''Wait till you meet him. You'll see.''

"Peter . . ."

"What?"

"I'm not going to try to talk you out of being there. During the action, I mean. I can see how excited you are. But listen, take care of yourself. Y'know?"

Tangent reached out to touch Tony Malcolm's arm.

"Thanks, Tony," he said softly. "Not to worry. I'm so skinny, they'll never hit me."

"Send me an update through Jon Wilson as soon as it's over. Win or lose."

"Will do."

"Hurry back," Malcolm said lightly.

28

THEY WERE ALL there in Yvonne Mayer's apartment at the Golden Calf: Anokye, Yeboa, Abraham, Duclos, Tangent, Fante, Leiberman—and Yvonne herself, withdrawn, saying little, listening. Her eyes followed Captain Anokye.

"The day after tomorrow," the Little Captain said. "The fifth of August. At oh six hundred. Is that clear to everyone? I will notify the Nyam myself, and my brother in Zabar. Minister, you, Duclos, Fante, and Sene will notify the others. Is that satisfactory?"

The men nodded.

"Now we will go through it once more," the Captain said. "The timing will make us or break us."

They clustered around the table, looking down at the map of Asante, studying the circles, the arrows, the routes of attack. Speaking in a cold, emotionless voice, Captain Obiri Anokye pointed out the sequence of actions that would culminate in the assault on the palace. It was his plan—no help from Alistair Greeley on this—but if he was apprehensive, nothing in his tone or manner revealed it. He spoke with steady authority, iron sureness.

There were questions: Leiberman wanted to know about transportation back to Mokodi from Gonja; Tangent asked about a weapon for himself; Duclos complained, briefly, of what he considered the trivial task assigned him—seizure of the Mokodi mosque. Even Willi Abraham had questions regarding his capture of the telephone exchange and cable office.

"Isolate the palace," Anokye ordered. "No calls can go out, but be sure they can receive calls. I suspect Anatole Garde may be in radio communication with Togo or Ghana from inside the palace, but there is nothing we can do about it. Any other questions?"

The men were silent.

"The important element is speed," the Little Captain said, studying the map. "With luck, all preliminaries should be concluded by noon, and the palace captured by nightfall. If we move quickly, if our complete control of Asante becomes obvious, I do not think the French will interfere. You know of the American warships off our coast. Mr. Tangent is to be thanked for that effort. But if the coup is not immediately successful, I believe the French may decide to come to the aid of Prempeh, regardless of the presence of those ships. So it is important to strike hard and strike swiftly. Avoid unnecessary killing, but do what must be done."

"Prisoners?" Leiberman asked.

"Preferably not," Anokye said shortly. "We do not have the men to guard them. But they should be given the opportunity to join us. Do not attempt to persuade them. Merely ask them—once. Do I make myself clear? Resistance must be met by annihilation. There is no other way. If you have no stomach for it, think of what *our* fate will be if we fail."

Little was said after that. There were handshakes, a few muttered words, and then the apartment gradually cleared as men slipped away. Finally, Anokye and Yvonne Mayer were alone, she in her corner chair, he still standing, hands

283

on hips, staring down at the map of Asante.

"I have tried to anticipate every possibility and to prepare for it," he said aloud, almost speaking to himself. "But I know how important chance and accident can be. Do you pray, Yvonne?"

"No," she said. "Not for years."

"Nor I," he laughed.

"I thought you went to church?"

"I do. For the meaning it has to others. Well, if neither of us can pray, then I suppose we must put our faith in Russian rifles and American grenades."

He turned to her, grinning, and she rose and came to him, arms stretched wide. They embraced, but when he turned again to the map, she moved behind him, pressing tightly against him, her arms about his neck.

"I can do it," he said, voice low and urgent. "I know I can."

"You can," she whispered.

"It's in me," he said. "A fire to command. To rule. It drives me. You know that?"

"Yes," she said.

"I must obey," he went on, his eyes on the map but not seeing. "It is a kind of duty. To myself. Not to God, King, or country. But to me, my own destiny. I know, Yvonne, I know I will not be killed. I know I will succeed in this. I would be a traitor if I did not act, a traitor to myself. As far as I can. Wherever it leads. I can see no limits, no boundary I cannot cross. Energy. The need to act. The will to act! I cannot disobey that. That duty. I wish I could make you understand."

"I understand, Bibi,"

"Do you?" he said. He laughed shortly, excited. "I wonder if I do? It is something I cannot resist. A fever. An

284

ache. How else can I describe it? That I was born for this. Auntie Tal cast the stones for me, and . . ."

"And what?"

"A great destiny. But that is all superstition. It means nothing. Still . . ."

They huddled quietly. He reached around behind her, gripped her buttocks so she came tighter to him, cleaving. She buried her face in his neck and shoulder. His stirring bull smell. She savored.

"How I wish I could see it," he mused. "All of it. My life outlined like this map. Circles and lines. Arrows and masses. The sequences and the climax. No, I would not want to see it. Where is the pleasure there? I must live it, make it unfold. Yvonne? You understand? Yes, you understand everything. I must believe in myself. Obey. My duty to myself. Follow it."

"I know," she murmured. "I know."

"I have no choice," he said. He turned slowly in her embrace until he was facing her. Widened eyes close. "No choice at all."

"Do you remember what I told you?" she whispered. "What I would do if you betrayed your promise to me?"

"I have not forgotten," he said.

"This future you see for yourself, this great destiny, it will all come to dust, Bibi, if you desert me. Do you believe that?"

"Yes," he said, shivering, "I believe it. But I shall not betray you, and I shall conquer. I swear it!"

In bed, he seemed charged with fury, a maniacal anguish he sought to exhaust inside her. He plunged, rutting, with a rage that drove her to a sweated convulsion, squirming slickly beneath him, trying to encompass and hold his frenzy.

He put a hand across her mouth to stifle her screams. Then he rent her brutally, oblivious to her pleasure or hurt, staring at her with burning eyes, gone from her and from himself, driven by a force he could not control, slave and master, crying out in pain in triumph.

29

COLONEL RAMON DE BLANCA, cousin of King Prempeh, CO of 3rd Brigade, Asante Royal Army, spent the evening of August 4th in his Mokodi home. He enjoyed a delightful lamb curry, with all the side dishes, at a table shared with his father, grandfather, two uncles, three male cousins, and his two eldest sons. Later, stirred by the curry, he took pleasure with his second wife, who was five months pregnant.

At midnight, the Colonel headed back to Gonja, carrying a box of dates, raisins, figs, dried apricots, and a hand of green bananas. He nibbled these delicacies on the trip north. He was chauffeured by a Muslim corporal who was actually a member of the palace guard but had been temporarily detached to serve as Colonel de Blanca's bodyguard. And to report his activities personally to General Opoku Tutu, the Colonel had no doubt.

But he had nothing to fear. He had obeyed Tutu's orders, bringing in his brigade from the field and from village garrisons to concentrate more than 300 men in and around Gonja. There would be more in another week, and by August 12th, Colonel de Blanca did not believe any combination of rebels and dissidents would dare attack. He had already established a perimeter defense about the garrison and arsenal, including heavy machine guns. He had also detailed a reinforced platoon under the command of Lt. Rafael Mohammed to protect the pump station on the freshwater pipeline to Mokodi.

So the Colonel slept well that night, naked under the mosquito net in his private bedroom in officers' quarters above the Gonja arsenal. His last thoughts, before sleep took him, were a fantasy in which he crushed the expected rebellion, was awarded a higher rank, a raise in pay, medals, gifts from the King. Then he could afford a third wife.

The morning of August 5th was hot, vaporous, the blue sky scrimmed with white gauze. The air was a thin ocean; men awoke with bodies already sweated, eyes gummed, throats clogged. It was a day to move slowly, seek the shade, speak softly to avoid the angers that flared so easily in such cruel weather.

At 0600, rebels under the command of the Nyam approached the Bonja barracks in two troops, guiding on the paved highway. They had made a night march of more than ten miles over rough ground, but morale was high, the new Kalashnikov rifles were feathers in their hands, they looked forward eagerly to what they were to do.

The Nyam led almost 100 men, women, and a few children. Not all were Marxist rebels; there were perhaps 30 trained revolutionaries. The others had been won over with the rifles and glowing descriptions of the splendid victory that awaited them. There had been little military discipline on the march, but much laughter, calling back and forth, songs, even a few shots. It was of little importance, the Nyam assured Katsuva. The animals knew how to point the guns and pull the triggers. Their number, and their surprise attack, would overwhelm Gonja's defenders. Then the King's men would all be killed. Then the arsenal would be looted. Then the Nyam and his loyal 30 would push on to Mokodi. Then . . . A day of glory.

The Nyam himself approached the guard at the gate, his

288

hands empty, stretched wide. He spoke in Twi, pleading for water, a scrap to eat, anything. As he begged, he moved slowly around, maneuvering the guard until the soldier's back was to the highway. Katsuva, running lightly on bare feet, came from the bushes, crossed the road, slid a knife into the soldier's back, to the left of the spine, upward, smoothly.

Then all the rebels came bursting across the road, shouting joyously, pointing their new rifles at the garrison buildings and firing at anything and everything. They screamed with delight at the noise of their guns. It was all as the Nyam had promised.

The wild rush carried them inside the fence. As planned, the Nyam and his trained men sprinted toward the corrugated iron building that housed the armory and officers' quarters. Katsuva led the recruits in a stampede to the main barracks, a long, low wooden building with wide screen doors and cloth netting nailed over open windows.

Alarmed by the shouting and firing, a few soldiers had come popping from the barracks. They saw the frenzied throng bearing down on them and turned to scramble back inside. A few made it; the bodies of the others fell on the porch, piling up in front of the doors.

The recruits rushed the doors, hurdling the dead and dying. Katsuva was first inside. He saw hundreds of men rising from plank benches and tables, from their morning meal. Most wore only shorts and singlets. Few had rifles. The NCOs carried sidearms. Almost all had razored glaives, swinging from belt scabbards.

The fire of the recruits slackened. They had been shown how to point their rifles and pull the trigger. They had not been taught to reload. It would not be necessary, the Nyam had insisted, not to surprise and destroy a garrison of 50 men. But here were hundreds of soldiers, staring wide-eyed at this civilian gang with red rags tied about their arms.

Then rifle fire dwindled and stopped. The recruits, laughing foolishly, began grabbing at the bread and rice and fufu and fruit on the tables. The soldiers roared, a single roar of fury, blood-lust. They surged forward with raised glaives, one animal, a steel porcupine.

They fell upon Katsuva and the recruits, glaives falling, cutting, piercing, slicing. Soldiers in the front ranks were pressed by those behind; the screaming mob was jammed out through the wide doors. Katsuva fell under a dozen blades, decapitated before his body ceased rolling.

The others, men, women, children, were pursued and cut down. New rifles were jerked from severed hands. Arms, ears, legs, heads sprang free and bounced. A woman was split upward to her waist, breasts sliced away. A child tottered fainting on bloodied legs until a mighty chop cut it in two. The lower half stood a moment, spouting, before crumpling.

Furious hacking continued even after the recruits, all, were dead. A red mist obscured the morning sun. Puddles soaked the dust. Pye-dogs nosed about ravenously. Flies gathered. Soldiers howled in their frenzy to find one enemy still alive. Glaives fell on lifeless limbs, on scraps of flesh. Heads were minced and flung, severed testicles kicked across the blood-soaked field. Soldiers' bare feet trampled hot meat. Then, at an officer's screamed command, maddened troops turned to the armory and with dripping glaives held high surged in a screaking charge.

Colonel Ramon de Blanca had been awakened by the crackling of rifle fire, by wild shouts. He lay a moment, sleep-fogged, struggling to understand what was happening. Then he rolled naked from under his mosquito net, rushed to the window. Men with red rags tied about their arms were running across the small parade ground. They were all carrying rifles and appeared to be led by a thin, mustached man waving them on.

The colonel was buckling his pistol belt about his bare waist when his bodyguard burst in to scream that the garrison was under attack.

"I know that, you fool," the colonel yelled at him. "Get the doors closed and barred. Put men at all the windows."

Then, realizing he was naked, Colonel de Blanca pulled on khaki pants, which meant he had to unbuckle his holster web, then put it on again over the trouser belt. Before he left his bedroom he ran to the window, cursing furiously, and fired two shots blindly at the advancing rebels. He hit nothing, he knew, but the action pleased him.

There was confusion downstairs. Men dashed about, pushing one another to find a firing position. The colonel got them sorted out, ordered a squad upstairs to fire from the windows there, unbarred the rear door long enough to send runners to bring in a machine gun crew from the perimeter defense and to recall Lt. Rafael Mohammed from the pump station.

The first grenade exploded outside the main door, but it held. The officers and men in the arsenal put up a steady fire from their window positions. Several rebels were seen to fall. The others sought what cover they could find behind trees and parked vehicles. A second grenade bounced off the arsenal wall and exploded. A splinter smashed the face of a soldier who had stood up to fire from a window.

The colonel estimated the attacking force at perhaps 40 or 50 men armed with automatic rifles. He hoped to hold

291

out until the machine gun and Lt. Mohammed's platoon arrived. But suddenly the men at the windows were screaming wildly, jumping with excitement. Colonel de Blanca peered cautiously from below a ledge and saw a mob of his soldiers sprinting across the parade ground, shouting, attacking the rebels from the rear.

The enemy turned to face this threat. The colonel ordered the doors thrown open, and he personally led a determined charge toward the attackers. The rebels scattered, ran, were shot or cut down. Finally, a few threw their rifles away and stood with arms raised. Within moments the assault on the Gonja garrison was ended.

Seven rebels, including the mustached leader, still lived, standing, blank-faced, arms stretched high as 3rd Brigade soldiers danced about them laughing, poking rifle muzzles at them, sending glaives whistling by their heads. Then the captives were knocked down with rifle butts. Their elbows were wired tightly behind their backs, their ankles crossed and wired.

Order was slowly restored. Third Brigade had 11 dead and 23 wounded. Almost 100 rebels had been killed. And there were the seven live prisoners. A good morning's work. The colonel thought of his fantasy. It was all coming true. He hurried to the telephone in the Duty Office to call General Tutu at the palace and report how he, Colonel de Blanca, had crushed the rebellion.

Something was wrong with the phone. Twice he was disconnected, and when he finally got through to the palace, there was so much crackling on the line and so much background noise, he could hardly hear. It was a long time before General Tutu came on, and when he did, he refused to listen to the story of Colonel de Blanca's great victory. Instead, he shouted that a coup d'etat was in progress, the palace was under attack, and the colonel was to come to Mokodi at once, bringing every available man and weapon.

It took the colonel and his harried officers almost two hours to organize the convoy. There were not enough trucks and personnel carriers at the garrison to transport all the 3rd Brigade troops, so men were sent into Gonja to commandeer trucks, cars, taxis—any vehicle that could make it to Mokodi.

Finally, Colonel de Blanca had his men uniformed, fully equipped, and loaded aboard transportation. He left twenty soldiers at the garrison, under command of a master sergeant. Before he took his place in the lead jeep, the colonel ordered the seven trussed rebels thrown in a heap. They were soaked with two gallons of gasoline and set on fire. The 3rd Brigade convoy moved off with soldiers laughing at the screams of the burning rebels and their frantic efforts to roll out of the flames.

They drove through Gonja, Asantis standing silently alongside the road, not responding to the soldiers' waves and whistles. Once outside the town, the convoy picked up speed. Colonel Ramon de Blanca stood upright in the lead jeep, an automatic rifle cradled in his arms. The hot wind tangled his hair, rippled his shirt. He looked back proudly to see the line of packed vehicles following him. Almost 300 armed men. A glorious moment.

But then, rounding a bend, the jeep slowed suddenly, and Colonel de Blanca had to grab the windshield top to keep his balance. There was an overturned produce truck, sideways across the road. It completely blocked the highway.

The colonel's driver pulled up until his front bumper was only a few meters from the underside of the tipped truck. The other vehicles in the convoy closed in tightly and stopped, bumper to bumper.

"Get some men and drag that thing aside," the colonel ordered angrily.

Then the mortars opened up.

Captain Obiri Anokye had planned the ambush, and assigned Sam Leiberman and Sgt. Sene Yeboa to command. The three men had walked over the ground and selected their positions.

"Emplace the mortars along this line," the Little Captain told Leiberman. He held his arms out straight from his sides. "I will detail my best men, but I want you to check elevations and corrections. You will be able to move along this slight dip with reasonable concealment."

"Yeah," Leiberman said. "Reasonable."

"After the initial barrage, Third Brigade will retreat into the wheat field on the other side of the road. They are poorly disciplined, and will run from the mortars instead of attacking toward them. Sene, you will place the Gonjan ABIs at the far edge of the wheat field, perhaps fifty meters beyond the grain, in the clear. Plan overlapping fields of fire for your machine guns. Leiberman, when you see them desert the trucks and run into the wheat field, increase your range and herd them into Sene's guns. Does it sound good?"

"They all sound good," Leiberman said. "What if they come off the road toward the mortars? What do I do then?"

"Run," the Captain said.

"Good," Leiberman said. "That's what I wanted to hear."

"But they will not do that," Anokye smiled. "I know my people. They will run into the wheat field, thinking to

294

escape. Continue mortar fire even after you hear Sene's rifles and machine guns. I think then that many will surrender. Ask them if they wish to join us. But do not ask until all the officers have been killed. Is that clear, Sene?"

"Yes, Little Captain."

"All commissioned officers are to be killed immediately, regardless of rank. *Then* the men can be asked. With no officers alive to witness their defection, I believe many will come to us."

"And then we go to you in Mokodi?" Sgt. Yeboa asked eagerly.

"First, ask of your prisoners how many Third Brigade soldiers were left to guard the Gonja garrison. Then detail enough ABIs to capture it. You know the one they call the Leopard?"

"Yes, Bibi."

"Put him in command. The remainder of your forces should then come to Mokodi in whatever vehicles survive the mortar shelling. Come as quickly as you can. I shall be with the attack group at the palace."

"If we're late," Leiberman said, "start without us."

The first volley of 60 mm mortar shells that fell on the stalled 3rd Brigade convoy was an almost perfect straddle. Leiberman had carefully paced off the range, and the mortar crews Captain Anokye assigned to him were knowledgeable and eager. Watching the results through binoculars, Leiberman called out corrections, and before long all four mortar tubes were right on target, crews working swiftly, explosions following one another in a regular crump-crump-crump. The whole line of trucks and troops seemed to go up in dirty flame.

The first volley knocked Colonel Ramon de Blanca out of his jeep. When he climbed shakily to his feet, dazed but unwounded, he saw his command, those still alive, spilling from the transports and running into the wheat field. The colonel made one screaming effort to turn them around, to lead them in an attack toward the mortars. But it was hopeless. He joined the flight, plunging into the wheat.

Mortar shells pursued them; it was impossible to make a stand. Bodies and parts of bodies went flinging up against the morning sky, pinwheeling, falling back. The air filled with chopped grain, dust, the stink of burning trucks, of scorched flesh. Keens, too, of the wounded and the fearful living. They ran, ran, ran, tripping, falling, gasping, choking, weeping, pounding over the dead, over the crawling, lurching wounded. The mortar shells came after them, bloody blooms in golden wheat.

Until those who made it through the grain burst into the clear, still running wildly, rifles and helmets lost, thrown away. Then, from across the clearing, a line of rifle fire began to wink at them, machine guns sputtered, and men flopped on their faces, dug fingers into the hot earth, knew they were dead.

It seemed to Colonel de Blanca the noise would never end. But finally the mortars ceased, machine guns stuttered to a halt. He raised his head cautiously to see a line of riflemen advancing slowly. Lt. Rafael Mohammed, lying close to the colonel, jumped to his feet to fire his pistol at the approaching men. He got off two shots before he was cut down, bullets plucking at him, his face dissolving into a raw sponge.

Then what was left of 3rd Brigade was sitting with hands atop their heads, surrounded by at least a hundred silent men carrying good automatic rifles, machine pistols, burp guns. Grenades were slung from their belts and from ropes around their necks. Colonel de Blanca had time to note that none of these men wore red rags about their arms, but then a husky Asanti sergeant wearing the insignia of 4th Brigade came up to him, placed the muzzle of his Uzi close to the colonel's left side, and blew his heart away.

30

At 0800 THE time lock on the vault of the Asante National Bank clicked off. M. Claude Bernard, the bank manager, spun the combination and twirled the big tumbler wheel. With the aid of Alistair Greeley, he swung the massive vault door open. Greeley entered to prepare the cash drawers. The assistant tellers began lining up at 0830, signed receipts for their trays, and went to their cages.

At precisely 0900, the manager nodded to the bank guard. The venetian blinds were pulled up, the front door unlocked, and the Asante National Bank was open for business.

First to enter was a 10-man squad of armed 4th Brigade troopers under command of a corporal. They knew exactly what to do: the bank guard was relieved of his revolver, two soldiers went immediately to the open vault and stood guard with rifles at port arms, and all employees of the bank were instructed to remain calm, leave the bank quietly, return to their homes, and listen to the radio for further news.

M. Claude Bernard, a plump, choleric man who wore white-piped waistcoats, demanded to know on what authority his bank was being seized.

"On this authority," the corporal said, showing the bank manager the muzzle of his rifle.

After the employees gathered their personal belongings and departed, they heard the front door being locked behind them and saw the venetian blinds rattle down.

"Madness!" the manager cried. "Madness! I must inform the palace at once."

Greeley watched him trot away. Then he looked about dazedly. The streets of Mokodi seemed calm, peaceful. Perhaps a few more people than usual, but nothing really extraordinary. Until two trucks loaded with soldiers rumbled by, heading toward the dock area. And softly on the morning breeze, Alistair Greeley heard a lazy popping of rifle fire from the direction of the palace.

Then a ramshackle flatbed truck came down the Boulevard Voltaire. There were at least a dozen shouting, singing civilians standing on the truck, throwing out handfuls of printed broadsides. One fluttered to the pavement at Greeley's feet. He didn't bother picking it up; he could read the headline easily: COUP D'ETAT!!! He felt sick.

He stood irresolutely outside the closed bank. The locked door and drawn blinds mocked him. He turned slowly away, eyes smarting with tears. The nigger had duped him. He, Alistair Greeley, an educated white man, duped and made a fool of by a smarmy nigger. It wasn't fair.

No hope of a bonus from Anatole Garde now. No hope of ridding his home of his whorish sister. No hope of anything. He'd be lucky to keep his position at the bank. Perhaps he would lose that, lose his home. Perhaps, even, lose his . . . Well, it was possible. If the Little Captain had deliberately fed him false information, then perhaps his relationship with Garde was known and he was on an "enemies of the state" list. Such things happened in these savage, uncivilized countries. Oh yes, it was possible.

He waited almost half an hour for his bus. He hardly saw the truckloads of soldiers trundling by. He was hardly conscious of the growing crowds of noisy, excited Asantis hurrying toward the palace. His own misery was a bile that sickened him. He retched dryly a few times, swallowing hard. His tongue felt swollen, teeth furry. He imagined he could smell his own tainted breath.

Then, when he realized the bus had not appeared, would not appear on this momentous day, he began the long walk home. He walked slowly, dragging that miserable boot that now seemed an intolerable weight holding him back, pulling him down. The sun rose slowly, sought him out, seared his eyes. He sweated through his black alpaca suit. Dust puffed from the unpaved road with every scuffling step, and the world wavered.

Three times he stopped to rest, twice in the shade of scrawny trees and once merely sitting on the open road, head bowed, tears making crazy rivulets in his mask of dust. He was staggering when his home came into view. The last hundred meters were a lurching nightmare. The glaring sun was inside his head, a molten core that threatened to grow, pulsing, until it consumed him.

He made it up the steps, but tripped on the worn rag rug on the porch and fell heavily to his knees.

"Maud," he called weakly. "Maud. Help me."

He made it inside on hands and knees, then clawed himself upright, pulling on the door frame. He stumbled into the kitchen, struggled out of his filthy jacket, pulled off his sodden tie, unbuttoned his shirt. He opened the tap, splashed water onto his face. Then he bent far over, letting the tepid water pour into his thin hair, onto his neck, soak his shirt and the cotton singlet he wore beneath.

He held a glass under the tap with a trembling hand, but could hardly swallow, it was so warm. He found a small bottle of Perrier water in the fridge. He struggled with the cap, almost weeping again with his weakness and frustration. Finally, he got it open, drank from the bottle, gulping greedily, water spilling from his mouth. He set the empty bottle aside, trying to catch his breath.

"Maud," he gasped. "Maud, where are you?"

He sat down on a kitchen chair to unlace and remove his boots. The molten core inside him was beginning to shrink, but he still felt fluttery. His hands still trembled as he filled a pitcher at the tap, then added a few broken slivers of ice from the laboring fridge.

"Maud," he called, louder now. "Are you home, Maud?"

The water was barely cooled, but he drank off half the pitcher and put the remainder inside the fridge. He shuffled into the living room, flopped into a morris chair with soiled cushions. He closed his eyes.

"Maud," he called once. Then stopped. She wasn't home. Jane wasn't home. Both probably in town to see the excitement. To see Captain Obiri Anokye make a fool of Alistair Greeley, an educated white man. Oh God. What would Garde say? What would Garde do? He had little doubt now that not only had Anokye lied about the date of the coup, he had lied about everything else: the numbers involved, the weapons available, the tactics to be used. Everything.

Telephone Garde. That was the thing to do. Call and explain that he was as much an innocent victim as Garde. Anokye had lied to him. Anokye had led him by the nose. The dirty wog had cheated him. It wasn't Greeley's fault. It was the treachery of the Little Captain. Yes. Garde could see that, couldn't he?

He dragged himself into his study. But when he picked up the phone, he heard nothing but the sound of his own heavy breathing. The line was dead. Groaning, Greeley let the phone slip from his grasp and dangle on its cord.

But then, for some reason, it reminded him of a hanged man, and he hastily hauled it up and replaced it in its cradle.

"Maud!" he yelled furiously. "Maud!"

He turned away and saw the white envelope. It was on a small end table, propped against a display case of two model soldiers.

"What?" Alistair Greeley said aloud. "What?"

The envelope was inscribed: Alistair—Personal. In Maud's spidery script. It was sealed. He tore it open and read it swiftly. He didn't understand.

"What?" he said again. "What?"

He read it twice more, the second time slowly because, somehow, it was gratifying to feel such complete anguish, to be so utterly abased, to be thoroughly and finally destroyed and have nothing left. There was a curious kind of peace in that. In annihilation. A blank quiet with foolish hope dead once and for all.

She and Jane had gone away together, and it was no use searching for them because he would never find them, and even if he did, they had no intention of returning to his house, and the best thing he could do would be to try to forget them and make a new life, as they intended to do, and she was sorry for any unhappiness this might cause, but things couldn't continue as they had been, could they, and this was the best way, and surely he could see that, and both of them wished him good luck and all the best and hoped he might find happiness in the future, and there was a beef pie on the bottom shelf of the fridge he might warm up for dinner. Sincerely yours. Maude.

He started to read it again, but his hands were shaking so, his eyes so smeary with tears, that he could make out none of it; the letter fell from limp fingers onto the floor.

He seemed to know instinctively what he must do, the

302

one effective act of an ineffectual life, and stumbled to the desk. In the lower drawer, far back, was a Webley .38 revolver, an enormous, long-barreled weapon he had owned for years and never fired. There was a small box of cartridges, but when he opened it he saw the bullets were green, furry with tarnish, and he had trouble sticking one into the cylinder. But he fumbled it into place, turned the loaded chamber into firing position and, using both hands, succeeded in pulling the rusty hammer back to full cock.

Moving quickly now, while his spasm of resolve lasted, he sat in the swivel chair behind the desk. He raised the heavy revolver. He pointed the wavering barrel at his right temple. He took a deep breath. He closed his eyes. He yanked the trigger.

There was an enormous explosion. He felt a blast of hot gas scorch his cheek. The lid of his right eye stung and quivered. His right ear rang shrilly. He smelled heat, gunpowder, burning hair. Dazed, he turned slowly and saw that he had shot the head off the antique model of an 1812 British captain of the King's Own Regiment of Dragoons.

31

THE JUNIOR OFFICERS and NCOs crowded into Captain Anokye's office leaned forward eagerly to hear his words. Never before had they seen him so tense, never had he spoken so fiercely.

"Do not think it will be easy," he warned them. "The palace, the city, the nation will not be won without a bitter struggle. Many of the King's men will die rather than surrender. I may die. You may die. Be prepared for this and be willing to accept it, knowing our cause is just, and our people look to us for a better life."

There was a murmur of approval from the assembled soldiers. They were uniformed, armed, ready to go.

"No quarter asked, none given," the Little Captain said harshly. "If we fail, we and our families perish. Our blood will soak the earth, vultures will feed on our guts. But if we win, the rewards of the victors will be ours. I promise you this: I shall never forget those who stood beside me on this day. Trust me! It is important that we move swiftly. Do not hesitate to kill those who offer resistance, even those who merely delay you. Carry out the orders you have been given. Strike hard and strike fast. Have no doubt of the—"

There was an interruption; Captain Anokye stopped speaking. The office door opened, Major Etienne Corbeil entered slowly, leaning heavily on a silver-headed cane. Behind him, hovering solicitously, came his aide, Lt. Lebrun.

The Major, a holdover from the days of French rule, was nominal CO of 4th Brigade during the extended absences of Colonel Onya Nketia, the King's youngest son, who preferred Paris to Mokodi. Major Corbeil was pushing 70, a small, frail, pale-haired, pale-skinned soldier, only somewhat senile. He looked about vaguely, eyes dimmed, frame wasted but still erect. He appeared startled when all the men in the room snapped noisily to attention.

"Would you care to join us, Major?" Captain Anokye asked softly.

"No, no," Corbeil said, making a short waving gesture. "Carry on, carry on. Forgive the intrusion. Just looking about . . ."

He was seen so rarely away from his air-conditioned office that Anokye's junior officers and noncoms stared at him curiously. He wore the old French colonial uniform: high choker collar, fitted tunic, braided kepi. Decorations from a dozen wars covered his left breast.

"We are planning an action, Major," Anokye said, "and I would deem—"

"Ah," the old soldier said, eyes suddenly gleaming. "An action!" He drew himself up, looked about sternly. "Soldiers of France," he said in a whispery voice, "on your brave shoulders rests the reputation of the French army. Do not forget the heroes who have gone before, and those to come. Napoleon, Foch, Pétain. Orléans, Austerlitz, Verdun. The roll call of great battles and great victories is a constant reminder of our heritage. And now, the eyes of all France are on you today as you once again prove the valor of French arms. Remember, you . . ."

They stared with astonishment at this antique as he spoke eloquently of la gloire! la patrie! urging them to attack with vigor, to fight with determination, and to have their gas masks with them at all times. They were to remember always that they were citizens of France, with the tradition of French courage and élan.

Captain Anokye was silent, letting the old man finish. The others, too, listened politely.

"Soldiers of France!" Major Etienne Corbeil cried out in conclusion, "I salute you:"

He raised a trembling hand to the brim of his kepi. Then he turned slowly and shuffled away, his aide close to his elbow.

They waited silently until the door was again closed. Then Captain Anokye took a deep breath, glanced at his watch.

"It is time," he said.

There were almost twenty men in the room, but he insisted on embracing and speaking a few quiet words to each. Lieutenants, sergeants, corporals. The room gradually emptied as officers and NCOs departed to join their commands. Finally the Little Captain was alone. He sat a moment at his desk. He heard the shouted orders outside, the grind of trucks starting up, the solid stamp of armed men advancing on packed ground. Then he stood, buckled on his pistol belt, donned his helmet. Concealed in the helmet, between liner and steel, was a small bundle of white feathers from the hackle of a cock, bound with a crimson thread.

The Asante Royal Tank Corps was quartered within a fenced compound large enough to contain a corrugated iron garage, a repair shop, a combination barracks and mess hall, and several small outbuildings. The Corps consisted of thirty men commanded by Capt. Jim Nkomo, with Lt. Seko second in command. The garage housed the two new French AMX-30 tanks that constituted the Royal Tank Corps. There was also an ancient British half-track personnel carrier, inoperative, and two jeeps of World War II vintage, both in working order but rarely used because of the Corps' limited fuel allotment.

The same shortage of fuel kept the tanks immobilized most of the time, though they were featured in parades and during the annual King's Day when all the armed forces paraded in review. The AMX-30 tanks were less than a year old and had been customized in France to operate in Asante's climate and on Asante's soft roads.

Captain Obiri Anokye pulled up outside the fenced compound, riding in the cab of a truck that held twenty-five 4th Brigade soldiers. The Captain alighted slowly and moved casually around to the back. He ordered Sgt. Sebako to get the men disembarked and lined up in two files outside the gate. While this was going on, several tankers inside moved up to the fence and stared curiously at the troopers wearing battle dress. Many of the tankers had been engaged in early morning housekeeping assignments, washing clothes, policing the Corps area. Most of them wore only shorts. All wore the dark green Tank Corps beret, a mark of distinction.

When his men were formed, the Little Captain approached the uniformed guard inside the fence. The armed tanker came to attention and saluted.

Anokye returned the salute. "Open the gate," he said.

The guard hesitated a moment, eyes rolling in indecision. Then he lifted the heavy steel bar on his side and pulled half the gate inward. Captain Anokye motioned to his men. He marched inside the compound. They followed him. No one was grinning.

The tankers watched in bewilderment as Sgt. Sebako stationed the men at three-meter intervals along the inside

307

of the fence. The soldiers stood at port arms. More half-clad tankers came out of the barracks building to stare at this unusual proceeding. At first there was a confused chatter. Then the tankers fell silent, moving uneasily, not taking their eyes from the armed men.

Captain Anokye waited patiently until Sgt. Sebako had placed the soldiers in a wide semicircle, all facing inward. They covered the fronts and sides of the compound buildings.

An unarmed tanker officer came hurrying from the garage toward Captain Anokye. It was Lt. Seko, a thin, pinched-face, light-skinned man, a Muslim, old for a lieutenant, wearing steel-rimmed spectacles. He looked in astonishment at the armed troopers inside the fence, his eyes flicking from Captain Anokye to the soldiers, then back again. Finally he saluted slowly, hand trembling slightly. Anokye returned the salute gravely.

"Captain," Seko faltered, "is there—"

"Is Nkomo on duty?" the Little Captain interrupted.

"Well, not exactly on," Seko mumbled. He licked his lips nervously. "In his quarters. I'm not sure. He may still be."

"Take me to him," Anokye said. "Now."

He motioned Sgt. Sebako to remain in position, then followed Lt. Seko to the barracks. They went to the far end where plywood partitions halfway to the ceiling formed small bedrooms for the two officers and an even smaller duty office.

They paused before one of the openings. Capt. Jim Nkomo was sitting naked on the edge of his bed. He was holding a shard of mirror, and with a small pair of mani-cure scissors, he was delicately trimming his heavy black beard. It was an enormous beard, covering his neck, almost reaching his chest. But it was difficult to tell where the beard ended; Nkomo's body was covered with a thick mat of black hair: chest, shoulders, back, legs. His penis and testicles were almost hidden.

He glanced up as the two men paused at the doorway. He looked at Anokye, looked at his helmet, looked at the pistol holster hanging from the web belt.

"Captain Anokye," he said. Voice loud, booming, echoing in the small bedroom. "Good morning."

"Good morning."

"To what fortunate concatenation of events do I owe the honor of this unexpected visitation?"

"His men are all around," Lt. Seko reported angrily. "Inside the fence. Battle gear."

"We have a de facto invasion of the premises, do we?" Nkomo said. He didn't seem perturbed. He held the mirror before his face again and continued clipping gently at his beard. "Captain Anokye, can you provide a reason for this unusual and somewhat incomprehensible course of action?"

"I want your tanks," Anokye said coldly. "Both of them. Fueled and manned. Under my orders."

Nkomo lowered the mirror to stare at the Little Captain. Then he tossed mirror and scissors aside. He stood slowly, unfolding to his full height. A heavy man, blue-black, straight up and down, no waist. Large teeth gleamed whitely in the tangle of mustache and beard. Anokye supposed it was meant to be a smile, but Capt. Nkomo's eyes weren't smiling.

"You want my tanks, do you?" he asked. "I presume you have a legitimate order from a superior officer to that effect?"

"No," Captain Anokye said. He withdrew his pistol, let it hang from his hand alongside his right leg. "I have no order. I have twenty-five armed men."

Nkomo's eyes flickered to the pistol, then rose again to Anokye's face.

"Precisely what the fuck is this?" he asked gently. "Surely you can't seriously believe I will turn over command of my tanks to you without a legitimate order from a superior officer?"

"Yes," Anokye said. "I seriously believe you would be wise to do exactly that."

There was silence, inside the little room and outside. The two tankmen looked at each other, then back to Anokye.

"The palace is presently under attack," Captain Anokye said. "I need the tanks for the final assault. I intend to take the palace, Mokodi, all of Asante. I have the men to do it."

There was a moment of silence again, the two tankers considering this. Then Nkomo sighed noisily.

"Oh-ho," he said. "Oh-ho. May I have permission to call the palace, Captain? The phone is right next door, in the duty office."

Anokye raised the pistol, trained it on Nkomo's hairy middle.

"Make your call," he said. "No sudden movements. From either of you."

"We are both unarmed," Nkomo shrugged. "As you can easily perceive."

The three men moved next door to the duty office. Capt. Jim Nkomo, still naked, stood at the desk, absently scratching his ribs, and called the palace. It took almost five minutes to get through to General Opoku Tutu. The conversation was brief. Nkomo listened, murmured a few words, replaced the phone slowly.

"Yes," he nodded. "It is as you stated. The palace is indeed under attack. Heavy rifle fire. I am ordered to bring up my tanks and drive off the attackers. Now that presents me with a rather difficult if not insuperable problem, wouldn't you say?''

"Don't do it," Lt. Seko cried furiously. "He can't use the tanks without us.''

Anokye shifted the pistol muzzle slightly toward Seko.

"A dead hero?" he asked. "Is that your wish? I could kill you both now. Your men would then do as I command. They would follow me.''

"Ah, yes," Capt. Nkomo agreed thoughtfully. "I rather imagine they would." He pondered a moment, head lowered, beard mingling with chest hair. "What about Third Brigade?" he asked finally.

"Being engaged right now at Gonja. By the Nyam's rebels and the Asante Brothers of Independence. All armed with automatic weapons. And mortars.''

"Oh-ho," Nkomo said again, teeth flashing. "Long planning, Captain?''

"Yes. Long and careful. The bank is being taken now. And the cable office, telephone exchange, radio station, dock area, newspaper. And Zabar.''

Lt. Seko cursed, a long stream of bitter futility.

"Ah, the coup I have heard rumored," Nkomo said. "But early. That, too, was part of your plan?''

"Yes.''

"And if you succeed, you become the new king?''

"No one will be king," Anokye said. "Asante will become a republic. A new constitution. Everyone will vote. An elected legislature. Well? Please decide quickly.''

"If I should choose to link my destiny with yours, Captain," Nkomo said, "to become your humble and obedient servant, how may I profit?''

"I suggest we discuss that at another time, in private.

311

Make up your mind, man. What is it to be?"

Capt. Nkomo turned to Seko.

"Fuel the tanks, Lieutenant," he said briskly. "I'll take the lead with A Team. You follow with B."

Seko stared at him, shocked.

"Captain—" he started.

Nkomo sighed. "Lieutenant, as I have reiterated to you on several occasions, you must discipline yourself to reason coolly and logically, as the white man reasons. If we refuse Captain Anokye's request, we are dead. And to no purpose, as he gets the tanks without us. If we join him and he is defeated, then we are also dead. Ergo, our only logical choice is to join him and exert our energies to the utmost to insure his success. Only then may we hope to remain alive."

Lt. Seko made a strangled sound, turned, ran down the barracks toward the garage.

"Now it is another time and we are alone," Nkomo said. "I repeat, how may I profit personally from joining this crusade of yours?"

"What do you want?" the Little Captain asked. "Money?"

"Always welcome, of course. But what I really desire is an expanded Tank Corps. Perhaps an armored brigade. More equipment, sufficient fuel, more men, a higher rank. *Colonel* Nkomo would be a great honor."

"Agreed," Captain Anokye said promptly. "You have my word."

"I know it is to be trusted," Nkomo nodded. "You may replace your pistol now. I assure you that—"

They felt the heavy explosion through the floor of the barracks. Then heard a reverberating boom that fluttered the walls. Somewhere glass shattered. They heard yells from outside, a few shots.

312

Capt. Jim Nkomo gave a great roar of fury and dashed naked down the barracks. Anokye ran after him.

Flames and heavy black smoke poured from the open doors of the garage. The roof had been blown twenty meters away. The tankmen were running about frantically, throwing canvas buckets of water onto the garage walls, trying to operate two small fire extinguishers. The heat drove them back. Finally they stopped trying; tankers and soldiers watched with awe as small explosions continued to belch. One wall fell inward, then another . . .

Sgt. Sebako and three soldiers were holding Lt. Seko tightly by the arms. His steel-rimmed spectacles had been knocked awry. They hung crazily from one ear.

"He did it, Captain," Sgt. Sebako said excitedly. "Went into the garage. Then came running out. He started for the back fence. I fired at him. But it was too late. The garage blew up. It knocked him down."

Capt. Jim Nkomo shielded his eyes, trying to peer into the smoke and flames. He turned slowly away.

"My beauties," he said to the Little Captain. "Oh, the lovelies. Not a scratch on them. Worthless junk now. He filled them with fuel all right. Down the hatch."

"Long live King Prempeh!" Lt. Seko shouted loudly. "Long live Asante!"

"But not long live you," Nkomo said grimly. "May I borrow your pistol, Captain?"

Anokye handed it to him, butt foremost.

"Stand aside," Nkomo ordered.

Sgt. Sebako and the other soldiers dropped Lt. Seko's arms and scrambled hastily out of the way. Capt. Jim Nkomo stepped close, aimed carefully, fired three times into Seko's genitals. The lieutenant crumpled onto the ground, still alive, still conscious. He looked up meekly.

"No one offer him succor," Nkomo commanded. "Let

the foul traitor decay slowly." He returned the Walther to Anokye. "Will you be able to assault the palace without the aid of the tanks, Captain?"

"Somehow," the Little Captain said. "But it will be difficult."

"Trucks," Capt. Nkomo said, grinning. "The biggest trucks we can find, and the bulldozer belonging to the Department of Transportation. Infantry can follow them up to the palace doors."

"Suicide for the drivers," Anokye said.

"Perhaps not. We may be able to rig wood shielding. Heavy planks."

"Excellent," the Little Captain nodded. "Will you see what can be done? My command post will be the telephone exchange across the Boulevard from the palace. Report to me there."

"As soon as possible. I'll get on it at once."

"I suggest you cover your nakedness first," Anokye smiled.

"Before I do that . . ." said Capt. Jim Nkomo, and began to urinate on the dying Lt. Seko.

Prior to his efforts at the Royal Tank Corps, Captain Obiri Anokye had led the bulk of 4th Brigade, more than 200 men, to the neighborhood of the palace. He had directed the placement of his troops, armed with rifles, machine pistols, machine guns, and rifle grenades, in previously selected positions. They were on the ground and higher floors of office buildings, stores, hotels, restaurants, cabarets, and residences surrounding the palace plaza.

These premises were commandeered, the occupants of the buildings told to leave immediately. Many of the positions selected were a floor or two higher than the palace. All windows overlooking the palace grounds were manned by armed troopers of 4th Brigade. Streets were cleared of pedestrians, and guards posted to prevent civilians from entering the siege area.

At 0800, the order was given to open fire, and the attack against the Asante Royal Palace began. All its windows were shattered almost immediately; doors were hastily slammed shut as the heavy barrage continued steadily. After making an inspection tour of the firing positions, the Little Captain temporarily turned command over to Lt. Solomon, a stolid, unimaginative officer who knew only how to obey orders. Captain Anokye then departed on his unsuccessful attempt to obtain the tanks.

Others active in the coup, including Minister of Finance Willi Abraham and Professor Jean-Louis Duclos, had been given subsidiary assignments and sufficient personnel to carry them out. Abraham, for instance, captured the cable office and telephone exchange. Duclos seized the Mokodi mosque. Certain employees of the Asante *New Times* and the national radio station took over control of their offices without military assistance. They had been beneficiaries of the Starrett Petroleum slush fund. Continuous radio broadcasts began at once, predicting the imminent downfall of King Prempeh in joyous tones. The presses of the *New Times* turned out broadsides informing the populace of the coup and hailing the birth of a free Asante.

Small additional detachments of troops had been sent to the homes of a selected list of high government and secret police officials. These included most of King Prempeh's relatives and ministers of his regime. The individuals were placed under house arrest with armed guards posted inside and out. Prime Minister Osei Ware was taken while tend-ing roses in his garden. Anatole Garde was arrested while sleeping with Sbeth in an upper bedroom of the Golden Calf. Soldiers sent to the home of Commander of the Armed Forces Opoku Tutu reported the general was absent. It was later determined that he was inside the palace when the attack started. It was determined by the simple expedient of calling him on the telephone.

During the previous evening, fragmentary and confusing reports had begun filtering into headquarters of the secret police, located in the palace cellar. The reports dealt with the observed movement of the Nyam's rebels toward Gonja, unexpected gatherings of several chapters of the Asante Brothers of Independence, unusual nighttime activities at the Mokodi barracks, etc. The chief of the secret police, an organization that also provided intelligence to the armed forces, thought it best to alert General Tutu at 0200.

The general, grumbling, left a pleasant party with several old friends and new boys being held aboard *La Liberté* and went to the palace to hear in person an assessment of the situation by the "Nutcracker," the chief of the secret police. Tutu then made the decision to alert the palace guard. The entire guard, with battle gear, was brought into the palace. When King Prempeh awoke, he was informed of this action. He and General Tutu were discussing at breakfast what further measures should be taken when, at 0800, the palace came under heavy rifle fire.

From the volume of shots, it was almost immediately apparent to both men that this was not the sniping of a few dissidents but the start of the coup that Anatole Garde had warned them was coming. They cursed the inaccuracy of the time schedule he had predicted as (with some difficulty on the King's part) they flopped onto the floor and crawled

316

under the dining table. In a few moments they cautiously raised their heads far enough to watch palace guards rush into the room and begin firing at targets of opportunity from the palace windows.

Stooping low, making a wild dash, and then sliding under the table to join them, the colonel of the guard told King Prempeh that his wives and children had been escorted to the cellar. He recommended the King and General Tutu join them there as soon as possible. No windowed room in the palace was safe, he said, and some of the bullets apparently were being fired from positions higher than the palace; plunging fire made even the floors unsafe.

It took the King and General Tutu almost an hour to make the perilous trip downstairs. It was particularly difficult for the obese Prempeh because he could not run; he could, at best, hurry. And bending double was impossible. The sight of several dead and unattended wounded lying on the palace floor did not increase his confidence; he was gray with fright, gasping for breath, and sweating profusely when he finally burst into cellar headquarters of the secret police. Slithering along corridors and down stairs had dislodged most of his medals. He was immediately surrounded by wives and children, all of them weeping, screaming, clutching at him for comfort.

He slapped his way through the frantic mob to grab up a phone and call the French embassy. But after several clicks and much static, the dial tone returned. The same thing happened when General Tutu attempted to call the Royal Tank Corps and the Gonja garrison. It was only when a call came through from the gendarmerie on Zabar, reporting they were under attack, that it became evident the telephone exchange had been captured; the palace could receive calls but not make them.

In the small inner office of the chief of the secret police, the colonel of the palace guard delivered his assessment of the situation. It was not reassuring. He said the palace was surrounded by a large force of concealed riflemen, and it appeared impossible to summon rescuers.

"So far they are using only rifles, Your Majesty," the colonel said. "If they have mortars and artillery, I cannot guarantee we'll be able to hold out."

"Can you send runners?" Tutu asked. "Slip them out back doors or terrace windows? To call Colonel de Blanca at Gonja?"

The colonel shook his head. "We tried it, General. Three men at different times. All shot down before they had taken ten steps."

"What about our ammunition?"

"Plenty of that, sir. And machine guns, grenades, and two bazookas. But at the moment we have no satisfactory targets."

"How many men have you?"

"Counting the secret police, about a hundred and sixty. Fourteen casualties at last count."

King Prempeh rose, and the other two men automatically jerked to their feet. The King slammed a pudgy fist down on the rickety table.

"I will not hide here and be threatened," he thundered. "Go out there and kill them!"

The two soldiers looked at him in astonishment. Even in this cellar room they could hear the constant crackle of gunfire.

"A sortie, Your Majesty?" the colonel asked. "Where? In what direction? Against what? They are all around us."

"I command you to go out there and kill them!" the King screamed. "I *command* you!"

"Yes, Your Majesty. At once, Your Majesty."

318

At the door, General Tutu whispered, "No more than ten men." The colonel nodded grimly and departed.

King Prempeh sat down heavily on a wooden chair that creaked and groaned beneath his weight. General Opoku Tutu stood at his right.

"The French embassy will learn of our situation, Your Majesty. They will come to our aid."

The King looked up hopefully. "Do you really think so?"

"Oh yes, Your Majesty. If we can just hold out, paratroops can be here in a few hours."

"How many hours?" the King demanded.

"I don't know the exact disposition of French forces," General Tutu acknowledged. "But surely by tonight."

"Tonight? We may all be dead by tonight. Who is it, Tutu? Who's leading them? That captain Garde told us about?"

"Probably, Your Majesty. Captain Anokye."

"We should have taken him," the King groaned. "We should have killed him. I was too kind."

"Yes, Your Majesty."

"Get me some food," Prempeh said nervously. "I am hungry."

General Tutu went to the door and motioned to the King's chamberlain.

"The King is hungry," he told him. "Bring some food."

The man was shocked. "But I'll have to go upstairs for it, General."

"Then go, you fool! Or send a servant. But get it!"

There was a heavier burst of firing from upstairs. General Tutu heard a few distant shouts. And dimly, he thought, he heard the chatter of machine guns. In a few moments the colonel of the guard came down the cellar steps, dark face coated with plaster dust. He was carrying a Colt .45.

"We tried, General," he reported. "Ten men. They didn't even get halfway across the plaza. Machine guns."

Tutu nodded glumly. "I heard," he said.

"Where's my food?" King Prempeh roared.

But 30 minutes later their plight didn't seem so serious. Colonel de Blanca had called from the Gonja garrison and Capt. Nkomo had called from the Royal Tank Corps compound. Both had promised to come at once to the relief of the palace.

"More chicken!" screamed King Prempeh IV.

The insurgents' command post was established on the second floor of the telephone exchange, captured by Willi Abraham's task force. Here, during the long morning of August 5th, the first results of the Asante coup d'etat were reported.

Other than failure at the Royal Tank Corps, events were proceeding as Captain Obiri Anokye had planned. By 1300, it was learned that the Nyam had been killed and his force of Marxist rebels destroyed. Third Brigade had been decimated south of Gonja; Sam Leiberman and Sgt. Sene Yeboa had already arrived in Mokodi, bringing 50 men on trucks with another 70 following on foot. The Gonja garrison had been secured, as had those at Kasai, Kumasi, and all the smaller towns and villages where chapters of the Asante Brothers of Independence existed.

The Royal Highway from Mokodi to Four Points was under control of insurgent forces, as were the freshwater pumping stations in the north. Property of the King's relatives had been seized, including the phosphate mines where many political prisoners were released. *La Liberté* and the Royal Navy's motor launches had been surrendered by their crews without serious resistance. The three planes and the small airfield used by the Royal Air Force were taken without a shot fired.

Finally, most gratifying to Captain Anokye, a telephoned message from his brother Zuni reported the island of Zabar captured and secured. Zuni's forces had suffered only two men killed and five wounded. He promised to send immediately 20 armed men to assist in the attack on the palace.

By 1400, the reinforcements brought by Leiberman and Sgt. Yeboa had been posted in additional firing positions; the palace was surrounded by a tight ring of riflemen reinforced by several machine-gun crews. Leiberman had brought along the mortars, but the Little Captain again refused to use them against the palace.

Meanwhile, the crowds of excited civilians had grown and were being restrained with difficulty behind army barricades. It was Leiberman who suggested using the civilians in an assault on the palace.

"There must be five thousand out there," he told Anokye. "Why don't you turn them loose? A human wave. The palace guard can't kill 'em all."

The Captain shook his head. "It would probably work," he said, "but politically it would be unsatisfactory. I want only the army to carry out this coup—carry it out to a successful conclusion. I want the nation to remember the courage and sacrifice of the army."

Leiberman stared at him a moment, then nodded. "I guess you know what you're doing."

Later, Leiberman murmured to Peter Tangent: "The black bwana is way ahead of us all. Nice to be on the winning side for a change."

Tangent, following instructions of Captain Anokye, had remained close to Willi Abraham during the early

321

hours of the coup. He had peeked nervously from a telephone exchange window while the armed cordon was thrown around the palace. And he had watched, fascinated, when a squad of guards, sallying bravely from the palace, were shot down in minutes. Some of the men, struck by the fusillade, had gone into balletic poses and steps, pirouetting, rising on their toes, whirling, arms lifted high, legs flung in their death leaps.

Tangent had made a determined effort to keep out of the soldiers' way and to refrain from asking too many questions. Sam Leiberman had told him of the action south of Gonja, and Willi Abraham had kept him informed as messages came in from outlying localities, reporting the insurgents' success.

Tangent did ask Willi Abraham: "Does Anokye intend to kill the King?"

"Oh yes," Abraham nodded. "It is necessary. A living Prempeh, in Asante or abroad, would represent a constant danger, a threat. He would never cease plotting his return to power. And, of course, by killing the King personally, the Little Captain inherits his strength, spirit, and wisdom."

"Do you believe that?" Tangent asked.

"Many in Asante do," Abraham said. "Captain Anokye is aware of it. So Prempeh must die."

Then, perhaps sensing Tangent's reaction, Abraham glanced down at the 9 mm Parabellum automatic Tangent was wearing in a brand-new leather holster.

"Surely, Mr. Tangent," the Minister of Finance said gently, "you did not expect this to be a bloodless coup? In South America perhaps. Not in Africa."

At approximately 1430, Capt. Jim Nkomo reported to the command post in high good humor. The bearded tank officer had been unable to obtain the Department of Transportation bulldozer—as usual, it was down for repairs—but he had rounded up six heavy trucks, military and civilian, and equipped the cabs with shielding: thick planks across the windshields with just a crack between them where the driver could peer out.

It took 30 minutes to plan the first truck assault on the palace. It would be driven across the plaza alongside the flagstoned walk leading up to the front steps and doorway. Driver and a man armed with a machine pistol in the cab. Twenty men standing on the truck bed, concealed but not protected by the canvas covering. Thirty men to follow on foot directly behind the truck. All the assault troops to be armed with automatic weapons.

Captain Anokye said he would command the assault personally. Attempts were made to dissuade him, by Abraham, Tangent, Capt. Nkomo. Sgt. Sene Yeboa begged permission to lead the truck assault. The Little Captain listened to them all patiently, then shook his head.

"This is my decision," he said firmly. "I will go. Willi, you will be in command here. The moment the truck starts, lay down fire against every doorway and window of the palace."

The truck assault was a disaster. As it rumbled across the plaza, going slowly to provide cover for the foot soldiers who followed, a heavy rifle barrage was brought to bear against the palace windows. But it did not prevent a well-directed return fire from the guards against the lumbering truck. The tires were shot out first and, as the truck wobbled forward, enfilade fire from the wings of the palace killed most of the men aboard the truck.

Then a lucky shot into the gas tank brought the truck to a flaming halt halfway across the parade ground. The few troopers on the truck still alive leaped off screaming, burning bundles. The soldiers following, led by Captain

Anokye, retreated to the protection of the telephone exchange. It was not an orderly retreat. Seventeen men returned safely, several with wounds and burns. The Little Captain was unharmed.

He first saw to the care of the wounded, then gathered his aides about the desk in the office of the director of the telephone exchange. Spread on the desk was a hand-drawn map of the palace, the plaza, the surrounding buildings.

"We will try again," the Little Captain said grimly. "This time we will use two trucks, one to the front door, one to the rear. To divide their fire. No men on foot following the trucks. So they will be able to speed across the plaza, as fast as possible, carrying as many men as we can squeeze aboard. Captain Nkomo, drain the tanks of surplus gas. Leaye just enough to get across the grounds to the palace itself. Everyone understand?"

The dual assault was organized by 1600. At 20 minutes past the hour, precisely, a truckload of soldiers raced across the plaza toward the front door of the palace as another truckload sped toward the rear entrance. The front truck was manned by 4th Brigade troopers, the rear by veterans of the ABI. A heavy covering fire was laid down by riflemen and machine gunners in the surrounding buildings.

The guard proved equal to the challenge. In the front of the palace and in the rear, bazookamen poked the snouts of their tubes over ledges of windows on the ground floor and fired their rockets at short range at the approaching trucks. The one speeding to the rear of the palace was destroyed by two direct hits. All aboard were casualties.

The truck lurching toward the front door evaded the first rocket, was stopped by the second, survived two close misses and another direct hit, and then was tipped over on its side by a sixth rocket. The soldiers came spilling out. Being closer to the palace than to the protection of the buildings beyond the plaza, about ten 4th Brigade troopers ran forward frantically and sought cover by throwing themselves onto the ground at the base of the palace terrace. Here they could not be hit by rifle fire from the palace windows.

But the guard solved this problem; they pulled pins from fragmentation grenades and rolled them across the tiled terrace to drop amongst the cowering soldiers on the far side.

Captain Obiri Anokye and the others watched this massacre from windows in the telephone exchange. After several grenades had exploded and no movement was seen amongst the attackers huddled at the base of the palace terrace, the Little Captain said tonelessly to Lt. Solomon, "Resume intermittent fire."

Then he stood somberly with folded arms as the fire against the palace from soldiers in protected positions dwindled to a light popping. Willi Abraham stepped to Anokye's side, murmured a few words, led him away from the open window back to the safety of the interior office. The others clustered about the desk again, looking down at the map, not wanting to see Anokye's face.

Finally: "The mortars, Captain?" Leiberman asked softly.

"We have three more trucks," Capt. Nkomo offered.

Captain Anokye took his familiar stance: hands on hips, torso bent slightly backward, chin elevated. The small vertical wrinkles appeared between his brows. He looked slowly around the circle of aides.

"We have several alternatives," he said quietly. "We could cut off their freshwater supply and simply sit here and starve them out. But time is the determining factor. I am certain the French are now aware of Prempeh's predicament. I want to present Paris with a fait accompli before they decide to come to the King's aid. Also, the guard will undoubtedly take advantage of darkness to make potentially dangerous sallies from the palace against our positions. So the palace must be taken as soon as possible. Certainly before nightfall. We will use every man available in a coordinated charge. The three remaining trucks will attack at the same time.''

"Casualties will be high, Bibi," Willi Abraham said.

"Yes," Anokye agreed, "but it must be done. It is the only way. I will personally lead the attack.''

There was silence again as all stared down at the map on the table, envisioning the raw, frontal attack. The palace grounds were already littered with the smoking debris of battle: burned-out trucks and burned-out men. They could hear the diminishing screams of the wounded. If they dared look, they could see, here and there, arms raised in supplication from the twisted and blackened heaps. They could imagine what reeking garbage the new attack would create.

Peter Tangent cleared his throat. "Captain," he said hesitantly, "may I make a suggestion?"

"Of course, Mr. Tangent."

"Starrett has a helicopter. A Sikorsky. Seats twelve plus two-man crew. We use it to transport personnel and matériel from the roof of the Mokodi Hilton to the helipad on the *Starrett Explorer*."

When they all looked at him, waiting, Tangent added: "The palace has a flat roof."

Then they all turned to look at Captain Anokye. He was staring at Tangent, large eyes partly lidded as he regarded the American thoughtfully.

326

"And Starrett would make the helicopter available to us?" he asked softly.

"I don't believe it would be wise for me to *volunteer* the copter, Captain. But if you commandeered it at gunpoint, I would have no choice, would I?"

Captain Anokye drew his Walther P38 and pointed it at Tangent. "I demand you make the Starrett helicopter available," he said.

"That's good enough for me," Tangent said hurriedly. "All of you are witnesses that I am complying under duress. Now let me call and see if it's at the hotel or out on the ship."

He put a call through to J. Tom Petty at the Mokodi Hilton.

"What the hell's happening?" Petty demanded excitedly. "We can hear the gunfire. There's soldier boys in the lobby. Where are you? Is Prempeh out on his fat ass?"

"Almost," Tangent said. "The palace is surrounded. Just a question of time. Where's the chopper?"

"What?"

"Where's the helicopter?"

"Right here. Upstairs. On the roof."

"The army wants it to land troops on the palace roof."

"Beautiful. You going to give it to them?"

"I have no choice."

"Oh-ho, it's like that, is it? Well, let them borrow it if it means getting rid of those royal shitheads."

"Where's the crew?"

"Down in the bar, hustling gash."

"You think they'll fly soldiers onto the palace?"

"Sure they will."

"Pay them as much as they want."

"Pete, they're *Australians*, for God's sake. They'll do it for a case of beer."

Sam Leiberman called the plan "organized chaos," but
seemed to think none the less of it for that. As improvised
by Captain Anokye, the attack on the palace would consist
of three elements:

Leiberman and Sgt. Yeboa would select 10 men of 4th
Brigade, soldiers known for their vigor and resourceful
ness. All twelve men, armed with submachine guns and
fragmentation grenades, would be taken by truck to the
Mokodi Hilton. There they would board Starrett's
helicopter for the trip back to the palace roof.

When the copter came in over the palace and was letting
down, the three remaining trucks under the command of
Capt. Jim Nkomo would begin their assault. All would
aim for the front entrance to the palace, hoping that one or
two might escape bazooka rockets by offering more than
one target.

After the trucks began their wild dash, Captain Obir
Anokye and Lt. Solomon would lead the charge of foot
soldiers. This attack would come from all sides, ringing
the palace. It would be preceded by a barrage of rifle
grenades aimed to land on the terrace and drive the defen
ders back from the windows.

By 1700, the three forces were organized, the helicop
ter squad on its way to board the Sikorsky at the Mokodi
Hilton.

"See you in the throne room," Leiberman said to Peter
Tangent.

"We'll be waiting for you," Tangent said, with more
confidence than he felt.

Then Tangent and the other aides, officers, and non
coms joined the Little Captain at the desk while Minister
of Finance Willi Abraham drew quick floor plans of the
palace, pointing out stairways, chambers, the entrance to
the cellar, the door to the armory, offices, and apartments

"After we are inside," Anokye said to Capt. Nkomo, "I will take my men down to the cellar. You and Solomon clear out the upstairs. Remember, Leiberman and Yeboa will be coming down from the roof. Be certain of your targets. Willi, please stay here with the reserve. If we need you, a messenger will be sent. Mr. Tangent, I suggest you stay with the Minister. There is no need to endanger yourself. Anything else? I think not. It will all be over in an hour. One way or another."

Then they waited in silence. The few soldiers remaining at the windows kept up a desultory fire against the palace. But most of the attacking troops were gathered out of sight on the ground floors of the protecting buildings. Captain Obiri Anokye let himself be seen as much as possible by the waiting soldiers, moving about, smiling, joking, slapping a few men atop their helmets, saying things to make them laugh. Several reached out to touch him briefly.

"Juju," Willi Abraham murmured to Tangent. "They think he has magic, that he is invincible. By touching him, they may share it."

Then, sooner than Tangent had expected, they heard the whump-whump-whump of the copter. It approached the palace from the rear, coming in low. It made a tight circle, tilting steeply downward, then straightened over the palace roof, slowed, hovered a moment, began to let down.

"Now!" the Little Captain shouted to Nkomo. "Go!"

The bearded tanker waved, swung into the cab of the lead truck. Its horn began blaring steadily. The three trucks ground into gear, accelerated across the Boulevard Voltaire, bounced over the curb, started speeding across the grassed plaza toward the palace.

"Rifle grenades!" Anokye shouted. "Fire!"

A few seconds later a ragged circle of explosions burst

around the palace. Only a few grenades hit the building itself or landed on the terrace. But their blooms of earth and flame served as a signal. With a feral roar, almost 200 armed men burst from cover, began a wild charge toward the palace, legs driving, knees lifted high, guns firing. In the forefront ran Captain Anokye, carrying a Thompson submachine gun. And close behind him, to his own amazement, pounded the tall, lanky figure of Peter Tangent, wondering just what the hell he thought he was doing.

At almost the moment the copter touched down, the door was flung open. Leiberman jumped onto the palace roof. After him came Sgt. Yeboa. Then the remainder of the squad, leaping, staggering, falling.

They heard the ragged crump of rifle grenades. Then the whine of truck engines. Explosions. The roar of the attack. The rotor began its dazzling spin again, the helicopter took off and tilted swiftly away. No escape now.

Leiberman glanced around the roof, led the way to a hutlike structure, opened the door cautiously. A narrow staircase led down to a dusty, dimly lighted attic. He started down, step by step, holding a Uzi chest-high. The others followed in file.

The attic was stacked with cartons and crates. At the far end, a three-sided railing marked the stairway. Leiberman ran forward. Almost there when head and shoulders poked above floor level. A startled face stared. A rifle barrel began swinging to level.

Leiberman triggered a short burst. The guard's head exploded like a hammered melon. Then, grenades into the stairway opening, down on the floor, explosions, up, rush, thunder of boots, down to the next floor, a corridor door, Yeboa and Leiberman working as a team, opened door, tossed grenade, slammed door, explosion, open again, debouchment into the corridor, guards popping from doorways, spray of bullets, all the squad in action now, spreading, kicking doors open, rolling grenades, automatic weapons chattering from hip, chest, shoulder, leaning into the kick, piercing smell of cordite, men rushing, falling, skidding on the polished floor, a guard clapping his eyes, screaming, out again, in, down a staircase, a soldier shot and looping over a banister to fall spread-eagled, curses, shout of triumph, shriek of terror, steel whispers in the air, glass shattering, solid thunk of bullets, defecation of the dying, invisible fingers plucking, two men straining against each other, embracing, bodies tight until one slides away, eyes glazing, down, guards rushing, doors smashed open, grenades floating upward, whine of splinters, and more doors, corridors, rooms, splinters from the walls and moldings, plaster dropping, a shrill whistle cut off suddenly, faces of fear, faces of fury, men clutching chests, throats, bellies, another staircase, wide, and Yeboa and Leiberman, sobbing, shivering, bloodied, sodden, halted their remaining men, reloaded again, knelt, peered downward, the noise of the battle below growing in intensity.

Two of Capt. Nkomo's trucks were taken out by bazooka rockets. The third, with Nkomo in the cab, hit the steps, front tires blew, rear wheels churned, the truck bounced up the steps, across the terrace, slammed into the front doors, smashed them open, stopped, steam rising from the cracked radiator.

Then Nkomo and his men were through the doors, into the palace. Down on the polished floor as an arc of fire from inside doorways poured into them. Grenades skidded back and forth, dead men were lifted and flung by the blasts, ropes of red festooned the walls. Nkomo sprayed

331

his gun ahead of him, deafened by the noise, despairing of gaining the wide stairway that led upward. But then Anokye's foot soldiers were pouring through the shattered doors behind him, through windows, and running, screaming from the rear of the palace. The guards retreated, some backing up the stairway, as more and more soldiers pressed them, closer, glaives flashing now, fingers, hands, arms, legs springing free and rolling. The screams were of victory, as more soldiers rushed the stairway, the remaining guards were trapped between death above and death below and stood in their last fury to club with rifle butts and went down to bloody puddles, kicked, stamped, riddled again and again, killed a dozen times, as a screamed chant of triumph burst from a hundred throats, and the head of a guard, kaffiyeh still in place, was booted the length of a corridor, glaived through an eye, hoisted aloft with a scream of exultation even as explosions from the cellar rumbled and walls quivered.

Running men following Captain Anokye took heavy casualties as they crossed the plaza. But they saw Nkomo's truck crash the doors, heard the sounds of battle from the helicopter squad. As they neared the palace, fire from the windows slackened. They knew the day was theirs.

Anokye came to the terrace wall, leaped for a handhold, slipped, fell back, and Tangent was beside him, bending over, hands on knees, offering his back. The Little Captain understood, stepped on Tangent's back, hauled himself up by the balustrade, leaned down to grab Tangent's hand, pull him scrabbling up. And the other soldiers leaped, formed human ladders, swarmed up and over to the palace windows and French doors, tossing grenades, firing at anything and everything, Anokye into the main ballroom, Tangent and others crowding him, skidding, sliding, falling, rolling, killing the guards who crouched and died along the walls, keening a battle cry. Out into the corridor, remembering the floor plan, around a corner, a dozen guns chopping down a guards officer who loomed, then blasting the lock from the cellar door, crushing it off the hinges, a stumbling rush downward, women and children cowering in a corner, a guards colonel coolly leveling his pistol as chunks of his shoulder shred away, his eyes and ears spouting blood, and melting down he goes, to another doorway, inner room, General Tutu smashed away with a rifle butt, fat Prempeh caught in the arms of his chair, struggling to rise, as Captain Obiri Anokye steps close and stitches the bulging belly and chest, bullets making neat holes like fingers poking deep in dough, slamming the King backward as one plump, beringed hand floats up in lazy protest and a final burst from the Little Captain's gun ends the reign of King Prempeh IV.

32

DURING THE EVENING of August 5th, following the capture of the royal palace at Mokodi by insurgent forces under command of Captain Obiri Anokye, Mai Fante escorted an unharmed Anatole Garde to the French embassy and delivered him to the Ambassador.

Fante spent an hour with embassy officials and, using his considerable forensic skills and even more considerable charm, assured them the new Asante government would desire nothing but the closest friendship with France. French investments in Asante were secure, the Asante National Bank could reopen in the morning with not a franc missing, no French assets would be seized, no French citizen would be harmed or threatened. And, Mai Fante reminded the Ambassador, Captain Anokye had been educated at the lycée and owed his military expertise to Major Etienne Corbeil. The Little Captain would not forget his friends.

Much mollified, the Ambassador immediately sent off a long cable to Paris. There, at a meeting on the second floor of L'escargot d'Or of those most closely concerned with the Asante problem, it was decided to make no decision for the time being. This, as Tony Malcolm later remarked to Peter Tangent, was a classically Gallic action: a decision not to make a decision. In any event, no intervention or opposition by French forces was anticipated, and none developed.

334

Also in the hours following the coup d'etat, a number of men and a few women were brought to the Mokodi barracks by armed guards. The prisoners included former Prime Minister Osei Ware, General Opoku Tutu, several high officials of the Prempeh regime, several of the late King's close relatives, the few members of the palace guard still alive, the chief of the secret police and all his subordinates who could be rounded up, and a mixed bag of police spies, informers, executives of the phosphate mines, etc.

Around midnight, the prisoners were marched to a distant field and executed by gunfire, but not before their captors had a little fun with them.

In the days and weeks following the coup, Captain Obiri Anokye moved swiftly to consolidate his power. He appointed an interim cabinet, including Willi Abraham as Premier, Mai Fante as Attorney General, and Professor Jean-Louis Duclos as Minister of State. Other official positions were fairly parceled out to animists, Christians, and Muslims. All were black. In addition to serving as president pro tem, Captain Anokye assumed the powers and duties of Commander-in-Chief of the Armed Forces.

A month after the coup d'etat, the new constitution was submitted to the electorate along with a ballot of candidates for election to the executive and legislative branches of the new government. Anyone who wished might run for national office, and several slates of candidates were submitted to the voters. The Little Captain and those he supported won easily.

During this period, Starrett Petroleum brought over two offshore drilling rigs and began sinking delineation wells to determine the size of the Zabarian oil field. When President-elect Anokye announced his intention to celebrate his inauguration with a national festival, Starrett (at

Peter Tangent's suggestion) offered to pay the cost of the entire celebration that would include free food and drink, fireworks, and dancing in the streets. Starrett also presented President-elect Anokye with a fine piece of Steuben glass depicting a lion, rampant, on a ground of dead serpents.

The inaugural ceremony and the celebration that followed were planned and carried out under the direction of a public relations expert Peter Tangent persuaded Anokye to employ. The expert, from PR Afrique in Monrovia, Liberia, suggested to the Little Captain that during the inaugural ceremony and afterward he continue to wear the uniform of an officer of the Asante army, but without any indication of rank or decorations. Anokye readily agreed.

It seemed to Tangent that the entire population of Asante gathered in Mokodi to witness the inauguration of Obiri Anokye as President of the Asante Republic. The crowds waited patiently while oaths of office were taken by the legislature and newly appointed judiciary. Finally, when the Little Captain swore to "uphold, maintain, and further" the principles of the constitution, the Asantis greeted their new President and new nation with such noisy joy that foreign correspondents, in their dispatches, could only use such phrases as "mad delight," "hysterical pleasure," "thunderous approval," and so forth.

That night the main boulevards of Mokodi were lighted by the blaze of the palace and the brilliant flare of fireworks overhead. There was, indeed, dancing in the streets, and a sense of unreserved delight as a whole people threw off the tyranny of the past and celebrated their limitless future. Food for all. Jobs for all. Fun for all.

During the early hours of the evening, President Anokye moved through the crowds of civilians thronging

336

the open ground floor of the palace and enjoying the free food and drinks, dancing to the music of three bands, singing the new National Anthem ("Asante, land of our fathers/our hearts belong to thee . . ."). The President was escorted closely at all times by several aides and an armed and alert Sgt. Sene Yeboa. He had refused promotion to officers rank but had accepted a large increase in salary and assignment as commander of President Anokye's personal guard.

Later in the evening, the President left the public chambers to join a smaller throng on the second floor of the palace. The damage caused during the battle of August 5th had been sufficiently repaired so that President Anokye was able to entertain friends and honored guests in elegant chambers and to join them at a generous buffet.

The President's family was present, of course, conducting themselves with quiet dignity. Squiring Sara Anokye was Lt. Jere Songo of the Togolese army, who had received a personal invitation to the inaugural from the President himself. Another recipient of a gracefully written request from the President was the Premier of Dahomey, Benedicto da Silva. He was accompanied by his daughter Beatrice.

The young girl's greeting to Anokye was a mixture of hesitant formality and youthful delight. "I left you a captain and find you a president," she laughed, holding out a soft hand. "Anyway, congratulations, Mr. President."

"Things have moved quickly," he smiled in return. "I am very happy to see you again. What a lovely gown!"

"Do you really like it? I had it made specially for your inaugural."

"I like it very much. As you said, green is your color."

"You remember!"

She glowed with pleasure. They stood a moment without speaking, looking into each other's eyes. But then Peter Tangent and Jonathan Wilson, the American cultural attaché, came up to offer their congratulations. They introduced a third man, Anthony Malcolm, described merely as "a resident of London." In turn, the President introduced Beatrice da Silva, and the five chatted easily a few minutes until the Little Captain excused himself and moved away to greet Jean-Louis Duclos and Mboa, who had announced their intention to wed.

It was almost an hour before the President was able to maneuver through the crush to the side of Benedicto da Silva.

"Premier," he murmured, "may I have a few moments of your time?"

"With pleasure, Mr. President," da Silva said, and followed Anokye out into the corridor and to a room at the rear of the palace.

"Please excuse the confusion here, Premier," Anokye said, switching on the overhead light and closing the door behind them. "This room is being redecorated as a study. I have an office downstairs, but I felt the need for more private quarters. For quiet talks, or just to be alone for a few moments."

"I understand, Mr. President. For a man in your position, public appearances can become onerous. One sometimes needs solitude to think."

"Yes, that is so."

"A cigar, Mr. President?"

"Thank you, I will."

They sat on a leather couch, lighted the long, thin cigars.

"Excellent tobacco," Anokye said. "Cuban?"

338

"Sumatran. I expect a shipment soon. Please accept the poor gift of a box."

"Thank you. With pleasure."

They sat in silence, puffing slowly, watching the white smoke bloom up to the high ceiling.

"I hope our nations may continue to enjoy cordial relations," Anokye said. "I see no reason why this cannot be."

"Nor I, Mr. President," the Dahomeyan Premier said. "I look forward to a closer relationship in the future."

"Yes. You have heard of the oil field found in our waters?"

"All Africa knows of it, Mr. President. And envies your good fortune!"

"Premier, I am aware of the economic situation in your country. We have not yet started to receive revenues from our oil. When we do, perhaps we may find a way to be of assistance to you."

"We would welcome such assistance with sincere thanks, Mr. President."

"But that is all in the future. I asked you to join me here to discuss a more immediate matter." President Anokye turned slowly to look at the Premier. "A more personal matter."

Benedicto da Silva said nothing, waiting. He was a tall, slender man, with gray hair naturally curled, lying in waves along his elegantly shaped head. The silvered Vandyke was beautifully trimmed, the mustache waxed. Like his daughter, his skin was dark with a rosy undertint. He smelled faintly of a woodsy cologne.

His black silk suit was artfully tailored, shoes gleaming, linen impeccable. His manner was assured. But behind the smooth urbanity, graceful gestures, fluent speech, were craggy jaw, firm lips, flinty eyes.

"Premier, I had the pleasure of meeting your daughter several weeks ago during a reception in this palace."

"So she informed me, Mr. President."

"I found her a lovely and charming young lady."

"Thank you, Mr. President. Since the death of my wife, Beatrice has taken over duties not usually the responsibility of one so young. I find her assistance invaluable."

"I am certain you do. Premier, I would like to see her more frequently. On a personal basis. I would not do that without your permission."

The Premier's eyes narrowed slightly. But he showed no obvious surprise. He did not smile.

"You do my daughter great honor, Mr. President," he said softly. "And show me great respect, for which I am grateful."

"I would do nothing to endanger our friendship, Premier. Or the friendship between our countries. In matters of this kind, I believe it is best to speak openly and honestly."

"I agree. I hope you will understand if I speak as openly and honestly."

"Of course."

"Your history and background, to my knowledge, are altogether admirable. With few advantages to start with, you have worked hard, developed your talents, and earned an enviable reputation in Asante. Knowing your past record, I am confident you will prove to be a wise and effective leader of your people. However, there *is* something that makes me hesitate to grant immediately the approval you seek."

"Oh? And that is?"

"Mr. President, please forgive my candor, but it has come to my attention that you are involved with a woman who is a subject of public comment. A public woman, in fact. A white woman. May I ask if this is true?"

"It is true."

"I appreciate your honesty. Ordinarily, your relationship with this woman, or any woman, would be no business of mine. After all, it hardly concerns me. But in view of what you are asking, it suddenly becomes my business and does concern me. Me and mine. Do I make myself clear, Mr. President?"

"Perfectly."

Anokye stood and began to pace about the littered room, head lowered, hands clasped behind him. The Premier sat quietly, knees crossed, the crease of his trousers precisely adjusted. Finally the Little Captain sighed, raised his head, looked directly at the other man.

"Premier," he said, "if I promised you to end the relationship to which you refer, if I gave you my word that never again will I meet with this woman, would you then grant me permission to see your daughter?"

"I would, Mr. President, and gladly."

"I now give you that promise and pledge my honor that I will immediately end my—my relationship with this woman."

"Then I welcome your friendship for my daughter. But I must warn you: My approval may not guarantee hers! She has a mind of her own, and in matters of this nature I would not attempt to influence her—unless she asks for my advice, of course."

"I understand that."

"So, in effect, Mr. President, you are on your own. But I cannot believe my daughter's love will prove more difficult for the Little Captain to capture than the royal palace of Asante!''

The two men laughed, shook hands, finished their cigars, and returned arm in arm to the inaugural reception.

By midnight, most of the guests had departed or were queuing up to leave. President Anokye stood at the doorway, shaking hands, embracing his family, exchanging salaams with Muslim guests, placing palms against palms with certain old friends who retained the ancient ways. To some men he murmured a few words, so that when the last visitor had departed and servants moved in to clean the room, President Anokye returned to his private study to find waiting for him Sgt. Yeboa, Peter Tangent, Sam Leiberman, Colonel Jim Nkomo, Willi Abraham, Jean-Louis Duclos, and Mai Fante.

As instructed, Sgt. Yeboa was serving brandy and black coffee. The men were gathered around a small table on which was displayed Peter Tangent's personal gift to President Obiri Anokye to commemorate his inauguration.

It was a set of handsomely designed and crafted model soldiers wearing the dress uniforms of a captain and nine enlisted men of the Asante army. Made by Bulwer & Knightley of London, the beautifully detailed models gleamed with bright colors and sparkling accoutrements. The gift had pleased the Little Captain enormously.

He joined the circle of men admiring the models and picked up the figure of the captain to hold it high in the air, turning it this way and that to catch the light, grinning unaffectedly with delight. He held on to the soldier even as he motioned the men into a circle about the desk and unfolded a large colored map of Africa.

They stared down, fascinated, at the mosaic of the giant continent.

"So many nations," said Willi Abraham.

"So many poor nations," said Jean-Louis Duclos.

"So many weak nations," said Sam Leiberman.

"Many small, poor, and weak nations," President Anokye repeated slowly. "Yes, they are that. With governments as evil as Prempeh's—and worse. With ignorant and greedy rulers torturing the land and the people. Africa, my Africa! How many nations now? I have lost count? Sixty? More? And singly they are nothing. Spits of impoverished land. Even those with natural riches see their children die and their spirit dwindle." He paused to look around the circle of silent, spellbound men. "You know I speak the truth. Some so poor they have nothing to offer but their thin blood. But Africans all! Our brothers. I have thought much on this. So when I stare at this map I no longer see the blotches of individual countries and the lines of boundaries. I see one Africa, one land, one great continent unified and strong. Wait! Do not say to me that this is an impossible dream. Was our resolve to free Asante impossible? Was our capture of this palace a dream? What we may conceive, we may do—if we believe in our destiny. I say to you we can create *one* Africa. We can weld all these fragile links into one mighty chain that no enemy can break. A chain of blood, of common heritage and tradition, a chain of history and culture that once joined might last a thousand years or for all eternity. I would give my life with joy to help create such a human monument. I ask you to think on what I have said, and you will know in your hearts it is so. Africa *can* be united. Africa *shall* be united. If not by us, then by others. As for me, I want only to end my days not as an Asante but as an *African*, a citizen of a great new nation. Tangent, there are profits awaiting you and the men you represent. Leiberman, there is adventure without end. Nkomo, there

343

is fame. Abraham, Fante, Duclos, there is opportunity to put your theories into practice, to create a world power of wise laws, prosperous people, and fertile lands. Sene, I know, shares my destiny and my dreams. The future is ours if we but have the strength and confidence and courage that won the Fifth of August. Together, we can create from this poor, shattered land one nation from the Indian Ocean to the South Atlantic, from the Mediterranean to the Cape. I *know* it can be done. I *know* I am the man to do it. I ask now for your help and your dedication. I need not spell out what such a resolve will demand of you. But if you make the greatest sacrifice a man can make, is there not content in that, for a man to give his life to such a cause? Compared to that purpose, all else seems feeble and without value. I can think of no better life—short or long—than one spent freely, gladly for the future of Africa. Think of it! One land, one government, one people. The world's second-largest continent become the world's first nation! How do you answer me?"

Transfixed by his words, they stood shaken and silent. If they thought they had guessed his ambition, their guesses were water compared to the blood of his true desire. Now they stared at him with wonder, seeing the fire, hearing the glory. They could not resist him.

"Whatever you ask," Peter Tangent said.

"I'm in," Sam Leiberman said.

"I pledge to you," said Nkomo.

And Abraham, Duclos, Mai Fante nodded their agreement.

President Obiri Anokye exhaled in a slow sigh, but gave no sign that he had ever doubted their assent. He turned the map of Africa until he was facing the west coast.

"When viewed from where I now stand," he said,

344

"Africa looks exactly like a gun, a cocked gun, and Asante is the trigger."

Suddenly he slammed the model of an Asante army captain onto the map of Africa.

"We turn south," he said.

"Yes *sah!*" said Sgt. Yeboa.

END